PENGUIN BOOKS

OUT OF THE SHELTER

David Lodge has published nine novels, including *Paradise News*, *Nice Work* (short-listed for the Booker Prize and winner of the *Sunday Express* Book of the Year Award, 1988), *Small World* (also short-listed for the Booker Prize in 1984), *How Far Can You Go?* (Whitbread Book of the Year, 1980), and *Changing Places* (awarded the *Yorkshire Post* and Hawthornden prizes). He is also the author and editor of several works of literary criticism, the most recent being *The Art of Fiction* (Viking). He is Honorary Professor of Modern English Literature at the University of Birmingham, where he taught from 1960 to 1987, and still lives in that city.

Out of the Shelter

DAVID LODGE

Revised edition
With an Introduction by the author

PENGUIN BOOKS

PENGUIN BOOKS
Published by the Penguin Group
Penguin Books USA Inc.,
375 Hudson Street, New York, New York 10014, U.S.A.
Penguin Books Ltd, 27 Wrights Lane, London W8 5TZ, England
Penguin Books Australia Ltd, Ringwood, Victoria, Australia
Penguin Books Canada Ltd, 10 Alcorn Avenue, Toronto, Ontario, Canada M4V 3B2
Penguin Books (N.Z.) Ltd, 182-190 Wairau Road, Auckland 10, New Zealand

Penguin Books Ltd, Registered Offices:
Harmondsworth, Middlesex, England

First published in Great Britain by Macmillan 1970
This revised edition first published in Great Britain
by Martin Secker & Warburg Limited 1985
First published in the United States of America by Penguin Books 1989

5 7 9 10 8 6 4

LIBRARY OF CONGRESS CATALOGING IN PUBLICATION DATA
Lodge, David, 1935–
Out of the shelter/David Lodge.—Rev. ed./with an
introduction by the author.
p. cm.—(A King Penguin)
ISBN 0 14 01.2279 6
I. Title.
PR6062.036098 1989
823'.914—dc19 89-30032

Printed in the United States of America
Set in Plantin

For Eileen
In Affectionate Memory

Introduction

In 1951, at the age of sixteen, I travelled unaccompanied to Heidelberg, West Germany, to spend a holiday with my aunt Eileen, my mother's sister, who was working there as a civilian secretary for the U.S. Army. A single woman, she had been employed at the American military headquarters at Cheltenham before D-Day, and volunteered for service in Europe during the closing stages of the war and the occupation of Germany. For her, the experience was a personal Liberation. From a life of limited means and possibilities, further depressed by the common privations of wartime on the Home Front, she was suddenly taken under the protection of the richest, most powerful and most privileged nation in the world, and launched into a life of travel, excitement and high living such as she had previously only dreamed of. A vivacious and attractive lady, who always looked at least fifteen years younger than her real age, she made friends easily and was socially popular. First in Paris, later in Heidelberg, her off-duty life was full of parties, restaurant meals, dances and excursions. As Europe recovered from the devastation of war, and tourism revived, Eileen eagerly took advantage of her opportunities to travel further afield. The American Army, and its civilian establishment, were almost alone at that time in having the money, and the freedom of movement, to make Europe their playground. For a few years, they had the run of its luxury hotels, fashionable resorts, first-class restaurants, golf-courses and casinos – years when most Europeans themselves were struggling to rebuild their war-scarred cities and coping with food rationing and other shortages.

In Britain, "austerity" seemed to continue longer than anywhere else west of the Iron Curtain. Many basic foods were still rationed in

1951, six years after the end of the war. The weekly meat ration was increased in August – to a value of one shilling and eightpence per person. The Government actually tried to *reduce* the cheese ration, in the same year, from three ounces to two, but was defeated by a snap vote in the Commons. Just across the Channel, in France and Belgium, food was plentiful, and even the Germans (who, it was often ironically observed, were supposed to have lost the war) were better off in some respects than the British, who were not even able to enjoy Continental fare on holiday because of the absurdly mean currency allowance for non-essential travel abroad. It was only because my aunt Eileen sponsored my visit and guaranteed to cover my expenses that I was able to make the trip to Heidelberg.

For a boy of my age and background (lower-middle-class-London-suburban) it was an unusual and somewhat intimidating venture. I had always enjoyed a good relationship with my aunt, and her reports of the American expatriate way of life in Heidelberg were inviting. But Germany, the land of the hereditary enemy, still perceived through the distorting lens of a wartime childhood, was not an inviting holiday destination: and the journey there by rail and sea, with all the unknown hazards of foreign languages, customs, currency, etc., was a somewhat daunting prospect for someone who had never made an unaccompanied journey of more than thirty miles from home in his life. My parents, inexperienced in such matters, could not offer much help or advice. I remember that I spent long weary hours queuing for a passport at Petty France and for a visa at the German Embassy, because I had left the completion of these formalities rather late. There were moments when I wondered whether I would ever get away by the appointed date, and times when I was half-inclined to abandon the attempt.

But I persevered – and how glad I was, subsequently, that I did so, for that visit to Heidelberg was one of the formative experiences of my life. The successful completion of the long and tiring journey; the initiation into a world of relatively sophisticated adult pleasures and pastimes under the auspices of my aunt and her friends; exposure to the historic and picturesque aspects of Germany, and a limited intercourse with Germans themselves – all this greatly strengthened my self-confidence (never very robust before), and opened new horizons for future aspiration. Two years later, as a university student, I returned to Heidelberg and had another enjoyable holiday; and in 1967, long after my aunt had left the place, I went back again to do some research for *Out of the Shelter*. But it was the first visit that was crucially important for me; and although I drew on impressions and experiences from all three visits to Heidelberg in my novel, I did not hesitate to set it at the time of the earliest, and to make my central character sixteen years old, as I then was myself.

Out of the Shelter is probably the most autobiographical of my novels, inasmuch as Timothy Young's early life, and the circumstances in which he comes to visit Heidelberg, correspond closely to my own. For Part I, I drew on my memories of the London Blitz of 1940: of being "evacuated" with my mother to the country for much of the war (though my father, unlike Timothy's in this and many other respects, was not a London air-raid warden but a musician in the Air Force); of growing up in the post-war austerity years in the unlovely environment of South-East London, on the borders of New Cross and Brockley, going to a grant-aided Catholic grammar school, and slightly surprising myself by my own academic success, which would eventually propel me into the professional middle class. For my aunt, I substituted the character of Timothy's sister Kate (I am an only child myself), physically and emotionally very different from Eileen. The adult relationships and intrigues in which Timothy becomes involved in Parts II and III are invented, but the context in which they unfold is based on personal experience and observation. I did, for instance, actually live clandestinely in a women's hostel on my first visit to Heidelberg, though not with the interesting consequences this entails for Timothy. Gloria Rose, I am sorry to say, though I badly needed someone like her in 1951, is a figure of imagination, and the birthday party on the Neckar that proves so memorable for Timothy was suggested by a poster advertising a boat trip that I did not take.

Out of the Shelter is, then, autobiographical in origins, but not confessional in intent. Generically, it is a combination of the *Bildungsroman* (the useful German term for a novel about the passage from childhood to maturity and the recognition of one's vocation) and the Jamesian "international" novel of conflicting ethical and cultural codes. James Joyce's *A Portrait of the Artist as a Young Man* and Henry James's *The Ambassadors* are its most obvious literary models.

(Some of the stories of Joyce's *Dubliners*, and James's *What Maisie Knew* also influenced the handling of the naive central consciousness.) What encouraged me to base a novel on my first visit to Heidelberg, and the domestic milieu against which it was foregrounded, was a feeling that my experience had a representative significance that transcended its importance for me personally. Perhaps I felt this all the more keenly because I was writing the novel in the late 1960s, when the generation gap between those who remembered World War II and those who did not was provocatively encapsulated in the slogan, *Never trust anyone over thirty*.

The war and its aftermath shaped my generation in a number of ways. Its epic scale and scope, seen from a childish perspective, impressed on us a simple patriotic ethic and mythology that were not to be easily or lightly discarded. (How the old emotions welled up again in the Falklands War!) Its anxieties and privations made us temperamentally cautious, unassertive, grateful for small mercies and modest in our ambitions. We did not think that happiness, pleasure, abundance, constituted the natural order of things; they were to be earned by hard work (such as passing examinations) and even then it cost us some pains to enjoy them. It seemed to me that by virtue of my encounter with the American expatriate community in Germany in 1951 I had been granted a privileged foretaste of the hedonistic, materialistic good life that the British, and most of the other developed or developing nations of the world, would soon aspire to, and in some measure enjoy: a life of possessions, machines and diversions, of personal transportation, labour-saving devices, smart cheap clothing, mass tourism, technologically-based leisure and entertainment – making available to a large section of society pleasures formerly restricted to a tiny minority. Is this a new freedom for man, or a new enslavement? I do not presume to give an answer, but the question is raised obliquely in Timothy Young's story.

The question has special point in relation to Britain in 1951, a year that, with historical hindsight, appears as one of crucial transition, the hinge on which our society swung from "austerity" to "affluence". When I made my journey to Heidelberg in the summer of 1951, the Labour Government, its landslide majority of 1945 reduced to six seats in the General Election of 1950, was on its last legs. The Party had been split by the resignation from the Cabinet of

Aneurin Bevan and Harold Wilson over the introduction of charges under the National Health Service, and its leadership weakened by the illnesses of Cripps, Bevin and Attlee. Other difficulties and embarrassments included the domestic fuel shortages, the confiscation of the oil plant at Abadan by the Persian Government, and the disappearance of the diplomats Burgess and Maclean, soon to turn up in Moscow. But the root cause of most of the Government's problems, as I discovered when I did a little background reading for my novel, was an economic crisis which it was unable to control, partly because of its political dependence on the United States.

The big swing against Labour in the General Election of 1950 was a clear sign that the electorate was fed up with self-denial and impatient for some of the cake they had been promised for so long. And at last the Government was in a position to hand out a little cake. Cripps' budget of April 1950 was based on a cautious economic forecast of a three per cent rise in industrial production, and estimated that an extra £200 million would be available for private spending. Three months later, this painfully earned bonus was dashed from his hands by the outbreak of the Korean War. Though the immediate conflict was in Asia, there was widespread fear that the Russians would escalate the Cold War in Europe into a hot one. The United States promised strengthened defences, but only on condition that European allies matched American aid with self-help. Thus, at the very moment when Britain was at last beginning to get its peacetime economy working smoothly, and easing the brakes on private consumption, it was forced by political circumstances to undertake a crippling burden of rearmament. On 4 August, 1950, the British Government undertook to increase its defence expenditure by £1000 million over the next three years. Since many other nations, including the United States, were doing the same thing, the result was a world-wide shortage of raw materials, which slowed Britain's industrial recovery, and caused balance-of-payments difficulties, falling dollar and gold reserves, and inflation. Gaitskell confronted these problems in his 1951 Budget by raising taxation, curbing private spending, and holding back expenditure on State welfare. It was probably the only realistic policy – the majority of voters were no more willing than they are now to embrace the unilateralist alternative – but it split the Party, and associated Labour more firmly than ever with "austerity".

It was no surprise when the Tories won the election of October 1951, though for their first two years of office they were no more successful than Labour in managing the economy. Then the crisis disappeared, as suddenly as it had arisen, with the ending of the Korean War and the swing of world markets against the producers of raw materials and in favour of industrialized countries like Britain. The Conservatives reaped the political harvest, epitomized in Harold Macmillan's 1959 campaign slogan, "You've Never Had It So Good" (a significantly American locution, which fell oddly from the lips of that quintessentially British politician) and the Labour Party languished in opposition for the next thirteen years. In this perspective, the qualified success of the Festival of Britain in 1951, which the Home Secretary Herbert Morrison (who had lent his name to the famous indoor shelter) described as "the people giving themselves a pat on the back", seems more like the people giving a final push, friendly yet firm, to the departing Government.

In 1951 most of these political and economic events were, of course, either hidden in the future, or simply not apprehended by a sixteen-year-old schoolboy, but they form part of the subtext of *Out of the Shelter*.

Out of the Shelter (1970) was the fourth of my novels to be published, coming between *The British Museum is Falling Down* and *Changing Places*, but it was conceived before the earlier of those books, and in tone and technique has much more in common with my first two works of fiction, *The Picturegoers* and *Ginger, You're Barmy*. That is to say, it is a "serious" realistic novel in which comedy is an incidental rather than a structural element, and metafictional games and stylistic experiment are not allowed to disturb the illusion of life. The production and publication of this book had, however, their moments of black comedy, though I did not see them as funny at the time. The story may be of interest to those who are interested in such things, and will allow me to explain why and in what respects I have revised the text for this new edition.

I wrote most of the novel in 1967–8, and delivered the typescript to my agent in December 1968, just before leaving Britain for a six-month stint as visiting associate professor at the University of California, Berkeley. It was under option to MacGibbon & Kee, who had published my first three novels with modest success. After a longish interval I heard that they had rejected *Out of the Shelter*, for reasons that were never spelled out, but had something to do, I believe, with the imminent departure from the firm of my editor, Timothy O'Keeffe, and the disappearance, not very long afterwards, of MacGibbon & Kee as a separate imprint, absorbed into the Granada empire. The novel was then submitted to Macmillan, who after another long delay offered to publish it on condition that I cut it by a third. I accepted that the novel was too long, but this seemed excessively drastic surgery, even to a demoralized novelist anxious to find a publisher. We agreed on a twenty-five per cent reduction. The publishers suggested that it should be made at the expense of local colour, historical contextualization and the discussion of ideas, throwing more attention on to the character and fortunes of the young hero, though they did not make any specific recommendations. In the event, I followed their advice, cutting a good deal from the first section about Timothy's childhood, and several scenes in Parts II and III which were more discursive or descriptive than dramatic in content. Also excised was a longish appendix in the form of an essay, purportedly written by the character Don Kowalski some thirteen years after the main action, about the social, political and economic life of Britain in 1951.

I completed this work in August 1969, after my return to England. The man at Macmillan chiefly responsible for accepting the novel had now left the firm, and my new editor had not read the original MS. He pronounced himself pleased with the cut version, but thought it could still be improved by some fine combing-out of redundant lines and phrases. When this was done, it was still a longish novel, and presented costing problems to the publishers. My editor wrote to suggest that it should be set by computer, "a new method which we have begun to use for several of our novels with considerable success". He assured me that it would be significantly quicker and cheaper than conventional printing. The drawback was that I would not be able to see proofs because, allegedly, they would be unintelligible to anyone who was not a computer expert. Such an expert would check the computer-coded tape on to which the text had been typed against my copy-edited MS. "He will, of course, take the utmost care: his reputation depends upon it." Eager to please, and to co-operate, I suppressed my misgivings and agreed.

By the end of December I had given the copy-edited MS. a final check and returned it to the publishers. At the beginning of January 1970 I had the first intimation of trouble to come. It seemed that the computer could cope with only a small amount of italic, and that titles of books, etc., would therefore have to be printed in roman inside quotation marks. This rather shook one's faith in the new post-Gutenberg technology.

Publication was scheduled for early June. In April the date was postponed till August; in May it was postponed again till 10 September; in August it was postponed again till 24 September. By this time, I had seen an advance copy of the book, and was appalled. The text was riddled with misprints, nearly all introduced by the printer, and many of them grotesquely obvious (like *u* for *you*). A pun had been removed, and a joke thus transformed into a meaningless banality, by the correction of a deliberate misspelling, in spite of the fact that I had written in the margin of my MS: *Joke! Do not correct spelling*. The lines of type were bumpy, the spaces between the words grossly uneven, and there were strange gaps within words, notably between the *o* and *th* of my central character's name, Timothy, which appeared two or three hundred times. Those lonely words at the beginnings of lines that printers call widows abounded, as did awkward word-breaks at line endings. In short, it was the most hideous piece of printing that I had ever set eyes on, and there was absolutely nothing that I could do about it.

My editor was suitably apologetic and sympathetic, but the sheets of the first printing were already being bound. I discovered many years later, through a chance meeting at a dinner party with someone who worked for Macmillan at the time, that this monstrosity was actually a second attempt: the first printout of my novel was so garbled that they had to discard the tape and start all over again. My editor concealed from me this fact (which explains the repeated postponement of publication), no doubt in fear of authorial rage. He need not have worried. Reviewing the correspondence in which this sorry story is recorded, I am dismayed by my own pusillanimity, the mildness of my complaints, my servile eagerness to please, the readiness with which I waived the right to see proofs. Nowadays I take nothing on trust, involve myself in every stage of a book's production, and insist on seeing, not only proofs, but the corrected proofs as well. (I am fortunate in having co-operative publishers and an editor as obsessively perfectionist as myself.)

Out of the Shelter was finally published on 1 October 1970, at the height of the season, in a week when, it seemed, every important English novelist had a new book out. It received relatively few reviews – fewer by far than my previous novels – and those that appeared, though generally favourable, were shortish and restrained in their praise. There was a long and appreciative notice in the *T.L.S.*, whose contributors were then still anonymous, which I later discovered was writtten by Bernard Bergonzi. He was well qualified to review the novel, having come from a Catholic lower-middle-class London background very similar to my own (in fact we grew up within a couple of miles of each other, though we did not meet until we were both university teachers). His review gave me great pleasure, as did one by James Davie in the *Glasgow Herald*, but they made little difference to sales of the novel, which were disappointing. Macmillan sold a little over two thousand copies and, a year or so after publication, pulped the remaining unbound sheets. The novel was never paperbacked, or published in America, or translated into another language. It was the least successful of my novels, and is certainly the least well known, though a few of my friends like it more than any of the others.

How far, and in what proportions, this relative neglect of *Out of the Shelter* was due to bad timing, poor production, or the literary quality of the text itself, would be hard to gauge and is, in any case, probably not for me to say. But I have always felt that this novel might appeal to a bigger audience than it managed to find on its first publication, and it therefore gives me particular pleasure to see it in print again. Since, for reasons already given, the text had to be re-set (rather than photographically reproduced from the first edition) I have taken the opportunity to revise it. I should not have taken advantage of the same opportunity had it arisen (it did not) in other reissues of my novels. As a general rule I would say that the point of reissues is to make available to interested readers the full range of a writer's work in its historical continuity, the imperfections and immaturities of early works being part of their identity and often of their charm. But I make an exception of *Out of the Shelter*. Of all my other novels I think I can honestly say that they were as good as I could make them at the time of their publication: but this one was written, and then drastically cut, at a time of considerable personal stress, when my critical judgment was not, I believe, altogether reliable. The original text was certainly far too long, but it now seems to me that the cuts I made were not invariably well-advised, and that some opportunities for further cuts and adjustments were missed.

Accordingly, in revising *Out of the Shelter* for this new edition, I have restored a small proportion of the deleted passages, made a number of new cuts, and, in the process of retyping the entire text, made many small stylistic alterations. I have, however, resisted temptations to change the story, and the narrative method remains as it was: everything is presented from Timothy's point of view, but narrated by a "covert" authorial voice that articulates his adolescent sensibility with a slightly more eloquent and mature style than Timothy himself would have commanded.

In short, I have not attempted to rewrite the novel, as if I were tackling its subject for the first time in 1984, but have endeavoured to discover the most effective version of the novel I wrote in 1967–8.

DAVID LODGE
August 1984

ONE

The Shelter

1

Almost the first thing he could remember was his mother standing on a stool in the kitchen, piling tins of food into the top cupboard. On the table there were more tins: pineapple, peaches, little oranges – you could tell by the pictures. He asked her:

– What are all those tins for?

The sun was shining through the bobbly kitchen window behind her head, and though he screwed up his eyes against the dazzle he couldn't see her face properly, but he remembered her looking down at him for what seemed a long time before she said:

– Because there's a war, dear.

– What's a war? he asked. But he could never remember what she answered.

Soon he found out that war was a Mickey Mouse gasmask that steamed up when you breathed and his father getting a tin hat and a whistle and Jill crying because her Dad was going away to join the Air Force and the wireless on all the time and black paper stuck over the front-door windows and sirens going and getting up in the middle of the night because of the raids. It was fun getting up in the middle of the night.

They didn't have their own shelter. He and his mother went up the road, to Jill's house, number 64, which had a shelter in the back garden. Jill's Dad had made it himself. His own Dad was usually on duty during an air raid, he was a Warden, making sure everybody was in a shelter, and not letting any lights show through their curtains. If the German planes saw a light shining through your curtains they would know where you were and they would drop a bomb on you. Sometimes in the middle of a raid his father would call in at number 64 and come down to the shelter to see that they were all right. Or he would come and fetch them after the All Clear had sounded. Sometimes he would carry Timothy home asleep, and he would wake up in the morning in his own bed without having heard the All Clear. The All-Clear siren was all the same noise, but the Air-Raid siren was up and down, *uhhhERRR* . . . *uhhhERRR* . . . *uhhhERRR* . . . It was clever to have two different sirens that sounded like what they meant. The All Clear was a tired, safe sound, like you felt going home, yawning, after a raid, but the Air-Raid siren sounded frightened.

Not that Timothy was frightened. After a while he got so used to the Air-Raid sirens that his mother had to wake him to go up the road to Jill's before the German bombers came over. Jill was the same age as he was, five, but he was older because his birthday came first. Jill was pretty. He was going to marry her when they were grown up. His sister Kath was much older than he was, sixteen, almost grown up, but she wasn't living at home any more. She had gone away to the country, with her school, with the nuns. Kath's school had gone away because of the raids. The raids were because of the War. They were called the Blitz. His mother said that if the Blitz went on much longer she would take Timothy to live in the country too. They lived in London, which was the biggest city in the whole world. Timothy didn't want to go and live in the country. He had been there once and stung himself on some nettles and fell into a cow's business. But he didn't want the raids to stop either, because it was fun getting up in the middle of the night.

– Timothy! Timothy! Wake up, dear.

He whimpered, and snuggled deeper into the warm bed.

– Timothy, wake up, it's a raid.

A siren started up very near, *uhhhERRR* . . . *uhhhERRR* . . . *uhhhERRR* . . . and he opened his eyes. His mother's face was bent over him, white and creased, a scarf over her hair.

– Hurry up, dear. It's a raid.

– I know, he said, yawning.

He sat on the edge of the bed, listening to the sirens, while his mother pulled socks over his feet.

– That noise, she said. She wore trousers for the raids, and an old jacket of his father's with a zip at the front. He liked his mother in trousers.

– Here's your siren suit, it's warm from the tank.

He wore the siren suit over his pyjamas. It was a blue one. Winston Churchill had one just like it. He felt brave as soon as he put it on. Pyjamas and dressing gowns had slits and gaps and unprotected spaces, but his siren suit had tight elastic round the wrists and ankles, and a zip at the front. When he was zipped into his siren suit he felt nothing could hurt him.

His mother laced up his shoes, tying the bow tight.

– There, you'll do. Have you got your toys?

He picked up the cardboard box that held his shelter toys and followed his mother down the stairs to the hall. She took their gasmasks from the hook by the front door and hung Timothy's Mickey Mouse one round his neck by its string.

– Turn out the light first, he reminded her as she started to open the front door. You'll get Dad into trouble.

She turned out the light and it was pitch dark in the hall. Outside the only light came from the searchlights that swept across the sky like great fingers wagging to and fro. Timothy dawdled going up the street, partly to show he wasn't afraid, and partly in the hope of seeing a German plane caught in the searchlights. Once he had seen one, a tiny silver cross it looked like in the bright beam, but it disappeared into a cloud before the guns could shoot it down. He could hear some guns now, thudding in the distance. His mother stumbled over the kerb.

– Sst! Can't see anything in this blessed blackout.

It was easier to see when you were coming back from the shelter after the All Clear, because of the fires. The fires were down at the Docks and they lit up the sky in a great red glow like a huge bonfire.

Suddenly there was a big bang from behind the houses in their street that made them both jump. His mother tightened her grip on his hand and began to run, tugging him behind her.

– Stop, you're hurting, he complained, it's only the railway gun.

– Come *on*, Timothy!

The railway gun went up and down the line behind the houses on Jill's side. You could see the railway from the end of Jill's garden, but only green electric trains went past in the daytime. His father went to work on the train. He worked in an office.

His mother had a key to the front door of Jill's house, but as she was fitting it into the lock the door opened and Uncle Jack was standing there.

– 'Allo, 'allo! he said. Just in time for the party.

– Why Jack! You gave me quite a turn, said his mother. What are you doing at home?

Uncle Jack closed the door behind them and switched on the light.

– Wangled a thirty-six. Thought I'd nip home and see how everybody was getting on.

Jill's Dad was wearing his blue Air Force uniform with the wings. He was big and strong and cheerful and Timothy loved him. He called him Uncle Jack, though he wasn't his real uncle. He wished his father had a proper uniform instead of just a tin hat and a band round his arm. His father couldn't join the Air Force because he was too old, which his mother said was very lucky because he wouldn't have to go away from home like Uncle Jack. Timothy was glad his father wasn't going away, but he thought it was better to be an airman than a warden.

– How's Tiny Tim, then? said Uncle Jack, ruffling Timothy's hair. Uncle Jack always called him that, or sometimes just Tiny. It was a joke between them. Timothy pretended not to like it. He clenched his fists and squared up to Uncle Jack like a boxer.

– Not now, Tiny, he said, you'd better go straight down to the shelter.

He led them through the hall and into the kitchen. Jill's house was just like his own, and yet it was different. All the rooms were the same size and in the same places, but they had different things in them and they smelled different, especially the kitchen. In the kitchen Uncle Jack picked up a torch that had a piece of paper stuck across half of the part where the light shone. That was to stop the light shining up in the air and showing the German bombers where you were. Uncle Jack turned out the kitchen light and opened the back door into the garden. He shone his torch out on to the path.

– Mind your step.

As he spoke a plane flew over the house, quite low. Timothy's mother shrank back into the house.

– It's all right, said Uncle Jack. One of ours. You can tell by the engine.

Timothy turned his face up in quiet worship of the man who could tell by the engine.

The shelter was at the bottom of the garden, which wasn't very far from the house. It was called an Anderson, and it was just a big hole in the ground, really, with cement walls and a curved iron roof. The roof was covered with earth and in the daytime it looked just like a little hill. Uncle Jack had planted some grass and flowers on top of it. Steps led down to a little door and inside there were some wooden steps. Uncle Jack called down and Auntie Nora opened the little door.

– Come along, my dears, she said, I was beginning to wonder where you'd got to.

– Can I stay and watch? Timothy asked, as he always did.

– Of course you can't, said his mother, come on down this minute, and mind you hold on to the rail.

Timothy went down slowly, staring up at the sky till the last moment. If only he could see just one German plane shot down, just one. But the bombers hadn't come over yet.

– There we are, said Auntie Nora, as they clambered into the shelter. She was knitting as usual.

It was cosy and warm in the shelter. Uncle Jack had fixed up an electric light and there was an oil-stove that smelled and a little stove called a Primus for making cocoa or tea. There were two bunks and some old chairs and boxes with cushions on them. There was an old carpet on the floor, all muddy and worn.

Jill was sitting on one of the bunks. Timothy went and sat next to her, carrying his box of shelter toys. Jill was dressing her doll, Susan, the black one. The other dolls were sitting up beside her. Timothy opened his box. In it he had One-Ear Rabbit, some coloured marbles, five toy soldiers, the fire engine with a ladder, and a toy gun on wheels that fired matchsticks. One-Ear Rabbit took up most of the room in the box, but he couldn't leave him at home with a raid going on.

– Susan is being naughty, said Jill, I had to smack her.

– The railway gun went bang just as we came, said Timothy, but I wasn't frightened.

– She won't sit still.

– I wanted to stay outside and watch with your Dad, but my Mum won't let me.

– My Dad's come home.

– I know.

– He's going to stay at home always.

Auntie Nora stopped knitting.

– Jill, you know Daddy's got to go back tomorrow. But he'll soon be home again. Her hands flicked at the red wool and the needles clicked again.

– He does very well for leaves, considering, she said to Timothy's mother.

– Said he was going to stay at home always, Jill sulked. She gnawed at one of her dark ringlets. Timothy pulled her ringlets sometimes, but he liked them really.

– He said no such thing. You mustn't tell fibs, Jill. Of course he would *like* to stay at home with us, but he has to go back to the station.

– Doesn't have to. Jill's lip trembled.

– She doesn't understand, said Auntie Nora to Timothy's mother.

– How can they, at their age? said his mother. I had a letter from Kath this morning.

– Did you? How is she? What about a cup of cocoa? said Auntie Nora.

– Would you like a cup of cocoa, Jill? Timothy?

– No, said Jill.

– No *thank you, Mummy*. What about a biscuit?

Jill hesitated.

– Can I have a cream one?

The biscuits were like sandwiches, with sweet yellow cream inside. Timothy nibbled all round the edges of his, first, where there wasn't much cream; then he had a smaller biscuit, richly packed with cream. Jill took the top off her biscuit, licked off the cream inside, put the two bits together again, and took one bite. Then she dropped the biscuit on the floor. Auntie Nora hadn't seen. She was bent over the little stove, heating milk for the cocoa, knitting still.

– How's Kath, then? How does she like Wales?

Timothy pretended to be busy with his biscuit, but he was listening to the talk about Kath. He was interested in his big sister. It seemed a long time since she went away. He found it difficult to remember what she looked like, except that she was fat and wore glasses, like his father.

– She's all right, said his mother. Well, so she says. Misses home, of course, and she says the food's terrible.

– Sst! Still, she's better off there.

– Oh, yes. And between you, me and the gatepost, I hope it'll teach her to appreciate home. She was getting too much for me. Couldn't do anything with her.

– It's the age, isn't it. How old is she?

– Sixteen. We thought we'd keep her at the convent till she's taken her School Certificate. Though the fees . . .

– It must be a drain.

– Mind you, she'll never pass. She's scatterbrained, and what with the school being evacuated . . . Timothy's another kettle of fish, we think he's going to be brainy.

– I wouldn't be surprised. Auntie Nora glanced across at him, and saw the biscuit on the floor.

– Jill! Why did you take the biscuit if you didn't want it?

– It's for Susan. Jill picked up the biscuit and pretended to feed her doll.

– You'd better not waste it, that's the last packet and there's no more at Shepherd's.

– Shopping's getting worse, isn't it? said Timothy's mother.

– Oh, shocking, I queued for three-quarters of an hour at Shepherd's this morning . . .

Timothy's attention wandered as the two mothers talked about food and rationing. Planes were droning overhead now, lots of planes together, German planes. The guns were banging loudly. Timothy aimed his gun up through the roof of the shelter.

– *Bang*, he went. *Bang! Bang! Bang!* Jill covered her ears.

– Timothy, there's enough noise without you, said his mother.

– Don't they sound near, said Auntie Nora, knitting faster, I think Jack ought to come down. It's silly risking it up there. She opened the shelter door a little and called up:

– Come down, Jack, it's silly to risk it up there. I'm making some cocoa.

Uncle Jack came heavily down the stairs. He was a big man and couldn't stand up straight inside the shelter. He sat on one of the boxes with a cushion on top. Jill ran to him and he sat her on his knee.

– Well, they've copped it all right down the Docks, he said. Sky's all red over there.

– Have they shot any German planes down? Timothy asked.

– 'Spect so, Tiny. They're throwing up enough flak, anyway.

– Did you see any shot down? he asked. But Auntie Nora was giving Uncle Jack his cocoa and he didn't hear.

While they were all drinking the cocoa, Timothy's father came into the shelter. He wasn't as tall as Uncle Jack, and he could stand up inside the shelter without bending. He took off his tin hat and wiped his forehead with a handkerchief. There was a red mark on his forehead where the tin hat had been. The top of his head hadn't got much hair on it. He wore an old raincoat with an armband that had letters on it, A.R.P. He said he would get a proper uniform soon, but it wouldn't have wings on it.

– They're copping it down at the Docks tonight, he said.

– I thought so, said Uncle Jack.

– Biggest raid yet, they reckon. Jerry's lost a packet of planes, they say. But they just keep on coming over in waves.

– Oh dear, I wish we didn't live so near the river, said Auntie Nora.

– We're all right here, ducks, said Uncle Jack. Must be three miles away, those fires.

– Well, I just hope we don't have any up this way tonight, said Timothy's father, because I reckon every fire-engine in South-East London's down at the Docks.

– Mine isn't! said Timothy, holding up his fire-engine with a ladder, and all the grown-ups laughed.

– 'Attaboy, Tiny, said Uncle Jack. He took out a packet of cigarettes and offered them round. Timothy's mother shook her head, but Auntie Nora took one.

– I don't usually, she said, but these raids . . .

The cigarette smoke hung in the air in curly shapes. Its smell mixed with the smell of the oil stove and the smell of cocoa. Timothy yawned.

– Time these children had a nap, said Timothy's mother. Looks as if we might be here all night.

– I'm not tired, said Timothy.

– And I'm not tired, said Jill, putting her arms round her father's neck.

– I'd better be off, said Timothy's father. You be a good boy now, Tim. I'll come back and fetch you when the All Clear's gone. He put on his tin hat and buttoned up his raincoat.

– I'll see you out, Geoff, said Uncle Jack. He got up holding Jill in his arms and carried her across to the bunk where Timothy was.

– You and Timothy have a nice sleep now, love. I'll see you in the morning.

– You're not going away tomorrow, are you Daddy? said Jill, keeping her arms round his neck so he couldn't stand up straight.

– Not straightaway, no, my precious.

– Not ever?

– You have a nice sleep now, my pet, or you'll be too tired to play with me in the morning.

– Can Timothy sleep in my bunk?

– We usually let them, said Auntie Nora.

– I suppose it's all right if he's going to marry you, said Uncle Jack, and the grown-ups laughed.

– Can't I go outside for just a little look? Timothy pleaded, as the two men were getting ready to go out.

– No, said his mother. Now get into bed, and let's have no more nonsense.

– Why can't I?

– Because you might get killed, that's why.

– What about Dad, then?

– Dad is grown up and he has a tin hat.

– Uncle Jack hasn't got a tin hat.

– And Uncle Jack ought to have more sense, said Auntie Nora, only he's not much more grown up than you are, Timothy.

– He is, he is grown up! He's brave, Jill said.

– Fact is, said Uncle Jack with a grin, you'd hardly know there was a war on at the station. I have to come home to see a bit of action.

– You're welcome to it, said Timothy's father, as they disappeared up the steps. Sixth night running, this is.

– Blimey, just look at that sky! they heard Uncle Jack say, as Auntie Nora closed the door behind them.

– Now, she said, let's get you two comfy.

His mother took off his siren suit and Auntie Nora took off Jill's dressing-gown. Then Auntie Nora tucked them in tight under the blankets. She put a shade over the light so that it didn't shine in their eyes. His mother gave him One-Ear Rabbit to hug and Jill had Susan. He looked up at the curved roof of the shelter and felt warm and safe. The two mothers sat over the oil-stove, talking in low voices. They were talking about Kath again. He couldn't hear properly, and he couldn't understand what he did hear.

– Wants to join the W.A.A.F.s as soon as she can but Geoff won't hear of . . .

– Don't blame you, Jack says the morals . . .

– Keep her at home if we can, plenty of useful . . .

– Wedding practically every week, Jack says, and mostly because they . . .

– That Roberts girl up the road . . .

The heads came closer together, the voices whispered, Auntie Nora's knitting needles went clicketty-click, clicketty-click. Shadows shifted on the roof of the shelter with the quick movements of her hands. The guns sounded faint now, a long way off. He pulled down his pyjama trousers and Jill wriggled beside him as she pulled up the skirt of her nightie. Then he felt her cool soft fingers on his thing and with his own finger he felt for the little crease between her legs. He was warm and safe and sleepy. He hoped there would be another raid the next night.

A big bang woke him. There was a buzzing in his ears, and although Jill was still in bed beside him it was as if she was crying a long way away. The first thing he did was to pull up his pyjama trousers. Some dirt had fallen on his head. The electric light was swinging in the air, throwing wild shadows over the walls and roof. The two mothers were standing at the bottom of the steps.

– Jack, Auntie Nora was shouting, are you all right Jack? Jack? Oh my God! She went up the steps, tripped, and crawled out of the shelter, calling Jack.

– Nora, don't, be careful, his mother said. He saw her make the sign of the cross and her lips moving silently as she closed her eyes tight.

– Mummy! Daddy! Jill wailed, hugging her doll. Where's my Daddy?

Timothy started to cry too, not knowing why. Jill jumped out of bed and ran to the steps. His mother opened her eyes.

– Jill! Come back!

But Jill was already through the door at the top of the steps. His mother scrambled after her. Timothy was frightened. He would be left on his own.

– Mum! he shrieked.

She stopped and turned round, saying something, but he couldn't hear. There was a loud whistling noise and a flash and a roar and just before the light went out his mother seemed to be flying across the shelter towards him. He felt her body fall across his and cried out because she had hurt him but he couldn't hear his own voice because of the buzzing in his ears. A lot more dirt had fallen on the bed. It was pitch dark and he was very frightened. Then he felt his mother move and her arms tighten around him. She was saying something but he couldn't hear properly. Then he could hear as if she was a long way away. She was saying:

– Timothy, are you all right, Timothy? She was crying.

After a little while he could see things. The oil stove, surprisingly, was still alight, and there was a dim red glow from the little window at the bottom and some yellow light coming through the holes at the top. The doorway of the shelter was blocked up with earth and stones, and some had fallen into the shelter. There seemed to be grass and even flowers in the dirt. And there were two eyes that shone in the dim light of the stove. He couldn't see any face, just the two eyes, very close together, and they frightened him. His mother tried to get up, but he wouldn't let go of her. She said:

– Timothy, if you let go of me I could light a candle and then we won't be in the dark.

So he let go of her, and she stumbled slowly round the shelter looking for a candle. She found one and lit it. Then he saw that the eyes belonged to Jill's Susan.

– Look, he said, pointing. Susan.

His mother picked the doll from the dirt and began to cry. There was a hole in Susan's cheek and one arm and one leg were missing and her dress was all torn and dirty. His mother went over to the doorway and began to dig at the dirt with her hands. More dirt and stones fell into the shelter. A brick fell on her foot and she gave a cry of pain.

– It's no use, she said, we'll have to wait here until they dig us out.

Daddy will come soon and dig us out. She limped over to the bed and sat down, putting her arms around him.

– I don't want to go out, he said, I don't want to go up there.

– Daddy will come soon. It'll be all right.

They used three candles before the men dug them out. His father wasn't one of them. But his Dad was all right, they said. It had been a shock, that was all. He was resting at home, waiting for them.

– Come on, son, your Dad's waiting for you, they said.

But Timothy didn't want to leave the shelter. In the end, one of the men had to carry him, kicking and screaming, out of the shelter, into the open air.

2

There were no more nights of getting up and going up the road to Jill's house. Jill's house wasn't there any more, and Jill had gone to heaven and so had her Mummy, and her Daddy had gone back to the Air Force. Timothy and his mother went to live in the country where they didn't have air raids. They lived in a place called Blyfield, in a dark narrow house near the gasworks. The house belonged to Mrs. Tonks, who was fat and smelled funny. They had the front room that was full of hard shiny furniture, and a bedroom upstairs. His mother shared Mrs. Tonks' kitchen, which was a drawback.

There were a lot of drawbacks at Mrs. Tonks, his mother used to say. There was no electric light in the house, and they had to light the gas when it got dark. His mother held a spill to the white lacy bit and it lit with a little pop and turned blue and red and then yellowy-white and burned with a faint hiss. You could make it brighter or dimmer by pulling on a little chain. Mrs. Tonks wouldn't have a gaslight burning on the stairs because it was a waste, so when his mother took him up to bed she held a candle in a candlestick, and she used to leave the candle burning on the bedroom mantelpiece because he didn't like the dark now. If the candle went out before he fell asleep, he called out and she came and lit another candle. It was cold in the winter and when you woke up in the morning there was ice on the inside of the window. He scratched it off with his finger-nail, and looked through the holes he had made, at the gasworks. Behind the gasworks there was a field with some cows in it. One day his mother wanted to take a short-cut through the field, but as they started across the field one of the cows looked at them and he was frightened and they went round by the road. In the mornings they washed in a basin in the bedroom. His mother brought the hot water upstairs in a jug from the kitchen. Mrs. Tonks' house didn't have a bathroom. His mother bathed him in a tin bath in front of the fire in the front room. It was nice having a bath in front of the fire, especially getting dried afterwards, but he wasn't allowed to splash; and when his father brought him his boats from home there wasn't really room for them in the tin bath. His father was still working at the office in London, but he came to see them at weekends.

He went to school at a convent near the village. He liked his teacher, Sister Teresa, she had a nice smile and rosy cheeks, but he was frightened of Sister Scholastica who had a big pimple on her chin with hairs growing out of it. Sister Scholastica taught the big girls, but sometimes she was in the playground. Her name was hard to say and once he called her Sister Elastica and the little girls laughed and Sister Scholastica looked cross. On Sundays he and his mother went to mass in the convent chapel. The priest came on a bicycle. The mass was very long because the nuns sang a lot. Sister Teresa sang the best and Sister Scholastica sang the worst.

There was a song they often sang on the wireless called *There'll Be Bluebirds Over The White Cliffs of Dover.*

There'll be bluebirds over
The white cliffs of Dover,
Tomorrow, just you wait and see.
There'll be love and laughter,
And peace ever after,
Tomorrow, when the world is free.

Nearly at the end of the song were the words:

And Jimmy will go to sleep
In his own little room again.

When he came to those words he always thought of his own little room in London.

One day they had a concert at the school and everybody had to sing a song or recite a poem. He sang *The White Cliffs of Dover* and Sister Teresa cried and gave him a kiss afterwards. Dover was a seaside place with tall white cliffs. He thought it would be nice to go there after the war was over and see the bluebirds.

One day his mother came to school with him to see Mother Superior, to ask if he could be a boarder. He didn't want to be a boarder, but his mother said she had to go back to London to work and it was too dangerous for him to go with her. Mother Superior said he would like it, the boarders had lots of fun, and she took a bag of toffees out of a drawer and offered him one. He took the toffee but he didn't eat it. On the way back to Mrs Tonks's he threw it into a ditch. His mother saw but she didn't say anything.

The next day she took him to the school with a suitcase with his clothes in it, but no toys except One-Ear Rabbit. Boarders weren't allowed to have their own toys, but Mother Superior said he could keep One-Ear Rabbit. His mother kissed him goodbye and told him to be a good boy. She was crying and he couldn't understand why she was leaving him all on his own. He didn't cry but he was frightened and unhappy. The boarding part of the school was cold and dark, with wooden stairs and passages that had no carpets and creaked when you trod on them. There was stew for supper with bits of white fat in it and watery gravy that made the potatoes all mushy. He didn't eat any of it, but he was frightened in case Sister Scholastica noticed. After supper they went into the chapel and sang hymns and said long prayers which he didn't know. He opened and closed his mouth soundlessly to pretend that he was singing and praying with the others. Then it was time to go to bed. His bed was in a big room with some other little boys. There was a place to wash, but only cold water. There was only lino on the floor and it was cold under his feet when he took off his shoes and socks, so he got in bed quickly. The Sister who was in charge asked him if he had said his night prayers and he said his mother let him say them in bed if it was cold and the other boys giggled. The Sister said next time he must kneel down beside his bed to say them like the other boys. She turned out the lights, except for a little one at the end of the room where she sat, saying her rosary. The rosary beads clicked as she fingered them. It reminded him of Auntie Nora's knitting needles in the shelter. He wished he was back in the shelter before the bomb fell. He didn't like being a boarder at the convent. He felt like crying, but the other boys would hear him and it wouldn't be any use. When his mother came to see him he would cry a lot and ask her to take him away. He pictured himself crying and saying to his mother *Take me away, take me away, take me away,* and she took him away. It was a nice picture. Thinking of it, he fell asleep.

The next morning a bell woke him when it was still dark. Someone had put his arms outside the blankets in the night and they were cold. He pulled the blankets over his head and tried to think of the picture of his mother taking him away, but it was no use. He couldn't believe in it, with the sounds of the other boys getting up and water running and shoes clattering on the wooden stairs. He got out of bed, shivering in the cold air, and put on his clothes. But he wasn't used to dressing on his own, and he couldn't manage the buttons on his shirtsleeves or his shoe-laces. He stood beside the bed with his shoe-laces trailing and his shirt cuffs hanging open until the Sister came to help him. She took off his shirt and told him to go and wash. When he came back she looked at his ears to see if they were clean. For breakfast there was porridge, but not nice porridge like his mother made. It was runny and there wasn't enough sugar to taste.

After breakfast they went to the cloakrooms to clean their shoes. A Sister in a blue apron gave him a tin of black shoe polish and a brush. He looked at them helplessly. Suddenly he began to cry, hopeless, useless tears, tears he had planned to save for his mother when she came to visit him, now wasted on the indifferent boys and girls around him, tears unheard, unseen in the dark, noisy cloakroom, smelling of boot polish.

– What's the matter, Timothy? Big boys mustn't cry.

He turned to look up at the Sister. He wiped his eyes with the back of his hand and sniffed.

– Don't know how to do it.

– Well, now, that's nothing to cry about. Here, I'll show you.

The Sister bent down over his shoes, brushing vigorously. Some of the other children sniggered and stared. Timothy was ashamed and looked away, through the barred window that faced the main gate, and suddenly saw his mother coming up the drive, carrying his Wellington boots. Without thinking he ran from the cloakroom and down the passage. A nun saw him coming and threw up her hands to stop him. Running in the corridors was not allowed. She was smiling, but he felt in his heart that if she stopped him he would not see his mother and he would be a boarder for ever and ever. He ducked under the nun's arm, felt her hand catch at his sleeve, wriggled free of her grasp and stumbled to the door. Another Sister had just opened it and his mother stood on the threshold. He threw himself into her arms.

It was lovely to be back home again. For days he went about the house in a trance of delight, scarcely daring to speak or play in case it would break the spell and send him back to the convent. But his mother promised him he wouldn't have to go back. There were not many raids in London now, and they had a shelter of their own. It wasn't in their garden, like Jill's; it was in the front room, and it was like a big iron table. You slept underneath the top, on mattresses. The shelter was called a Morrison, and it nearly filled their front room. His father said it wouldn't save you from a direct hit, but nothing much would. Anyway, Timothy felt safe as soon as he had crawled into the shelter. It was lined with mattresses and cushions and the sides were joined with wire mesh so you could breathe, but if the ceiling fell on top of you you wouldn't be hurt. Timothy slept in the Morrison every night, and if there was a raid his mother came downstairs and crawled in beside him.

Uncle Jack sometimes stayed with them when he was on leave, because he hadn't got a house any more. Where Jill's house had been, and the houses on each side of it, there was just a big space and piles of bricks and twisted pipes. Grass and weeds had grown over them while Timothy had been away. One day he saw Uncle Jack standing on the bomb-site with his hands in his pockets, staring at the ground. Timothy nearly called out to him, but decided not to. When he got home he told his mother, and later he heard her telling his father. His mother said it was only natural but he shouldn't brood. His father said Jack blamed himself but what was the use. From their talk he found out what had happened on the last night in the shelter. When the first bomb fell in the next street, the one that had woken him up, Uncle Jack ran off to help. He shouted first to Auntie Nora, but she didn't hear him. When she came out of the shelter to look for him, with Jill behind her, their own house was hit by a second bomb and they were killed in the garden. Killed meant you were dead and buried in the ground, but your soul went to heaven. You were happy in heaven but the people you left behind were sad, like Uncle Jack. Timothy missed playing with Jill, but he wasn't as sad as he had been boarding at the convent.

There were lots of bomb-sites in the streets around. You weren't supposed to go on them, though the big boys did. There might be unexploded bombs and if you trod on one it would go off and kill you. The big boys went on the bomb-sites looking for shrapnel. Timothy found a piece of shrapnel one morning on the way to school. It was lying in the gutter and when he picked it up it was still warm. It was heavy in his hand and rough to the touch, like the pumice stone in the bath when it was dry. Jean Collins tried to make him throw the piece of shrapnel away, but he kept it even though she pinched him. The piece of metal, warm and rough and heavy in his hand, excited him strangely: a piece of the war that had fallen out of the sky. He began to collect shrapnel. You were supposed to collect it to give to the Government, to make new shells; but Timothy kept the pieces he found, in a cardboard box under his bed.

He went to the parish school. He was a bit frightened at first – some of the boys were rough and the teachers shouted and hit the naughty children – but it was better than being a boarder at the convent. Gradually he came to feel at ease in the violent, overcrowded playground. The thing he disliked most was being bossed about by Jean Collins. She took him to school and brought him back and was supposed to look after him because his mother was working on the ration books. Sometimes when she was cross she would say that Hitler would catch him one day and do horrible things to him. He didn't believe her but he didn't like her to say it. Hitler was the head of the Germans. He had started the war. He was a nasty man with a black moustache. Another name for Germans was Nazis, which sounded like Nasties, so it was a good name.

One day Timothy went with his mother and father to see a film about Hitler. It was supposed to be a funny film, making fun of Hitler. The man strutted about and shouted and screamed and spluttered and everybody in the cinema laughed, but Timothy laughed a little bit after the others, for he was secretly frightened. He couldn't feel sure that it was just a man dressed up to look like Hitler, because he looked so real, and all the other people and the places in the film looked real. Not real, exactly, but like a dream or a nightmare which you thought was real until you woke up. After that he sometimes dreamed of Hitler and woke up crying in the night with the black-and-white pictures of Hitler still flickering before his eyes like the film.

One day in the school playground some big boys chased Jean Collins, pulling up her skirt from behind and shouting:

– Blue knickers! Blue ones! Jean Collins' face went all red and she cried and all the big boys laughed and Timothy laughed too, he was pleased to see Jean Collins being bullied for once. But the Headmaster had seen it all from his window and next day the big boys were caned, and Timothy crept about the school in fear and trembling in case the Headmaster had seen him laughing.

When he was seven he made his first Holy Communion. Before that you had to make your First Confession. You went into a little dark place at the side of the church, like a cupboard, where there was a wire mesh and one of the Fathers was sitting behind it and you told him your sins and he forgave you, only it was Jesus really. Then your soul was washed clean of the stains of sin and was bright and shining. Sins were things like telling lies or cheeking your parents or missing mass on Sundays. There were also sins of impurity. Miss Marples never explained properly what sins of impurity were but he knew it was doing rude things, like the drawings some of the big boys did in the lavs, or pulling up Jean Collins' skirt to see her knickers. Timothy was glad he hadn't done any of these things, because it would be awful to have to tell them in confession.

He tried not to think of what he had done with Jill, when they had looked at each other in her bathroom, and when they touched each other in the bunk in the shelter. He could never tell that to the Father. The Father wouldn't tell anyone, and he wasn't supposed to know who you were, because it was dark in the confessional and you whispered. But suppose he recognized your voice, even though you were whispering, or peeped through his curtain and saw you kneeling with the other boys and girls and counted to know when it was your turn? He tried to think of how he would tell the Father about himself and Jill, but his insides felt funny just thinking of it. He couldn't. But you were supposed to confess all the sins you could remember before you made your First Communion, or it was sacrilege, which was the worst sin of all.

He slept badly the night before his First Confession, and dreamed the Hitler dream. Lying awake in the Morrison shelter, as the room slowly got light, he decided he would confess a sin he hadn't done to make up for not confessing about Jill. He invented a sin about stealing some money from his mother's handbag, though he had never stolen anything in his life, ever. The Father said:

– How much was it, my child?

Timothy had not expected this question and said one pound, which was the first sum that came into his head. The Father seemed to think this was a lot of money and talked to him for a long time about how wicked it was to steal, until Timothy got quite frightened and wished he hadn't said it was so much money. But anyway, he thought afterwards, he had surely made up for not confessing about Jill, and he made his First Communion without worrying too much.

His sister Kath came home, because she had left school. She was seventeen. Timothy was shy with her at first, because it was a long time since he had seen her. She was very fat. When she walked about in her bedroom upstairs the things on the dining-room sideboard rattled and his father would lift his head from his newspaper and say:

– My God, she'll come through the ceiling one of these days. Never mind, we can claim it as war damage.

The back bedroom looked different now with Kath's photos of her school-friends and postcards of film stars, and it smelled of scent. She had lipstick too, though she wasn't supposed to use it. One day he looked through the crack between the door hinges of her room and saw her putting lipstick on her face in front of the mirror. He supposed that she washed it off before she came downstairs, though it seemed funny to wear lipstick when nobody was looking at you.

After she had been at home for a little while, Kath started to go to work. She went up to the City with his father, every morning on the train, to work in an office. There was a woman in charge of her office called Miss Harper, who Kath called the Old Battleaxe. Kath wanted to join the W.A.A.F.s, the girls' Air Force, when she was eighteen, but his mother and father didn't want her to, and there were big rows in the dining-room after he had gone to bed, which usually ended with Kath stomping upstairs to her room and slamming her door. Timothy was on his sister's side. If he were grown up himself he would be a pilot and fly a Spitfire and shoot down lots of Germans.

His model planes were his favourite toys. Uncle Jack gave them to him. A friend of his in the Air Force made them out of wood, painted with camouflage markings and red, white and blue circles on the wings. He had Spitfires, Hurricanes and Wellington bombers. The top of the Morrison shelter was his airfield. There was a dark brown sideboard in the front room which he had never liked because of its stiff drawers and sharp corners, so he called it Germany and sent his Wellingtons to bomb it. Uncle Jack was a tail-gunner in a Wellington now. He came to see them after he had finished his training and he was quite excited. He said he was looking forward to giving the Jerries a bit of their own medicine. It was Kath's eighteenth birthday and she asked Uncle Jack didn't he think she should join the W.A.A.F.s, and that started another row. Uncle Jack didn't say anything at first, but after dinner he said to Timothy's father that he thought Kath ought to be allowed to join the W.A.A.F.s if she really wanted to, because it was more useful than working in an office. Timothy's father sighed, and said:

– Well, I suppose you're right, Jack. All right, then.

Then Kath threw her arms round his neck and kissed him, and then she did the same to Uncle Jack, and then his mother came in from the kitchen and cried a bit, and Uncle Jack said:

– As long as you don't think it's going to be like Worrals.

Kath said she didn't read that stuff any more. The next day she went to the place where you joined the W.A.A.F.s, but she wasn't allowed to join up because she failed the medical. She came home and cried for three days and nights and then she went back to work at the same office, and everything went on as before, only duller.

Kath was sulky and not much fun. Uncle Jack didn't come and see them any more. His mother said it was because his station was a long way away, but one day she told him that Uncle Jack was missing. Missing meant his plane hadn't come back from a raid. But probably Uncle Jack had jumped out of the plane with his parachute on and been taken prisoner. When the war was over he would come back to England. Timothy felt sorry for Uncle Jack being a prisoner in Germany. He thought it must be like being a boarder at the convent, all on your own and being afraid you would never go home again.

For the war went on and on. His mother and father often talked about pre-war, but Timothy found it difficult to remember what it was like. He could remember going to the seaside and eating a banana which was gritty because he had dropped it in the sand. That must have been pre-war because you couldn't get bananas any more.

And he remembered a Christmas tree with lights on it in a shop window, and that must have been pre-war because it was dark and the lights were shining out on to the pavement, so there couldn't have been a blackout. His parents talked a lot about pre-war at Christmas time, and the things you used to be able to get to eat: bananas and oranges and grapes and figs and dates, and as much mincemeat as you liked, without points. All these things would come back after the war. But the war went on and on.

Kath gave Timothy an atlas one Christmas. There was a map of the world spread over the first two pages, and Great Britain and all the countries in the British Empire were coloured pink. Britain was very small but there were a lot of pink countries and some of them were very big. Germany was a small yellow country and Italy was a small green country. When he looked at the size of the pink countries, and of America and Russia, the war didn't seem quite fair, though he didn't like to think about that. We were fighting Japan, too, but that was another small country. Germany and Italy and Japan had started the war, so it was their own fault if they got beaten, but it was taking a long time to beat them. Timothy liked to do paintings of races – car races, aeroplane races and boat races. Each car, plane or boat had a little flag to show what country it belonged to. The picture showed the end of the race, and the order was always the same: England was first, America was second, Russia was third, France was fourth, Italy fifth, Germany sixth and Japan last. Sometimes Germany and Japan crashed or sank and didn't finish.

One day Kath brought home an American airman called Rod whom she had met at a dance. He was sun-tanned and his uniform was very smooth and soft, not like Uncle Jack's which was rough and hairy. Rod had chewing gum called Juicy Fruit in great long strips which he gave to Timothy. The strips were so big that you only needed half a piece at a time. He had a big loud laugh that showed his white teeth, and he called Timothy *Junior* and his father *Sir*. The second time Rod came to their house he brought milk chocolate for Timothy and his mother and cigarettes for his father. Timothy liked Rod and was glad the Americans were fighting on the same side as England. But Rod didn't come to see them any more. There was a big row about it which he heard from the landing when they thought he was in bed. His father shouted at Kath that she wasn't to go out with a married man, and she ran upstairs almost before he had time to scuttle back to bed, and slammed the door of her room.

Then one day Kath left home. She went to work for the American Army as a secretary in a place called Cheltenham. His mother and father didn't want her to go but she pestered them till they agreed. She wrote them letters saying she was having a great time and the Americans were very nice to work for and she was getting all kinds of things to eat that you couldn't get in the shops. His mother said she would get fatter than ever. His father said the Yanks knew how to look after themselves. Kath was working in the Chaplains' Department, and his mother said that was a comfort anyway. Kath said she couldn't say anything more about her work because of security. That meant spies and so on, and Timothy was rather impressed.

Some time after Kath went to Cheltenham there was D-Day. Everybody was very excited and they had the wireless on all day at home. His father said the war would soon be over, and Timothy said, *Good-oh*, because Uncle Jack would come home. But that night when he went to bed his mother said Uncle Jack wouldn't be coming home. They had known all along that Uncle Jack had been killed when his plane was shot down, but they hadn't told Timothy because he was too young. But now he was getting to be a big boy and must understand that people got killed fighting in wars, which was why they were very terrible things. And he must say a prayer every night for the repose of Uncle Jack's soul, like he did for Jill and her Mummy. Timothy felt as if he wanted to cry but couldn't. But he was full of hatred for the Germans because they had killed the nicest man he had ever known.

Then the buzz-bombs started, and it was more like the beginning of the war again than the end. The buzz-bombs were like aeroplanes, only they had no pilots and they went very fast, so it was difficult to shoot them down. Their proper name was V.1s, but they were called buzz-bombs because they buzzed as they flew overhead and when they stopped buzzing you knew that there would be a big explosion just afterwards. One fell on a Woolworth's not far away and killed a lot of people, and his father said it was getting too dangerous for Timothy and his mother to stay in London, so they went back to Blyfield again. Not to Mrs. Tonks this time, but to another house that belonged to Mr. Barwood. He was an old man whose wife had died and he let them live in his house for nothing because Timothy's mother cooked for him and cleaned the house.

Every day and every night the bombers flew over Blyfield on their way to bomb Germany. He would be in the garden, or in the field behind it, catching butterflies, and he would hear the distant hum of engines and drop his net and stare up at the blue sky, shading his eyes. Slowly the hum grew louder and louder until it seemed to fill the whole sky, but it was funny because you couldn't see any aeroplanes at first. And then you would see one, high, high in the sky, a tiny silver speck; and once you saw one you would suddenly see them all, hundreds, it seemed, flying steadily in formation. Sometimes they ruled chalk-white lines of vapour behind them, and then they were easy to see. They were American bombers, called Flying Fortresses because they had so many gun turrets. The British bombers were mostly Lancasters and they had one turret fewer. He never saw a Lancaster because they flew at night, but he saw pictures of them and he heard them. The throb of their engines made his bedroom windows rattle. He also heard them coming back in the mornings before it was light, but they didn't make so much noise then because they didn't come back all together. And some didn't come back at all, like Uncle Jack's.

His father sometimes came down to Blyfield at weekends. Now they were getting V.2s as well as V.1s in London. V.2s were rockets and they were so fast that you couldn't shoot them down. There wasn't even time to sound an Air-Raid siren. All you saw was a flash in the sky and then the next second there was an explosion. Thank God Jerry didn't get them before, his father said. He said they were well out of it, and he was glad Kath was in Cheltenham.

Then they had exciting news from Kath. She had missed sending her usual weekly letter and his mother was getting worried and thinking of trying to phone her, when they heard she was in Paris, which had been liberated only three weeks before. The American Army had wanted secretaries in France and they had asked for volunteers and Kath had volunteered without telling anybody. She said they hadn't been told where they were going and they didn't know it was Paris until the plane started circling and they saw the Eiffel Tower and then all the girls in the plane cheered, even the ones who had been sick. She said she was safe and well and it was the most exciting thing that had ever happened to her. Timothy thought she was rather brave to go to France when they were still fighting the Germans there. Supposing the Germans started winning again and took her prisoner? He thought that his mother was worried about that too. She said she didn't like to think of Kath in Paris all on her own, she was too young and they should never have let her go to Cheltenham in the first place. Every day his mother ran to the door as soon as the postman came to see if there was a letter from Kath. The letters were written on a single sheet of paper which folded over to make its own envelope. It was called V-Mail, and it had red stripes on the outside and a place for the Censor's stamp.

The V on the V-Mail stood for Victory. Winston Churchill made the V for Victory sign with his fingers when they took pictures of him, and he held his cigar in the other hand. Everybody liked Mr. Churchill, and they called him Winnie, which was usually a girl's name, but was short for Winston. Churchill was head of the British and Roosevelt was head of the Americans and Stalin was head of the Russians. The Russians were winning too, now, on the other side of Germany. Timothy had some comics about a little boy Cossack who played all kinds of tricks on the Germans as they were retreating.

Timothy went back to school at the convent where he had been before. Usually they didn't take boys over seven, but as it was wartime they made an exception. It felt strange going back again, though the nuns he remembered best, Sister Teresa and Sister Scholastica, had left. It was boring being in a class of all girls except one other boy his age, but it was better than having to go to the village school. He feared the rough village boys, but at the same time he despised them. They had been in Blyfield all their lives, and they didn't know anything, really. The war to them was just the odd V.1 being shot down and the bombers droning overhead. They had no idea what it was like in London, where there were bomb-sites and shelters and shrapnel in the streets. Timothy pined for the streets of London and the shops and the red buses and trams. East Grinstead, the nearest large town to Blyfield, wasn't really very big, but Timothy liked going there with his mother on the Green Line bus. There was a hospital in the town for mending the skins of airmen who had been burned in plane crashes, and you often saw them walking about the streets in their bright blue hospital uniforms and white bandages. Sometimes they had bandages covering all their faces, with just holes for their eyes and mouths; and sometimes they had no bandages, and no faces, really – as if their faces had been made of wax, and melted. When they met these men on the pavement, his mother took his hand and hurried past. She said it was rude to stare at the poor men's faces, and he supposed she was right; but it also seemed rude to walk past and look the other way. It was difficult to know what to do. He wondered which the men preferred.

Timothy was overjoyed when his mother said they would be going home for Christmas and would probably stay there. The V.1s and V.2s had practically stopped now, and his father thought it was safe. The news was good and everybody thought the war would soon be over. But when his father met them at Victoria Station, the first thing he said to Timothy's mother was:

– I see we're losing the war again.

He meant it as a joke, but Timothy could see that he was a bit worried. The Germans were fighting back and the Americans were having to retreat. The newspapers called it the Battle of the Bulge. It spoiled Christmas, because his parents were worried about Kath. But on Boxing Day the news was better. The wireless said the Americans were fighting back and the Germans were retreating again. Then they had a letter from Kath. His mother read it out at breakfast:

I am having the time of my life here in Paris. I enjoy working for the Americans – they are so friendly and we have a lot of fun. We are looked after very well – good billets, good food, entertainment, etc. We had a heavy snowfall yesterday and Paris looks really lovely covered in thick snow. Paris is a beautiful city. The streets are much wider than they are in London. I hope you had a nice Christmas together at number 33. We were looking forward to having Midnight Mass in Notre Dame cathedral, but it was cancelled owing to the turn of events.

The turn of events meant the Battle of the Bulge.

– You wouldn't think there was a war on, otherwise, his mother said. The way she talks, you'd think she was on holiday.

– She ought to worry about her own battle of the bulge, if you ask me, his father said, with all that Yank food she's getting.

The war with Germany came to an end in the spring. They listened to every news broadcast on the wireless, and each time there were the names of new towns captured by the Allies. Every day Timothy looked at the maps in the *Daily Express* and followed the movement of the great white arrows of the Allied armies cutting into Germany. The British and the Americans were advancing from the west and the Russians from the east. Soon they would join up and Germany would be beaten. He was excited and impatient for the end. He felt as he felt when some bully was called out from assembly at school and caned – a mixture of elation and relief and righteousness. When the first news of Belsen came out and pictures appeared in the newspapers of starving men in tattered pyjamas with arms and legs like sticks, ribs sticking through their skins, some lying dead in heaps, limbs all tangled together, Timothy felt almost glad – glad that the Germans had been shown to be wicked beyond all imagining, for it confirmed the righteousness of the war. It was as if all the evil and nastiness and cruelty in the world had been drawn into one place and was now being punished and stamped out, crushed between the mighty armies of the Allies.

He resented any imperfection in the victory, and the death of President Roosevelt, just before the Germans surrendered, seemed to him a piece of mismanagement on the part of God. He had had some vague picture in his mind of Churchill, Roosevelt and Stalin marching in triumph into Berlin and shaking hands with each other on a pile of rubble under a blue sky, while the soldiers of the three nations unslung their rifles and took off their helmets and grinned and cheered. And he had a picture, too, of Hitler being dragged before them, frightened and guilty and pleading for mercy and then being hanged or something. But Hitler killed himself, before the Allies could capture him, and that was another imperfection. Then they couldn't find Hitler's body and the papers said perhaps he had escaped after all and was hiding somewhere. The boys at school argued about whether he was dead or not, and Timothy took the side of those who said he was, because he couldn't bear to think that Hitler had escaped, and he was a bit afraid that, if he had, he might reappear one day with an army. For to Timothy there had always been something superhuman about Hitler, as if he were like the Devil. Otherwise, how could a small country like Germany have nearly beaten so many other countries?

But Germany was beaten, and they had V.E. Day, which meant Victory in Europe, for the war wasn't over yet, because there was still Japan. The Japanese were like the Germans, they were cruel to their prisoners; and they were more difficult to beat in some ways because they didn't mind getting killed. They had suicide pilots who would crash their planes on to a ship to sink it even though they got killed themselves. Then the Americans dropped the atom bomb, and the Japanese surrendered. That the Allies had invented the atom bomb seemed to Timothy the final proof that the good people were the cleverest people and would always win in the end. It was a pity that they hadn't invented the atom bomb before, though, because they could have just dropped it on Berlin and a few other German towns and then Germany would have surrendered much quicker.

Between V.E. Day and V.J. Day there was something called a General Election, and afterwards a man called Mister Attlee, whom Timothy had never heard of before, was Prime Minister instead of Winston Churchill. Timothy couldn't understand it, because everybody liked Churchill and he had won the war. His father said it was politics and he was too young to understand. But Timothy was shocked by what seemed to him ingratitude and treachery. Besides, it was stupid to get rid of Churchill before the Japs were beaten. Mister Attlee didn't look like a war-winning man. In fact he looked rather like Timothy's father.

But the Japs surrendered and on V.J. Night they had a bonfire in the street, on the bomb-site. Everybody came out of their houses and stood around the bonfire laughing and talking and drinking beer and lemonade out of bottles. Like all the children, Timothy had a red, white and blue ribbon pinned on his coat in the shape of a V. There were bonfires that night on lots of bomb-sites all over London. They lit up the sky in a red glow like the Blitz. Then a man let off some fireworks that he had saved from pre-war.

There were so many grown-ups round him that Timothy couldn't see the fireworks properly, and he moved away from the crowd till he found a high place to stand on. The last firework was an especially bright flare that lit up the whole bomb-site like daylight and he realized that he was standing on the grassy roof of Jill's old shelter.

The glare of the firework faded and he was in the dark again. The figures of the people below him were dim silhouettes against the red glow of the fire. He felt strange: solemn, yet baffled, as if something should be said, or thought, at this moment, but he didn't know quite what it was. He scrambled down from the roof of the shelter and, stumbling over rubble and twisted pipes, made his way back to the circle around the fire.

– Oh, there you are, said his mother. What have you been doing with your best trousers? She slapped at them with her hand.

He stared into the glowing embers.

– Mum . . .

– Your face is filthy, too. What?

She took a handkerchief from her handbag, spat on it and rubbed at his cheek. He put up with this childish treatment because he had a question to ask.

– Mum, is the war really over?

– Yes, thank goodness.

– What will it be like now?

– What will it be like? Goodness, you do ask questions. I suppose things will go back to normal in time. She closed her handbag with a snap.

– What's normal?

– Well, all the soldiers will come home, and go back to work. There won't be a blackout . . . and there'll be more food in the shops, and no rationing.

– Will there be bananas?

– Yes, there'll be bananas, and oranges and pineapples, and all those things.

– When will you buy me a banana?

His mother laughed.

– Oh, I couldn't say. It'll all take a certain amount of time.

3

– It's all taking a lot longer than I bargained for, his mother used to say, for she often recalled Timothy's questions on V.J. Night. It was two years before Timothy tasted a banana, and then his mother had to queue for an hour to get a bunch. Rationing went on, and in some ways it got worse.

In fact life changed surprisingly little after the war. The street-lamps were turned on one night, and Timothy and his two friends in the road, Jonesy and Blinker, walked round the streets for so long, experimenting with their shadows in the strange bluish light, that his mother sent his father out to look for them; but the novelty soon wore off. The soldiers were being demobbed, and every now and again one of the houses in the neighbourhood would be plastered with hand-painted signs saying *Welcome Home Dad*. But his Dad had never been away from home, and Uncle Jack, for whom he would have liked to paint a *Welcome Home* sign, was not coming back from the war. He thought of putting up a sign for Kath when she came home, but he was afraid that Jonesy and Blinker might tease him about it, because she was only a secretary.

But when Kath arrived she was wearing a special uniform, a very smart khaki one made of smooth cloth, like Rod's, with a red, white and blue badge on her sleeve. To everybody's surprise, she wasn't half so fat as she had been when she went away. Her hair was done differently, and she didn't wear glasses any more, except for reading, and she wore lipstick and nail varnish. She smoked cigarettes, too. When he walked up the road with her, Timothy saw the dim shapes of the neighbours moving behind their lace curtains like fish in an aquarium, drawn to the windows to look at his glamorous sister.

Jonesy and Blinker said she was smashing, and Timothy wished he had put up a *Welcome Home* sign after all.

But Kath was only on leave, and she made it clear that she had no plans to come back to London for good. She was working in Frankfurt now. His parents wanted her to come home, but she said she was better off where she was; well paid and well looked after, and she was seeing life. They were all sitting round the dining-room table after tea. His mother muttered something about some people being selfish, and Kath looked upset.

– That's a silly thing to say, Mum. What good would I be at home? We always got on each other's nerves.

– What nonsense, said his mother, pinching her lips together.

– It isn't – is it, Dad?

His father shifted uneasily in his chair and drew from his pocket a packet of Lucky Strike that Kath had given him.

– I don't know, Kath. But I know that your mother and me would like to have you a bit nearer home.

Kath took a cigarette and lit it, and her father's, with a dainty gold lighter.

– Look, if there's an emergency, I can always hop on a service plane and be home in a few hours.

– That's not the point, said his mother.

– What is the point then? If it's money I'd be glad to –

– We don't need your money, girl, said his father impatiently. There's nothing to spend it on, anyway.

Timothy's mother began to pile the plates in front of her.

– Well, I suppose I'll have to resign myself to running this house all on my own.

– Oh, Mum! Tell you what. (Kath stubbed out her cigarette in a saucer; the butt, crimsoned with lipstick, was so long that it buckled under the pressure, and Timothy saw his father cast a scandalized glance at the waste.) Tell you what: let me pay for a woman to come in and clean.

– A woman! What would I do with a woman? I can manage perfectly well on my own in this house, thank you very much.

Kath exploded with laughter:

– Mum, you're impossible!

Timothy and his father joined in the laughter. His mother gave an uncertain, unhappy smile. Undecided whether or not to take offence, she stood up and carried the pile of plates out to the kitchen.

Kath had brought a lot of presents home with her. It was as if a fairy godmother had visited the house. For Timothy there were American sweets, or candies as she called them, with strange, inexplicable names like *Baby Ruth* and *Oh Henry!* There were American cigarettes in huge packets of 200 for his father, and a new kind of stockings called nylons for his mother. And there were special expensive presents as well: a watch for Timothy, a camera for his father and earrings with real pearls for his mother.

– Kath, you shouldn't be so extravagant, his mother said, turning the earrings in her hand. I'll never dare wear them. They must have cost the earth.

– I saved my cigarette ration, Kath explained. You can buy anything in Germany for cigarettes. Or food.

– You mean you got these things on the black market, Kath? his father asked, with a hint of disapproval in his voice.

Kath shrugged.

– Everybody does it. Why, only the other day the Chaplain's driver came into the office tossing a tin of ham in his hands. I asked him what he was doing with it, and d'you know what he said? *Chaplain told me to go out and get some flowers for the altar.*

– The Catholic Chaplain? his mother said.

– Yes.

– Goodness. I suppose it must be all right, then.

Timothy was curious to know how many cigarettes his watch had cost, but he thought it might be impolite to ask. It was a Swiss watch with a sweep second hand and it was shockproof, waterproof and antimagnetic. He imagined a German handing over the watch for a carton of cigarettes and smoking them one by one and, when there were only a few left, wishing he hadn't swapped his watch because a watch lasted and cigarettes didn't.

– What are they like, the Germans? he asked Kath, on her last day at home. They were sitting in the back bedroom, which he had given up to Kath for her leave. She was varnishing her nails, an operation he liked to watch.

– Well, we're not supposed to fraternize – you know, mix with the Germans. In fact at first they kept us behind wire, you weren't allowed out without a pass. So it's difficult to say. But they seem just like other people. Except that you see a lot of cripples, injuries of various kinds.

– I s'pose they hate us for winning the war?

– They're pretty bitter about the bombing, and nobody likes to be occupied, of course. But they're better off under the Americans than they would be in the Russian zone, and they know it.

– Well, anyway, they asked for it, didn't they? The bombing, I mean.

– I suppose so . . . But the Blitz was nothing to Frankfurt. I've never seen such devastation. Block after block, completely flattened.

– You know our Woolworth's was hit by a flying bomb? Timothy asked her, feeling obscurely that Kath was underrating the battle-scars of her own country.

– Yes, wasn't that terrible? All those people killed, children too. Well, thank God it's all over now.

– I wonder you want to go back to Frankfurt, he said.

– Oh well, I might get posted to a nicer place. You never know. There!

Kath had finished her nails. She replaced the bottle cap with its little brush, stood up, and waved her hands in the air to dry the varnish. She walked to the window and stared out.

– My God, she murmured.

Timothy followed her to the window to see what had provoked this comment. But looking out, he saw only the familiar rows of narrow back gardens with their coal sheds and washing lines, a tram stopping in the street beyond, and the smoky expanse of roofs blurring into the distance. A fine drizzle was falling, and the smoke rose slowly from the chimneys. He went back to the bed where he had been sitting and turned the pages of an American magazine Kath had brought home with her. It was thick and heavy and shiny, and there were a lot of pictures in it of pancakes dripping with syrup and tall drinks full of fruit and lumps of ice and huge streamlined cars, spread across two pages so that they seemed to bend in the middle. The magazine was called *Life*.

– Can I keep this, Kath, or do you want to take it back with you? he asked timidly.

– Mmm? she murmured abstractedly. Oh, yes, keep it Timothy, I get it all the time in Germany.

She was still standing at the window, moving her hands up and down, like some large bird struggling into flight.

When he was ten, Timothy went to a grammar school, St. Michael's. The teachers were called Brothers, and they were like priests except that they didn't say mass. They wore black cassocks and big white collars. There were also some teachers who were not Brothers and wore ordinary clothes, like the Art master. Timothy liked Art best. They had a double period of Art on Friday afternoons, which was a nice way to end the week. His best subjects were art and maths. At the end of term they had tests, and Timothy usually came third or fourth in the class, though he was one of the youngest. At first his parents paid for him to go to St. Michael's, but when he was eleven he took a special test and after that it was free.

There were two things he didn't like about his school. One was the caning, of which there was a lot, not just for being naughty but for getting your lessons wrong; and the other was games. Timothy was keen on sport, especially football, which everybody played at break. Being light and agile, he was rather good at playground football, where you needed to dodge not just the opposing players, but other players in other games sharing the same pitch. But the school game was rugby, which he hated. He didn't like getting banged and knocked like you did in rugby, and he didn't have the courage to tackle other players round the legs when they were running. He learned to run about on the edge of the play, looking as if he were interested, without actually touching the ball or another player. Sometimes he would fall over on purpose to get his knees muddy so that it would look as if he had tackled somebody. It was the same with cricket in the summer. He enjoyed playing in the playground, and with an old tennis ball that had had most of the fur rubbed off it he could turn off-breaks quite sharply. But cricket with a real ball, hard and deadly, was a different matter. The only other school sport was running, and he was no good at that either. Usually he was eliminated in the heats before Sports Day, and so he would sit with his parents to watch the races, and see the winners go up at the end to receive their cups.

– It's a shame they don't give cups for lessons, his mother would say. Then you'd win something, Timothy.

But Timothy coveted athletic success, and coming first in Art or

Maths gave him only a fleeting satisfaction. Sport was his chief interest in life. Sometimes his father took him to watch Charlton Athletic in the football season, and Surrey in the cricket season. He followed the fortunes of these teams in the *Daily Express* with passionate interest, and enacted their triumphs in fantasy, kicking a ball in the street against the front garden fence, or batting, for hour after solitary hour, a sorbo-rubber ball suspended by a string from the clothes-line in the back garden. But his achievements stopped short in the street or the playground. They passed into no records, were engraved upon no trophies, brought no credit to his school, and reflected no glory upon himself. He was resigned to a life of humble obscurity.

Kath came back for Christmas 1947. Timothy and his parents went up to Victoria Station to meet her. The train was late, and while his parents sat in the buffet drinking cups of tea he walked about the station to keep warm, investigating the automatic slot-machines that stood, empty and neglected, near the entrances to the platforms. They bore faded legends offering chocolate bars and caramels and nuts and raisins for one penny. The slots of the pennies were sealed up. Behind their grime-encrusted windows there were only empty metal racks, but he pulled experimentally on the drawers, hoping, though not really hoping, that one of them would open and yield up a piece of forgotten pre-war confectionery.

At last Kath's train came in, drawn by a Battle of Britain class locomotive, and she alighted like an exotic bird on to the grey winter platform, slippery with mud and litter. She wasn't wearing her khaki uniform, but a green tartan costume with a cape and fur hat. The costume had a very long skirt, reaching almost to her ankles.

– You've gone in for the New Look, then? was his mother's first comment.

– Yes, like it? Kath pirouetted on the platform. She had a lot of cases with her of all kinds and shapes, round ones and square ones as well as the usual oblong ones. She hired a taxi to take them home, and she talked all the way. Timothy thought she was talking posher than she used to, and when he answered her questions she mimicked his accent and said:

– You're a proper little Cockney, aren't you, Timothy?

Kath had brought them a lot of presents again. Some were not to be opened till Christmas morning, but she brought out at once bottles, tins of food and cigarettes and sweets. Some of the sweets were British kinds that you couldn't buy in the shops even on points, because they were for export only: Olde English Butterscotch and Mackintosh's Toffees and Original Pontefract Cakes, luxuriously packed in stout painted tins and gay wrappings. The sweets had travelled halfway round the world, via America and Germany, before coming into his hands. He consumed them reverently, like a persecuted Christian receiving the sacrament.

– I don't know what Christmas would be without you, Kath, his father said. There's nothing in the shops.

– Rationing's terrible – worse than the war, said his mother. Bread's the latest, if you don't mind.

– I don't understand it, said Kath. You seem to be no better off than the Germans.

– That's what I say, said his mother. What use was it winning the war if we still have to pinch and scrape for every meal?

– It's this Government, said his father. You won't catch me voting for that lot again.

His father was always grumbling about the Government. So was the *Daily Express*. Timothy picked up the sarcastic phrases of his father, and the caricatured likenesses of Strachey, Shinwell and Cripps in the newspaper became part of his private mythology, like Hitler, Goebbels and Goering in the war, less evil bogeymen, but equally available for ridicule and abuse. Timothy was also aware of another, more disturbing variation on the emotions of the war. It seemed that the Russians, and Stalin (Uncle Joe, as people used to call him) were not friendly any more. They were Communists, which meant that nobody was allowed to have anything of their own in Russia, and they wanted to take over other countries so that nobody could have anything of their own there, either. Sometimes they sounded as bad as the Nazis. They were atheists, and persecuted the Church. Every Sunday, at the end of Mass, there were prayers for the conversion of Russia.

Despite all the presents that Kath had brought, it wasn't a very merry Christmas. There was a power-cut on Christmas Day which spoiled the dinner. Kath kept complaining of the cold, but they didn't have much coal and his parents kept bickering about the fire, whether it should be poked or not. Kath didn't stay for very long because she wanted to get back to Germany for a fancy-dress ball she was going to, as the Statue of Liberty, on New Year's Eve. She was living in Heidelberg now, which she liked much better than Frankfurt. She said it was a picturesque little town on a river, between mountains, with a ruined castle and lots of old buildings, and it had hardly been damaged at all in the war. She lived in a hotel converted into a hostel, and had lots of nice girl friends.

– Any boy friends, Kath? his father asked.

– Well, I don't have any trouble getting escorts for parties and so on. There aren't so many girls around, you see – apart from the German ones, of course. So I do all right for dates. It's a good place to be for a fat girl, I always say. The girls in the office get a laugh out of that.

– I wouldn't say you were fat now, said his mother.

– Well, I'm not exactly slim, am I? Kath smoothed her skirt over her hips.

– As long as you don't go marrying a Yank, his father said.

Kath laughed.

– All the nice ones are married already, she said. And the others aren't interested in marriage.

– What are they interested in? Timothy asked.

Kath laughed again, but didn't answer, and his mother told him it was time he went to bed.

It was rather dismal seeing Kath off at Victoria. She had a cold and kept blowing her nose and complaining because she couldn't get any paper tissues in London.

– I think it's disgusting the way people use these cotton hankies. Just carrying a lot of germs around with them.

– I'm sorry if I disgust you, his mother said huffily. She too had a cold.

– Oh, I don't mean you, Mum.

– And I always boil them to get rid of the germs, his mother went on fretfully.

– Kath, what about coming over in the summer, when it's a bit warmer? his father said.

– Well, I don't know, Dad. A girl friend of mine in Heidelberg . . . we were thinking of making a trip to Italy this summer.

– Italy?

– I've always wanted to see Rome and Florence and all those places.

– Oh well . . . You've got to do these things while you're young, I suppose. He picked at a hole in his glove.

– We thought we'd try and get a holiday this year, his mother said to Kath.

– Oh good – where?

– Worthing. We used to go there before the war – Mrs. Watkins, remember?

– Yes, I remember, said Kath.

– She's still there.

– Why don't you go somewhere new?

– Oh, I wouldn't like to go somewhere I didn't know.

A whistle sounded shrilly and doors began to slam.

– You'd better get in, Kath, his father said.

– I'll let you know about the summer, she said, as she kissed them goodbye.

Timothy ran beside the train until he couldn't keep up with Kath any more. He walked slowly back along the platform to where his parents waited disconsolately, breathing plumes of steam into the cold air. It was snowing and a few flakes were falling through the holes in the station roof that had been made by the war. He looked up at the roof to see where the snow was coming in, but in the grey, dirty light it was impossible to distinguish the panes that were missing from the panes that were in place. Against the expanse of grey glass the snowflakes themselves looked a darker grey as they floated down towards him. It was funny standing under a roof while the snow fell on you.

Kath didn't come home in the summer. She went to Italy with her girl friend, and they had a succession of postcards from Lake Como, Florence and Rome, and later a letter with a photograph of Kath and her friend pretending to be holding up the Leaning Tower of Pisa. She said she wouldn't come home for the following Christmas, because it was so cold in England in the winter, but wait for the spring. But in the spring she was invited to join a party on a Mediterranean cruise, which was too good a chance to miss; but that used up her leave and her money, so her visit would have to wait for another year.

Kath sent them long typewritten letters describing her holidays and weekend trips. Timothy found them boring – catalogues of foreign places and foreign meals – but he derived a vague satisfaction from having a sister who led such an exotic and adventurous life. In part he acquired this attitude from his parents. Kath's letters and postcards, kept behind the clock on the dining-room mantelpiece and produced for the enquiring visitor, were a source of quiet pride, evidence that they had lines of communication with a larger and more glamorous life than their own. Yet at the same time he knew that his parents missed Kath, and his mother, particularly, was bitter sometimes about her long absence.

They decided to go to Worthing again that summer, 1949. Timothy was pleased. It seemed natural and inevitable, part of the rhythm of his life, a rhythm so simple and orderly that it was difficult for him, looking back over a year, to distinguish one week from the next, except by the seasonal changes of sport. School was always much the same, and he arranged his weekends so that they conformed to a timetable almost as rigid. On Friday evening he got most of his homework done and had a bath. Saturday was given over entirely to pleasure. In the morning his mother brought him breakfast in bed, and he lay in, reading comics, until about eleven o'clock. In the afternoon he and Jonesy and Blinker went to watch Charlton Athletic, or Charlton Reserves if the first team were playing away, and he asked for no greater happiness than to watch Charlton win. He hadn't, of course, been able to watch their greatest victory, against Burnley in the Cup Final of 1947. He listened to the radio commentary in an agony of suspense as the game went into extra time with no score. Then Duffy, the little bald-headed left-winger, scored a fantastic goal right out of the blue, taking a cross from the right wing on the volley, and with his right foot too. Duffy ran the length of the pitch to embrace Sam Bartram, Charlton's goalkeeper, the commentator said. Charlton never rose to such heights again, but they were always an interesting team to watch, fickle and unpredictable, but capable of heartwarming flashes of brilliance. More than once he and his friends had left the Valley a few minutes before the end of a game, dispirited by their team's poor performance, only to hear, as they passed through the quiet, car-lined streets, a huge explosive roar filling the air behind them, indicating that Charlton had scored a last-minute goal and snatched a point.

Coming home on the smoke-filled top deck of a swaying tram, he would dispute the critical points of the game with Jonesy and Blinker. Usually, instead of changing trams at New Cross, they would get off at Deptford High Street, and walk the rest of the way home through the back streets, kicking an old tennis ball between them, for watching a good game produced a kind of ache in the legs, a longing to kick and dribble, that had to be satisfied. They would play in the street until it got dark, and then, tingling from the exercise in the cold, damp air, he went in for his tea, baked beans on toast with a rasher of bacon, usually, on Saturdays. After tea he took down the football results from the wireless and helped his father check his pools coupon. In the evening he would meet Jonesy and Blinker again – they went to each other's houses in turn – to play cards or Monopoly.

Sunday was mainly devoted to Church. They usually went to the ten o'clock Mass on Sunday mornings, unless they were going to Communion, in which case they went to the eight-thirty, because of the fast. Sometimes they went to Benediction in the afternoon. On Sunday evenings, after high tea, there was usually some homework to finish off, and after that he would listen to Variety Bandbox on the radio, with his parents. It was a safe, orderly life.

So he was glad that they went to Worthing again for their holiday. It was a change from home, but it was also familiar. They had the same rooms at Mrs. Watkins' and the same table in the dining-room, at the window. It looked out on to the bus shelter and the bowling green. Everything was the same.

But somehow, after the first few days, it wasn't as enjoyable as the year before. He was fourteen, too old to play with the sand at low tide – on his own, anyway; and he was too shy to make friends with other children on the beach. He was too old to paddle, and he couldn't swim. There seemed to be nothing much to do except mooch about the pier playing the pinball machines. In one part of the pier they had machines that you looked into to see pictures of bare women. He walked past them every day, longing to have a look, but afraid that people would stare, or his parents come past by chance. One afternoon when there weren't many people about, and his parents were listening to a concert at the bandstand, he sidled up to one of the machines, inserted a penny, and pressed his face to the viewer. The machine whirred and a succession of faded sepia photographs flicked past, depicting young women larking about on swings and seesaws. It was true that they were bare, but the parts you wanted to see had been blanked out. The hairstyles reminded him of snaps of his mother and her friends when she was young, in the album at home. He left the pier feeling both guilty and cheated, and went to sit on the beach. Sometimes when the mothers changed their little girls out of their wet swimming costumes, you could glimpse the little cleft between their legs. But the big girls kept towels wrapped carefully round them when they changed and stared if they caught you looking.

The second week of the holiday was better. His parents made friends with a Mr. and Mrs. Clements, who were staying at the same guesthouse. Mr. Clements was a big man, with hair on his shoulders as well as his chest. He offered to teach Timothy how to swim, at the baths, and Timothy was so bored that he agreed. He didn't enjoy the lessons, but by the end of the week he suddenly got the hang of it, and could swim the width of the pool. Next year, he thought, as the train drew out of Worthing station, next year the holiday will be more fun because I can swim.

But the next holiday was just as disappointing. It was a bad summer all round. Kath had been going to come home at last, but her leave was cancelled at the last moment because the Korean War broke out. The English football team, incredibly and humiliatingly, was knocked out of the World Cup, by America of all countries, one-nil. And he should have taken his O-Levels in June, but the Government had passed a stupid rule that you couldn't sit the exam unless you were fifteen before the first of January that year, and he was fifteen on the tenth of January. Timothy now had a personal grievance against the Government, and took a keen interest in the election in February. Labour won again, but with such a narrow majority that everybody said there would have to be another election before long. Timothy drew some satisfaction from the swing against Labour, but it didn't help his personal situation. He sat the mock O-Levels at Easter with the rest of his class, and his teachers reckoned he would have passed with several credits. With those results he could have left school and started his apprenticeship as a draughtsman. If that was what he was going to do. There was a certain amount of doubt about it.

On his fourteenth birthday his Uncle Ted had asked him what his best subjects were and he had told him Art and Maths, and Uncle Ted said that in that case he had better be a draughtsman. Somehow the idea had stuck. Timothy liked drawing and making diagrams of things, and it pleased him to have some definite idea of the future, something to tell people when they asked, as they were always asking, what he was going to do when he left school. *I'm going to be a draughtsman*. It sounded quite impressive – something a little out of the ordinary: professional, specialized, and yet sensible, not too ambitious, something he could be reasonably sure of attaining. His father thought it was a good idea. His mother wasn't so sure. She had always wanted Timothy to be a teacher.

After Timothy had taken the mock O-Level exams, the Headmaster, Brother Augustine, asked to see him with his parents. He said there was no point keeping Timothy in the Fifth Form for another year. He suggested that he should go into the Sixth Form and sit his O-Levels at the end of his first year, then A-Levels the year after that, when he would be seventeen.

– We hadn't thought of keeping him on at school for another two years, said his father. He's set on being a draughtsman, and he might as well start his apprenticeship as soon as he can.

– A draughtsman? Brother Augustine raised his eyebrows. I think Timothy might set his sights a bit higher than that. I want to get a proper Sixth Form going at St. Michael's – put the boys in for University. Timothy's one of the boys I had in mind. What d'you think, Timothy?

– I don't know, Timothy said, truthfully. He knew nothing about universities apart from the Oxford and Cambridge Boat Race.

– Would it, er, cost a lot? his father asked.

– It shouldn't cost you much at all, Mr. Young, perhaps nothing. University education is free now, and the maintenance grants are quite generous. Getting in is the difficult thing.

– I think it's a good idea, said his mother. But his father wanted to know what it would lead to.

– We thought draughtsmanship was a good idea, Art and Maths being his best subjects. It sort of combines them. That's what his Uncle Ted said.

– Yes, well, what about architecture?

– Architecture?

In the end they left it that Timothy would go into the Sixth Form in September, take his O-Levels the next summer, and make up his mind in the course of the year what he wanted to do. Riding home, on the bus, the word *architecture* echoed in his mind, mysterious, alluring, intimidating. To be an architect was certainly a pleasing notion, but beset with difficulties and uncertainties. His mother was elated at the prospect of Timothy going to University, but his father was not so keen. He discovered that you could become an architect through an apprenticeship and that many people thought it was the best way – you got practical experience from the beginning. Timothy would have found it easier to make up his mind about the future if he had been allowed to sit the O-Level exams. As it was, he existed in an academic limbo, neither passing nor failing.

Other, less definable and less discussable frustrations weighed on Timothy's spirits when they went to Worthing again in the summer of 1950, making him, as his mother said, moody. He was lonely and bored – bored with his parents' company and bored with Worthing; bored with the promenade and the pier and the putting green and Mrs. Watkins' Spam salads. Though he could swim quite well now, it wasn't much fun swimming on your own. He usually went in as soon as they settled themselves on the beach in the morning, to get it over with. After that there wasn't much to do except to sit on the beach and read and watch the girls covertly from behind his sunglasses. There was one girl with dark curly hair and a pale blue swimming costume that he thought was rather pretty. He used to watch her tiptoeing over the pebbles to go swimming with her father, plucking at the bottom edge of her swimming costume, and then, as she came back again, pulling her shoulder straps straight and taking off her rubber cap to shake out her hair. But she never took any notice of him.

In the evenings he dressed in his new brown gaberdine trousers and the yellow pullover his mother had knitted for him at his request. As he stood before the wardrobe mirror in his room to slick down his dry, salty hair with Brylcreem, he admired the effect of the clothes, the first he had chosen himself. But putting them on only created a sense of expectancy that could not be satisfied. After supper there was nothing to do except to take a stroll along the promenade with his parents as the sun set beyond Littlehampton and a chill breeze blew off the sea, or perhaps go to the pictures. He preferred to go to the cinema on his own, and to walk back along the front afterwards in the dark, brooding on certain scenes in the film he had just seen, or on the girl in the blue bathing suit, or on both, in some confused way, together. One night there was a gale which blew the waves in great rollers against the sea wall and sent spray lashing over the promenade. He walked for miles that night, soaked to the skin, the phrase *defying the elements* ringing in his head.

The next morning the sea was calm under a hazy sky, and the beach was strewn with pieces of driftwood. Some of them were branches of trees stripped, bleached and worn smooth by the sea. They were strangely beautiful and he amused himself by sketching some of them. He was alone: his parents had gone shopping and would join him later. The girl in the blue bathing costume and her family came and settled themselves nearby, and he was conscious that she was sneaking curious glances at him. Close up, she wasn't as pretty as she had seemed before, and when she was drying herself after a swim he noticed, with a slight shock of disgust, that she had hair under her arms. The recent appearance of his own body hair had made him uneasy, particularly the growth that had suddenly sprouted at his groin and swayed in the bathwater like seaweed. He knew that men usually had hair there, but he thought his was appearing abnormally early and copiously. The hair in his armpits didn't worry him so much, but it looked ugly on a girl.

The sun dissolved the haze and it grew hot. He took a long swim, going further from the shore than he had ever done before, then threw himself down on his towel, cradling his head on his arms. Gradually the hot sun dried his skin and a delicious languor poured through his limbs. He dozed. After a while he heard his parents' voices, and the sound of deckchairs being dragged across the shingle.

– Give your mother a hand, son, his father called. Reluctant to stir, to disturb his delightful relaxation, he kept his eyes shut.

– Don't bother him, Geoff, I think he's asleep.

– In the middle of the morning?

– He's been in the water. I expect he tired himself out.

– Hmm. Got no energy, that boy.

Timothy stayed immobile, feigning sleep. The trivial chat of his parents, as they settled themselves in their deckchairs, came to him like a radio play.

– Well, this is a bit of all right.

– Lovely. Why don't you take your jacket off?
Pause.
– You got a paper, then?
– Last one. Last *Express*.
Pause.
– What did you think of the kippers this morning?
– I think I *will* take my jacket off.
– I thought they were a bit dry myself.
– What?
– The kippers.
– Oh, yes, they were a bit dry, I suppose.
– I didn't like to say anything.
Pause.
– Anything in the paper?
– MacArthur says he's confident.
– MacArthur?
– In Korea.
– Oh, yes.
– They're talking about calling up the Z Reserves.
– Sst! Like the war all over again.
– They'll be putting petrol on ration again soon, I wouldn't be surprised.
Pause.
– It'd be nice to have a little car, Geoff.
– Twelve months' waiting-list for most models.
– I didn't mean a new one.
– New one or old one, it doesn't make much odds. We can't afford to run one, anyway.
– Kath said she was thinking of learning to drive.
– When was that?
– In her last letter. You read it.
Pause.
– Pity she couldn't come over this summer.
Pause.
– She wouldn't have come anyway.
– What?
– She'll never come over. She'll always find some excuse.
– But she was all booked to come. It was this Korean business that stopped her. You read the letter.

– If it hadn't been that it would have been something else.

– I don't know what you're talking about, Dorothy. What are you talking about?

– When was the last time she came home?

– I know, but –

– Nineteen forty-seven. Three years ago.

– Two and a half.

– All right, two and half. But this is the third year running she's got out of coming home.

– What are you getting at?

– I don't know. But there's something funny going on over there.

– What d'you mean, something funny?

Timothy was now fully alert, though he kept his eyes shut and didn't move. His mother dropped her voice and he had to strain to hear her reply.

– Some affair, some man, something she doesn't want us to know about.

– What, our Kath?

– She's not our Kath any more, Geoff, you might as well face that. She's only spent three weeks at home, all told, in the last three years.

– Well, I know, but that doesn't mean . . . She's still a decent Catholic girl.

– Is she?

– What do you mean, *is she*?

– How do we know? Remember that Rod?

– Oh, that was just . . . she thought he was lonely. She didn't even know he was married when she first met him.

– So she said.

– Anyway, just because she hasn't been able to get home lately, you've no right to . . . More likely it's *you* that's put her off.

– Me!

– Yes, you, Dorothy. You were always getting at her when she was at home. You can't deny it.

– Well, that's a nice thing to say!

– What I mean is, just because she hasn't been home for a while, you jump to conclusions . . .

– I don't suppose I'm the only one.

– What d'you mean?

– When a daughter goes away, stays away from home for three years –

– Two and a half.

– Never gets married and shows no signs of doing so.

– She's young yet.

– The neighbours think it's funny.

– The neighbours should mind their own bloody business.

– There's no need to use language.

– What are you getting at, anyway?

– You remember that Wilkes girl, up the road. Veronica?

– What about her?

– She disappeared suddenly and never came home. They said she'd got a job up north. Then someone saw her in Manchester, pushing a pram. And she hadn't got a wedding ring.

– Are you suggesting . . .

– I'm not suggesting anything, I'm only explaining to you why people talk.

– You're mad, Dorothy, that's what you are.

– Well, we'll see. Now let's drop the subject. I'm going to wake Timothy up, his back's getting quite red. Timothy!

He felt his mother's hand on his shoulder. He went through an elaborate mime of waking up, yawning and squinting at the sea, sparkling in the sun.

– I've got some Nivea in my bag. Shall I put some on your back?

– No, I'm going to get an ice cream.

He didn't really want an ice cream, but he wanted to be on his own.

Timothy sometimes wondered whether he really had been asleep that morning on the beach, and dreamed the conversation between his parents. The idea of his big sister Kath, plump, heavy-footed, convent-educated Kath, being involved in the most spectacular sort of sin, seemed to him almost incredible, even if she did smoke and paint her nails. But if it *was* true (and he had little doubt that the conversation, anyway, had really happened) then it domesticated the sin, brought it excitingly, disturbingly out of the realm of fiction, or moral theology, into real life, his own life. For if it was possible for Kath to do it, if his mother could actually acknowledge that possibility, then it was possible for him to do it, too, perhaps, one day.

And he had never thought of it as a real possibility before – without being married, that is, a condition too remote to imagine very vividly. You might think about it, you might want to do it, but it was so enormous a sin that you would never actually do it. It was whispered that two of the boys in the Sixth had done it, with two girls they met on a camping holiday, all together in one tent, and it excited him just to think of it, but he didn't believe the story. They were just boasting. They had made it up. And yet, if Kath had done it . . . perhaps lots of people did it. It was still a sin, of course, a mortal sin. If you died suddenly with such a sin on your soul you would go to hell. It was a terrible risk. But if lots of people did it . . . There was a kind of safety in numbers.

He recalled his guilt over what he had done with Jill when they were five, and how he had been too ashamed to confess it, and wondered for years afterwards whether all his confessions had been void because of that one suppression of the truth, and all his communions sacrilegious. Until one day he was reading a book, a grown-up's book he had taken at random from the shelves of the local library, and started to read. And there suddenly was the whole episode, as if the writer were describing himself and Jill – the two children left alone in the house, I'll show you mine if you'll show me yours, and the boy looking but not wanting to show his own, it was all exactly as it had happened. And although it was only a story, it showed that other children had done the same thing. And it wasn't described as anything very awful, or surprising, but as if it were quite ordinary. The relief had been tremendous. He was not alone. He belonged to a community, curious about the bodies of the opposite sex. It had been quite easy, then, to mention the business with Jill in a general confession he made during a school retreat, and the priest had made no comment.

Until now, the limit of his sexual ambition had been to see a grown-up girl bare, like he had seen Jill. To see the part that was always hidden, somehow, in paintings, or photographs, like the ones in *Razzle*, the magazine that was passed from hand to hand at school, and that he would sometimes glance at with affected scorn. But now, with the new possibilities revealed about Kath, his mind moved on, uncertainly, hesitantly, to the act itself, only to collapse from a simple want of information. He knew that you put your thing into the girl's. But what happened then, how long did you do it for, what did it feel like, did it hurt the girl, how did it make a baby, and how did the baby come out? He didn't know, he didn't know. It was partly his own fault. A year ago his father had come out into the garden where he was reading (he remembered it vividly, he was sitting in the red deckchair and there was a plane high in the sky making a vapour trail) and started a conversation on the subject that had never previously been mentioned between them. But he had been surprised by the suddenness of it, and embarrassed by the sight of his mother shooting anxious glances at them from the kitchen window. He had given the impression that he already knew everything he needed to know, and his father, visibly relieved, had let the subject drop.

For the rest of the holiday at Worthing, he kept away from his parents more and more, to think. His favourite place for thinking was the western end of the promenade, towards Littlehampton, where the cafés and hotels petered out into ordinary suburban houses and the road swerved inland towards the downs. Few holidaymakers walked that far, and there was a Corporation shelter, the last one on the front, where he could usually sit undisturbed.

He walked along the front to his shelter on the last evening of the holiday, after supper, leaving his mother packing their cases, and his father reading the evening newspaper in Mrs. Watkins' lounge. The sun had set, but still cast a rosy, reflected glow on the clouds, which in turn were reflected in the sea. The tide was coming in, and the waves churned the shingle on the beach. A poem in the book they had done for O-Level English came into his mind. He had answered a question on it in his mock examination.

Listen! you hear the grating roar
Of pebbles which the waves draw back, and fling,
At their return, up the high strand,
Begin and cease, and then again begin,
With tremulous cadence slow, and bring
The eternal note of sadness in.

He had written:

The poet, hearing the sound of the waves on the shore, feels sad. There is a good onomatopoeia in this verse. We seem to hear the sound of the waves on the beach. Note the alliteration of the hard *g* in the line *Begin, and cease and then again begin.*

But repeating the line to himself now, and listening to the waves on the beach below him, he thought that the best word in the line was *cease*. It was like the hiss of the wave as it broke and spent itself on the beach: *cease*. And there was a rhythm about the whole verse that was just like the rhythm of the waves, regular, but not monotonous, because each wave came just before, or just after you expected it. He wished he had thought of this before, so that he could have brought it into his examination answer. It was a good poem, *Dover Beach*. By Matthew Arnold. Whoever he was. There was a funny word at the end of the poem – *darkling*.

And we are here as on a darkling plain . . .

He hadn't been able to find *darkling* in the dictionary at home, but you could guess what it meant. It was darkling now: the pink had faded from the clouds, they were grey now, and the sea a darker grey. Over to the east it was quite black, except for the lights of the two Brighton piers twinkling in the distance – and as he looked, the lights of Worthing pier came on suddenly, and extinguished, by their brilliance, the last natural light of evening.

And we are here as on a darkling plain . . .

Something, something . . .

struggle and flight,
Where ignorant armies clash by night.

That was before they had radar. It was radar that won the Battle of Britain. Fighter Command watched the German planes coming over on their radar screens and sent our squadrons to intercept them. The Jerries must have had a nasty surprise when the Spitfires and Hurricanes came zeroing in out of the sun, their machine guns hammering: *der-der-der-der-der-der-der-der-der-* . . .

Alone in the shelter, under cover of night, safe from observation, Timothy lapsed into a heroic dream of his childhood. The dark shelter became the cockpit of a Spitfire. Crouched in his seat, he eased the joystick forward and squinted through the spider's-web gunsight at a Heinkel bomber. He pressed the button on the joystick and eight streams of bullets, marked by tracers, converged on the enemy aircraft, which burst into flames, tilted over, disintegrated and fell, in spinning, burning fragments, into the sea. Leaning back against his seat, he pulled the Spitfire out of its dive and banked steeply, scanning the skies for his next target. His back was to England, and his face, set in an expression of watchful defiance, was turned towards Europe.

TWO

Coming Out

1

One morning late in July 1951, Timothy Young woke early from a dream-troubled sleep. Half awake, he tried to recall his dream. He had been trapped in a convent run by some crazy nuns who thought the war was still going on and that he was a pupil left in their charge. When he attempted to escape, they chased him through the dark echoing corridors of the convent, and a huge nun loomed up out of the shadows and tackled him like a rugby full-back. Her face was unpleasantly familiar, and just before he woke up he realized that it was Hitler's, with the moustache shaved off, and that all the nuns were Nazis in disguise. It was a ridiculous dream, but he was left with an oppressive sense of anxiety and foreboding that he was soon able to trace to its source: he was leaving for Germany that morning.

He heard the muffled sound of the alarm clock ringing briefly in his parents' bedroom. Shortly afterwards he heard his mother padding downstairs in her slippers. It was scarcely light, and couldn't be much later than six o'clock. His train didn't leave Victoria until eleven, and he was all packed and ready to leave; but his parents had an exaggerated fear, which he recognized in himself, of missing trains. They always liked to be early. When they went to Worthing they were sometimes so early that they caught the train before the one they had intended to catch.

Worthing. It was funny – he knew he'd been bored with the place these last two summers, but now, at this moment, he couldn't recapture that sense of boredom, however hard he tried. In his imagination Worthing seemed the most charming holiday place in the world: bright, clean, familiar, safe. Only two hours in the electric train and you were there, the sea sparkling at the end of the street, the pier brightly painted and inviting, the lawns and flower beds on the front neatly groomed. What did he want to go to Heidelberg for, a whole day and night's journey away? Well, he had only himself to blame.

He remembered vividly the day the invitation had come, a bolt from the blue. He had read Kath's letter many times since, hoping to find in its vague, casual phrases some clue as to what he had let himself in for, so that he now had it off by heart.

I'm afraid I shan't be able to get home after all this year, as I've used up all my leave on the skiing holiday at Christmas and my trip to Seville this Easter. I was hoping to wangle another week's leave this summer, but my boss won't wear it, and I can't blame him. Anyway, what I want to suggest is, why doesn't Timothy come out here for a holiday this summer? If you could pay his fare, I could look after the rest of his expenses. I'd like to give him a treat – he deserves something after all that hard work at school, and I think he'd enjoy himself here. Heidelberg is a charming old town, and there's lots to see and do. I'm sure he could amuse himself in the daytime, and I'd be free in the evenings and at weekends. Do think about it seriously. Of course you could all come if you think you'd enjoy it, but frankly accommodation might be a bit of a problem as it is very scarce and v. expensive. But it shouldn't be difficult to find somewhere just for Timothy, and I'm hoping to get him a PX card so that he can use the American eating-places and so on.

– He's too young to go all that way on his own, his mother said, when the letter had been passed round the breakfast table. Timothy agreed, but was silent.

– What do you think, son? his father said.

– Why don't we all go? Timothy said

– Your father wouldn't enjoy it. Foreign food doesn't agree with him.

– What d'you mean, Dorothy?

– You remember what you were like on that day trip to Boulogne, before the war.

– That was the crossing. Nothing to do with the food.

– That's another thing. You're not a good sailor.

– Well, anyway, Kath seems to think it would be difficult to put us all up.

– It's plain as a pikestaff she doesn't want you and me there, said his mother.

His father looked unhappy. He turned to Timothy.

– What d'you think, son? D'you fancy going on your own?

– What about the fares? he said.

– I expect we can manage it. And you've got some money in the Post Office, haven't you?

– I was saving it, he said.

– Of course he's saving it, said his mother. The idea.

– Well, what's he saving it for, then?

– Not to fritter it away on Continental holidays, anyway. If Timothy wants to go, we'll pay his fares. *I've* got some money of my own.

This phrase was one his mother uttered from time to time with the air of making a dark threat. Nobody knew how much money she had or where she kept it. She had never been known to actually spend any of it.

– I'll have to think about it, Timothy said.

– Well, don't be too long making up your mind, said his mother. I'll have to let Mrs. Watkins know if you're not coming with us this year.

– All right, he said. He had already decided that he wouldn't go, and was only seeking some dignified excuse.

But that day, at school, he was betrayed into changing his mind. It was a free period for the first-year Sixth. The ten boys sprawled across the desks, or perched on the radiators. Study proceeded slowly and erratically, interrupted by occasional questions, arguments, and sporadic outbreaks of mock-serious fighting.

– What's the past participle of *carpo*?

– *Carpsum*.

– *Carptum*.

– You ignorant twat, Morrison!

Then two of them would wrestle for a few minutes, locked together like young bulls, staggering round the classroom, colliding with desks and knocking over chairs.

Timothy, sitting at the back of the room, complained uselessly:

– Oh, pack it in, will you?

He was trying to revise his O-Level English texts. His exams were only a couple of months away, but his classmates had no public exams that summer and were indisposed to work. The bright spring sunshine that poured through the windows and glittered on the teeming dust-motes in the air of the classroom made them restless and quarrelsome. After a while they gave up the pretence of private study, and gathered at the windows to gossip. They were talking of their plans for the summer holidays. One was going to a Butlin's camp, two more were going youth-hostelling, and several tried to conceal the fact that they weren't going anywhere at all. Gerry Bovington, the athletic, curly-haired darling of the Sixth, worshipped from afar by numerous boys in the lower forms, the only son of well-to-do parents, announced that he was going to France.

– France?

– Dinard. It's in Brittany. My Ma and Pa used to go there before the war.

– You'll have to go on a ship, won't you?

– Of course he'll have to go on a ship, twat. Don't you know England is entirely surrounded by water?

– Twat yourself. England is joined to Scotland and Wales, in case you didn't know.

And then there was another scuffle, in which the boys tried to conceal their envy of Gerry Bovington, and their ignorance of everything to do with Abroad. When they had finished, Bovington said:

– We're taking the car over. He unwrapped a toffee and tossed it into his mouth.

There was a silence, then somebody said:

– I wonder what old Young is doing this summer.

– Swotting for his A-Levels, I 'spect.

Timothy ignored their taunts, until Bovington screwed up his toffee paper, dropped it on to his foot, and kicked it accurately in a high arc on to Timothy's desk.

– Three points, said someone mechanically.

Timothy picked up the toffee paper between finger and thumb with an expression of studied distaste, and dropped it on to the floor.

– As a matter of fact, he said, I'm going to Heidelberg this summer.

The immediate effect of this announcement was gratifying.

– Heidelwhat?

– Where's that, then?

– Germany.
– Who you going with?
– Nobody.
– You going on your own?
– That's right.
– What you want to go to Germany for?
– To see my sister.
– What's your sister doing in Germany?
– She works for the American Army.
– Lying bastard!
– No, it's true, that's where he gets all those Yank sweets from.

Bowed over his books, pretending absorption in study, Timothy felt their glances playing over him with a new curiosity and respect. But already he was beginning to count the cost of his small act of self-assertion, and bitterly to regret it. His only hope was that his mother would have thought of some serious objection to Kath's proposal during the day. But to his surprise and dismay, when he announced that evening that he thought he would go to Heidelberg, she seemed pleased.

– Good. I've been thinking: it'll do you good to have a change, after all this studying. You've been looking peaky lately.

And that, as far as Timothy was concerned, was the point of no return. He had accepted Kath's invitation freely, and was considered lucky by friends and neighbours to have received it. Among the people he knew, a holiday on the Continent was a rare and adventurous undertaking, difficult to achieve even for those who could afford it because of the currency restrictions. Timothy himself believed that these were not the real disincentives – that like himself, other people quailed at the perils and problems of foreign travel: frontiers, passports, tickets, timetables, foreign languages, foreign food, foreign money, foreign customs. But the pretence had to be kept up. Retreat was out of the question, and he could not even admit his misgivings without a serious loss of face.

The door of his bedroom swung open. His mother shuffled backwards into the room, carrying a cup of tea in one hand and some clean washing in the other.

– Oh, you're awake then? she said. I've brought you a cup of tea.
– Thanks.

He sat up in bed to sip the sweet scalding tea. The rim of the cup chafed a sore place at the corner of his mouth, probably the beginning of a pimple. His mother drew back the curtains and looked out with her habitual suspicious frown.

– Looks like a nice day, she said grudgingly. Here's your clean shirt for this morning, I ironed it last night. And I've washed you some extra socks and pants. I'll put them in your bag.

His bag was on the floor. They both regarded it dubiously. His parents would need the family suitcases for their own holiday at Worthing, which was due to commence the following weekend, so it had been decided to buy a new one for Timothy. But then his mother had remembered that there was a large Air Force grip in the loft, which Uncle Jack had left with them at some stage of the war. It had been mildewed and thickly coated with dust when his father brought it down, but after a good scrub it seemed still serviceable. It was made of blue canvas, and fastened with a long zip. Timothy thought it would be lighter than an ordinary suitcase, and decided in favour of it. It was certainly big enough for his purposes, but as it was packed it seemed slowly to lose its original shape. The two handles scarcely met over its swollen girth, and, when lifted, its two extremities drooped limply towards the ground. Overnight, it had settled on the floor like the bloated carcase of a beached infant whale.

– They had lovely cases at Marks' last week, his mother sighed. I expect they've all gone by now.

– It'll be all right.

– Well, you'll just have to get a porter if you can't manage it.

– How much should I pay him?

– Oh, about one-and-six, I should think. Two shillings. I don't know about the Continent.

Neither do I, Timothy thought gloomily. I don't know anything about the Continent.

His mother, crouched on the floor, fussed and fidgeted, poking the socks and underpants into vacant spaces, wondering aloud if he had enough woollies, or too few.

– It could be hot there, she said. And then again it might be chilly in the evenings.

– I'd better get up, he said. He didn't really want to get up yet, but his mother irritated him, fussing with his bag. At last she zipped it shut and rose stiffly to her feet, tugging her dressing-gown across her narrow chest. Then, with one hand on the door handle, she paused and looked at him speculatively.

– I hope you'll be all right.

– Why shouldn't I be? he asked, disingenuously.

– It's a long way to go all on your own, at your age. Perhaps we should have got you a sleeper.

– It was expensive, wasn't it?

– Shocking.

Secretly, Timothy was glad they hadn't got him a sleeper. It would have been another unfamiliar ritual, that he was glad not to have to cope with. And it would have increased the risk, which already haunted him, of sleeping through the stop at Mannheim, where he had to change trains for Heidelberg, and of being carried on into the depths of southern Europe, unable to communicate, short of money, hopelessly lost, hurtling at sixty miles an hour further and further away from home, family, friends.

His mother still lingered at the door.

– Kath won't recognize you.

This was a problem he hadn't reckoned with.

– Perhaps I should wear my school cap? he suggested anxiously.

– Oh, she'll pick you out all right. I only meant you've grown a lot since she last saw you . . . D'you want me to send on your results?

– I 'spect I'll be back before then. I'm only going for three weeks. Better not send them, anyway, in case they're rotten.

– Oh, they won't be . . . Why do you think Kath hasn't been home since forty-seven?

The question took him by surprise.

– Don't ask me. She seems mad keen on travelling around Europe. I s'pose she thinks it's a waste of time to spend her holidays at home.

– But it's not natural, is it, Timothy? You wouldn't be like that if you had to live away from home, would you? You'd come home and see your mother and father from time to time, wouldn't you?

– Well, yes, I s'pose so. Course I would.

He was embarrassed, and flinched from meeting the sad appeal of his mother's pale grey eyes. There was something wrong with the tear duct in the left one, and there was usually moisture gathering in the corner of it. Her lined, unwashed face, surmounted by the turban covering her curlers, reminded him of the face that hovered anxiously over his bed in the nights of the Blitz, urging him to wake up and hurry along to the shelter.

– I'm worried about Kath, Timothy.

– Worried, what about?

– I don't think she can be happy. There's something wrong with her life out there.

– What makes you think that?

– If she was happy, she'd want to come home occasionally, to show us. It's only natural. If you've done well at school, come top or something, you like to come home and tell us, don't you?

– Well, yes, I s'pose so.

– Well, then . . . She closed the door and came to sit on the end of his bed.

– Timothy, I want you to try and find out what's the matter with Kath. Why she never comes to see us.

– You mean, ask her?

– I don't know. Perhaps. She probably wouldn't tell you. Just keep your eyes open. You're a clever boy. You don't miss much.

They heard his father come out of the next bedroom and go into the lavatory.

– There's your father. I'll have to go and get his breakfast, I'm all behind. Why don't you have yours in bed?

– All right, thanks, Mum.

– What would you like, bacon and tomatoes? I'll do you a bit of fried bread to go with it, she said, getting up from the bed. I wonder what you'll be eating this time tomorrow.

As he ate his breakfast, Timothy mused on the conversation he had overheard on the beach at Worthing a year before. Without that, he wouldn't have had a clue as to what his mother was driving at. But it was all too clear, now, why she had encouraged him to go to Heidelberg, and the realization made him uneasy. He had enough problems to face without having to spy on his sister, on whose companionship and protection he would be totally reliant in the next few weeks.

He ate his breakfast slowly, putting off the moment when he would have to rise and prepare himself for his journey. The sun inched its way into the room, moving slowly across the threadbare carpet, fading the stain where he had spilled a bottle of ink two years ago, climbing the walls where he had hung the best of his paintings and sketches, together with a photograph of Charlton's Cup-winning team of 1947, his First Holy Communion Certificate, and a diploma awarded by the *Daily Express* for his entry in a children's painting competition. His eyes lingered on these and other familiar features of the room – the small table at which he did his homework, the drawing board and easel he had been given last Christmas, the crucifix on the wall, the balsawood model Spitfire on the chest of drawers, the bookcase mostly filled with books he had outgrown but was reluctant to throw away – *Just William*, *Biggles*, a complete set of *The Boy's Book of Soccer* from 1946 to 1950, and comic annuals, *Beano*, *Radio Fun* and *Champion*. There were a few Penguins more recently acquired: Homer's *Odyssey*, Herbert Read's *The Meaning of Art*, *Contemporary Verse*, and Voltaire's *Candide* (certain pages of which he had read several times).

One advantage of his sister's absence from home was that this room was permanently his, and the small, narrow one in which he had slept as a child was used as a box room. He liked his room, he had grown used to it; and although he added to its furnishings from time to time, he subtracted nothing. He liked the sense of continuity his possessions gave him, each object linking one year to the next in an unbroken succession, back to his earliest memories. Even One-Ear Rabbit peeped discreetly from the top of the wardrobe. His father was going to redecorate the room while he was away, but Timothy had stipulated that the same pale blue distemper was to be used on the walls, and that every picture should be returned to its original position. He knew how glad he would be to return to this familiar room. He looked forward to doing so already. He wanted nothing changed in his absence.

When Timothy came downstairs his father had finished his breakfast and was rolling his first cigarette. It was a quarter to eight and soon he would be leaving for work. Timothy's mother was to see him off from Victoria.

– Well, son, all ready?

– More or less, Dad.

His father ran the tip of his tongue along the edge of the cigarette paper, twirled the little rubber and metal machine, and ejected a cigarette, still damp with spittle along the seam.

– I should leave yourself plenty of time to get to Victoria. You know what those thirty-sixes are like.

– I thought we'd leave about ten.

– Before, if I were you. Better early than late.

His cigarette was loosely packed and a few shreds of tobacco trailed from the end. When he applied a match, the paper flared up in a brief flame and glowing fragments of ash fell on to his knees. He brushed them off vigorously.

– You might bring us back a few packets of fags if you have room.

– Sure, Dad.

– Sure, Dad, his father mimicked him. He's talking like a Yank already, Dorothy. Have a real twang by the time he gets home, I bet.

– I don't know, his mother said. It hasn't happened to Kath. I thought how nicely she spoke when she was home last.

– A bit too posh, if you ask me, said his father. I think she puts it on to impress the Yanks. He winked at Timothy and changed the subject:

– Had a letter from Stubbins and Gillow, this morning, son.

– The architects?

– They're still keen to have you, if you want to start in September. Five pounds a week to start with, plus luncheon vouchers. Not bad for a sixteen-year-old. Of course, once you're qualified it jumps up to . . . quite a lot.

– I think Timothy should stay on at school and try for University, said his mother.

– Let the boy make up his own mind, Dorothy. It's not as if he's giving up his education, anyway. He'll be taking examinations all the time, going to night school and so on. What shall I tell them, son?

– I dunno, Dad, I still haven't decided. I want to see what my results are like first.

– Yes, wait till you get your results, said his mother. There's no hurry. Stubbins and Gillow can wait.

– All right, we'll leave it till you come home, said his father. He picked up his newspaper and went upstairs.

– Don't sit in there all morning, his mother called up the stairs. It's gone eight already.

– All right, all right, he muttered from the landing. They heard the door of the lavatory shut.

– Don't forget to thank your father when you say goodbye, said his mother. It costs money, you know.

When his father came downstairs again he was fully dressed for work. His mother handed him his sandwiches, which he put in his attaché case.

– Thanks dear. Well, Tim, have a good journey, and let us have a card to say you've arrived safely.

– I will, Dad. And thanks for the fares and everything.

– That's all right, son. Give our love to Kath. Tell her to come over and see us soon.

– I will.

– Goodbye, then, son.

They shook hands solemnly. It was a strange sensation. Timothy couldn't remember shaking hands with his father before. The last time they had been separated for any length of time was in the war, when he had been young enough to kiss his father goodbye. The handshake was like casting off a rope that had held him for a long time in safe anchorage. But he was relieved when his father left the house. The strain of maintaining a mask of imperturbable confidence about the journey before him was increasing, and the fewer observers there were, the better. Now he had only his mother to cope with.

– I'll make some sandwiches for the train, she said.

– Make a good few will you, Mum? Then I can save some for tea-time.

– They won't be very nice by then, she said doubtfully. You should be able to get something hot on the boat. Or on the train the other side.

The idea of his ordering himself a meal on a foreign train was so preposterous that he didn't offer a comment.

Timothy was ready long before his mother. He was washed and dressed, his bag was packed, and his documents checked. There was nothing else to do, but it was too early to leave. He prowled restlessly round the house, and tried unsuccessfully to read the paper. The headline story was about Burgess and Maclean: B & M – WHERE ARE THEY? But there was nothing new in the report, and he couldn't concentrate on the words anyway. He scanned the cricket scores, and threw down the paper. He went out into the back garden.

It was a bright day. The sun shone on the grey slate roofs of the houses beyond the garden fence, and dappled the coalshed with the shadows of the rose bushes. A sorbo-rubber ball still hung from the clothes-line by a grimy, weather-stained string, though it was a year or two since he had last played with it. He went back into the house and took his cricket bat from the cupboard under the stairs. Its bottom was splintered and worn down by years of street cricket, the rubber covering the handle was perished and sticky. He went back into the garden and began to practise his strokes: off drives and on drives, leg glances and forward defensive pushes with a dead bat. From time to time he indulged in a hook, which invariably snagged the string in the rose bushes, and brought a shower of petals fluttering to the ground.

Carrying his bag between them to the bus stop, each holding a handle, they took up the whole width of the pavement. Halfway along the street the paving stones were newer, where the bomb had dropped. The houses had been rebuilt, in exactly the same style. Except for the unweathered look of the brickwork and roof tiles you would never have guessed that there had been a gaping hole there for nearly ten years. A young woman with a scarf round her head opened the bedroom window of Jill's house (as it used to be) to shake out a mop, and a little girl's face peered down at them through the next window pane: new people, whom they didn't know.

They waited nearly fifteen minutes for a number 36 bus. Conversation was desultory, and contributed mainly by his mother.

– Did I pack your green shirt? she wondered. Did you remember to put in your toothbrush? It's going to be hot. I should have given you more apples, they're thirstquenching. I wish I'd bought something for you to take Kath, but what can you give her, she's got everything, and better quality. These buses! Aren't you too hot in those trousers? You should have packed them and worn your best ones, they're lighter. Don't slouch, Timothy.

He gave curt answers to these remarks, if he bothered to answer at all. He stood with his hands in his pockets, taking in the familiar scene, the little row of shops opposite the bus stop, where he had bought his comics and expended his sweet ration for so many years, the hardware store that smelled of carbolic and paraffin, the watch repairers that had been closed and empty as long as he could remember, its big clock outside stopped permanently at twenty minutes past two, the time the bomb had fallen just along the street. The houses that adjoined this row of shops were small terraced cottages with front doors that opened straight into the front rooms, and a bare yard of space between the windows and the pavement. Their own house, though not much bigger, was more modern and semi-detached, with a pebble-dash façade and some decorative woodwork which his father, like their neighbours, kept brightly painted in two colours, green and cream. These terraced cottages, whose roofs he looked at from his bedroom window, were mostly grey stone and brick, encrusted with soot, streaky with rain as though tear-stained. They had a tired, over-worked look, like the stout, scarved women who went in and out of them with their babies and shopping baskets.

The whole journey to Victoria was like that. From the window of the bus the familiar streets took on a strange visual clarity and resonance of association. He felt that he was seeing them for the first time as they really were, that he was responding with all his senses to the special character of South-East London, its soiled, worn textures of brick and stone, its low, irregular skyline, its odours of breweries and gas and vegetables and tanneries. He noticed how old and neglected it all was: if you raised your eyes above the modern shop-fronts, you saw that they had been pasted on to buildings crumbling into decay, with cracked, grimy windows and broken-backed roofs and chipped chimney pots. The predominant colours were black, brown and a dirty cream. Guinness tints. Those were the tints to use if you were to try and paint it – and he was suddenly filled with the urge to try.

He felt strangely stirred; and it seemed more than ever foolish to be going abroad – for that was the point of going away, wasn't it, to see your home with a fresh eye when you returned? But the bus rolled on inexorably to Victoria. Now it was skirting the Oval. From the top of the bus he could see over the wall, but play hadn't started yet. Groundsmen were taking the covers off the wicket, and the scoreboard showed the overnight score: Surrey 247 all out, and Northants 21 for 1. The bus left the Oval behind, swept under the railway arches at Vauxhall and turned on to Vauxhall Bridge. A pleasure boat passed beneath them ferrying people from the Festival of Britain on the South Bank to the Festival Gardens at Battersea. Vauxhall was not the most impressive place at which to cross the

Thames – the buildings here, except for the Tate Gallery, were undistinguished. But the river glinted prettily in the sunlight, and downstream you could see Lambeth Bridge and the Houses of Parliament, and beyond them the great expanse of London with the dome of St. Paul's shimmering in the haze. London. They said it wasn't the biggest city in the world any more, that Tokyo had a bigger population. But it was still the greatest, and he often thought how lucky he was to have been born there. It was just chance. He might have been born in one of the towns and villages you saw from the train on the way to Worthing, dim little places that seemed to have no reason for existing. Or he might have not been born in England at all. He might have been a French boy, or a German . . . What would *that* have been like? To grow up in that benighted country, knowing that everybody in other countries hated and despised you, because of Hitler, because of the concentration camps, because of the war which your country had started and lost.

Actually, when he thought of the Germans, the ones living in Germany now, he felt no hatred, only a kind of embarrassment. It was far more likely that they hated *you*. And that was what made him, at the deepest level, apprehensive about the weeks to come. A solitary English boy, he thought, would not be particularly welcome in occupied Germany. They would think he had come to gloat. It wasn't a place any normal person would choose to go to for a holiday, a country soaked in blood and guilt and ugly memories, a country your own side had been fighting only six years ago. The only consolation was that he was not going to Germany to see the Germans, but to see Kath and her American friends. The idea of Americans was a reassuring one. He remembered watching convoys of American tanks and lorries rumbling through Blyfield in the months before D-Day, and feeling a lift of the spirits at the mere sight of them, their tanned, untired faces, the functional smartness and sophistication of their uniforms and equipment, the glamour of their general style, as irresistible as a Technicolor film, a little larger than life.

– You're very quiet, Timothy. Is anything the matter?

– No, why should there be?

– You don't need any medicine, do you?

– No, he said irritably. This was his mother's usual way of enquiring about the regularity of his bowels.

– I'll get you some Bile Beans at Victoria. They have a Boots there.

– I don't need any, Mum. Come on, ours is the next stop.

They had left the bag in the space under the stairs. The conductor helped them off with it.

– Wotcher got in there, a body? he quipped.

Timothy smiled feebly from the pavement. His mother muttered:

– Sauce!

It was already obvious, though the journey had scarcely begun, that the bag had been a mistake. It was too wide to go on the luggage rack of his compartment, and too fat to fit under his seat. Eventually they left it in the corridor, and the other passengers struggled over it as best they could. Timothy put his raincoat and sandwiches on a corner seat and joined his mother on the platform, where a party of schoolgirls in brown blazers trimmed with gold hummed and heaved like a swarm of bees. About half a dozen of them broke away and ran past him tittering and shrieking vacantly. They had discs pinned to the lapels of their blazers. A giggle of schoolgirls, he thought; like a gaggle of geese. He felt a kind of aloof pride in confronting the perils of Continental travel alone, without teachers and an organized party, at the same time that he envied them that protection. His mother wondered where they were going.

– It says Innsbruck on their luggage. Austria.

– Fancy that. What a long way to go.

– I hope they're not on my train to Mannheim, he grumbled. The noise they're making.

– Well, they're excited, I expect. Are you excited?

Timothy shrugged.

– I dunno. Not excited, exactly.

– I'm sure I would have been, at your age. But you never were one to show your feelings.

Thank God for that, he thought, looking miserably at the clock that showed it was ten minutes to eleven. The train was already full, and some passengers were standing in the corridors.

– You were lucky to get a seat, his mother said.

– I'd better get in, in case someone takes it.

She kissed him goodbye, and he took his seat. Through the glass his mother mouthed last-minute instructions and questions, to which he replied with a nod or shake of the head. Tiring of this absurd mime, he stood up and opened the ventilator window.

– I should go, Mum, there's no point in waiting.

– Oh, no, I must see you off.

– Have they closed the gates yet?

She squinted down the platform.

– I'd need my glasses . . . There's a mobile canteen down there. Shall I get you something extra to eat?

– No, don't bother.

– They've got some Lyons' Individual Fruit Pies. I saw them as we came past.

Timothy hesitated. He was rather partial to Lyons' Individual Fruit Pies.

– Alright, he said, and immediately regretted it. This was just the kind of last-minute rush, unsettling and entirely unnecessary, that he had tried to avoid, and had so far succeeded in avoiding.

He opened the window to its fullest extent. By standing on tiptoe and turning his head sideways, he could just see his mother hurrying down the platform towards the mobile canteen. As she reached it and fumbled in her handbag, a whistle shrilled and doors began to slam along the length of the train. His mother came away from the canteen at a trot, then stopped and retraced her steps. Timothy groaned under his breath: she must have forgotten her change. Now she was running along the platform, holding outstretched the pie in its cardboard box, like a relay-runner's baton. He withdrew his head from the window, and extended his arm in its place. When she was about ten yards away the train began to move. For a few seconds the gap remained stable, then began to grow wider. His mother staggered to a halt, gasping for breath, clutching her side with her free hand. He waved and smiled, trying to convey that it didn't matter. But that was the last view he had of his mother: standing on the platform, gasping for breath, disappointment lining her face, still holding outstretched, like a rejected gift, the Lyons' Individual Fruit Pie.

2

At first, everything went smoothly. He declined the offer of a porter at Dover, and, although the bag bumped awkwardly against his knee and made his arm ache, he managed the long walk along the quay to the ship with only two pauses for a change of hands. He dragged his burden aboard, and up three flights of stairs, until he found an open deck high up at the front of the ship, with plenty of deckchairs marked *Gratuit*. He collapsed, perspiring, into one of these, until the ship shuddered and began to move.

It turned in the middle of the harbour, giving him a fine view of Dover, its grey slate roofs spread out beneath the battlements of the castle, gleaming dully in the sunshine. Some holidaymakers who had walked out to the end of the harbour mole, where there was a small lighthouse, waved to them as they passed. Then he felt for the first time in his life the slow, deliberate roll of a big ship at sea. It was a strange, unsettling sensation, to feel the solid mass of the deck, which in harbour had seemed as firm as dry land, tilting silently and mysteriously under your feet. It was the very movement of risk and adventure.

For a while the boat sailed parallel to the coast. A song from his childhood came into his head.

There'll be bluebirds over
The white cliffs of Dover,
Tomorrow, just you wait and see.

He remembered planning to go and see the bluebirds when the war was over. Well, it had taken him a long time to get here, and there weren't any bluebirds, only scavenging seagulls that swooped and glided round the ship with shrill cries. The cliffs were a rather dirty white, too, but they confronted the blue sea with a kind of peaceful serenity that fitted the song.

The ship changed course and the coast slipped out of his view. He was looking over the bows of the ship, dipping and rising gently as it carved a path through the waves. A brisk wind blew off the sea, flipped his tie over his shoulder and set it fluttering by his ear. The wind, and the bright light bouncing off the waves, made him half-close his eyes, and drew his mouth into a smile. He was enjoying himself.

– Sailing card, sir?

He turned to find a uniformed officer at his side. He handed over his ticket and the man frowned.

– This is the first-class deck, he said coldly. Kindly go to the rear of the ship, which is reserved for second-class passengers.

Mortified, cringing with embarrassment under the glances of the other passengers in the vicinity, Timothy picked up his bag and staggered as quickly as he could along the side of the ship, until he came to a little gate which gave access to the second-class deck. It was crammed with people and baggage. Most of the passengers sat or stood or lay on the deck, eating sandwiches and drinking cups of tea; or, if fortunate enough to be in possession of one of the few deckchairs, lolled in attitudes of abandonment, eyes closed and mouths sagging open, faces turned towards a sun that glowed dully behind the screen of the ship's smoke. Five nuns sat shoulder to shoulder on a bench, holding on their fluttering veils with both hands, and smiling timidly. There was a buzz of conversation, laughter, children's cries and babies' howls. Every now and again a gust of wind blew smoke down from the funnels. Timothy could see nowhere for himself and his bag except at the foot of the nuns, around whom the other passengers had left a respectful space.

The afternoon passed slowly. He ate the remainder of his sandwiches, then got out the current number of *Cycling*, which he had kept unread for this purpose. His subscription to this magazine dated from two years ago, when he had suddenly developed an enthusiasm for cycling. He had pestered his parents into buying him a sports bike which he had gradually equipped with all the approved accessories – water flasks, bored alloy hubs, 4-speed derailleur gear, etc., and which he rode to school, striving to cut seconds off his best time by such dangerous expedients as using buses for pacemakers. With Jonesy and Blinker he had sometimes attended the cycle races at Herne Hill, and gloried in the triumphs of Reg Harris, the only British athlete who seemed to be able to win anything against foreign competition. His enthusiasm for the sport had gradually ebbed away – not quite to the point, however, where he felt impelled to cancel his subscription to *Cycling*. Its appearance on the doormat every Wednesday still lit a feeble flicker of interest in him, and the very predictability and monotony of its articles, blurred photographs and pages of small ads, soothed his study-wearied brain. But this afternoon the spell seemed finally broken. He realized he was deeply bored with *Cycling*, and would not be sorry if he never saw another copy again.

Then there was nothing much to do except watch the other passengers. The party of schoolgirls was much in evidence, jumping up and down restlessly, brushing back their hair and holding down their skirts in the breeze, leaning over the rails and pestering their teachers with questions. There was one girl among them whom he thought was rather attractive, a girl with a long black pony-tail and a pale oval face, but she sat next to one of the teachers most of the time and did not join in the general skirmishing. Then someone called her to the side of the ship, and she rose to her feet and threaded her way gracefully through the crowd. He stood up himself and saw, with a shock of surprise and excitement – land! He pushed his way to the rail and stared at the long, low shoreline that divided sea and sky. Was it Belgium already, or France? It was Europe, anyway, his first sight of it, palpably foreign even at this distance, low and yellowy-brown, very different from the grass-topped white cliffs of England.

He stayed there for the rest of the voyage, elbows on the rail and hands cupping his chin, gazing pensively at the foreign shore, trying to extract from its indistinct outline some clue or guide for comporting himself upon it. As they entered Ostend harbour he could see the people on the jetty clearly, bathed in the yellow light of the slanting sun, their elongated shadows stretching towards the ship as they smiled and waved. They seemed very friendly; but the Belgians were, after all, our allies in the war, he thought, gazing over their heads at the foreign-looking streets and squares, the gaily-striped umbrellas on the pavements outside the cafés, the advertisements for Martini and Belge cigarettes. Nothing could happen to you in Belgium.

The water churned and the boat vibrated as the propellers brought it to a halt. They were about to dock. With a spasm of panic he realized that he had forgotten all about his bag. But, pushing through the crowd, he found it safe where he had left it. There was, on reflection, little chance that anyone would try to steal it. The staircases were jammed tight with people waiting to get off the boat.

Muffled shouts rose from the bowels of the ship, and the throng at the head of the stairs began to heave and sway as a group of Belgian porters, dressed in coarse blue denim, forced their way through. *Porteur! Porteur!* they cried, with an elongated vowel that hovered between French and English. A high, confident voice called:

– Yes, these two here, please!

Timothy, curious to observe the transaction, turned his head, but a squat porter with a bristly chin interposed himself

– *Porteur?* he demanded.

– Er . . .

Timothy hesitated. The man snatched his bag, heaved it on to his shoulder with what sounded like a curse, and forced his badge under Timothy's nose.

– *Dirty Floor*, he appeared to say, and disappeared into the crowd.

– Hey! Timothy protested weakly. Helplessly he watched his bag receding over the heads of the other passengers, until a sudden movement of the crowd pitched him down the staircase. As he shuffled in line off the boat he wondered miserably how and where and even whether he would recover his bag. For all its inconvenient bulk, it was a comforting presence. Its labels were proof that he had come from somewhere definite and was going somewhere definite – as long as he hung on to it he felt that he would eventually end up, like a parcel, either at Heidelberg or back home. *Dirty floor* must have meant thirty-four, for that was the number on the man's badge – but where was he supposed to meet him?

The porter wasn't at Passport Control. He wasn't in the Customs shed, where passengers were being quickly waved through – it seemed to be a formality. Timothy moved on and found himself in the station. It was very big and crowded, and looked more like a street into which railway engines had strayed, with lots of shops and cafés with tables outside them, and a rich foreign smell in the air.

Impossible to find anyone here. Perhaps the porter had read the labels on his bag and was waiting for him at the platform. But which platform? He spotted a large indicator board and, after struggling with the twenty-four-hour timetable, identified his train, which was leaving from number seven platform. Pleased with this feat, he hurried to platform seven. The train was filling up, but there was no sign of his porter.

He was suddenly conscious of a very full bladder, and cursed himself for not having gone to the lavatory on the boat. To go now would increase the risk of missing his porter, but he didn't think he could last for another twenty-five minutes, when his train was due to depart. He looked around desperately for a Gents, remembered that it wouldn't be called that, and picked out a sign saying *Hommes* above a stone staircase. He ran down, came face to face with a woman in a white coat sitting at a table, and retreated rapidly up the stairs. He inspected the sign again. It indubitably said *Hommes*. He went round to the other side, where there was another staircase marked *Dames*. Was there some perverse Belgium custom of calling Gents, Ladies, and Ladies, Gents? He peered cautiously down the stairs and glimpsed the same woman in the white coat. He gave up the mystery, and the attempt to relieve himself, for time was running short. His train would be leaving soon, without him, or without his bag, or both.

It was the nightmare he had always feared, from the moment the journey had been decided upon. He took out his school cap and put it on, as though raising a distress signal. He had to get someone's help, somebody who spoke English, for his confidence in his French, never strong, had melted away in the crisis. He stopped a man in the uniform of a Cook's courier.

– Excuse me, but have you seen a porter, number thirty-floor, anywhere? With a blue bag?

The man regarded him haughtily.

– Are you a Cook's tourist, sir?

– No, but I'm English, he pleaded.

At that moment he heard the sweet, the indescribably sweet cry of *Dirty Floor! Dirty Floor!* just behind him. The porter threw up his hands and gave vent to a rapid stream of French. Timothy could guess what the gist of it was.

– *Pardon*, he said, *je ne sais pas*.

– *Bruxelles?* the man demanded.

– Mannheim. The porter looked at Timothy as if he doubted whether he would get so far.

– *Wagon-lit?*

– No. *Non.*

The porter shook his head and set off, muttering under his breath, Timothy following humbly behind. He gave the man his smallest-denomination Belgian note, worth about ten shillings, and waited hopefully for change. The man pocketed the note expressionlessly and marched away. There were no seats left on the train and he had to stand in the corridor. But at least he was aboard, and probably lots of people would get out at Brussels.

The train stopped three times in Brussels, but nobody got out. On the contrary, hundreds more people got in. The corridor filled up. His bag disappeared under a mountain of other people's baggage, and he was unable even to reach it. The air was thick with pungent cigarette smoke, the odours of cheese, garlic and perspiration, and a mixture of foreign accents – French, German and something in between which he thought was probably Flemish. The prospect of the night's journey looked increasingly grim. On the way to Brussels there had at least been something to look at – the long, flat fields, where people were still working in the fading light, straightening up to wave as the train rushed past, and the neat little farmhouses, white-walled and red-roofed; but when they emerged from the tunnels of Brussels, it was quite dark. Now and again the lights of a town flashed past, and at Liège the sky was dramatically lit by the red glare of factory furnaces, reminding him of the docks burning in the Blitz. But for the most part he could see nothing but his own wan reflection in the windows.

The window ledge had on it a small notice in three languages:

Ne pas se pencher au dehors
Nicht hinauslehnen
Do not lean out of the window

But he heard no English voice in the corridor, except when the brown-and-gold-blazered schoolgirls (they were still dogging his tracks) emerged from their reserved compartments and squeezed past on their way to the W.C. They came in pairs, usually, lifting their brown-stockinged legs over the luggage like ponies, nervously tossing back their manes of hair, and giggling inanely. They seemed to spend hours in the W.C.

The girl with the black pony-tail made her visit alone. She was carrying a small tartan toilet bag. As she passed, the train swerved across some points and she was thrown against him.

– Oh! Sorry! she exclaimed. But she looked more vexed than sorry.

– It's all right, he said, and then wished he had said something more gallant, like, *Are you all right?* He might even have steadied her with a deftly placed hand. Perhaps she would say something to him on her way back.

Using the window as a mirror, he combed back his long forelock; it fell forward across his brow almost immediately. He straightened his school tie, but little could be done to improve its appearance, for the fabric was strained and creased just under the knot. His shirt collar was grimy and curling up at the points. He pushed his spectacles back on to the bridge of his nose – they had always been a little too big – and fingered the pimple at the corner of his mouth exploratively. Even in the poor reflection of the window he could see the dark shadow on his upper lip where a downy moustache was beginning to grow. He heard the door of the W.C. open and shut, and straightened himself to his full height against the wall of the corridor.

The girl passed him without a glance.

Timothy went into the W.C. There was a faint smell of scent in the air, soap or perfume, and a long black hair in the washbasin. He urinated and washed his hands. The receptacle for used paper towels was already overflowing, but there was a white enamel bin low down on one wall. He flipped up the lid with his foot and, as he tossed in his towel, glimpsed at the bottom what looked like a bloody bandage. It was a strange, disturbing sight. Was somebody ill on the train, he wondered – or injured? Some criminal on the run, staunching his wounds and biting his lip until he reached safety? Anything, he felt, could happen on this train.

He sat down on the seat of the W.C. to ease his aching legs, and wondered how long he could stay there before people began knocking on the door. Someone knocked on the door.

It was the ticket collector. Timothy yielded the W.C. to another pair of schoolgirls, and presented his ticket for inspection. He felt very thirsty. There was an apple left in his bag, but the bag was at this moment crushed irretrievably under the weight of two large suitcases and an even larger woman. He glanced at his watch. Six hours still to go, and he already felt exhausted. He leaned against the wall of the corridor and closed his eyes, letting his head roll with the swaying motion of the train. He thought about the girl with the black pony-tail, and the soft concussion of her body against his when the movement of the train threw her against him. He rehearsed the incident a hundred times in his mind, varying and perfecting his responses each time, until gradually he invented a whole relationship springing from the encounter, that turned on the girl somehow having a reserved compartment entirely to herself, which she invited him to share, where they talked and talked through the night until she dropped asleep with her head resting on his shoulder and the train broke down at Mannheim and her school party went to Heidelberg instead of Innsbruck and . . .

A sudden deceleration of the train threw him off balance. When it stopped they did not appear to be in a station, for there were no lights to be seen outside the windows. Then a door opened and two uniformed men climbed into the carriage and called out something in thick, guttural accents. The passengers standing in the corridor began to fumble in their pockets and handbags for passports. They must be at the German border.

As he watched the two men, who were dressed like soldiers, moving slowly towards him under the dim lights of the corridor, thumbing through the documents offered to them with, it seemed to Timothy, an unduly suspicious scrutiny, the ghosts of old half-remembered films about Nazi-occupied Europe, the Gestapo and the S.S., escaping prisoners of war and the Resistance, walked across his heart. The corridor was hushed, apart from the curt questions and replies. It seemed to him that the passengers were cowed and anxious, as if any of them might expect to be dragged off the train for some irregularity in their papers. He felt a twinge of anxiety about the poor likeness of his passport photograph, and looked again at the visa for which he had queued two weary hours outside the German Embassy in Kensington: a smudgy black imprint of ugly, unpronounceable words, like *Grenzübergangsstelle* and *einschlieblich*, stamped with the insignia of a scrawny eagle that seemed to be flexing its wings menacingly and squawking in spiteful rage. A fitting, if sinister emblem for Germany, he thought. Now it was his turn.

With a thumping heart, he offered his passport. The man glanced at his photograph, flipped to the visa and stamped the opposite page. Timothy felt a surge of relief. Then the other uniformed man addressed him in German. Timothy stared blankly. Was there something wrong with his passport after all? The other man showed it to his colleague.

– *Englisch?* said the latter.

– Yes, said Timothy. *Ja*, he added helpfully. This was a mistake, for another long, incomprehensible question in German followed. His knowledge of the language was limited to a few words derived from comics and war-films – *Achtung, Schweinhund, Dummkopf, kaput* – none of which seemed useful at the moment.

– I'm sorry, he said. I don't speak German.

A man standing beside him leaned over and said:

– They want to know vat smuggle you haf.

– No smuggle, said Timothy.

After a few more questions, interpreted by the man, the two officials moved on. Half an hour later, the train rolled into a large, bleak station.

– *Aachen . . . Aachen . . . Aachen!* blared the loudspeakers. The harsh, catarrhal syllables were a violence to the ears and the spirit. The signs, for some reason, said *Bad Aachen*, and it seemed appropriate. Bad Aachen. Bad Germany.

His last hope of getting a seat vanished. More crowds besieged the train and surged aboard, pushing and struggling, impeding the few passengers who wanted to alight. Then, when the carriages and corridors were packed tight, and the platforms empty, the train stood stationary for another half-hour.

They moved off at last. The lights of Aachen fell away. Conversation in the corridor became muted as the passengers began to compose themselves for the night, squatting on suitcases, or on the floor, cradling their heads on their knees. Soon Timothy and a young man further along the corridor, who was reading, holding up his book to catch the dim light of the corridor lamps, were the only passengers who were upright and awake. Some instinct restrained Timothy from sliding to the floor. As long as he remained upright, he felt, he resisted the nightmare of this journey, held it precariously at a distance, as some threatening spell or ordeal which would presently pass, restoring him to the ordered, English-speaking daylight world to which he belonged, where journeys were not a long struggle for suvival. His fellow-passengers evidently had lower expectations. He had a sense that, in Europe, life had always been like this, like an endless train journey through the night, across frontiers, loudspeakers blaring harshly over bleak platforms, uniformed men waking you up to examine your papers, no more immediate end in view than to make a little space for yourself and snatch a little sleep. He wondered if the young man reading the book was English too.

Then gradually weariness overcame his resistance. He sank to the floor, folding his raincoat to make a cushion. His head rested against someone's canvas grip. With a final abandonment of reserve, he loosened the shoelaces on his swollen feet and stretched out his legs. He closed his eyes and dozed.

The train picked up speed. The percussion of its wheels drummed in his ears, shifting in rhythm and resonance as it clattered over points and rumbled across bridges. He rolled and swayed unresistingly with its motion. He was dimly conscious that people were stepping over him, but he did not bother to move. It was the schoolgirls, going to the lavatory again. They stepped over him in a steady procession and he was looking up under their skirts, at their dark blue knickers, with handkerchiefs tucked under the elastic. The girl with the black pony-tail had no knickers on. Unable to move forward, she straddled him, and he saw all the smooth pearl-pink fissured wedge of flesh between her thighs and a delicious warmth welled up inside him and spilled over.

He woke, feeling wet and sticky at his crotch, but couldn't be bothered to go to the W.C. to clean up. In his present state, the extra discomfort was negligible. After a time his skin dried and he fell into a deep sleep.

He woke again with a pain in his back. His arm was twisted under his body and, as he sat up, tingled painfully with pins and needles. He struggled stiffly to his feet and staggered in the swaying corridor. He yawned, rubbed his eyes and checked his watch: 4.15. That was all right, then – he hadn't gone past Mannheim.

The corridor was empty now, except for his bag, which looked as though it had been trampled by a herd of buffalo, and there were two vacant seats in the nearest compartment. He slid back the door and sat down. The seat was hard and narrow in comparison with English trains, but the relief to his aching limbs was delicious. In the corner opposite the young man he had noticed earlier was still reading.

– Hi, he said over his book. I nearly awakened you when the seats were vacated, but you looked so peaceful.

– When was that? Timothy asked.

– Most of the people got out at Mainz. Tired?

Timothy nodded. The young man, who seemed to be American to judge by his accent, returned to his book. Timothy picked out the word *Europe* on the jacket.

Outside the window Europe was acquiring a little definition with the first hint of dawn. The dim shapes of houses and trees flicked by. In the distance he could see the lights of some distant town or factory. He turned his head to look in the other direction, across the corridor, and looked straight into the eyes of the girl with the black pony-tail. Did she smile at him, or was it his imagination? She lowered her eyes at once and moved on past his compartment. She looked pale and tired and her uniform was crumpled, but at least she'd had a seat through the night. He was mildly disappointed that she had not come past earlier, in time to get the full effect, the pathos and endurance of his prone and sleeping figure. But perhaps she had – perhaps that was why she had smiled at him. He chose to think so.

He felt light-headed with hunger and fatigue, but in better spirits than at any time since he had left home. In little more than an hour the ordeal would be over: he would be safe in the capable hands of his sister. That hour included the trickiest part of his journey – the change of trains at Mannheim – but somehow he faced it with unaccustomed calm. Having survived this extraordinary night gave him confidence.

When he alighted at Mannheim the only person on the platform seemed to be an old man in grey denim with a broom and bucket.

– Heidelberg? Timothy asked.

The old man nodded over his shoulder and said something incomprehensible.

– I'll show you, said a voice from behind him. I'm going to Heidelberg myself. It was the young American.

– Oh, thanks very much, said Timothy, picking up his bag.

– That looks kind of heavy, let me give you a hand, said the young man, taking one handle. His own luggage consisted of a small duffle bag which he carried easily over his shoulder.

Timothy stepped out with a light heart: his luck had decisively changed.

– It's jolly nice of you, he said. I couldn't understand that old man.

– You don't speak German?

– No, they've only just started doing it at our school. This was the answer he had prepared to a question he expected to be asked frequently in the coming weeks. It was true; though it was also true that until very recently he would have regarded the idea of learning German as absurd and, in a way, unpatriotic.

– Would that be Junior High? Or don't you call it that?

The train they had just left was leaving, sliding past with gathering speed. Timothy scanned the windows for the girl with the black pony-tail.

– I go to a grammar school, he said. I'm in the Sixth Form.

– That would make you, what, seventeen?

– Sixteen.

A blind was pulled back as if someone were peering out. Timothy straightened his shoulders.

– Sixteen. That's kind of young to be travelling all this way alone.

– Oh, there's nothing to it, really, said Timothy nonchalantly, as they descended the steps of the subway.

3

The young man's name was Don Kowalski, which matched Timothy's idea of the typical American no better than his appearance. He was tall and thin and sallow. He had a long nose and a cleft chin. His black, crinkly hair was short, but not crew-cut; it fitted his head like a skull cap. The Americans Timothy had seen in London were immediately recognizable by their pastel-coloured draped suits and gaudy ties. Don wore a tweed jacket and rather grubby cotton trousers and a white shirt open at the throat.

– So what brings you to Old Heidelberg, Timothy? he asked, as they settled themselves in a compartment of the short, antique-looking local train.

Timothy told him.

– You should have a great vacation, he said. Heidelberg's an interesting old town.

– D'you know it well?

– Pretty well. I've been there for over a year.

– Perhaps you know my sister, then.

Don shook his head.

– I don't think so. I was a G.I. until last month. I guess your sister moves in more exclusive circles.

– National Service?

– Same thing, except it's selective. I understand everybody has to do it in Britain. That's fairer.

– You can get deferment, though, if you go on studying.

– Are you planning to go to college?

– I might. Or I might do an apprenticeship. I'm waiting to see what my O-Level results are like.

– But it's free, isn't it – college education in England?

– If you can get in.

– And that's not easy – I know, I'm trying to get into the London School of Economics myself. In fact I've just been to England for an interview. You look surprised.

Timothy was indeed surprised: Don looked far too old to be a student, but it seemed impolite to say so.

– I just wondered why you wanted to study in England, instead of America.

– I like England. I've spent a couple of furloughs in London. I don't want to go back home just yet. And L.S.E. is a good school, especially for graduate work.

– It won't be free for you, though, will it?

– No, but we have a fine institution called the G.I. Bill. Just about the only thing to be said in favour of the draft.

As Don was explaining the G.I. Bill to him, and what graduate work was, the train moved out of Mannheim station. It was light now, though misty, and Timothy was astonished at the amount of war damage still in evidence. On both sides of the railway tracks there were many rubble-strewn open spaces and half-destroyed buildings. In the grey dawn light, with the mist drifting like smoke, the town looked as though a battle had only recently passed through it.

– Was there much fighting here in the war?

– That's bomb damage, mostly. As a matter of fact, Mannheim was the first target of the British area-bombing offensive, some time in 1940 or '41. And I expect they came back, or we did.

– It's worse than London.

– This is nothing. You should see Frankfurt. Or Hamburg . . . But Heidelberg wasn't touched. I guess that's why we based our Headquarters there. So we wouldn't have any ugly reminders of what we'd done.

Timothy glanced at him curiously. It seemed a queer thing to say – surely nobody need feel guilty about bombing the Germans? But it would be different for an American, he reflected. They wouldn't know about the Blitz – wouldn't know what it had been like.

– I s'pose there weren't any factories or stuff like that worth bombing in Heidelberg? he speculated.

– I guess not, but that didn't save Dresden. They say it was the Student Prince that saved Heidelberg.

– The Student Prince?

– Yeah, d'you know it? Kind of a light opera. *Drink! Drink!* and all that jazz. Real schmaltz, but it always went down very big in the States. Lots of Americans sent their kids to college there, just because of the opera. They say that if they'd ordered Heidelberg to be bombed, the Air Force would have mutinied.

Timothy laughed. He had never heard anybody talk about the war in this way before.

The train was rolling across flat, open country now. The mist lay thickly on the fields.

– Are there mountains behind this mist? he asked. My sister said there were mountains.

– Small mountains, yes. Tree-covered. They start just at Heidelberg, where the Neckar comes out into the Rhine plain. Mannheim is where it meets the Rhine. He demonstrated the junction of the rivers with his long, bony hands. The Neckar valley is very scenic . . . Your sister will be meeting you, I guess?

– I hope so, said Timothy. He dragged out his school cap and put it on. So she'll recognize me, he explained.

– How long since you last saw her?

– Three and a half years.

– That's quite a time.

– She doesn't seem to want to come home, Timothy said. The remark seemed indiscreet when he had made it, but Don seemed unsurprised.

– Heidelberg is full of people who don't want to go home, he said.

The train began to slow down.

– Well, here we are.

– Heidelberg? Already? Timothy jumped up from his seat and leaned out of the window. The air was mild and damp on his face. Straining his eyes he thought he could discern the vague shapes of mountains through the mist.

– The sun will soon burn off the fog, Don said behind him. Then you'll see it all.

Timothy couldn't help wishing, ungratefully, that Don would disappear and leave him to meet Kath alone. The company of a protective adult, he felt, diminished the heroism of his journey. He had, after all, managed it unassisted for all but the last half-hour. He wanted Kath to see him like that: alone, tired, dishevelled, but unbowed. However, it was impossible to refuse Don's assistance, and as they walked along the platform, with the heavy bag swaying between them, he saw Kath.

– There she is! he cried, and waved.

She didn't react at first; then she ran forward with a broad smile of recognition, her large breasts bouncing under her white jumper. Timothy was more aware of her breasts than of anything else for the first few minutes. If they had been like that before, he hadn't been of an age to separate them from the general amplitude of her figure. Now they hypnotized him. They were big, very big. Almost too big, but not quite. He was crushed against them as Kath embraced him, and felt the stiff material of her brassiere buckle against his bony chest.

– Timothy! It's marvellous to see you! How you've grown!

– So've you, he said thoughtlessly.

– Timothy! And I've been on a diet! How was the journey?

– All right.

– I didn't recognize you at first. I was looking for a little boy about so high (she held out her hand about three feet from the ground) and on his own. But I see you've had company. She glanced at Don.

– Only from Mannheim, said Timothy.

Don stepped forward and extended his hand.

– Don Kowalski, he said. You must be Timothy's sister.

– It was very kind of you to look after him.

– My pleasure. I wish we'd gotten acquainted earlier in the journey.

Kath returned her attention to Timothy.

– Are you tired, my pet? You must be, and hungry too. We'll get you some breakfast just as soon as we've dropped your bag somewhere.

– Can I give you a hand? said Don.

– That's very kind of you, but I think I'll get a porter, said Kath firmly.

– Well I'll leave you, then, said Don, but still lingering.

– Thank you *so* much, said Kath. Her manner was becoming a little bit what his father called *lah-di-dah*.

– Well, have a good vacation, Timothy, said Don, picking up his duffle bag. Maybe I'll see you around the town one of these days. It's not such a big place. You too, er . . .

– Kate Young.

– It's been a pleasure meeting you, Kate. You, too, Timothy.

They watched him lope away, swinging his duffle bag over his shoulder.

– Who is he? Kath asked in a low voice.

– I dunno. He said he'd just come out of the Army.

– I guessed he was a G.I. Seemed nice though.

– He was jolly nice. Why didn't you let him help us with my bag? It's terrifically heavy.

– You've got to be careful with these G.I.s. Another couple of minutes and he'd have been trying to date me. She grinned at him and tugged her sweater down over her breasts. Give them an inch and they'll take a mile, I always say. Now, what I suggest is, that we drop your bag at the Left Luggage and have a look at the room I've got lined up for you, and then we'll go and have some breakfast. I've got to go to work this morning, but probably you'd just like to rest and have an easy day, huh?

– I feel I'd like to sleep for about a week, he confessed.

– Poor darling, you do look tired. What time did they wake you up?

– Wake me up? he repeated, puzzled.

Kath gave him a searching look.

– You *did* have a sleeper, didn't you?

– No.

– You mean you sat up all night?

– No, I stood up most of the time. Then I lay on the floor. I couldn't get a seat. He grinned at the look on her face.

– My God! Kath screamed faintly. You must be half-dead! What time did you leave London?

– Eleven o'clock yesterday morning.

Kath groaned.

– And they sent you off without even a reserved seat . . . Of course, I should have known. Mum and Dad have no idea. Well, no use crying over spilt milk. You're here, and you don't look too bad, considering. Now, let's get a porter. *Träger!*

A man in grey denims, pushing a trolley along the platform, nodded and veered in their direction. Kath looked at his bag, and poked it experimentally with the toe of her white, high-heeled shoe.

– Where did you dig this up from?

– It used to be Uncle Jack's.
– Uncle Jack?
– Jill's Dad . . . you remember. He left it in our loft.
– Oh, poor Mr. Martin. What an extraordinary idea.
– Why?
– Well, you must admit, it's a bit morbid.

The porter came up and heaved the bag onto his trolley. She gave him an instruction in German, and they set off.

– You speak German, then, he said respectfully.
– Just a bit. You'll find most of the Germans speak English around here, because of the American presence. We're their bread and butter, you see. And their jam, too, I always say.
– You consider yourself American, then, Kath?
– No, why?
– You said *we* just now.
– Oh, it's just a manner of speaking. After all, I work for them.
– And you told Don your name was Kate.
– That's what everybody calls me here. It started with *Kiss Me Kate*. Did you see that show? I think it's been on in London.
– No, I haven't. What should I call you, Kath or Kate?
– Whichever you like. I always think of myself as Kath at home and Kate out here.
– Two different people?

She looked at him quizzically.

– I suppose you could say that, yes.

The porter led them to the Left Luggage counter.

– I'm going to check your bag in here, Kath explained, and then we can walk across to the guest house. I don't want to take the bag with us until we've seen the room. I'm afraid it won't be very luxurious.
– Anywhere with a bed will do, he said.
– Poor darling. She gave him a sympathetic hug. But it's so good to see you. And of course I want to hear all the news from home. How are Mum and Dad?
– Fine. They send their love, of course.
– Good, you must tell me everything when you're rested.

She tipped the porter and led Timothy out of the station. They passed through a colonnade and came out on to a broad street with a square to the left and gardens to the right. Blue single-decker trams, some coupled together, were cruising past, bells clanging. A huge, tree-covered mountain, startlingly near, heaved up in the mist behind the roofs. Timothy stopped and took it all in.

– Gosh! he said.

– Wait till the sun comes out, then you get all the colours. The green mountains and the blue sky and the coloured roofs. I never get tired of it. This is the Rohrbacherstrasse, she said, as they crossed the tramlines. That's Bismarckplatz, where all the trams are.

– I know about Bismarck, he said. He came into History this year.

– Your guest house is just down this street. I hope it's going to be all right. Accommodation's like gold-dust in Heidelberg. It's a tourist resort, you see, but nearly all the hotels are requisitioned by the Americans for their personnel – I live in one myself – so, as you can imagine, it's very difficult finding anywhere at the height of the season. The requisitioning is the big grudge the Germans have against us.

Timothy let her chatter on, too tired to say much on his own account.

– It was only as a special favour that I managed to get the offer of this place. It's price controlled, but I'll have to tip the woman.

– With cigarettes?

– Dear me, no. Those days have gone. The Germans are getting back on to their own feet now . . . it's amazing, they really know how to work. Here we are.

They stopped outside a tall, shuttered house, and Kath rang the bell. After a few moments, they heard the sound of bolts being drawn, and a stout, middle-aged woman in a flowered overall ushered them into a dark hall. Kath introduced him, in a mixture of English and German, to Frau Himmler. Though she nodded and smiled amicably enough, Timothy thought the name was a bad omen. His misgivings increased as she led them up four flights of stairs, each flight darker and more dilapidated than the one before. Carpet gave way to lino, and lino to bare boards. Frau Himmler unlocked a door on the top landing and pushed it open. They went in.

It was an attic room. It was clean, but that was about all you could say for it. The floor sloped almost as much as the ceiling, and the heavy furniture looked ready to slide down to one end of the room. There was an iron bed covered with a mountainous quilt, and a small window through which he could see a neighbouring chimney. Kath walked round the room, testing the bed springs and opening the chest of drawers.

– What d'you think? she murmured. A bit grim, isn't it?

He shrugged.

– It's all right.

In the end Kath decided that he would rest in her own room that day, and come back to Frau Himmler's in the evening if she hadn't been able to find anywhere better. This plan appealed to Timothy, who didn't look forward to being left in Frau Himmler's charge.

They had breakfast in a low-built, tree-shaded restaurant quite near the station, called the Stadtgarten. It was a cafeteria, but not a bit like a Lyons or an A.B.C. Under Kath's instruction, he loaded his tray with orange-juice, cornflakes, eggs and bacon, toast, and something called hot cakes, which looked like fat pancakes.

– You'll have two eggs, won't you? Kath asked him.

– Can I?

– Of course. How would you like them – fried, poached or scrambled?

– Fried, please.

– Sunny side up? the cook asked Timothy, as he broke the eggs into a frying pan. Timothy looked at Kath for interpretation.

– D'you like your eggs sunny side up – with the yolks showing – or turned over and broken into the pan?

– Sunny side up, he said, grinning at the childish but cheerful phrase.

Only one item of his meal disappointed him. When he asked for tea he was given a cup of hot water with a cardboard ticket on the end of a string hanging out of it.

– What's this? he asked, lifting the string and discovering a sodden little bag on the end.

– It's a tea-bag, said Kath, giggling.

– Can you take as much sugar as you like? he asked, unwrapping two lumps from the bowl on the table.

– Of course. There's no rationing.

– None at all?

– Not for American personnel.

– Gosh! he said, and took another lump.

– I can see you're going to enjoy the food, anyway, Timothy.

Their conversation remained on this level, light and casual. There was a little shyness between them, Timothy felt, and they were both trying each other out. It was not only that they hadn't seen each other for over three years. In those three years he had narrowed the age difference between them. Sixteen was nearer to twenty-seven than thirteen to twenty-four. Throughout his childhood, Kath had been almost indistinguishable from the grown-ups around him, more like an aunt than a sister. That relationship was no longer possible, but he wasn't quite sure what would replace it.

Towards the end of the meal, when Timothy was eating more out of greed than real hunger, and Kath was smoking her second cigarette, a woman who was passing their table stopped and greeted her.

– Kate, honey! Hi!

– Dolores! Haven't seen you for ages. What a gorgeous costume!

Dolores smirked and smoothed her skirt over her hips.

– Don't tell anyone, but I got it at the Thrift Shop.

– I don't believe it! Oh, Dolores, this is my brother Timothy.

Dolores, who had been shooting glances at him from under her thick eyelashes, stared.

– Well, how *marvellous!* Hi, Timothy, I'm so pleased to meet you. She extended a limp, manicured hand, adorned with a heavy jewelled ring and a gold bracelet. Is this the kid brother who sends you all those cute letters, Kate?

– Yes, just arrived from England to spend a vacation with me. Won't you sit down a moment?

– Thanks honey, but I'm just starting a vacation myself. Well, perhaps for just a second. I'm taking the eight-thirty train to Frankfurt, and flying to Rome.

– Heavenly! For how long?

– Five whole weeks, my dear. I've been saving it up. She flashed her smile between them in a wide arc, like a torch beam. I'm having two weeks' sightseeing – you know, really *doing* all those old churches and museums, and then three weeks on Capri, just lazing on the beach.

– Sounds marvellous.

– Should be, as long as I get some company, you know what I mean? She winked suggestively at Timothy. How was your journey, Timothy?

– Oh, don't talk about it, Kath broke in, and related the whole story. Dolores drew back her head and kept him covered with a wide-eyed stare throughout the narrative.

– Well, she exclaimed at intervals. How *ghastly* . . . all those *hours* . . . it's a wonder he's still on his feet . . .

Then Kath went on to describe Frau Himmler's room.

– The poor kid, it sounds just awful. Couldn't you find him something better, honey?

– I've been searching everywhere for the past three weeks. This was my last hope. You know what Heidelberg is like at high season, unless you pay the earth.

– It seems a real shame . . . My room will be empty for the next five weeks, Kate, if that's any help.

– You mean . . . ?

– Sure, he's welcome to use it.

– Did you hear that, Timothy? Kath said excitedly.

– It's jolly nice of you, he mumbled, completely taken aback. He'd just been thinking what a bore this woman was, when she came out with this extraordinarily generous offer.

– Well, why not, for heaven's sake? As long as he doesn't mind living in a women's hostel.

– A women's hostel? Timothy repeated faintly.

– That's right. Dolores turned to Kath. You'd have to figure out some way of sneaking him in in the evenings. The mornings would be no problem – he could just stay in the room until all the girls had gone to work.

– *I* know, said Kath. I could go in with him at night pretending he was my boyfriend seeing me home. He looks old enough, doesn't he?

– Sure he does, said Dolores, inspecting him doubtfully.

– Thanks very much, but I'd rather not, said Timothy firmly.

The two women cajoled him for some time, but he refused to be budged.

– Well, take the key, anyway, Kate, said Dolores, getting to her feet. Just in case he changes his mind. Timothy, have a great vacation.

He thanked her again, and they watched her prance across the floor of the restaurant, waving her braceleted hand to another friend.

– Timothy, said Kath, in a low voice, I hope you won't mind my mentioning it, but don't you know that you should stand up when a lady leaves the table?

– Sorry, he muttered. I forgot.

– Only these little things are important. And I want you to make a good impression on all my friends.

– I said I forgot.

– Now you're cross.

– No, I'm just tired.

– Poor darling, of course you are. You must get some sleep and I must get to work.

When they left the restaurant, the mist had nearly cleared, and it was quite warm though not yet eight o'clock. He felt sluggish and sticky, and it was an effort to keep up with Kath's brisk pace and conversation.

– Dolores is very sweet, don't you think? I think she overdresses, though, don't you? Most American women do. You'd be much more comfortable in her room, you know. Well, see how you feel when you've had a sleep.

He reminded her that his bag, with his pyjamas in it, was still at the station. She glanced at her watch.

– I don't think we've got time to pick it up now, or I'll be late for work. I can lend you some pyjamas, if you like. She giggled. They'll be a bit big for you.

– It's all right, I can sleep in my underwear.

– I'll get Rudolf to bring your bag across during the day. That's our porter at Fichte Haus. Charming boy, speaks English fluently.

Rudolf was operating the switchboard in a little office by the door when they entered Kath's hostel. He smiled through the glass and motioned them to wait. He was a handsome young man, with clean-cut features and fair hair combed straight back from his forehead. When he came out of the office, Timothy saw that his left arm was missing below the elbow, and the sleeve of his jacket was pinned neatly to his chest.

– This is my brother, Timothy, Rudolf. You remember, I told you he was coming to visit me.

– Indeed, yes, Miss Young. Rudolf made a slight bow that seemed oddly formal because of the folded sleeve, and shook Timothy's hand.

– He's going to rest in my room today until I've sorted out his accommodation.

– I will make sure he is not disturbed.

Timothy thanked Rudolf and Kath asked him to bring the bag over from the station later in the day.

– Will he be able to manage it? Timothy whispered, as they ascended the carpeted stairs. With his arm, I mean?

– Oh, yes, he has a trolley. I could get a cab, but he'll be glad of the tip.

– How did he lose it?

– His arm? In the war, I guess. I don't like to ask him. I know he was a prisoner of war in England. That's where he learned English.

– He looks too young to have been in the war.

– I expect he was called up at the very end. The Germans were drafting schoolboys by then.

– You'd never guess . . . I mean, he seems jolly nice.

– It's a shame, he's far too intelligent for this job, but the Germans can't pick and choose, especially with a disability like that. Well, here we are, *chez* Young.

She slotted a key into one of the flush-fitting doors spaced out down the corridor, and pushed it open.

– Good, she said, looking round, they've made the bed already.

– You mean somebody makes your bed for you?

– Yes, we're really spoiled here. I never even touch a duster.

– It's a smashing room, Kath, he said, looking round, taking in a divan scattered with bright cushions, a drop-leaf table and two upright chairs, an easy chair and coffee table, fitted cupboards in varnished wood.

– Hey! he exclaimed. That's one of my sketches on the wall.

– That's right, I had it framed. I show it to all my friends.

– I'd forgotten all about it. The perspective is all wrong. I can do much better than that now, he said. But it pleased him to see his work – a pen-and-wash sketch of Tower Bridge, done from a photograph – handsomely framed on Kath's wall. It didn't look at all bad, actually.

– Well, I like it, anyway. Perhaps you could do some sketching while you're here. There are lots of nice views.

– Maybe. I brought my pad and some watercolours with me.

She pulled back the coverlet on the divan bed.

– Now, would you like to take a shower? I should think most of the girls will have finished with the bathrooms by now.

– No, I don't think I'll bother.

– Want to hit the sack right away, huh? Well, I can't blame you. You can have a wash here. She opened one of the cupboards to reveal a fitted washbasin and mirror.

– Er, is there a lavatory anywhere?

– Halfway along the passage. The white door.

When he returned to Kath's room she had taken off her jumper and was buttoning up a white blouse.

– Looks as if it's going to be a hot day, she said. I'll pull down the blinds and leave the window open.

She tugged at a string behind the curtain, and the Venetian blind, pale green to match the walls, dropped down, quenching the sunlight. Timothy sank into the easy chair and took off his shoes, wriggling his toes inside his woollen socks. Kath stood before the mirror, ran her tongue over her lipstick, and dabbed at her hair, turning her head from side to side.

– Well, she said, dropping the lipstick into her handbag and closing it with a snap, have a good rest, Timothy, and don't worry about a thing.

– As long as I don't have to live in that women's hostel . . .

– You don't have to do anything you don't want to do, my pet, she assured him, stroking his head. This is *your* holiday, and I want you to have a really good time. I haven't been much of a sister to you, have I?

– I wouldn't say that, he said awkwardly.

– Well, anyway, I want to make it up to you now you've come all this way. She bent to kiss him on the forehead. Now I've put lipstick all over you. I'll be home about five-thirty, she went on briskly. We'll eat out with Vince and Greg – two of my particular friends. They're dying to meet you. If there's anything you want, ask Rudolf. There's an icebox in the hall with Coke and suchlike. Now, I really must fly.

– 'Bye, Kath. Kate.

She grinned, and was gone.

Timothy locked the door, took off all his clothes except his pants and vest, and bathed his feet one by one in the wash basin. They were red and swollen, imprinted with the ribbed weave of his socks. Then he washed his face and hands and climbed into the bed. The sheets were cool and crisp and clean. He stretched luxuriously.

Though he was tired, he felt too excited to go to sleep at once. Not excited, exactly, but strange: strange to his surroundings, and strange to himself. In this sleek, comfortable, tidy room, suffused with a green underwater light, he floated free of time and space. Home seemed infinitely remote, and the self that belonged there just as distant. Between them and himself, here, now, the journey had intervened; but the journey itself scarcely seemed real in retrospect, perhaps because it had been a night journey. In the daytime you could watch the miles flow past the window, and the changing scene kept pace with the changes inside you. But at night you could see nothing except your own reflection in the glass. Had he dreamed the whole journey? Was he dreaming now? No, he wasn't dreaming. He could feel the starch in the fresh sheets. He could see the lines of light thrown on the ceiling by the Venetian blinds. He could hear the murmur of the traffic, punctuated by hooters and tram bells. These things were real. And yet they weren't enough to establish the reality of Heidelberg. He hadn't seen enough of the place to form a coherent picture; and the people he had met – Don and Dolores and Rudolf and even Kath herself – were like figures in a dream landscape, like the characters in *The Wizard of Oz*, eccentric and unpredictable and slightly alarming even when they seemed friendly. And he couldn't say to himself, well I've finally arrived, this is my place for the next three weeks, because this room was only a waiting-room, a stage on the way to his final destination, Frau Himmler's guest house. Or Dolores' hostel. That was a daft idea, and yet . . . Frau Himmler's was not an inviting prospect. Not only was it bleak and unwelcoming, it was also unmistakably *German*.

Timothy had already acquired a sense of two communities living in Heidelberg: underneath, the Germans, and on top of them, floating, or skimming over them with minimum contact, like dragonflies or water-boatmen, the Americans. From their point of view the German surface looked docile and calm as a millpond. But who knew what dark shapes moved in the depths below? To stay at Frau Himmler's would be to sink at least partially into those depths, and Timothy shrank instinctively from their cold contact. Even

Kath, he thought, had seemed less at ease in the dark forbidding house, less certain in her dealings with Frau Himmler, than she did elsewhere.

Kath had certainly changed. She had a poise and a self-confidence and a fresh clean health about her that made him feel dowdy and uncouth at her side. And she was almost what you might call good-looking now. She was still on the fat side, but you weren't so much aware of it – it was something to do with the way she dressed and carried herself. And if her bust was enormous, it wasn't in the droopy way of fat women on seaside postcards, but more like Jane Russell, or the bare women in *Razzle*, who made boys at school double up and groan as if in pain when they looked. She held her breasts high, like her head. And her face was quite pretty, really; though the chin was just a little too big, it gave a warm, good-humoured expression to her face. And her hair – he couldn't remember, now, exactly how her hair was done, except that it was neat and framed her head attractively. Her new-found attractiveness made his mother's suspicions, that she had had some kind of affair, and perhaps a child, seem more plausible. But in that case why had she invited him out, risking discovery? It could only be, he realized, with a sudden flash of intuition, because she *wanted* him to find out.

Yes, some time in the next three weeks Kath would take him, without explanation, to some home or orphanage – he visualized it as an old house in the country near Heidelberg, run by gentle, soft-spoken nuns, with children toddling about in the garden, digging in sandpits and playing on swings . . . and there would be one little girl (for some reason he was sure it would be a girl), dressed in a smock like all the others, but somehow different from them, a pretty little girl with dark ringlets, like Jill, who came running across the grass as soon as she saw Kath, and Kath caught her up and swung her round in the air and said to him, *What d'you think of this one, Timothy?* and he said, *She's sweet*, and Kath said, *She's mine, Timothy, she's mine* and burst into tears. And he was very grown-up about it and not a bit shocked but full of sympathy and understanding. And he promised to help her bring up the child as soon as he had a job and to persuade their parents to accept it. And Kath was amazed and overjoyed and grateful. *Oh, Timothy*, she said . . .

But though it was her voice that he heard, she would not say what she was supposed to say, and it was as if she were speaking to someone else, talking right through him.

– Sixteen . . . a real English schoolboy. It brought it all back to me as soon as I set eyes on him. You know those terrible raincoats they make them wear in England? . . . No, of course you wouldn't, well, they're navy blue and they're too hot in summer and too thin for winter and they don't keep the rain out anyway, and they're tied up in the middle like a sack of potatoes. And thick grey flannels and black shoes and a cap – wait till you see the *cap* . . . And he looked so pale and tired, poor kid, stood up all night because he couldn't get a seat . . . Absolutely packed, he said . . . Well, they probably thought it would be extravagant, that's one of their favourite words, *extravagant* . . .

He realized now that Kath was not speaking to him in his imagination or in a dream. She was in the room, speaking to someone else. She must have come back for something. He opened his eyes and saw her sitting curled up on the armchair, with her back to him, wearing a flower-patterned dressing-gown. She had a cigarette in one hand and the telephone receiver in the other. The light in the room had changed, and the air felt warmer. Was it possible that he had been asleep – that it was afternoon already, and Kath was back from work? It felt as though it was only a moment ago that he had got into bed.

Now she was talking about the offer of Dolores' room.

– Well, the trouble is, he's dead set against it, you know what boys are like at that age, the idea of living in a girls' hostel just makes him curl up. Yes I'm sure you would, but not everybody's . . . well, I wish he would . . . quite, and not only that but it would save me quite a few Marks . . . You'll have to help me persuade him, but *tactfully*, now. Right, see you about seven. 'Bye.

Kath put down the telephone and Timothy hastily shut his eyes. He heard a click as she switched on the radio, and dance music filled the room. Then the music stopped and a mellow American voice announced:

– A.F.N. Frankfurt, and this is Staff Sergeant MacCabe with the news at eighteen hundred hours. First the headlines. Korea: truce talks continued at Kaesong today, but no progress was reported on the exchange of prisoners. Two US airmen died and three others were

seriously injured in an automobile accident on the Frankfurt–Mannheim autobahn last night. At home, Senator Joseph McCarthy made new allegations of Communist infiltration of the State Department at a press conference in Washington . . .

Timothy sat up in bed and yawned.

– Oh, so you're awake at last, said Kath. I put the radio on purposely.

– It's funny listening to the news and hearing nothing about England.

– Did you sleep well?

– Like a log. Kath, I've been thinking. Maybe I ought to take your friend's room.

Kath beamed.

– I'm so glad! What made you change your mind?

– Oh, I dunno. It seems silly not to take the offer.

– Well, I'm sure you'll be more comfortable there. I didn't like to think of you in that dismal attic. Rudolf has brought your bag over, by the way.

– Good. You'll find a pair of trousers, brown ones, near the top. Bung them over.

– Wouldn't you like to have your shower straightaway?

– No, I don't think I'll bother today, he said. Catching a look of consternation on her face, he added: I had a bath the night before last.

Kath exploded in a mixture of amusement and protest.

– But you've been travelling hundreds of miles since then. In all those dirty trains.

– Oh, all right then, he said hastily. Where's the bathroom?

– Just next to the toilet, where you went this morning.

– Won't there be some women about?

– There might be, yes. Kath pondered. I know . . .

She dressed him in an old dressing-gown of her own, and covered his head with a plastic shower-cap trimmed with artificial flowers.

– There, she giggled. It's a good job you haven't started to shave yet.

She opened the door, looked out conspiratorially, then signalled to him that the corridor was clear.

Clutching the buttonless dressing-gown across his chest and

knees, Timothy slunk along the corridor and slipped into the bathroom. He bolted the door and leaned against it. His grotesque image confronted him in a mirror at the other end of the room. He dragged off the shower-cap and threw it to the floor. Already he regretted changing his mind about Dolores' room. It would be like this all the time there. If it hadn't been for Kath's reference to money on the phone, he would have changed his mind once again.

When he returned the bed was made, and Kath had changed into a black silky dress with a deep neckline that showed a lot of what the *Daily Express* called cleavage.

– Smashing dress, Kath.

– Well, thank you, Timothy, coming from you that's quite a compliment. Have a nice shower?

– I had a bath. I don't go much for showers.

– Oh, I find showers so much more refreshing. And it's cleaner, I always think.

Kath obviously had a bit of an obsession about washing, he thought to himself, as he turned his back and, preserving modesty with the aid of the dressing-gown, put on his brown gaberdine trousers. He dressed with more than usual care, for the remarks he had heard about his appearance rankled somewhat. He put on his best white shirt, his brown Harris tweed sports jacket and a wine-coloured tie.

– Well, you do look smart, Kath said. But he sensed a certain reserve in her voice.

– I don't have a suit, he said. Is this all right?

– It's fine, Timothy, fine. I'm just thinking that you may find that jacket a little warm here. It's a wonderful piece of material, isn't it? She fingered his lapel.

– Harris tweed. Utility.

– You haven't got anything lighter?

– Only my blazer, but that's a bit dirty.

– Is that a nylon shirt?

– Yes, you sent it to me two Christmases ago.

– Did I? And it still fits you?

– It's a bit tight round the neck, he admitted. Mum moved the button on the collar.

– Yes, said Kath, I can see . . . We'll have to get you some lighter clothes. A lightweight jacket, and maybe a pair of pants.

– I've got plenty of pants, he said. Mum washed me four pairs.

– Sorry, I mean trousers, Kath laughed. The American boys call them pants. You pick these words up.

– You don't have an American accent, though.

– I'm glad you think so. Between you and me, a good English accent goes down very well with the Americans. It's my biggest social asset.

One up for Dad, Timothy thought to himself.

– You must be getting pretty hungry, Timothy, but the boys will be here soon. I'll go get you a Coke and some ice and we'll fix ourselves a drink while we're waiting.

When she was gone he took off his jacket. Kath was perfectly right – it was too thick for the weather. He was perspiring already. His blazer was lighter, but when he tried it on in front of the mirror it looked wrong with his brown trousers, and anyway it was filthy from the journey. He flung the blazer aside and scowled at his reflection. He had dragged nearly his entire wardrobe with him to Germany, and here he was with nothing suitable to wear on his very first evening.

Kath served the drinks with some ceremony. She poured the Coca-Cola, already well chilled, to judge by the condensation on the bottle, over several cubes of ice in a tall glass, added a slice of lemon and two straws.

– How's that?

He sucked long and deeply on the straws and felt the drink pierce his thirst like an icicle.

– Delicious! What are you drinking, Kath?

– Martini on the rocks. The experts would shudder, but I can't be bothered to get out the shaker. Want to try it? No? Well, perhaps you'd better not. I don't want Mum and Dad accusing me of leading you into bad habits.

– Where'd you get the ice from?

– There's a communal kitchen on each floor. We share a big fridge.

– I wish we had a fridge at home.

– Why doesn't Mum get one?

– I dunno. Export only, I s'pose. Or it's too expensive. Everything in England's one thing or the other. He helped himself liberally to the salted nuts that Kath had put on the table beside him. As well as peanuts there were almonds, walnuts and brazils. Every day seemed to be like Christmas here.

– I don't know how Mum manages without a fridge, said Kath. Or rather I do know, only too well. Keeping the butter and milk in the sink in the summer, with the tap running. Sniffing the food in the larder to see if it's gone off . . . She sighed humorously, blowing out a plume of cigarette smoke.

– And she never throws anything away. She eats it up herself if nobody else will.

– Ah, yes, eating up. *This needs eating up*. It's a wonder she hasn't poisoned herself before now.

– Oh, well, I s'pose it's rationing that made her like that, said Timothy, making up for some obscure feeling of disloyalty.

– I feel so guilty sometimes, when I think of rationing still going on at home. We eat so well out here. Even the Germans are better off, and in France or Belgium you can get any food you like.

– It's the Government.

– I read in *Time* the other day they think there'll be another election soon.

– Old Attlee's hanging on 'cos he knows he'll be chucked out.

– You think the Conservatives will win next time, then?

– It's a dead cert, said Timothy confidently.

– That will please the Americans. They adore Churchill. What do you think of this Burgess and Maclean affair? The Americans are furious about it.

– I don't see how anybody could have guessed what they were doing. I mean, why should two Englishmen spy for the Russians? It just doesn't make sense.

– Perhaps they did it for the money. Or they think Russia's going to win the next war, Kath said lightly.

On the radio, to the background of lilting violins, an American voice drawled:

– *Music by Candelight . . . A.F.N. presents background music for dancing, dining or just eeeeeeasy listening.*

– So you can cook for yourself here, then? said Timothy.

– Yes, but I'm not much of a cook, I warn you. Vince suggested – he was on the phone just now – that we go to the Molkenkur tonight.

I think you'll like that. It's halfway up the Königstuhl – that's the big mountain you saw from the station this morning.

– A restaurant, is it?

– Yes, and a club for officers and civilian personnel. We go there quite a lot. They have a regular band. D'you dance, Timothy?

– No.

– Too bad, I'll have to teach you.

– I don't see much in dancing, myself, he said guardedly. Vince is an American, I s'pose?

– Yes, Greg too. They're great fun – you'll like them. I must have mentioned them in my letters.

– Are they in the Army?

– They were during the war, but now they're civilians working for the Army.

– Sort of civil servants, like Uncle Ted?

Kath smiled.

– Well, sort of civil servants, yes, but not a bit like Uncle Ted. They have very good jobs – high salaries – and I think Vince must have a private income of his own. He comes from an old Washington family – his father was an ambassador or a consul or something like that. But whatever they have, they spend. Easy come, easy go.

– Are they married?

Kath looked startled.

– Good heavens, no. What gave you that idea?

– I was just wondering, he said.

– No, they're real bachelor boys. I can't imagine either of them settling down and getting married. They enjoy high living too much.

She drained her glass and gazed thoughtfully at the olive in the bottom. Timothy wondered whether to throw in some leading question, like, *And what about you Kath?* But the moment passed. There was a knock at the door.

Timothy's first impression of Vince and Greg was that they were positive and negative versions of the same person. Vince had startlingly blond hair, a tanned complexion, and was wearing a dark blue suit. Greg had black hair, a pale face, and was dressed in beige. But on closer inspection they were quite different. Vince was strikingly handsome and athletic in build and had a moustache: he looked like a film star. Greg was shorter and stouter, and his snub nose, slightly protuberant eyes and hint of a double chin gave him the appearance of a genial baby. Timothy found himself smiling as soon as he saw Greg, who advanced into the room with his arms outstretched.

– Kiss me, Kate! Honey, you look wonderful.

Kath obliged him with a peck on the cheek, smiling over his shoulder at Vince.

– Greg, Vince, this is Timothy.

– I'm always glad to meet a fellow artist, said Greg, as they shook hands. Oh, you may laugh, Kate, but let me tell you, I used to draw moustaches on the New York subway posters that were very widely admired. That was my moustache period. He threw himself down on the sofa and crossed his plump little legs.

– Take no notice, said Vince, smiling at Timothy. He's always like this.

– How about a drink, boys? Martini on the rocks O.K?

– You know how Vince likes it, honey, said Greg. Just pass the Martini bottle once over the gin.

– Kate tells me you had a rough trip, Timothy, said Vince.

– Yes, I didn't have a seat.

– Gee, no seat? That's terrible, said Greg. Whaddya do, give it up to a lady?

– No, I just couldn't get one, said Timothy, seeing too late that Greg was joking.

– Oh, Kate, said Vince. We brought you a corsage. He presented her with a small bunch of purplish flowers in a cellophane box.

– Oh, how sweet of you. Aren't they lovely, Timothy? She went to the mirror and pinned them to her dress.

– Mind you don't puncture your falsies with the pin, honey, Greg said.

– That's one artificial aid I don't need, Gregory Roche, Kath retorted, flushing slightly.

– I'm only kidding, honey. Say, did you hear about the guy who discovered on his wedding night that his bride wore falsies? He said, *There seems to have been a misudderstanding*.

– Greg! I'm going to have to censor your jokes while Timothy is here, said Kath, laughing.

– Aw, come on, said Greg. Timothy knows about falsies, don't you Timothy?

– Yes, he admitted with some embarrassment.

– Are we going to the Molkenkur? said Vince.

– Yes, said Kath. It's such a lovely view from the terrace. I want to show Timothy.

– Gosh! Timothy exclaimed, as they walked out on to the terrace.

– Isn't it beautiful?

– Fantastic.

He leaned on the parapet and gazed down. The green, thickly wooded mountainside fell away sharply beneath them till it met the red, grey and brown roofs of the town, quaintly shaped and densely packed together, with the spires of churches sticking up here and there. Beyond the roofs was the river, broad and calm, spanned by two bridges. There was only a thin sprinkling of houses on the other bank, and behind them another wooded mountain rose steeply into the sky. To his right, the river passed out of sight between more mountains; to his left it lost itself in the sunset haze of an endless plain. He could see trams and cars moving slowly through the streets below, but only the faintest murmur of traffic carried up to this height. He had never seen a town so completely before.

– It's like a toy town.

– It's so romantic, I always think, said Kath. All those old buildings, and so unspoiled. You can just see the edge of the Castle over there. Down below is the Old Bridge, the one with the two towers on this side. The Americans built the other one, after the war. The Germans were ordered to blow up all the bridges as they retreated.

– But not the old one?

– Yes, even that one, said Vince. But only the middle span, and they restored it soon after the war. The Burgermeister was telling me just the other day, it was the first bridge to be restored in the whole of Germany. You can see the bricks in the middle are a different colour when you're close up.

– Folks, this is a fascinating travelogue, said Greg, but if Timothy is as hungry as I am . . .

– Yes, let's eat, said Kath.

As it was so warm, they decided to eat outside on the terrace. A waiter handed Timothy an enormous menu, which he stared at blankly. The only item that looked familiar was ham 'n eggs, but this was cried down as too unenterprising. Eventually he settled on Chicken-in-the-Rough as his main course, and after being assured that a shrimp cocktail contained no gin (an innocent enquiry that was received as a great witticism) he consented to try one as a starter. The shrimps seemed to him more like oversized prawns, but it was the fried chicken, served in a basket overflowing with chips, that really astonished him. Incredulously he counted the joints.

– Blimey! he said. There must be a whole chicken here.

– Think you can manage it? Kath said, smiling.

– I just pick it up and eat it in my fingers?

– That's right.

– Here goes, then.

He grasped a drumstick and bit deeply into the meat. The three adults delayed starting their own dishes to watch him.

– So that's what it's like to have an appetite, said Vince. I'd forgotten. He began to cut up his food into small pieces, which he then ate with a fork held in his right hand. Timothy was intrigued to see that Greg and even Kath also ate in this fashion.

– Chicken is a luxury in England, remember, Kath said.

– Yes, the last time we had chicken at home was Easter Sunday, said Timothy, and then it lasted us for three days.

– How about that? said Greg. But where d'you get your eggs from if you haven't any chickens?

– Don't you know anything? said Vince. Laying hens aren't good to eat.

– They do say eggs will come off ration soon, Timothy said.

– Eggs on ration? I don't believe it, said Greg. The hens must be constipated.

The meal passed quickly and pleasantly. The conversation kept Timothy constantly diverted. It wasn't that any of the remarks were roaringly funny in themselves; but each joke derived an impetus from the previous one, so that conversation rode forward on little waves of hilarity. Greg was the chief comedian, but all three adults treated conversation as a kind of team game, passing the ball deftly between them, never letting it drop to the ground. Timothy, used to meals consumed rapidly, and often alone (he and his parents rarely sat down together at the table except on Sundays) found this new style of social intercourse fascinating. As he listened, he watched the river turn a dull gold in the rays of the setting sun, thrown into relief by the dark face of the mountain on the further bank. Then the stars came out and the lights of the town twinkled in the valley below. An illuminated pleasure boat sailed up the river, disturbing its own reflection, so that it seemed to turn up a furrow of gold in the dark water.

The others took no dessert, but Vince, who insisted that the meal was his treat, ordered for Timothy something called Baked Alaska, a hot pudding miraculously filled with unmelted ice cream. The windows of the restaurant were open, and music carried out on to the terrace. Kath danced in turn with the two men. She tried to persuade Timothy to take a lesson from her, but he declined.

Conversation flagged while Kath was dancing with Vince. Greg became guarded and taciturn, as if he had no intention of wasting his witticisms on Timothy alone. When Timothy asked him about his work, he replied briefly that he was in the Real Estate Department, and declined to elaborate. When Timothy enquired about Vince's work he replied, almost rudely, that he had better ask Vince himself. Eventually they fell silent, and watched the other two figures swaying to the music, moving in and out of the shadows and patches of light on the terrace. Timothy noticed with interest that Kath danced cheek-to-cheek with Vince; but looking through the open windows he could see that the couples on the dance floor, even quite elderly ones, danced in the same fashion. And when it was Greg's turn, his face, too, was pressed to Kath's.

– You should take up Kate's offer to teach you to dance, Timothy, said Vince. She has a natural sense of rhythm.

– Does she? We always used to think she was rather heavy-footed at home. That's what Mum used to say.

– No, she's a great dancer. A great girl in many ways, your sister.

– She's changed a lot, Timothy confided, since she came out here.

– For the better, I trust?

– Oh, yes. Heidelberg seems a smashing place, what I've seen of it. Do you like living here?

– I guess so. It gets a little claustrophobic at times. But it's conveniently located. Yes, I like it fine.

Vince was sitting with his back to the lighted windows of the restaurant, and his face was a dark, inscrutable mask except when he drew on the cigar he was smoking. Then a faint red glow momentarily illuminated his handsome features, and tinged his blond moustache with fire.

– What's Real Estate? Timothy asked him. Greg said that was his work.

– Oh, property. The Army has to buy up land for its building programmes, requisition accommodation, pay compensation – it's quite a big operation. Greg's a genius at it.

– Why do they call it Real Estate? Is there such a thing as Unreal Estate?

Vince chuckled in the darkness.

– Say, that's good. Maybe that's what I should go in for. *Vincent Vernon, Unreal Estate Agent. Castles in the air, ivory towers . . . heavenly mansions. Unusual commission. Loans arranged.*

– Do you have an interesting job? Timothy asked.

– Yeah.

There was a long silence, and Timothy had just decided that Vince was going to be as uncommunicative as Greg, when he added:

– Officially I'm a liaison official with the German government. Off the record, I'm concerned with de-nazification in this area. D'you know what that means?

– Getting rid of Nazis, I s'pose. You put them in prison, or something?

– The really criminal ones are tried and sent to prison, but there aren't many of those around now. Mostly my job is checking on government personnel to see that they have a clean political record, and supervising re-education programmes in schools and colleges. Officially all that's the responsibility of the Federal government now, but we like to keep a friendly eye on things. Hence my somewhat ambiguous job.

– Is it dangerous?

Vince laughed.

– Not a bit.

The music shifted into a Latin-American rhythm. Kath and Greg began to jig up and down energetically, laughing and calling encouragement to each other.

– It was difficult finding German administrators with clean records to run the country after the war. Mostly they were Communists who'd managed to survive somehow. Now, of course, the Communists are even less acceptable to Uncle Sam than the ex-Nazis.

– Weren't there any other Germans against Hitler?

– Yeah, but most of them were liquidated after the July Plot.

– What was that? Our history syllabus stops at 1914, he added apologetically.

– Well, there were several attempts to assassinate Hitler – by Germans, I mean, but the one that came nearest to success was in July 1944. A group of German officers tried to kill Hitler by blowing him up at one of his conferences. A guy called Stauffenberg planted the bomb in a briefcase, but after he left the room somebody moved the bag with the bomb in it, quite accidentally, and Hitler survived, just badly shaken.

– Gosh! said Timothy, fascinated.

– Of course, Hitler was pretty mad. Ordered a purge of everyone suspected of disloyalty. They reckon five thousand people were arrested and executed. Just about the five thousand people best qualified to run the country after the war. Stauffenberg was court-martialled and shot immediately after the assassination attempt. Luckily for him.

– Why?

– The other ringleaders were hanged from meathooks with piano wire. Not the quickest of deaths. Hitler had a film made of it for private viewing in his bunker. They say even Goebbels had to cover his eyes to stop himself from throwing up.

Vince drew on his cigar and the red glow came and went on his handsome, impassive features.

– Whew! Timothy whispered.

Kath and Greg came hilariously back to the table.

– Gee, I bet that samba has taken an inch off my waistline, said Greg, collapsing into a chair. And a year off my life.

– You two seemed to be very deep in conversation, Kath remarked.

– I've been giving Timothy a little history lesson. About the July plot.

– Oh, Vince, really!

– It was jolly interesting, said Timothy.

– Well, you've discovered his hobby-horse pretty quickly, Timothy, said Kath, putting a cigarette between her lips. He's always reading about Hitler and the Nazis.

– It's my job, honey, said Vince, leaning across the table and snapping his Ronson.

– Well, I know, but you might have picked a lighter topic of conversation for Timothy's first evening. Who wants to think about all those horrible things on a night like this? She threw back her head and blew smoke towards the stars.

They had come to the restaurant in Greg's enormous black Buick. Vince had a car, too, but it was, he said, a little cramped for four.

– It's a pre-war Mercedes, a white one, said Kath. Just wait till you see it, Timothy.

The Buick was wide enough to take them all on the front seat. It purred down the twisting mountain road, tyres squealing softly on the bends, headlights tunnelling through the woods. One of the corners was so sharp, and the car so long, that Greg had to stop, reverse, and take it again. He pushed a button on the dashboard, and throbbing, squealing jazz filled the car.

– Stan Kenton! he said. *Peanut Vendor*. This really sends me. He took a pencil from his pocket and tapped on the rim of the steering wheel to the rhythm.

– Just watch the road, maestro, said Vince.

– Yes, be careful, Greg, Kath agreed.

– Aw, this automobile drives itself. Power brakes, power steering, automatic transmission . . .

– Why don't you get an automatic pilot? said Vince. Then you could just sit here and play the radio.

– It'll come, said Greg. You can't stop progress.

He called at Fichte Haus to collect Timothy's bag, then drove them the short distance to Dolores' hostel.

– Well, Timothy, he said, as they got out of the car. I'll come over here one night and we'll organize a pantie-raid. You have pantie-raids in England?

– Certainly not, said Kath. English boys wouldn't dream of it. And Utility knickers wouldn't be worth stealing, believe me.

Vince offered to take Timothy's bag into the hostel, but Kath thought they would be less conspicuous on their own.

– I like your friends, said Timothy, as the Buick surged away, leaving them standing on the pavement with the bag between them.

– They're fun, aren't they? What I like about them is that they really make an effort to enjoy life. There's never a dull moment.

– I can see that.

– Now, let's see what Dolores' room is like. Hold yourself upright and try to look as if you're my boyfriend. I'll take one handle and you take the other.

The hostel was a larger, more impersonal place than Fichte Haus, with stone floors and long, rather bleak corridors. Kath said she thought it had been converted from a military barracks. As they waited for the lift, three women passed them without a second glance.

– You're doing fine, Timothy, Kath whispered.

– Are men allowed in here, then?

– Oh, yes. There's probably some rule about being out by midnight, but I don't suppose anyone bothers all that much.

The lift hummed and creaked as it rose to the second floor.

– Who lives here?

– Civilian secretaries, nurses maybe . . .

– Americans?

– Mostly, but there are all sorts of nationalities working for the Americans. British, Canadians, Australians, French, Dutch . . . Like me, they started working for the Americans in the war, or just after, and hung on to a good thing. Here we are.

Dolores' room looked more like a bedroom than Kath's, but a very comfortable one. The bed was made, with clean sheets, but there were a few women's things scattered around, signs of a hasty departure. Kath went round the room, tidying up, putting things away in drawers, pausing to inspect, with covetousness or curiosity, items of clothing and jewellery.

– Well, you should be pretty comfortable here, she said.

– It's smashing, he said. But what will happen if they find out I'm here?

– Nobody will find out, Timothy. And nothing terrible can happen, anyway. Don't worry.

– I'm not worried, he lied. What about tomorrow morning? When is it safe for me to get up and go out?

– All the girls will have to be at work by 8.30, so I should say the place will be empty by 8.15. You'll need to have breakfast and lunch . . . Here.

She took a long envelope from her handbag, and gave it to him. Inside was what looked like an identity card, with a photo of himself she had asked him to send in advance.

– That's your P.X. card. It admits you to the Stadtgarten and all the other restaurants and canteens for American personnel. Also to the P.X. itself, that's like a big store, and to the swimming pool. I'll show you where all these places are at the weekend. You can use Army buses with the card, too. Don't lose it, whatever you do.

– I'll look after it.

– And you'll need some money. She opened her purse.

– I've got some traveller's cheques . . .

– Keep them. Or change them into Marks. You have to use scrip in the American places – special money for the occupation forces. They change the colour of it every now and then, to stop currency rackets. Here. Take fifteen dollars to start with, and let me know when you want some more.

– Thanks very much, said Timothy, examining the notes with interest. They reminded him of Monopoly money.

– And here's a key to my room. I think you'd better not keep coming in and out of here during the day. Use my room if you want to rest or take a shower. I've told Rudolf. I don't think there's anything else, is there?

Timothy was wondering what he would do about going to the lavatory, but there was only one solution as far as he could see, and he didn't care to discuss it with Kath.

– What will you do tomorrow? she said.

Tomorrow suddenly yawned in front of him, an awful blank of solitary time.

– I dunno. Take a walk around the town, I s'pose.

– That's right, get the feel of the place, find your way around. Oh, that reminds me (she rummaged in her bag). Here's a map of Heidelberg. It tells you where the interesting buildings are and so on. Why don't you go and have a look at the Castle?

– Good idea.

– I'll be back from work about the same time as today. Now I'll love you and leave you.

She kissed him on the cheek.

– 'Night, Kath. And thanks for the super evening.

– I'm glad you enjoyed it. I thought you did very well.

– How d'you mean?

Kath looked a little embarrassed.

– Well, it must be all very strange to you. Lots of kids of your age and backgr . . . I thought you seemed quite grown up, she concluded, in some confusion.

Timothy shut the door behind her, locked it, and listened to her high heels click-clacking down the corridor. The lift gate clanged shut and the machinery whirred as the lift descended. Then it stopped. Silence. He was quite alone.

The first thing he did was to urinate in the sink, with taps running. There was no alternative: it would be madness to go wandering round the corridors in search of a lavatory. But if Kath escorted him to the room every night, that meant he had to make only one unprotected journey through the hostel each day, in the mornings. Otherwise he was secure.

The sense of being quite alone, and yet quite safe, was novel and exciting. He could do anything – like peeing in the sink – and no one would ever know, or find out. An unspecific licentiousness possessed him. When he had undressed for bed, he did not put on his pyjamas immediately, but walked about the room with nothing on, enjoying the coolness and freedom of his nakedness. He examined himself in a long mirror on the wall. As he looked, his thing stiffened and swelled and rose of its own accord, until it was trained on the ceiling like an ack-ack gun. He traversed to examine the phenomenon in profile. It always puzzled him. He didn't know quite what to make of it. There was something rather impressive about the powerful, spontaneous movement of the flesh, but something rather disgusting too. It looked ugly and brutal, all flushed, with swollen veins, and wiry black hair sprouting from the root.

The ugliness and the size worried him somewhat. It was bound to happen when he finally did it with a girl, when he got married, or whenever it was. When he was alone with her, in a bedroom, and they undressed, it was bound to happen, because it happened just thinking about it, and she would be disgusted and frightened and it would hurt her.

He had formed the theory that you slipped your thing into the girl's while it was small and limp, then it got big inside her; otherwise it would hurt. A girl's was so pretty in comparison, pale pink and smooth and hairless.

On impulse, he took a pair of nail-scissors from the dressing table and snipped away at the hair at his crotch, throwing the black, wiry clippings into the sink. He nicked his skin painfully once or twice, but he persevered, until there was only a sparse, whiskery stubble left. It didn't look much better. He tried to flush his hairs down the sink, but they wouldn't go, so he lifted the soggy tangle out, sealed it in an envelope and placed it carefully at the bottom of the waste paper bin, under a number of lipstick-stained tissues.

He put on his pyjamas, but still felt restless and indisposed to sleep. He wandered round the room, examining Dolores' possessions boldly but circumspectly, opening drawers containing scarves, sweaters and underwear, but not disturbing the contents, sniffing bottles of perfume and sampling jars of face cream, but replacing the lids carefully. In one of the drawers there was a white box with the cryptic legend, *Countess Comfort Extra*, that provoked his curiosity. He opened it and discovered inside a number of white, sausage-shaped bandages like the ones he had seen in the train W.C. They had little loops at each end. His mind, rapidly associating a number of hitherto unconnected observations and enigmas – remarks overheard at school, perplexing advertisements in his mother's magazines – began to formulate a theory, hesitated, tried again, and retired baffled. He closed the box and the drawer.

He looked at himself in the mirror again, drank a glass of rather tepid water, opened and shut drawers abstractedly. He pulled open a cupboard door and looked inside. It was a deep walk-in wardrobe: a room within a room, a shelter within a shelter. He stepped inside and pulled the door almost shut behind him. It was dark and smelled of mothballs. Rows of wire hangers clashed softly as he moved further in. A man's voice said distinctly:

– Is that your neighbour?

Timothy's heart seemed to stop. His thing shrivelled and wilted. A woman's drowsy voice said:

– What, honey?

– I thought I heard somebody next door.

– No, I told you, she's on vacation. That's why I let you come up this evening. Oh!

The *Oh* seemed to have nothing to do with the words before it. It was a sharp exclamation, a mixture of surprise and pleasure and pain. Timothy's flesh began to stir again. He heard the rhythmic creaking of bedsprings, grunts from the man, and gasps from the woman.

– Hold on, baby, I'm coming, said the man hoarsely.
– No, don't, not yet . . . Oh!
– Coming . . .
– No! Oh! Oh!
– Now.
– Oh! Yes! Now! Fuck me now! Oh. Oh. Oh. Oh. *Oh!*

Timothy ejaculated uncontrollably into the close, mothball-smelling darkness of the cupboard. The sensation brought him neither pleasure nor relief. His pyjamas were soaked in a cold sweat. He felt sick and very frightened. Slowly, with extreme caution, he bent his knees until he was crouching on the floor. He stayed there for what seemed an age, until all was quiet behind the back wall of the cupboard. Then he crept out into the room, shut the door quietly behind him, and crawled into bed. He turned off the bedside lamp and covered his head with the blankets. He wished he was at home.

THREE

Out of the Shelter

1

The picture postcard was divided into six small sections. There were views of the beach, the promenade, the bowling green, the pier, the flower-gardens and the war memorial. In the middle, inscribed in capital letters, was the name *WORTHING*. The photographs, in smudgy black and white, appeared to have been taken before the war; for on close inspection it could be seen that the male bathers had tops to their swimming costumes, and the cars were of antique design, with spare wheels strapped to their sides. It was an ugly and unprepossessing card – the fussy little segments distracted and repelled the eye – but he could mentally trace the motives behind its purchase with perfect confidence, for it was just the sort of card he had bought himself in past years to send to friends or relatives. Six pictures for the price of one was good value for money and eliminated the problem of choice.

He turned the card over and re-read the message, written unevenly in pencil:

Dear Timothy,
So glad you arrived safely. What is the weather like? It has been wet here, but the sun is out this morning so can't complain. Mrs. Watkins asked after you. How is Kath? Give her our love. Will she see to your washing? Expect you are having an interesting time. Dad sends his love. Love from, Mother

There was a P.S.: *What a shame about the pie.*

It had taken him some time to place this reference. It seemed to have happened a long time ago.

He took from his pocket the coloured postcard he had purchased earlier in the day in the Market Square, from one of the souvenir stalls that clung to the skirts of the Holy Ghost church. He was sitting, now, in almost exactly the position from which the picture had been taken, on the north bank of the river, just downstream from the Old Bridge, looking over its pinky-brown arches and creamy, helmet-capped towers, at the rambling, ruined castle beyond, that seemed to grow out of the green mountainside as naturally as the trees. The colours of the postcard were not quite true – the greens were too vivid, losing the bluish haze that seemed to smoke from the trees all day, softening the outline of the castle. All the lines in the picture were too sharp. Whether it was because of the atmosphere, or the weathering of centuries, there wasn't a hard edge to be seen in old Heidelberg. Nevertheless his postcard, he felt, would put sad, segmented, black-and-white Worthing in the shade.

He turned it over and took out the ball-point pen he had purchased at the P.X. to scribble a message to his parents. But the pen remained poised above the blank space. He couldn't put into words, even with much more space than a postcard afforded, all that he had seen and experienced in the past ten days. He put the card aside, and took up his drawing pad, with its half-finished sketch of the Old Bridge. Perhaps he should just send them that, with *Love from Timothy* on the back. But then, he thought to himself, if he were to send a purely pictorial message, it would have to be like the Worthing postcard after all, with several little pictures: not only the Old Bridge and the Castle, but also the riverside swimming pool, a white Mercedes coupé racing dangerously down a twisting mountain road, the gilded, mirrored Grande Salle of the Baden-Baden Casino, the glittering counters of the P.X., and a basket heaped with Chicken-in-the-Rough and French Fries.

At first, most of all, it was the food that impressed him. He had never eaten so much or so well in his life. He went initially for plain American fare – chicken, steaks, hamburgers, banana splits and apple pie with ice cream. Then, when he had sated his first, astonished appetite, he became more adventurous, tried food he had never had before – trout, lobster, venison, and even German dishes like *Wiener Schnitzel*, which usually turned out to be much less alarming than they sounded. Among desserts, nothing quite equalled the sheer magic of Baked Alaska, but he had enjoyed *crêpes Suzettes*, fresh pineapple steeped in kirsch, chocolate mousse and *baba au rhum*.

He ate a good breakfast every morning in the Stadtgarten, and then managed with a snack or two until the evening, when Kate took her main meal. Usually they ate out, at a restaurant, but once they stayed in her room and she prepared steak and salad. Even if it was, as she half-jokingly said, the only meal she could cook, it was jolly good. She talked a lot about food that evening, blaming her fatness on a bad diet in childhood and youth.

– It was partly the war, of course, you couldn't get enough nourishing food, so we filled ourselves with stodge, potatoes and bread-and-jam. It was terrible at school. I remember when I first joined the Americans at Cheltenham, I couldn't believe my eyes. I went into the canteen, and they were all eating steaks, great big juicy steaks, and looking as if it was the most natural thing in the world. And when I saw some of them get up from the table leaving their portions half-eaten, it made me quite angry. I used to steal food while I was at Cheltenham . . . Oh, just little bits and pieces, sugar lumps and butter pats and cookies. Sometimes a chicken leg. Dropped my napkin over them and slipped them into my handbag. I used to give them to some friends in the town. It was hardly worth the trouble, but it made me feel better.

– But didn't it make you fatter, all that food?

– It didn't make me any slimmer. I just lived from one meal to the next. Then one day I had a medical. The doctor said I was seriously overweight. That put the wind up me. I was terrified that I'd lose my job on medical grounds. So the doctor put me on a crash diet, and I lost ten pounds in three weeks. I still diet, but I'm not a fanatic. Now the American girls, they either eat far too much or live on crackers and lemon juice. Always extremes. But I like them.

One of the strangest meals he had was at a place called the Headquarters Club (it was inside a barracks, and they had to show their P.X. cards to an armed guard to get in). It wasn't the food that made it strange, but the fact that you ate a meal while you were watching a film. Between the rows of seats were rows of small round tables, and while the film was going on waiters moved about quietly in the half-darkness, taking orders for food and drink. Kate ordered sandwiches because they were easier to eat in the dark – though not all that easy, because they had three layers, and he nearly dislocated his jaw trying to bite through them all at once.

The film was an American one, about the War in the Pacific, as most American war films were in Timothy's experience. He preferred them to British ones, which were usually about Bomber Command. They were in black and white, and there were shots of bleak airfields and Lancasters taxiing for takeoff in the dusk, their chins lifted mournfully to the skies, and then coming back at dawn in ones and twos, riddled with bullets or with their undercarriages shot away, and always there was a plane missing. These films usually made him feel rather weepy, perhaps because they reminded him of Uncle Jack. The American films were much less upsetting, although they were more bloody and violent, and the blood was in Technicolor.

The film he saw with Kate at the Headquarters Club was called *The Halls of Montezuma*, which was the first line of a marching song; and it ended with a terrific battle scene, with the Marines advancing over a grassy plain, and the Mustangs roaring overhead firing rockets into the Jap emplacements, with the music of the march swelling in the background. He watched it with his blood pounding and the mayonnaise from his club sandwich dribbling down his chin. Later he realized that it was a Friday and that there had been chicken and bacon in the sandwich. Kate told him not to worry, there was no fasting or abstinence for Catholics in the Army, because they were considered to be on active service. He sniffed a little sarcastically at that.

A place where he often ate during the day was the P.X., a huge store in the American quarter of the town. Kate took him there on his first Saturday morning to buy him some lightweight clothes. They took one of the yellow Army buses that served as public transport for the U.S. personnel. You had to show your P.X. card to the driver of the bus, and to the soldiers at the gates of the P.X. store. It seemed funny at first to Timothy to have soldiers guarding a shop, but when he got inside it didn't seem so strange. He could imagine a stampede of people from outside trying to get in if they ever discovered what was there. He had never seen such an intoxicating profusion of goods in his life: food, clothing and sweets and gramophones and cameras and toys and sports equipment and suitcases and gadgets of all kinds that he had never seen before and whose functions he could only guess at. In his first week he went to the P.X. nearly every day, just to walk round the loaded shelves and counters in an orgy of curiosity and covetousness, appeasing his greed by the purchase of some small item like a ball-point pen or a pair of nylon socks.

On his first visit, Kate bought him a lightweight sports jacket made of mohair, a pair of cool, silky trousers to go with it, and three drip-dry shirts, one white, one pale blue, and one of yellow and brown checks that fastened under the collar with a little loop so that it looked neat buttoned up even without a tie. The shirts had the long pointed collars that were the height of fashion at home. He felt guilty about letting Kate buy him all these clothes, but he couldn't resist them. It wasn't just the expense that troubled and excited him like a sin, but the idea of buying so many things all at once. But then Kate started to do her own shopping, casually picking up six pairs of nylons here, four hundred cigarettes there, without even breaking off their conversation, and he began to realize that he was in a whole new world of buying and selling. Outside the store there was a ramp where people drove up and young men helped them to load their cars because they had too much to carry across the car park. The boots of the cars (only the Americans called them trunks) opened greedily like the jaws of whales until they were gorged with paper bags and cartons, then snapped shut, and the cars rolled away across the vast macadamed space where the multicoloured roofs of every make of American automobile shimmered in the sunshine.

Before they left the store, Kate had a coffee and Timothy a chocolate milk-shake at the snack bar.

– Isn't that the ex-G.I. you met on the train? Kate said.

It was indeed Don, reading a book over a cup of coffee on the other side of the horseshoe-shaped counter. He smiled his recognition, and came round to greet them.

– Well, hi, Timothy! How d'you like this temple of conspicuous consumption?

– You mean this shop? It's smashing.

– Seen much of the town yet?

– A bit, yes. I've been to the Castle.

– Are you still living in Heidelberg, Don? said Kate. Timothy tells me you've just been discharged from the Army.

– That's right. I'm supporting myself by doing some teaching at the Army School.

– In no hurry to get home, then?

– Don's going to the London School of Economics, Timothy explained.

– Are you! Kate said with interest.

– Well, I'm hoping to, said Don. I haven't heard the result of my interview yet. What about your exam results, Timothy?

– I'd forgotten all about them, he said honestly. But aren't the schools on holiday here?

– I'm teaching a special class of slow learners – or lazy learners. If the kids fail to get their grades in the school year, they have a chance to make up by doing a summer session. It's only mornings . . . Maybe I could show you around the town one afternoon, Timothy?

Kate welcomed this offer enthusiastically, and they made an arrangement to meet.

– What a nice boy, she remarked, as he loped off, with his book in his hand. I thought he was well-educated when you first introduced him. Some of the G.I.s are pretty crude. He may turn out to be a very useful friend, Timothy. Of course, he's nearer my age than yours, but I don't know any teenagers . . . I know one or two officers with families – perhaps I could find you some friends that way.

– I'm all right, said Timothy. I like being on my own.

The American boys and girls of his own age that he saw, mainly at the open-air swimming pool down by the river, seemed to belong to another race. The boys were like seals in and out of the water, strangely smooth and sleek with their cropped bullet heads and tanned, fleshy torsos. The girls tended to be plump, too, and wore curiously old-fashioned swimming costumes with skirts to mid-thigh that billowed out as they plumped heavily, feet-first, into the water. They arrived and departed in large groups, boys and girls together, dressed in bright shirts worn outside their jeans, talking loudly and unselfconsciously, though what they were talking about he could never quite catch. He felt that it would be almost as difficult to communicate with them as with the German boys he saw swimming in the river.

– They're not supposed to, Kath remarked, as they walked to the pool after their shopping expedition, but you can't blame them in this weather.

– Why not?

– The river's polluted. There's a risk of typhoid. The Americans requisitioned the only pool in town, and the Germans are pretty bitter about it. There's talk of building them a new one on the outskirts of town.

You needed your P.X. card, of course, to get into the pool. In a few days, Timothy had developed a superstitious attachment to this small square of cardboard. It seemed like a talisman of magical powers that admitted him to a world of privilege and pleasure. His constant fear was that he would lose it and find himself excluded from the friendly, protective enclaves of the Americans. The swimming pool, the Stadtgarten, the P.X., Kate's room – these were his bases, safe barricaded positions between which he carefully plotted his daily movements so that he always found himself near one or the other when he needed rest or refreshment. For, though he responded to the beauty and charm of Heidelberg and its setting, a measure of unease, an indefinable sense of risk, never left him as he strolled the public German streets. It was not that people looked hostile, or resentful. They didn't even look particularly defeated. On the whole they seemed quite ordinary, decently clothed and well fed, bustling about the town on their business, not given to smiling overmuch, perhaps, but placid and self-possessed. Only once did Timothy glimpse the Germany of his imagination. But that occasion affected him deeply.

He was walking up one of the cobbled streets behind the University that led to the Castle. About halfway up there was a recess in the wall on the right-hand side where water trickled from a spout above a little stone bowl. The man walking in front of Timothy stopped to drink, stooping and twisting his head to catch the water in his mouth. It was a hot day and the climb was tiring. Timothy slowed his pace, intending to cool his face and hands in the water, if not to take the risk of drinking it. Then, as he approached, the man straightened up, and turned to face Timothy, wiping his mouth with the back of his hand. It was a face of such coarse brutality that, in spite of the warm day, Timothy turned cold with fear. A bumpy, shaven iron-grey skull, small bloodshot eyes, flared nostrils, thick lips elongated into a sneer by a scar that curved down to the jawline – he took in this much as he swerved aside and stumbled on up the hill.

He glanced fearfully over his shoulder as, panting for breath, he reached the brow of the hill, but the man had disappeared, presumably up one of the steep lanes that branched from the road. Timothy passed into the cool shade of the Castle grounds, but did not stop until he had reached the sunny parapet of the western wall. There he sat, feeling the warmth of the stone through his trousers. The roofs and steeples of the town shimmered beneath him; long, low barges plied up and down the river, threading the arches of the Old Bridge; somewhere a clock or church bell chimed. But it was a long time before the peaceful scene calmed him. Meeting the ugly man had been like kicking a stone in a summer garden and uncovering a loathsome nest of insects – it made you distrust the smiling surface of things. The face had been the very image of the concentration-camp commander – the Beast of Belsen and other bogeymen who had scowled and strutted through the newspapers and nightmares of his childhood.

It was a heatwave, Kate said. You could feel the heat coming even in the early morning, when the mist was still rising from the river. By midday the sun was beating down fiercely out of a clear sky, and you took care to walk in the shade. The heat made the swimming pool not a place for exercise, but an oasis for rest and refreshment. He found it strangely voluptuous, this living dangerously in the heat – letting the sun daze and dehydrate you, then cheating it by slipping into the pool, or tipping an ice-cold drink down your throat in the shade of a tree. Kate had warned him not to sunbathe for more than a few minutes at a time at first, but he was impatient to be tanned like her friends. Beside them he felt as white as a root just plucked from the soil. On that first Saturday afternoon they swam immediately, and afterwards Kate rubbed some pleasant-smelling suntan lotion into his back and shoulders. He lay face down on his towel, with his eyes shut against the glare, rapt by overlapping sensations of warmth and coolness. His blood was still cool from the swim, but his skin was already warm from the sun; the sweet-smelling lotion was chill on his skin, but the firm pressure of Kate's hand was warm.

Afterwards, he performed the same service for her, kneeling at the side of her prostrate body, anointing her back and shoulders. Her flesh was warm and malleable, it flopped under his hands like water slapping a rock. He was embarrassed when she asked him to oil the backs of her thighs. They were her least attractive feature, colossal pillars of flesh, a legacy of the old fat Kath that she normally concealed under her skirts.

Most of Kate's closest friends seemed to be at the pool that afternoon, grouped in a circle: Vince and Greg, an American couple called Melvin and Ruth Fallert, and two girls from Kate's office – Dorothy, an Australian called Dot for short, and Maria, who was Dutch. Mel and Ruth were an oddly matched pair. He was a rather quiet, heavily-built man, good-looking in a grizzled sort of way. His wife was small and round and ugly, and her appearance was grotesque. She was stuffed into a gold lamé swimsuit several sizes too small for her dumpy figure, and her toenails were painted gold to match. She wore sunglasses whose frames were encrusted with sparkling synthetic stones, and a white plastic shield like a beak over her nose to protect it against sunburn. She looked like a fat little bird that had tricked itself out in stolen trinkets and she had a tireless, grating voice to match.

– Ruth's a real New Yorker, Kate whispered to Timothy. Jewish, of course, but she's got a heart of gold. It's her third marriage and his second . . .

Ruth was certainly humorous and good company, but Timothy couldn't imagine what had possessed Mel to marry her. Intercepting some of the looks he directed at hs wife, Timothy suspected that Mel found it equally puzzling.

Dot was a tall bronzed girl, whose excellent figure was sadly let down by her features: small eyes set rather close together, a long nose, and buck teeth projecting in a goofy smile. Maria was a neat little person with straight, cropped hair and a turned-up nose. She smiled all the time, but her eyes looked sad and anxious, as if she was uncertain of pleasing, or belonging.

Ruth was playing some kind of patience, sitting on a towel with her spindly legs crossed under her fat torso like a broody bird. She turned up a card and frowned.

– Jeeze, I need that like a hole in the head.

Timothy laughed.

– Whaddya laughing at, Timothy? Never hear anyone say that before?

– No.

– You'll hear it again, I can promise you that, said Mel dourly.

– Wise guy, said Ruth.

– Say, is that right you've got a new car, Mel? said Greg.

– Yeah, that's why he's in such a lousy mood, said Ruth. Some limbless driver scratched his fender in the Hauptstrasse this morning.

Vince giggled.

– Ruth! A limbless driver, for God's sake?

– That's right. Some poor German bastard with his legs shot off, or his arms, or something. Had this car with special controls, you know? Mel didn't notice. He jumps out of our car to blow this Kraut to about a thousand feet for scraping his fender – then he sees the guy is mostly hardware, steel claws and what have you. Mel collapsed like a balloon. Psssss! Like a balloon. Ruth chuckled hoarsely.

– I still say he shouldn't be allowed on the roads, said Mel.

– Is it a brand new car, Mel? Kate asked.

– Yeah, a new Olds. Picked it up from Antwerp last weekend.

– We stayed in a great hotel in Brussels, said Ruth. What was the name of it, honey?

– The Metropole.

– Yeah, the Metropole. You been there, Maria?

– No, said Maria, smiling. Was it nice?

– It was fabulous.

– The bill was fabulous, said Mel.

– Well, it was worth it, said Ruth.

– How much, Mel? Greg asked.

– Thirty dollars a night.

– Wow! said Dot from under her straw hat.

– Each, Mel added.

– More wow, said Dot, lifting her hat off to stare. You been breaking the bank at Baden, or something?

– Talking of Baden, said Vince, Greg and I were thinking of taking a trip down there next weekend. What about it, Kate? Timothy would find it interesting.

In a few minutes they had made up a party for the following

weekend. Only Maria was unable to come. She asked Ruth if she had liked Brussels, and the conversation turned to which was the most attractive European capital. Kath and Ruth chose Paris, Vince and Greg, Rome; Maria's favourite was Vienna, and Mel's Stockholm. Dot chose Lisbon, putting a stop to the argument, because no one else had been there.

There was a café in one corner of the swimming pool. Timothy collected orders for Coke, ice cream and coffee, and went off to get them with a five-dollar bill Vince gave him. When he returned with his loaded tray, he was surprised to see Don talking to Kate. The others were looking at him curiously. He had evidently just climbed out of the pool, for water was still coursing down his face and body, drawing the black hairs on his legs into straight lines, and forming a small damp patch on the grass. As Timothy came up, Kath began to introduce Don to the others. His skin was pale, almost as white as Timothy's, and he looked conscious of his moist appearance, wiping his hand ineffectually on his bathing shorts.

– I'm afraid I'm making everybody wet, he apologized, but my towel's over on the other side of the pool.

– Here! Vince tossed him a folded towel, which Don caught at the second attempt, nearly colliding with Timothy and his tray.

– Thanks! Oh, hi, Timothy. We meet again.

– Do you come here often, to coin a phrase? Greg asked Don. I know I've seen you before.

– You probably saw me over at G.H.Q. I used to work in the Orderly Room there.

– You mean, you're a soldier?

– I was.

Kate intervened.

– Don has finished his service. He's teaching at the Army School now.

Mel suddenly came to life.

– You just got your discharge from the Army?

– That's right.

– Then the best years of your life are over, fella.

– That's not the way I look at it, said Don with a smile.

– Of course he doesn't, said Ruth scornfully. This is a cultured guy – a teacher, dincha hear?

– Sure I heard.

– So what should he get out of the Army?
– A free trip to Europe? Vince suggested quietly.
– The strings spoil it, Don said.
– Well, I learned a helluva lot in the Army, said Mel. But that was wartime. I guess it's different now.
– Yeah, tell us what you did in the war, Daddy-oh, said Ruth. Tell us how you liberated Paris single-handed.
– Did you really fight in the war, Mel? Maria asked.
– Yeah, Ruth said. Mostly W.A.A.C.s, unarmed combat.
– I was with Patton's army, said Mel.
– I tried to join the W.A.A.C.s, said Greg, but I failed the medical.
– I tried to join the W.A.A.F.s, and I really did fail the medical, said Kate. But am I glad now! She raised a Coke bottle to her lips and tilted it towards the sun.
– How's that? Don asked her.
– Well, I shouldn't be here, otherwise. I'd probably be darning my stockings and saving my clothing coupons and looking forward to a week at a holiday camp as the highspot of the year.
– You make England sound grim, Don said.
– Well, it is, isn't it? You've just been there.
– Oh, I don't know. I kind of like London.
– I'm glad somebody does, said Timothy. Nobody had a good word to say for it just now.
– Aw, isn't that too bad, said Ruth, we've hurt Timothy's feelings. Sure I like London, kid. It's just that the food is so goddam awful and they don't seem to have invented ice yet.
– Say, Timothy, what's this Festival of Britain all about? said Greg.
– Jolly good.
– Worth making a trip to see it?
– I should think so, he replied guardedly.

Timothy had mixed feelings about the Festival. Taking their lead from the *Daily Express*, his family had tended to regard it as a prime instance of governmental folly, and enjoyed gloating over the successive scandals and setbacks of its preparation. But when he finally visited the Exhibition on the South Bank with a school party, all his scepticism and scorn had been swept away by a rush of wonder and delight, and he had gone back on several occasions. Now, in this exotic setting, so far from home, among these travelled, witty people, the Festival seemed to shrink again in significance. He tried to think of some feature that would appeal to his new friends.

– They have dancing in the open air in the evenings, he said.

– That's right! said Dot. Girl I know was over in London a few weeks back. She said they were dancing in the rain.

– Sounds wild, said Vince.

– Oh, they weren't carried away, if that's what you're thinking. Just a few couples, plodding round and round in the puddles, quick quick slow, pretending it wasn't raining.

– Ah, that's what made Britain Great, said Vince.

Kate laughed.

– You're so right. Dancing in the rain – that's typical.

– I thought the Festival was pretty good, myself, said Don. Considering the limited budget they had to work with, it's a very good show.

– Did you go to the Fun Fair at Battersea? Timothy asked him.

Don nodded without enthusiasm.

– That, I'm afraid, is something we definitely do better in the States. Coney Island, for instance . . .

– Coney Island! Gee, that makes me homesick, cried Ruth. You from New York City, Don?

– No, but I went to college there. Columbia.

– Well, that's a very good school, said Ruth, impressed.

– Vince went to Yale, didn't you, Vince? Kate said.

– Yeah, but I quit to join the Army. Never went back.

– Too bad, said Don.

The sun flashed on Vince's sunglasses as he turned to face Don.

– I've no regrets.

– That's fine, then, said Don.

– Where d'you come from originally, Don? Mel asked.

– My folks moved around a lot: Chicago, Columbus, Philadelphia. Now they've moved to California.

Ruth threw up her hands.

– California! Everybody I know is moving to California. There's only negroes and Puerto Ricans left in New York as far as I can make out.

– Your parents will be looking forward to seeing you, Don, said Maria, smiling.

– I'm afraid they'll have to wait longer. I'm planning to do graduate work in England before I go back home.

– Why doncha do it in the States? Mel asked.

– Oh, it's a long story. In my field, political science, it's all computers and consensus politics these days. I'm kind of attracted to the eccentric, amateur approach you get in England.

He talked a little more about his studies, but Timothy had the impression that no one, except perhaps Vince, could follow him. Then he said he had to be going. He folded the towel and returned it to Vince. Then he loped off, shoulders slightly stooped. He waved at them from the far side of the pool.

– Nice boy, said Dot. Where d'you find 'em, Kate?

– He was helping Timothy with his bag at the station when he arrived. I gave him the brush-off – I thought he was just one of those G.I.s on the make.

– You could still be right, honey, said Ruth. He has a lean and hungry look. If he's too much for you, pass him on.

Kate laughed.

– He's more Timothy's friend than mine.

They stayed at the pool until late afternoon that Saturday. In the evening they piled into Mel's vast glittering car and drove up the Neckar valley to a little inn for dinner. Afterwards, Kate saw him back to his room.

– I'll pick you up tomorrow morning, she said. I hope you don't mind a late breakfast. I usually lie in on a Sunday.

– What Mass d'you usually go to?

Kate looked a little confused.

– Oh, yes, you'll want to go to Mass.

– Won't you, then?

– Oh, yes, I'll go with you, of course. There's a church just round the corner from me. There are plenty of masses, non-stop all morning.

So that's it, he thought, as the door closed behind her and he heard the click-clack of her heels receding down the corridor. She's lapsed. That's why she hasn't come home. She's lapsed and she doesn't want Mum and Dad to find out.

Timothy had been told many times at school that the great advantage of the Latin liturgy was that it was always the same, all over the world. Wherever you were, you could always walk into a Catholic church and feel at home with the service – an amenity that was denied to Protestants. The Catholic Church was the universal Church: *Catholic* meant universal. He walked to Mass with Kate in the agreeable expectation of confirming this theory by experiment. In fact, he found the service disconcertingly strange.

Kate had made a mistake about the times, and they were late. The church was crowded and they had to stand in a press of people at the back. It was an old building, crammed with gilt statues, and huge dark oil paintings that looked more like the kind you saw in art galleries than the simple, crudely coloured devotional objects that decorated the redbrick parish church at home. It wasn't a High Mass, but there were two singers up in the gallery, a baritone and a soprano, who sang from time to time, solo or in duet. He couldn't tell whether they were singing in Latin or German, but it certainly wasn't the Kyrie, Gloria and Agnus Dei he was familiar with. It sounded more like a concert on the Third Programme than a mass, especially when somebody played a long virtuoso piece on a violin, an instrument he had never heard played in church before. Kate left the church at the Communion, and Timothy followed her.

– Whew! she exclaimed as they came out into the street. Wasn't it stuffy in there? I couldn't bear it another moment.

He restrained himself from pointing out that technically they hadn't heard Mass, since they had left before the Ablutions.

– I need some air, said Kate. Let's go up to the top of the Königstuhl, it's always cooler up there. We can take the funicular from the Cornmarket.

They sat in the rear compartment of the queer, crooked little train, in which each compartment was higher than the previous one, like steps, and looked down the track at the dizzily receding terminus. The train creaked and groaned. He could feel through his bones the enormous tug of gravity upon it. If the cable should snap. He turned his head and studied the wild flowers on the embankment at the side of the rails, wondering if he was in a state of mortal sin because of having come out of Mass early.

After they had walked a little way along the path at the top of the Königstuhl, he asked Kate straight out.

– I wouldn't say lapsed, exactly, she said. I mean, I still go to church occasionally, when I feel like it. I don't see the point of going otherwise. I had enough of that at the convent.

– Do you make your Easter Duties?

– No.

– Then you're lapsed, he said firmly.

Kate bit her lip, but didn't look particularly distressed. They were standing on a terrace near the funicular station. The Neckar valley was spread out beneath them like a relief map in the Geography room at school.

– Oh, dear. D'you think I'm a lost soul, Timothy?

– Course not, he said uncomfortably.

– Do you believe in Hell?

– We don't have to, he said evasively. Not with flames and things.

– I know. It's really the pain of loss, isn't it? I used to think at school that I wouldn't mind if I could be sure that was all – I thought I could put up with that.

Timothy sniggered, having had the same thought himself.

– I s'pose you'd rather Mum and Dad didn't know? he said.

To his surprise she seemed to be considering the point for the first time.

– I guess you're right. They wouldn't understand, and it would only upset them.

Not that, then.

Don proved to be a good guide to Heidelberg, and when Timothy met Kate that evening he was full of the information he had assimilated.

– I'd forgotten that Heidelberg was right in the middle of the Thirty Years' War, he told her over dinner. We did that for History in the Fourth Form.

They were eating at the Headquarters Club and were going to play Bingo afterwards.

– Which war was that?

– You know, in the seventeenth century, about the succession to the Holy Roman Empire. Catholics against Protestants.

– Who won?

Timothy reflected.

– Nobody, really.

– Like all wars, said Kate.

– We won the last one, didn't we?

– Sometimes I wonder . . . Only six years later, and we're on Germany's side against Russia. What will you have for dessert? Ice cream? Maple Walnut is good,

– You see, Frederick, the Fifth I think he was, of the Heidelberg Palatinate, was a Protestant, and the Protestants of Bohemia tried to make him Emperor. That's how the war started. Frederick married Elizabeth, the daughter of our James the Sixth – that's why the English Building in the castle is called that — he built it for her.

– Goodness, what a lot you know,Timothy.

– I got it all from Don.

– It's very good of him to spare the time.

– You know, Kate, he said hesitantly, I think Don's a bit keen on you.

– What makes you think that? she said, smiling.

– He said something about taking us out one evening, together. I said I'd mention it.

Kate frowned slightly.

– Hmm, it's a bit awkward.

– Why?

– Well, you see, I have my own social circle here, and Don doesn't exactly fit in.

– Why not?

– It's difficult to explain but . . . well, for one thing, he's still a G.I. in a way. I mean, I know he's been discharged, but that's his background as far as Heidelberg is concerned. If I introduce him into our circle, he's likely to keep meeting people, officers and so on, who used to be his bosses. It could be awkward for everybody. Heidelberg's a very small place. And I don't really think he's got much in common with us, anyway. We're not intellectual types, except perhaps Vince, and he's not exactly what you'd call . . . I know I should think twice about going out with Don. I'd be scared to open my mouth in case I put the Thirty Years' War in the wrong century. Now finish up your ice cream or we'll be late for the Bingo.

– What is Bingo, anyway?

Bingo turned out to be the game he knew as Housey Housey, but the different name seemed appropriate, more exciting and sophisticated. The players sat at tables, eating and drinking, and the stage was heaped with a glittering mountain of expensive prizes: refrigerators and radios and electric toasters and toys and bottles of liquor. Neither of them won anything, however, and Kate was disappointed.

– Perhaps we'll have better luck next Saturday, at Baden, she said. What's your lucky number?

– I don't have one, he replied.

Going home in the jolting yellow bus, she suddenly remarked:

– It would be easier if he had been an officer – Don, I mean. But they don't usually commission enlisted men.

– I don't think he would have wanted it. He was a conscientious objector.

Kate looked startled.

– He was telling me this afternoon.

– What happened to him then?

– Well, he went to prison.

– *Prison?*

– Only for a few days. They wouldn't let him be a conscientious objector because he hadn't got a religion. It seems you have to have a religion, in America, anyway.

– Did he change his mind, then?

– Sort of. They didn't really want to keep him in prison, so they promised him he could be a whatd'youcallit, non . . .

– Non-combatant?

– Right. So he decided to give in.

– Well, what a story! Why was he a conscientious objector, then?

Timothy shrugged.

– I didn't ask him. I s'pose he thinks war is wrong, or something.

– Perhaps he didn't want to get sent to Korea, said Kate, a little harshly.

– Well, you can't blame him. You said yourself that the last war didn't achieve anything.

– I didn't say that. What I said was . . . oh, I can't remember, she exclaimed irritably. But I think that if a man's called up, he ought to make the best of it.

There was silence between them for a while. Timothy wondered why he had tried to defend Don, since he inclined towards Kate's opinion of conscientious objection.

– What are you doing tomorrow? she asked at length.

– I'm going for a walk with Don. The Philosophy Way, he said, or something.

– Oh, the Philosophers' Way. You get a wonderful view of the town from there.

He had almost got used to living in the hostel. Going out in the mornings was the trickiest part. He usually waited till nine o'clock, but there was always the risk that someone would see him coming out of Dolores' room. Usually there were two or three cleaners swabbing the tiled floor of the lobby as he stepped out of the lift. They knelt back on their heels to wring out their cloths, and he sensed their curious, covert glances as he walked past them. He wondered if they thought he had been spending the night with one of the girls in the hostel. The idea amused, embarrassed and piqued him by turns. He had added to his experience lately, but as regards sex the additions were abysses concealing more than they revealed. Perhaps the most astonishing thing he had learned, on his very first evening, was that a woman might say the forbidden word aloud in her love, or lust.

For the next two nights he kept the door of the cupboard locked and undisturbed. On the third he opened it again. He could hear nothing. Emboldened, he stepped inside and pulled the door almost shut behind him. Immediately he heard the sound of a radio. High up in the corner of the cupboard there was a chink of light, caused by a crumbling of the plaster where some pipes passed through the wall. Evidently the sounds from next door came through this hole, and were amplified by the cupboard when the door was closed.

He listened again the next night before he went to bed, and the night after that. But he only heard the woman moving about her room, opening and shutting drawers, running water in the basin, turning on the radio, winding up a clock. On the following night there was dead silence at first, and he was about to leave the cupboard when he heard the woman come into the room. She had a man with her, a different one from last time, he thought. They sounded merry and slightly drunk. The woman kept saying *Shh!* and giggling. He heard the clink of a bottle against a glass. The voices dropped to a low murmur, interrupted by an occasional giggle or guffaw. The light went out behind the chink in the wall. He waited with bated breath for it to begin again: the woman's moan of pleasure and pain, the no no no no, and then yes, the blunt word of abandonment. But all he heard was the man panting and saying, *Oh Jesus!* again and again like someone wrestling in prayer. There was silence for a while, and then the woman said, *Would you pass me that pack of cigarettes?* and the man said, *I'm sorry, honey, I really am*, and she said, *Forget it*, and he said, *Too much damned bourbon*, and she yawned, and he said, *I can't understand it*, and she said, *Honey, I'm tired, I think you'd better go*, and the man said, *Maybe if we wait awhile*, and the woman said peevishly, *Look, let's forget it, it can happen to anybody*. Then the light came on again in the chink, and he heard the taps running, and the man arguing in a low earnest voice, and the woman's voice hard and clipped. Eventually a door opened and closed and the room was silent except for the noise of a jar dropping in the sink and the woman cursing. Timothy withdrew from the cupboard, mystified and frustrated. He tried to fit pictures to what he had heard, but his speculations petered out in a row of dots, like the interesting passages in the paperback books on Dolores' bookshelf.

In the course of his imaginings, he gradually invested the woman next door with a particular physical appearance. He created her out of words and phrases that he associated with sensual love. She was voluptuous, her breasts were like ripe fruit, her hair was lustrous, blue-black, drawn up from the nape, her movements were langorous, she had pouting, sensual lips. It was something of a shock when he actually set eyes on her. He and Kate were in the lift – she had just fetched him to leave for Baden-Baden – when the woman came out of her room. The lift was already descending as she came into sight. Looking up from almost ground level, he glimpsed legs like sticks on steep wedge-heeled shoes, a long skinny figure in a bright green fitted suit, a white triangular face and a coarse hank of ginger hair hanging down over one eye. Then she was gone. It wasn't exactly, in the phraseology of Dolores' library, a body made for love, yet it was, in its way, vivid and provocative. He glanced slyly at Kate, but she hadn't taken any particular notice of the woman.

– I hope you slept well, she said, it's going to be a long day.

– I always do.

– Quiet here at night, is it?
– Oh yes, very quiet, he assured her.

Two cars were drawn up outside the hostel: Vince's milkwhite Mercedes, with its hood down, and Mel Fallert's huge grey Oldsmobile, his *new Olds*, as he quaintly called it. Mel was leaning forward in the driver's seat, with his chin resting on the steering wheel, revving his engine with a wanton disregard for petrol consumption. Dot waved from the back seat as Kate and Timothy emerged from the hostel, and Ruth hopped out to greet them.

– Hi Kate! Hi Timothy! How d'ya like my leisurewear?

She was dressed entirely in an electric shade of blue – slacks, sweater, high-heeled sandals and a baseball cap with a long peak. Even her earrings were blue — two large discs with a number imprinted on them in gold.

– Marvellous, Ruth, said Kate politely. Where did you get the earrings?

– See what they are? Ruth cocked her head to one side like a parakeet. Cute, huh?

– Why, they're chips! Casino chips!

– Right. Hundred-Mark chips. I brought them back with me last time we won at Baden. Mel was furious. He said, *Only my wife would spend two hundred Marks on a pair of plastic earrings*. She emitted her harsh cawing laugh.

There was some discussion about who should travel in which car. Eventually Timothy was awarded the privilege of riding with Vince, and the rest of the party got into the Oldsmobile.

– No speeding now, Vince, Kate cautioned.

– O.K., honey.

Speed restrictions were very strict for American drivers in Germany, Vince explained, because of the high accident rate. Sometimes he took his car over the frontier into France just for the pleasure of putting his foot down. But even at the permitted miles-per-hour, the low-slung, open car gave an exhilarating sensation of speed, and when they got among the mountains of the Black Forest, and the road coiled itself in tight loops, Vince did not slow down. The long white bonnet seemed to be pointing straight at a continuous curving wall of trees that swept round Timothy in a blur, first this way and then that. Sometimes he closed his eyes, but always he had complete confidence in Vince's driving. Cradled in the deep, soft seat, he felt a seamless part of the car, and the car was an extension of Vince's strong brown hands. No tension was visible in his face, except a slight, elated baring of the teeth under the fair moustache.

After a while, Vince slowed down to allow the others to catch up with them. The noise of the engine, and the rush of wind, subsided and made conversation possible. They got talking about Hitler and the Nazis again.

– Nobody's satisfactorily explained Hitler, as far as I know, said Vince. He's a mystery, an enigma. What d'you think of when I say, *Hitler?*

– I dunno, said Timothy. I suppose I think of his face – you know, the toothbrush moustache and the cowslick of hair.

– Right, said Vince, as if he were putting Timothy through some kind of test. And the face, does it seem like an ordinary human face?

– No, not really. More like a Guy Fawkes mask.

– A mask, exactly! No matter how many photographs of Hitler you look at, you always get this sense of a mask. Never a human expression. Always that fixed, frozen look, even when he's smiling, which wasn't often. You don't get that with any other war leader – Churchill, Roosevelt, Stalin. You always feel that they were people as well as being quote *great men* unquote. Hitler always looks ridiculous in pictures.

– He used to frighten me, Timothy said. I used to dream about him.

– Yeah, frightening too. Ridiculous *and* frightening. He was so ridiculous it wasn't funny any more, you know what I mean? Take the cartoonists — he must have seemed like a gift, with his little moustache and all, but nobody really succeeded in caricaturing him. He was a caricature already.

– In that case, said Timothy, why did the Germans obey him?

– Oh, said Vince smiling, now you've asked the sixty-four-thousand-dollar question . . . The thing about Hitler, if you look at his record, on paper, up to about 1942, he'd not only gotten Germany off its knees – he'd gotten control of most of Europe, too. Well, just going on the record, he looks like some kind of genius, like Napoleon or Alexander the Great and those guys. But when you get close and look at the man himself for some kind of *explanation* of how he did it, it all just dissolves. You've got some ratty little guy, with no education, no humanity, no background, no ideas of his own, just hollow really, a hollow man spouting crazy slogans about blood and iron and the *Volk* and the Jews being in league with the Communists . . . He didn't even have any vices – he didn't smoke, didn't drink – d'you know what he got his kicks from?

– No?

– Cream cakes. *Cream cakes*, for Chrissake. Every time some country collapsed, all the Nazis went off to celebrate with coffee and cream cakes.

– What about Eva Braun? Timothy said.

– Ah, Eva Braun . . . I often wonder if Hitler ever screwed her. Did you know he only had one ball?

An organ-like car horn blared behind them. Vince glanced in the rear-view mirror.

– They've caught us up.

Timothy turned round to see the great grey car rising and falling slowly on its springs like a raft. Kate, sitting on the front seat between Mel and Ruth, smiled and waved. Not for the first time, his mind returned to the questions about her that he had brought with him to Germany, along with his Harris tweed sports jacket and four changes of underpants. That she was no longer a practising Catholic made it easier to imagine that she was having some illicit affair, but if so, who was it with? Vince seemed the obvious candidate – even Timothy could feel the magnetism of his blond good looks, his casual mastery of life. But that was just the problem: Timothy had to admit that, although Kate's looks had improved, she was still no great beauty, and never would be. Why should Vince, who could surely have any girl he liked come running to him at the beck of his finger, choose poor old Kate, with her almost too big breasts and her definitely too big legs? True, there was no apparent rival to Kate, and he seemed to spend much of his spare time with her – but always in the company of Greg, and usually others too. Surely, if there was anything between them, they would want more privacy? But he had never felt that his own presence was an embarrassment or encumbrance; or, if he had, it was in relation to all three of them. There was nothing which suggested an understanding between Kate and Vince which didn't include Greg too. Were they both in love with Kate, then, and she unwilling or unable to choose between them? If so, they were remarkably relaxed in their rivalry. Then could it be – the thought suddenly flashed upon him – that they were *both* her lovers, that they were *sharing* her between them? He tried to speculate how such an arrangement might work out in practice, and was surprised to realize how little shocked he was by the idea. Everything seemed so strange and new to him here, everyone seemed to live by notions so different from those that obtained at home, that almost anything was imaginable.

– Why do they call it the Philosophers' Way? he asked Don.

– I suppose it was always a favourite walk with the faculty at the University. A good place to muse on the eternal verities.

– It's a stiff climb.

– It levels off in a moment.

They tackled the last steep bend of the road in silence. Years ago, at school, a boy had asked in class what *philosopher* meant, and the master had said that a philosopher was a man who tried to explain what was real and what was true. Some philosophers had believed that nothing was real, including themselves. The class had roared with laughter.

– There you are, said Don, as they came out on to a level path. They took a rest leaning on a stone wall, looking down across the river at the castle on the far side. Wherever you stood, Heidelberg composed itself effortlessly into a picture. Don pointed out the buildings of the University.

– Which university will you go to, Timothy?

– I dunno. I might not go to university at all. My Dad wants me to do an apprenticeship instead.

– What kind of apprenticeship?

– Architectural drawing.

– You could study architecture at a university, couldn't you?

– Mmm. But you'd have to be terrifically good to get in.

– Well, you never know – maybe you *are* terrifically good.

Timothy made no comment, and Don went on:

– If you were an architect, what would you want to build?

– I dunno. Churches, maybe.

– Churches? Don seemed amused.

– What's wrong with churches? Timothy said defensively.

– Nothing. Nothing at all. I just wonder whether we need any more churches.

– We do in England – Catholic ones, anyway. The ones we've got are crowded out.

– If I were an architect, I'd go in for building schools and universities – they're the churches and cathedrals of our age. I guess you must be grateful that you came along just as the British educational system began to expand?

– I don't know about grateful. They wouldn't let me take my O-Levels when I was ready for it.

– Who are *they*?

– The rotten Government, of course.

– Hitler, said Vince, stroking the Mercedes round a hairpin bend, you have to admire him in a way. He had the true nihilist spirit. Death and destruction. And he was consistent to the end. D'you know what he said? *We may be destroyed, but if we are, we shall drag a world with us, a world in flames*. And, by God, he did. You should have seen Berlin in '45. A world in flames. *Götterdämmerung*.

– What's that mean? Timothy asked.

– *The Twilight of the Gods*. It's an opera by Wagner. Hitler was very fond of Wagner.

– *The Twilight of the Gods*, Timothy repeated slowly. The words were strangely stirring.

– It ends with whatsername, Brunnhilde, throwing herself on Siegfried's funeral pyre.

– Wasn't Hitler's corpse burned with Eva Braun's?

– Right. In the Chancellery garden, with the Russians half a mile away. Buildings on fire and shells exploding all over. All it needed was the music. And d'you know something? The name of the guy who married them was Wagner. Can you beat that?

– But they never found the bodies, did they?

– So the Russians say. Vince grinned, glancing across at Timothy. You think he may still be alive, holed up somewhere?

– No, said Timothy, looking at the endless waves of trees, dense and impenetrable. Where had he read or heard a story about Hitler and his staff hiding in a convent, disguised as nuns? He couldn't remember. A cloud passed over the sun and darkened the foliage. He could see why they called it the Black Forest.

Don laughed.

– You're a real little Tory, aren't you, Timothy?

– It's not that, he said. But Attlee is such a drip. It would be all right if Churchill was Prime Minister.

– You admire Churchill?

– He won the war, Timothy said, simply. It was a rotten trick to throw him out.

– There's not another country in the world that would have done it. That's what was so splendid about it.

– Splendid? I call it rotten.

– But do you realize what it means, Timothy? There's not another country in the world that would have voted out a man who had just led them to victory in a major war. Can you imagine the Germans doing it, even if they'd had the chance? Or the French? Or the Americans? It means you British put politics above patriotism, that's what it means. That's why you could never have a dictatorship in Britain.

– What about America?

– We have a contender, said Don. His name's McCarthy.

Baden-Baden was a holiday town of brightly painted buildings, green lawns, flower beds, fountains and flags. A narrow river rushed helter-skelter through the centre of the town in a series of shallow falls, and everywhere there was the murmur of running water. Baden was in the French Zone, and slim, sallow French soldiers, with flashes of scarlet on their tight-fitting uniforms, mingled with the civilians sitting in the sun or strolling by the river.

They checked into a hotel, halfway up one of the steep cobbled streets in the centre of town, with an atmosphere of dignified, old-fashioned luxury. Thick carpets and high ceilings muffled the excited chatter of their party, and the heavy gilt-framed mirrors on the walls of the long corridors seemed to reflect their jazzy sports clothing almost reproachfully as they passed. Timothy had a room to himself with its own adjoining bathroom. The bath had three sets of taps, marked *Brause*, *Susswasser* and *Thermalwasser*; and on the wall was a large thermometer with a wooden handle, and an hour-glass. He was playing absorbedly with this apparatus when Kate came to fetch him to drive to the golf club. On the way she pointed out the Casino: a huge, white, neo-classical building with Corinthian columns, unexpectedly chaste and decorous. He had expected something more lurid.

The golf course was in the foothills about two miles outside the town. They had lunch on the clubhouse terrace, overlooking the last green, where white tablecloths were spread under gaily striped umbrellas. German, French and American accents mingled with the soft clash of cutlery and the chinking of glasses. The long green fairways sprawled beneath them, and to their left he noticed a small timbered hotel, buried up to its eaves in trees, with a small oval swimming pool winking in the sun.

– This is the life, eh Timothy? said Kate.

They ordered trout with salad and sauté potatoes. Vince suggested some white wine to go with the meal.

– I'll just have a beer, said Mel. We're playing golf this afternoon, remember.

– What the hell, said Ruth. I can't hit the ball when I'm sober, so what have I got to lose?

Mel and Vince were serious golfers, and played against each other. The others formed a foursome, Kate and Greg playing against Dot and Ruth. Dot seemed to be a reasonably skilful player. The others were beginners whom Timothy quickly ranked in a descending order of competence: Kate, Greg, Ruth. They hired little trolleys to carry their golf bags, and Timothy volunteered to pull Kate's for her.

Vince and Mel whacked their balls high and straight down the fairway, and strode off shoulder to shoulder. It took the others much longer to get off the first tee, and their progress round the course was slow and erratic. They swung and missed, they hacked great divots out of the turf, they lost innumerable balls in the rough, or sliced them into the wrong fairways and got mixed up in other people's games. They giggled and cursed and tried to cheat on the score.

Timothy was bored until Kate allowed him to putt for her. He had considerable experience of putting on the bumpy Municipal green at Worthing, and as a result of his skill Kate and Greg began to draw level with Dot and Ruth.

– You're terrific, Timothy, said Kate, as he sank a sixteen-foot putt. You ought to take up the game.

Greg, who was lying on the grassy bank that half enclosed the green, applauded.

– The grass is like velvet, you can't miss, said Timothy modestly.

– Well, it *is* one of the finest courses in Europe, said Kate. Golfers come from all over the world to play here. Look out!

Timothy ducked as a ball whizzed past his head and disappeared into the rough grass on the far side of the green. Ruth limped over the rim of a bunker, a cigarette dangling from her lip, her baseball cap askew.

– Hey, didya see that? I actually hit it! Pow! She scowled and looked round with her hands on her hips. Now were the hell is it? Don't tell me it went straight down the hole?

– Maybe it did, Ruth, said Greg. But not down this hole. Try one of the other holes.

– O.K., Sam Snyder, you're not doing so good yourself. Jesus, it's hot! She sat down on the green and took off her right shoe, wriggling her toes. These new shoes are killing me.

– That pool looks a treat, doesn't it? said Dot, looking over towards the hotel Timothy had noticed earlier. And no one seems to be using it.

– Pool? Did someone say *pool?* Ruth squawked. Lead me to it. Carry me to it.

– Water, water, Greg croaked, crawling up the grass bank on all fours.

– How about it, gang? said Ruth. What say we call this game quits and go have a swim?

– But we've no costumes, Kate pointed out.

– This is no time for prudery, said Greg. Besides, I've always wanted to see Ruth in the raw.

– Brother, you haven't lived! Ruth cawed delightedly.

– Maybe they'll lend us some costumes, said Dot. I could sure do with a dip.

– Who says they'll even let us swim? said Kate. After all, it is a private pool.

The manager of the hotel shook his head bemusedly at first, but after a few notes had changed hands they were given permission to use the pool and some costumes were produced. The costumes were ill-fitting and of old-fashioned design, and their appearance, when they emerged from the dressing cubicles, threw them all into hysterics.

– I hope you kept your bras on, girls, said Ruth. I tried this on without, and for one horrible moment I thought I'd lost 'em. She mimed feeling herself for her breasts like a man searching for his wallet.

They ordered iced tea to drink while they were drying off in the sun. It was casting long shadows when Mel and Vince arrived, looking hot.

– What in hell are you doing here? Mel demanded of his wife. I've been looking all over the goddam course.

– He lost, said Ruth. You lost, didn't you, sweetie-pie? I can tell with my woman's intuition.

Vince confirmed this guess:

– Three and two. I offered him a few strokes before we started, but he was too proud to take the offer.

– My handicap's the same as yours, Mel growled. I just had an off day. My putting was all to hell.

– You should get Timothy to give you some lessons, said Ruth. He's the greatest.

– Wheredya get those swimsuits?

– A nice man in the hotel gave them to us.

– Looks like he got them out of a museum or something.

– You're just jealous, lover. Why don't you get yourself one and join us?

– Come on, it's getting late.

– Maybe we should go, said Vince. Or we'll never get to the Casino tonight.

– You talked me into it, said Ruth, jumping to her feet.

– You don't like Kate's friends, do you? Timothy said.

Don looked a little taken aback.

– I expect it's mutual.

– Why don't you, though?

Don seemed about to speak, but hesitated. They walked on in silence, apart from the buzzing of insects in the grass beside the Philosopher's Way, and the hum of traffic from the town far below.

– Let's drop the subject, he said at last. They're your sister's friends.

– I won't tell her, said Timothy.

Don grinned.

– I like your sister, anyway. Is that mutual?

– I dunno . . . I think so. You don't think she's too fat?

– No, said Don, laughing. I don't think she's too fat. You can tell her that, if you like.

They went back to the hotel to shower and change; then drove off again to a little restaurant in the mountains that Vince and Greg had discovered. It was an old, crooked-roofed little inn, with space for only twenty diners, and Greg said you had to book a table several days in advance. The meal seemed to go on for ages, and included venison, hunted in the Black Forest with bow and arrow, according to Vince, and rum omelettes which gave Dot hiccups. *Pardon me*, she kept saying, and Greg said had they heard the story about the American at a dinner party in Paris, where one of the ladies farted.

– A Frenchman sitting next to this American guy stood up and apologized. *Whaddya do that for, it wasn't you that farted*, said the American in a whisper. *Ah, M'sieu*, said the Frenchman, *in this country we have a reputation for gallantry*. A few minutes later the same lady farted again. The American jumped to his feet and said, *Folks, have that one on me!*

Timothy, who had never heard a grown-up say *fart* before, and had drunk two glasses of wine, thought this was very funny, and laughed a lot. The others began to tell stories, some of which made Kate look quizzically at him. He avoided her glance and cultivated an absent-minded smile which left the extent of his comprehension an open question – which indeed it was.

It was eleven o'clock by the time they left the restaurant. The lights of Baden-Baden twinkled in the valley far below. Ever since he had come out from England it seemed to him that he had been looking down from heights, being shown the kingdoms of the world, like Jesus in the Bible. The crisp night air quenched his yawns and cooled his overheated body. He would have liked to ride in the open Mercedes with Vince, but Kate threw a scarf over her head and jumped into the front passenger seat. The rest of the party got into Mel's Oldsmobile and followed the Mercedes down the twisting mountain road, its brake lights glowing and fading like cigarettes in the dark as Vince slowed at the sharp bends. Greg, on the front seat of the Oldsmobile, twiddled the knobs of the radio, sweeping the needle on the dial through a spectrum of gabbled languages, snatches of music, symphonies, marches, opera, until he found some jazz. Timothy was once again impressed by the insatiable appetite for diversion Kate's friends possessed. Their aim seemed to be to make life an endless succession of pleasant sensations, more than one sensation at a time if possible. He pictured whimsically to himself the six-armed Indian gods and goddesses he had seen in art books, with a martini in one hand, a cigarette in the other, one hand wielding a fork, another tuning a radio, while the third pair held a dancing partner round the waist.

This style of living was difficult to adjust to, for it affronted his deepest instincts and principles. The whole system of prudent rules and safeguards, painfully learned in the school of scarcity – saving up, keeping things for best, postponing pleasure, or ekeing it out morsel by morsel, living in anticipation or recollection, never by impulse – this system was impossible to operate in an environment of excess. What profit was it to save half the chocolate bar he got on Monday, if Kate gave him a whole new one on Tuesday? What point in rationing yourself to one Coke, when you had enough money in your pocket for two? What use looking forward to a treat next week, when today might produce something more exciting? Already *this* day had contained enough novelty and indulgence to satisfy a year's longing at home, and still it was not finished. They swooped down the spiralling road towards a new goal of pleasure. Half an hour ago he had been ready for bed. Now, refreshed by the cool night air, he had got his second wind, he entered into the spirit of excess, he wanted the night to go on. He marvelled at himself, and looked back with a certain scorn at his former existence. It seemed to him that for years he had been doing things that he hadn't really wanted to do, out of timidity and ignorance of anything better. Now he had discovered that there was another world to join, one that was abundantly pleasurable.

– You've heard of camp followers? said Don. When every army drew a second army in its wake. Living off the first army, protected by them, tolerated by them, scavenging for what the first army hadn't looted or destroyed . . . I'm afraid that's what the civilian establishment out here reminds me of, sometimes. Camp-followers. Only they don't wear rags and carry bundles on their backs. They wear Brooks Brothers suits and have matched luggage and they ride about in big shiny Buicks.

Timothy glanced covertly at Don's frayed cuffs and scruffy cotton trousers.

– But it's not their fault if they're well off, he said mildly.

– Maybe, but they don't deserve it, either, said Don. Why should *they* inherit the earth?

– Why d'you mean?

– They live like the aristocracy used to. But give me the aristocracy of blood over the aristocracy of the dollar any day. Back home most of these people wouldn't rate a second glance, and they know it. I don't mean your sister, now.

– No, said Timothy, though he couldn't see why not.

– I mean my compatriots. Back home they'd be nobodies, sitting in their backyards, wondering if they could afford to change their cars this year, planning a vacation in Atlantic City. Out here they can live like kings. Europe is their playground. They just struck it lucky.

– Being here, you mean?

– Being here at the right time. Just when the Germans – and not just the Germans – began to crawl out of their cellars, clear away the rubble, rebuild their cities, open up the hotels and restaurants and the sights and the casinos – they happened to be the only people around with enough money to take advantage of it. The only people with no currency problems, no passport problems, no visa problems. Of course, they can't travel East, but they wouldn't want to, anyway. No pleasure there. It's mostly rubble still, there.

– You mean, behind the Iron Curtain? Have you been there?

– I was all fixed to go to Warsaw once. I had my visa, everything.

– Why didn't you go, then?

Don shrugged.

– It's considered un-American to go to Communist-sponsored conferences – that's what it was, a youth conference. They said, *You can go, buddy, but we won't let you back in*. They would have confiscated my passport.

Don raised his hand and shaded his eyes. Timothy followed the direction of his gaze, along the line of the river eastwards, upstream.

There was a shallow dam or waterfall where water foamed, and a lock to one side. The river beyond the lock was quickly lost to view between the steep green mountains of the Neckar valley.

– Difficult to imagine, isn't it? said Don. Couple of hundred miles east and you wouldn't know the war had ended. Rubble. Food lines. Secret police.

– Why d'you want to go there, then?

– It's hard to say . . . I guess, when you think of what happened in Europe only a few years ago, sackcloth and ashes seem more appropriate than Waikiki shirts.

Timothy considered this for a moment.

– Is that why you like England? he asked.

When he woke in his hotel room in Baden he found that in the course of the night he had rolled himself tightly in the down quilt which, absurdly, seemed the only form of bed-clothing provided, so that he was soaked in perspiration. He was also extremely thirsty, and his head ached. Was this, he wondered, a hangover? He had only had two glasses of wine, and a Tom Collins at the Casino.

The memory of that drink released a stream of other mental images of the Casino. The gaudy magnificence of the décor – mirrors, chandeliers, murals. Gigantic naked women painted on the ceiling, labelled *Richesse*, *Noblesse*, *Industrie*, and *Agriculture*, with wisps of drapery concealing their private parts. The whirring rattle of the roulette wheels and the clicking of chips being shuffled and sorted, an incessant background noise, like the sound of crickets. Kate standing on the threshold of the *Grande Salle*, with flared nostrils and bright eyes, murmuring, *Isn't it fabulous, Timothy?* And, hours later, as they dragged their weary legs out to the car park, whispering: *Don't ask Vince how he made out. He had bad luck.*

His watch had stopped at twenty past seven, but he guessed it was much later than that, for bright sunlight glinted through the chinks in the window shutters. He went over to the washbasin, drank recklessly from the tap and splashed his face with cold water. When he threw back the shutters, sunlight and fresh air burst into the room, and he looked with an irresistible lift of the spirits over the roofs and walled gardens of the town, at the green mountains and the intensely blue sky.

He found Kate on the terrace of the hotel restaurant. She was sitting alone at a table, smoking a cigarette and reading a magazine through her sunglasses.

– Hi! she greeted him. Sleep well? I didn't like to wake you.

– What's the time?

– Nearly one.

– Blimey! What about Mass?

Kate grimaced. I think it may be too late for that. I'll ask a waiter. And order you some brunch.

– What's brunch?

– What d'you think?

– Breakfast and lunch, I s'pose. Is it a real word?

– It's an American word.

– It's typical.

The waiter told them that the last mass in the town was at twelve.

– You don't really mind, do you, Timothy?

– No, I don't mind. It wasn't my fault I overslept. What do you eat for brunch?

– Anything you like. That's the beauty of it.

He ordered fresh grapefruit, scrambled eggs with ham and sausage, *Apfelstrudel* and coffee. Kate told him that the others had gone off to play golf again.

– I hope you didn't stay behind just for me.

– No, I have a little errand to do this afternoon. Something I always do when I come to Baden. You can come with me, if you like.

– Where?

– It's an orphanage I discovered when we were here last summer.

The appearance of the waiter with his grapefruit enabled Timothy to conceal his excitement. He spooned out a neatly separated segment of the fruit and swallowed it.

– Orphanage? he repeated casually.

– I saw this crocodile of darling little children coming out of the church here one Sunday, and I got talking to one of the nuns who was with them. Well, I'd been lucky at the Casino the night before, so on impulse I gave her a hundred Marks for the home. Conscience money, Greg called it, but she was so grateful. She cried, Timothy. I felt awful – after all, what was a hundred Marks to me?

Kath sniffed and blew her nose daintily on a paper tissue.

– Well, to cut a long story short, the nun invited me to visit the home, and I've been going there ever since. I always take some candies for the kids and sometimes a little donation. The boys usually give me something, too – they're very generous like that, though they kid me about it. Lady Bountiful, Greg calls me. Would you like to come this afternoon?

Her tone was light, but he thought he detected an anxious plea in her eyes.

– Oh, yes, he assured her, I'll come.

– I've always had a thing about Eastern Europe, said Don quietly – so quietly that Timothy could barely catch his words. I've never been there, but I feel as if I know it, as if it were my home. I mean Poland, East Prussia, that part. The part that's been fought over so many times the soil must be like bonemeal. And sometimes the towns have Polish names and sometimes they have German names and another time it's Russian names. But they're the same places. There's a curse on that land. All the worst things happened there.

He fell silent, but Timothy had nothing to say.

– It's very grey. And cold – it's always winter there, in my mind. With a grey sky and a thin layer of dirty snow on the ground. Flat and marshy. Smoke hanging in the air, and a fine wet ash falling like drizzle – but we won't go into that. And somewhere there's a locomotive shunting, only you can't see it, only hear it, hear the freightcars clanking, and the freightcars – but we won't go into that either.

He paused again. Timothy, puzzled, remained silent.

– When I tried to go to Warsaw, I didn't really want to go to Warsaw at all, or the conference. I just wanted to go to Auschwitz.

Some response seemed to be expected of him.

– I've heard the name somewhere, he said. Wasn't it one of Napoleon's –

– That's Austerlitz. Jesus Christ! Don turned slowly to face him. D'you mean you don't know about Auschwitz?

– Was it a concentration camp? Like Belsen?

Don nodded.

– An extermination camp. There was a subtle difference.

– I thought it was that at first, but I couldn't think what you wanted to go there for, said Timothy defensively. That was the trouble with Don's company – it was something of a strain, like taking an examination all the time.

– I wanted to see if I could stop dreaming about the place if I actually saw it.

– You dream about the concentration camps?

– Regularly. I'm in the camp, you see, and the question is, am I Polish or Jewish? Actually I'm both. My grandparents were from Cracow – it's not far from Auschwitz. They met in the States – they couldn't have gotten married in Poland. He was Christian, or ex-Christian, and she was Jewish. The Poles hate the Jews as much as anyone else. The Poles also hate the Germans and the Russians, and the Germans and the Russians hate the Poles and each other. The only thing they have in common is that they all hate the Jews. The Jew is underneath the lot. Know that poem? No? Well, anyway, in the dream, I'm always denying that I'm a Jew. *No, no, Herr Kommandant, I'm not a Jew. Aryan, pure Aryan. Put me in a camp by all means – I understand – time of war – measures must be taken – but don't mix me up with those filthy Jews.* Of course, I hate myself like poison, but I want to survive, see? It's every man for himself. There's no point my going to the ovens if I can avoid it – it's not going to save anybody else's life. Besides, I'm not really Jewish, only my grandmother on my father's side. Well, they're not sure, so they let me off. I become a kind of camp character, like the school janitor, you know what I mean? Old guy in dungarees, hanging around in the background. Always got a broom in his hand – something to lean on, and you can always get very busy sweeping, very energetic all of a sudden when they march the women and children away to the disinfection block. Sweep sweep. I don't see anything. Too busy sweeping. *Like to keep the place looking clean and tidy, Herr Kommandant. Is there any chance at all of getting a new broom, Herr Kommandant? These bristles are quite worn out.* The officers find they can get a rise out of me by shooting a question in Yiddish every now and again, but they don't really want to catch me out. I'm too useful to them. I know all the camp gossip. But it scares the shit out of me when they do it.

After a while, Timothy said:

– How does the dream end?

– It doesn't end. That's why I want to go to Auschwitz.

It all happened exactly as he had dreamed or imagined it would: the old house, smelling of polish, on the outskirts of Baden, and the garden with sandpits and swings, and the children in their smocks clustered round Kate as she handed out candies, and the nuns smiling fondly, and the little curly-haired girl that came running over the grass after the others had dispersed, and Kate catching her and swinging her high in the air and saying to Timothy, *What do you think of this little girl, isn't she cute?* His answer came pat on cue:

– Is she yours, Kate?

She nearly dropped the child.

– What? she said blankly.

He felt his insides caving in with embarrassment, but managed to force a smile.

– Just a joke, he said.

– Oh. She shot him a puzzled glance.

– Where do these children come from, actually? he asked. He put on an earnest expression designed to stress the flippancy of his previous question.

– Some of the older ones lost their parents at the end of the war, in raids. Or they just got lost – there was terrible confusion in Germany, then, with refugees running away from the Russians. Of course, this one wasn't born until after the war – were you, my pet?

Kate put the child down on the ground and presented a chocolate bar. She proffered her cheek for a kiss, but the child ran off at once to show her prize to a nun. Kate laughed and shrugged at the nun, who mimed her own amusement and disapproval.

– I shouldn't be surprised if that little girl's father was a G.I., or a French soldier, said Kate.

– Or a Tommy, said Ruth. Why not a British soldier? Why blame the Frogs and the G.I.s for all the bastards?

Kate had been describing the little girl, in the Oldsmobile going back to Heidelberg. Trees flashed by in the twilight, but it was almost as calm and quiet as a living-room inside the huge car.

– The British soldier is a man of honour, said Timothy from the back seat. He had discovered that defending the clichés of British patriotism was the surest way of amusing his American friends, and amusement seemed to be the only currency in which he could repay them for the dollars and Marks they expended on his behalf. True to his expectations, Ruth croaked with delighted laughter.

– That's not what my friends in Hamburg tell me, said Dot. They say the Reeperbahn is like the Old Kent Road these days.

– What's the Reeperbahn? Timothy asked.

– Never you mind, Kate said.

Ruth chuckled.

– Kate wants to protect your innocence, Timothy. But I guess there's not much you don't know, eh?

He evaded the question by putting another:

– Don't the German girls mind . . . going with the Occupation troops?

Mel, hunched over the driving wheel, snorted.

– Most of 'em would give their right arms to hook a G.I.

– It's not their right arms that the G.I.s want, honey, Ruth tittered.

– Mind you, said Dot, the German girls are more choosy than they used to be.

– Right, said Mel. There was a time when you could have any Fräulein you liked for a Hershey bar.

– Yeah, said Ruth, now it's two Hershey bars and a Milky Way. Inflation, it's the same everywhere . . . Anyway, Timothy's not interested in Fräuleins, are you Timothy?

– No.

– What you want is a date with a nice young all-American high-school girl, right?

– Wrong, he said. I'm quite happy as I am.

– Leave it to me, Timothy, said Ruth. I'll fix you up.

– Lay off the kid, Ruth, said Mel. He's got plenty of time for dames. No darn good to you anyway, Timothy, take it from me. And whatever you do, don't get married.

– Now just a minute! Ruth protested.

– Take Hitler, for example. He was doing fine while he was single. He marries Eva Braun, and what happens? Next day he loses the war.

Ruth, laughing in spite of herself, punched her husband, and the car veered slightly.

– Take it easy willya? he shouted. But he was grinning, pleased with the success of his witticism. He flicked a switch on the dashboard, and headlights stabbed through the gathering dusk.

– Any sign of the boys? Kate asked.

– Huh, they'll be in Heidelberg by now, he muttered. When Vince has lost a stack at the Casino, he works it off in that car.

But why did God let Hitler live to the very end? Till so many were killed getting to him, or defending him. Or caught between the two, refugees. Or in the camps, ten thousand a day at Auschwitz alone, Don said. If the July plot had succeeded, maybe a million would have lived. More. But someone moved the bomb and Hitler survived. And there had been other attempts, Vince said. But the bombs failed to explode, or Hitler changed his programme at the last minute. And once a V.1 turned round and landed on Hitler's bunker, but he wasn't hurt. *You couldn't have blamed him for thinking he was under some sort of divine protection, could you?* Vince said. But why should God have protected Hitler?

– That's your problem, Timothy, said Don. I'm not a Christian, I'm not anything. But if I was a Christian I shouldn't be wondering what God was doing at the time, I'd be asking what other Christians were doing. Like the Pope, for instance.

– He was neutral. The Pope has to be neutral.

– I'm not talking about the war. I'm talking about the camps. How can you be neutral about the camps?

– Well, perhaps he didn't know. Nobody knew till after the war, did they?

– He knew. Plenty of people knew. Perhaps they didn't believe it. That's the only excuse I can think of. It's hard enough to believe now, God knows.

– But what could he do? He was shut up in the Vatican.

– He could have spoken out. He could have gotten himself crucified.

– That's not fair.

Timothy was hurt, baffled. The Pope couldn't be to blame. The Pope was a good man. They said he was a saint.

– No, it's not fair. But only because I say it. I have no right to say it. Leaning on my broom.

Mel dropped them at Fichte Haus at about 9 o'clock.

– See you two next Friday, if not before, said Ruth.

– I haven't told Timothy yet, said Kate.

– Oh, you'll love it, Timothy, said Ruth.

– What was all that about? he asked, as the Oldsmobile swept away.

– Next weekend we're all going on a trip to Garmisch – it's in the Bavarian Alps.

– Gosh! How far is that?

– Oh, I don't know, several hundred kilometres. We'll go by train, in sleepers, on Friday night, arrive back Monday morning. The Army has a Rest Centre there. It's absolutely out of this world: mountains, lake . . .

– What are we resting from – *this* weekend?

Kate laughed.

– You say the funniest things, Timothy. It's for the soldiers, really – a place for them to spend their furloughs. Everything is laid on: swimming, sightseeing, skiing in the winter and water-skiing in the summer. Ever tried that?

– No.

– Vince is very good at it. I can never seem to get started. Let's see if there's any mail.

Rudolf's little office was empty, but the door was unlocked, and Kate helped herself to her mail from the pigeonholes on the wall.

– Card for you from Mum, she said, passing him a picture postcard of Worthing, six views in black and white. He turned it over and scanned the message. Something about a pie.

– By the way, said Kate, leading the way to her room, Rudolf offered to take you out one day this week, on his day off. A bicycle ride in the country, he said. I said you'd like that. You would, wouldn't you?

– I dunno. What would I do for a bike?

– He said he could borrow one for you. He's such a nice boy. You've talked to him, haven't you?

– Just a bit. I don't know what to talk about, really.

– Talk about England. Rudolf's very fond of England.

– I'd feel embarrassed. Him being a prisoner of war, and that.

– You don't have to talk about the war. I never talk about the war to Germans. They want to forget about it, like most people. Phew! It's stuffy in here!

Pulling up the blind and opening the window in her room, Kate threw back over her shoulder:

– Any news from home?

– Nothing much. They send you their love. Want to read it?
– Later. I'll just make some coffee and sandwiches.
– Can I help?
– Well, that's very thoughtful of you, Timothy.

He liked going to the communal kitchen, with its sparkling white and stainless steel surfaces, its gadgets, its huge, humming fridge. When you opened the door of the fridge the inside lit up like some dream of a pre-war shop window. Kate let him open a tin of tuna fish with the wall can-opener that had a little magnet attached to it to hold the severed top.

– Can you buy these tin-openers here?
– At the P.X? Sure. Why?
– I thought I might take one back for Mum.
– Good idea. D'you think she'd use it?

He thought for a moment.

– No, he said, and they both laughed.

Kate took a wrapped loaf from the fridge and peeled off several slices.

– Is the kitchen at home just the same?
– How d'you mean?
– Does the cupboard door still catch on the back door handle?
– I s'pose so, yes.
– And does the drawer of the green table still stick?
– Yes.
– You've *still* got that old green table? And the same check oilcloth, I'll bet.
– It's sort of white now. The pattern's rubbed off.

Kath sighed.

– It doesn't sound as if things have changed much. Does the cold water still run slow when somebody flushes the toilet?
– Yes, but if you give the pipes a bang it comes on again. Trouble is, that brings down the soot in the boiler chimney sometimes.

Kate laughed and shook her head.

As usual, he was still eating when Kate had finished her share of the snack. She lit one of her long Pall Malls, and sat back in her armchair.

– Did you enjoy the weekend, Timothy?
– It was super.
– I hope the orphanage wasn't a bore for you.

– No, it was interesting.

Kate was silent for a moment. He had a premonition of what was coming. He took a large bite from the last sandwich.

– What did you mean when you said, *Is she yours?* About the little girl?

– I dunno why I said it, really, he mumbled.

– Oh, come on, Timothy. You must have meant something.

She waited patiently, inexorably for his reply. He shifted uncomfortably in his seat.

– Well, why haven't you been home all this time? he said finally.

Kate burst out laughing.

– So *that's* it! That's what you've been thinking? That I'm an unmarried mother? Oh dear, you don't know how funny that is. She shook her head, laughing, though the laughter was a little forced. I'm very likely the last virgin left in Heidelberg.

She flicked her cigarette at the ashtray, though there was no ash to speak of on the end.

– It wasn't my idea, he said.

– You needn't tell me that. It was Mum's, wasn't it?

– I heard her talking to Dad one day. She didn't know I was listening.

– And what did Dad say?

– He didn't believe it, I think. But he was worried. I didn't really believe it, but when you took me to the orphanage, it sort of put it into my head. And you must admit . . .

– What?

– Well, it seems funny that you haven't been home for so long.

Kate stubbed out her cigarette and lit another.

– I'll tell you why I haven't been home. For two simple reasons: firstly because I can't stand it, and secondly because I was afraid they'd try and make me stay.

– Make you?

Kate gestured impatiently, leaving a trail of smoke in the air.

– Well, of course they couldn't *make* me, against my will. I mean I couldn't face the arguments, the reproaches, the recriminations. I didn't want to hurt them by telling them what I really thought.

She didn't, she explained, want to have to tell them that she hated their poky little house, with rooms so small that you kept bumping into furniture every time you moved, where everyone was trapped in the back living-room for half the year because the rest of the house was cold as a tomb, and as damp.

– D'you know that the last time I was at home a pair of my shoes got *mildew* on them, just up in my bedroom? I can't tell you how depressed I felt that Christmas.

She couldn't wait to get back to Heidelberg, counting the days till her leave was up, and finally inventing an excuse to go back earlier than she had intended. Just to draw back the curtains of her bedroom in the morning was enough to give her a feeling of panic, as if she were drowning. Just to look down at all those mean, shabby little back gardens with their sheds, coalsheds and toolsheds and bicyclesheds, sagging and rotting away in the damp. And to see the women in old jumpers and skirts, with scarves over their curlers, clutching themselves against the cold, gossiping over the fences about the cost of potatoes, or hanging out sodden washing, with smoke falling from a thousand chimneys, so that if you ran your finger along a window ledge an hour after it had been dusted it came off black. The cold and the damp and the dirt.

– I couldn't stand it any longer. I realized that I'd never felt really warm or clean, in the winter, till I left home; and coming back to it again was too much.

Trying to keep out of the draughts, hunched over a fire so that your legs burned and your back froze, and every time someone opened and closed the door the fire belched a little cloud of smoke into the room and the Christmas cards fell off the mantelpiece.

– The work that wretched fire makes! And the arguments! And it doesn't even make you warm. I used to think about this cosy little room and taking a hot shower in a warm bathroom, and wonder how much longer I could stick it at home. I only had one bath the whole time I was there. Once was enough. But how could I explain to Mum and Dad?

How could she explain that it wasn't anything personal, that she wasn't getting at them, she knew it was how most people had to live because of the war, and the post-war shortages. But she had got used to a different standard of living, and it was no use pretending that she could readjust.

– One day that leave I went up to the West End to do some shopping – not that there was anything in the shops worth buying, but it was an excuse to get out. I left it late coming back, and got caught in the rush hour. I'd forgotten what it was like.

She thought she was going to faint, crushed into a compartment where a dozen people were standing in the narrow space between the two benches, hanging on to the luggage rack to keep their balance and trying to read newspapers at the same time. The reek of stale cigarette smoke and human bodies. The windows streaming with condensation. And she thought how narrowly she had escaped being one of those pinched, weary travellers, condemned to make this journey twice a day for the rest of their working lives, and she vowed that she would never come back.

– Never?

– You've been out here long enough to see why, haven't you, Timothy? Just think of this past weekend. Could I ever live a life remotely like this in England?

– Well, I know, but . . . never?

– I mean, for good, to settle there again. I don't mean visits, though I know I keep putting them off. I was secretly relieved when the Korean business stopped me coming home last time. Isn't that an awful confession? But it's no use pretending. You're supposed to miss home and family, aren't you, but, d'you know, I've never missed them, not even when I was evacuated. I used to wonder, when I was a kid, whether I was adopted, because I never felt I really loved my mother and father as you were supposed to.

– Seriously?

– Seriously. Of course, your being the favourite at home just added to it.

– Was I the favourite?

– Well, of course you were! And there was such a big age difference between us that I was sure they'd adopted me because they thought they couldn't have any children of their own, and that you came along unexpectedly – which was true, actually.

– Was it?

– Oh yes. Mum was warned not to have any more children after me – it was a difficult birth, apparently. But when you came along it all went off all right, and she's had a soft spot for you ever since.

Kate took another cigarette from the pack and offered him one.

– Oh, I keep forgetting.

– I think I'll try one, he said.

– My, I'm really leading you astray, aren't I. Have you ever smoked before?

– Once or twice.

Furtive drags on shared Woodbines in the bicycle sheds at school, little acrid shreds of tobacco left on the tongue. This was different. Cloudy cottonwool feeling in your mouth. He coughed.

– I used to wonder why I was fat when none of the rest of you were. It all seemed to add up. Then one day I found out I really was Mum's child. But it was a bit of a shock.

– Why?

– When I tried to join the W.A.A.F.s, I had to take my birth certificate along to the recruiting office. I'd never seen it before. Well, that proved it. But in the same envelope was Mum and Dad's marriage certificate. And looking at the dates I realized I was born six months after they were married.

She looked at him meaningfully.

– So what? he said.

– Oh, Timothy, I thought you knew a bit more about the facts of life than I did at your age! It means that I was conceived out of wedlock, as they say.

– Good Lord, he said, blushing.

– Makes you think, doesn't it? As a matter of fact, the idea rather tickles me. Makes Mum and Dad seem more human. But I was very shocked at the time. I thought they were such hypocrites, on at me all the time about wearing lipstick and staying out too late. Of course that's just why they *were* like that. It's classic. What's the matter with your cigarette?

– It's gone out.

– Cigarettes don't go out, she giggled, flicking her lighter for him. When you've finished it I must take you back. It's getting late.

But somehow she didn't take him back to Dolores' room, not for a long time. Too many barriers had gone down, too many doors had been opened, for them to stop easily. They slid together down an endless slope of disclosure. He could almost feel himself growing older as she talked, feeling his brain swelling under the pressure of so much new information – as he felt, when he stretched in his bed at night, those aches in his limbs his mother called growing pains. And when he did finally get to bed, although it was very late, and he was very tired, he couldn't sleep for a long time, going over in his mind different parts of their conversation, hearing Kate's voice saying:

– I don't know how I survived that year in Paris intact. I think I was so innocent that it took the men's breath away. They just didn't know how to seduce a girl who knew so little. I mean, I'd let a fellow take me out on the town, give me a meal, which was all black-market and cost the earth, and then take me to a night club, and then at the end of the evening, I'd shake hands. Shake hands! What they must have thought . . . Only one of them got really nasty about it. He called me up at the office once and called me a prick-teaser. I didn't even know what he meant. I remember I asked him, *Would you please repeat that?* in my best secretarial manner, and he did too, in the Army signal code – you know, P for Papa, R for Roger, and I wrote it all down and stared at it and sort of guessed what it meant and slammed the phone down. I thought he was some kind of maniac. But I suppose he was right, really. Of course, I was still a good Catholic girl in those days. Just a cuddle in the back of a taxi was enough to send me rushing off to Confession. The idea of going to bed with a man never entered my head.

– Then I fell in love. The real thing. Boom. His name was Adam. A Captain in the Army. I'd never met anyone like him in all my life. He wasn't a bit brash, but gentle and sophisticated and courteous. He was older than most of the men I knew, and I thought the sun and moon shone out of his eyes. There was a vague understanding that we should get married one day, when the war was over, but I didn't dare think about it – you lived from day to day then, because the fighting was still going on and you never knew what might happen. So when he told me one day that he was being transferred to the front line, and would I spend our last weekend together with him at a hotel near Paris, I said I would. I didn't know what it entailed, exactly. I knew it meant that we were going to do *it*, whatever *it* was. But I didn't care. I felt more like a bride than a mistress, anyway, all solemn and shy as the day approached. Then quite by chance his file came into our office, and I saw that he was married with a wife and four children back in the States. And he wasn't even going to the front – he was posted to Brussels, which had been liberated weeks before.

– I was bitter and resentful and full of self-pity for a long time, even after I was posted to Germany. What pulled me together was coming home, that first time after the war. I realized how dreary life was in England, and how lucky I was to be out of it. So I was a fat girl whom nobody wanted to marry – who cared? I could still have a good time, live in comfort, see the world. And what was so great about marriage anyway? I didn't think Mum had had much of a life. And I'd seen enough broken marriages, infidelities, divorces and so on in the Army (being in the Chaplain's Department, we saw a lot of that sort of thing). When I was posted to Heidelberg, I started a new life, made new friends, with people like Vince and Greg, Dot and Maria. I have a feeling that all of us, at some time in the past, were badly hurt. We never discuss the past, or our families, it's just a feeling. But we have something in common. We want to forget, perhaps that's it. We want to live in the present. We want fun and companionship without emotional involvement, without the risk of getting hurt again. And we do have a lot of fun, you've seen that. But it can't go on for ever.

– I decided about a year ago that I wouldn't wait to be fired. I'm going to emigrate to the States, Timothy. I can go at any time. My papers are all filed, my sponsors laid on. I haven't told anyone except Vince and Greg, and now you. The main thing that's holding me back is that Mum and Dad won't understand. They'll think that I'm deserting them. I'm hoping that you'll support me, Timothy, that you'll be able to make them understand. I can't stay here indefinitely, and I can't go back to England. You see that, don't you? I must go on, not back, and the States is the obvious place. Of course, I may hate it and want to come back, but I don't think so. You don't think I'm being selfish, do you? What could I expect if I went back to England? A shorthand-typist's job at ten pounds a week, if I was lucky. It's different for you, you're clever, you'll have all kinds of opportunities. Perhaps by the time you grow up, England will be a different place. But there'll never be opportunities for me. Whereas in the States a good secretary can earn five thousand dollars a year. I'll be able to fly back to see you all from time to time. Or you could fly out to America and see me, have another holiday like this one. That would be fun, wouldn't it? You do see that it's the only thing for me to do, don't you Timothy? Don't you?

He added a little more shadow under the arches of the bridge, softened the effect with his eraser, blew the crumbs of rubber away, and held up the sketch pad. The drawing was finished. It was quite good. The statue on the bridge looked a bit odd, but he had never been much good at figures. Otherwise it was all right. Kate and her friends would be impressed. But it looked a bit dead, grey and lifeless, in pencil.

He got out his little box of water-colours. Water. He scrambled down the bank to the river and filled his water container. It was a pleasing idea to paint the river with the river. He climbed back to his original position and began carefully to tint the drawing, testing his colours on the back of the Worthing postcard, until his mother's words were nearly obliterated.

He glanced at his watch: time to go. He wanted to take a shower at Fichte Haus before Kate got back from work. Don was coming for them at seven. It was a full life he was leading. There were times when he thought it must be the fullest life in the history of boyhood.

2

Don had suggested taking Timothy and Kate to one of the old inns where the Heidelberg students congregated, and they had made a date for Monday after the weekend at Baden. But when Kate came in from work she said:

– Would you mind very much going with Don on your own this evening? I feel absolutely done in after the weekend. And all that talking last night

– It won't be much fun without you, he said doubtfully.

– And it won't be much fun with me, I've got a splitting headache.

– Have a shower – you'll feel better.

She grinned wearily at him.

– You've become a shower enthusiast already. What did you do with yourself today?

Timothy showed her his drawing of the Old Bridge.

– Why, that's beautiful, Timothy! Can I add it to my collection?

– I thought I'd send it to Mum and Dad. I'll do you another one. Kate, Don is borrowing a car tonight, specially.

– Is he? Who from?

– Some friend in the Army. He'll be disappointed if you don't come.

She considered, sighed.

– Oh, all right.

The car that Don had borrowed was a battered Volkswagen. It seemed cramped and noisy after the cars Timothy had been riding in lately. When the engine was going, conversation was hardly possible. Fortunately they didn't have to drive very far. Don took them first to a floating restaurant, on a boat moored near the New Bridge. Timothy had often seen it, lit up at night, looking down from the terrace of the Molkenkur, and had asked Kate about it. *Looks pretty, doesn't it?* she had said. *But I'm told the food's not terribly good. Germans go there mostly.*

– Well, doesn't this look pretty, she said, as they drew up and Don hopped out of the car to open the door for her. All these lights and the water. I've always wanted to come here.

Timothy hoped Don could not detect the note of insincerity in her voice, or the speculative sniff she gave as they seated themselves on the deck. There *was* a bit of a pong coming off the murky water. When Don quipped *Fresh from the river!* as he filled their water glasses, the joke was a little too close for comfort, and he noticed that Kate didn't drink any of hers.

Timothy didn't enjoy the meal very much, partly because the food wasn't particularly good, but more because he felt somehow responsible for the social success of the evening. Conversation was sticky at first. After they had tried one or two fruitless topics – gambling, in which Don wasn't interested, and politics, in which Kate wasn't – they got onto the pros and cons of life in Europe and America.

– What about California, Don? said Kate. Did you say your family had moved there?

– Yes, but I've never been. They seem to like it, especially the climate.

– It sounds like the Mediterranean with all mod. cons., said Kate. If I ever emigrate to America, I think I'll go to California.

– Is that what you plan to do? said Don.

– Oh, it's just an idea, said Kate airily. You never know what the future holds.

– What would your folks say?

– What do yours say? she countered.

– *Touché*, said Don. Shall we go and explore some of these inns?

– I think one will be enough, if you don't mind, Don. Timothy and I had a heavy weekend.

– Sure.

There was an embarrassing little wrangle over the bill. Kate wanted to pay for herself and Timothy, but Don had his way, counting out the notes and coins carefully from a leather purse.

The Germans in the bar all looked up when they entered. There were some young women present, in blouses and skirts, but Kate stood out exotically in her cream-coloured linen suit and high-heeled shoes, like visiting royalty. The young waiter who found them a place at one of the long trestle tables dusted the bench down solicitously with his apron before she sat down.

The bar comprised two rooms, one at a lower level than the other, both furnished with long bare wooden tables deeply scarred with initials and mottoes. The ceiling was dark with smoke and heavily beamed: the grimy walls were almost covered with posters, banners, and old-fashioned photographs of young men in strange clothes and funny hats. The drinkers sat on the benches with thick mugs of beer before them. Most wore open-necked shirts with rolled-up sleeves, and some wore grey leather shorts.

– So this is a students' beer-cellar, said Kate, peeling off her gloves and looking curiously around.

– You mean you've never been to one before? said Don. After all your time in Heidelberg?

– Well, a girl can't very well come in here on her own, can she? And my friends don't go much for this sort of thing.

– Do *you?*

– I don't know, yet, she laughed. Give me a chance!

After a while, the singing started. A man sitting at the head of one of the long tables rapped on it with his beer mug and intoned a phrase. The rest of the men at the table took up the song in resounding chorus, sitting up very straight and staring before them with stern concentration. When they finished the other people in the bar applauded, and went on with their conversation. The singers smiled modestly at each other and took deep draughts of beer. Then, after a few minutes, the leader rapped on the table again and started another song.

– I guess it's some kind of society, Don explained. They probably have a regular meeting here, and the people come along to hear them sing. Usually it's more casual – everybody joins in.

– It's certainly not much like a knees-up at an English local, is it Timothy?

– Knees-up? Don enquired, intrigued. But as she was starting to explain, the singers struck up again. When they had finished, Timothy asked Don what the song had been about.

– It's about the castles of the Rhine. Which reminds me, Kate, don't you think Timothy should see the Rhine while he's in Germany?

– Well, yes, that would be nice, but the pretty part is a good way away.

– I was wondering whether we might take a little trip, the three of us, next weekend. Take a cruise up the Rhine, and stay over some place. They have boats that leave from Mainz. It's very scenic.

– Oh, I know! But unfortunately, Don, we've got something planned already for next weekend. I'm taking him to Garmisch, with some friends, to the Rest Centre there. And I'm afraid that will be Timothy's last weekend.

– Oh, well, it was just a thought, said Don.

– My last weekend, said Timothy, to fill the awkward silence that followed. I'd forgotten that.

– Cheer up, said Kate. There's plenty of time before you have to go home. Which reminds me, I fixed up some company for you tomorrow. Some boys of your own age for a change.

– Who? he asked suspiciously.

– Sons of a Captain I know, Ralph Mercer, he often comes into my office. He's got a sweet wife out here with him, in married quarters, and three children. I mentioned you were visiting me, and Mrs. Mercer rang me at the office today and said why don't you go over to their apartment tomorrow. You can have lunch with them, and her boys will take you somewhere in the afternoon.

– Do I have to?

– No of course you don't *have* to, said Kate, and pinched her lips together in a way that reminded him of his mother when she was displeased.

– Oh, all right, then, he said. How old are these kids, anyway?

– Larry is fifteen, I think, and the other boy is a bit younger. I'm sure you'll be glad when you go. You've had so much grown-up company lately, it will be a nice change.

– How would you like to meet the kids in my class? Don asked him. Maybe you could give them a little talk about England.

– Who, me?

– Yes, why don't you, Timothy, said Kate. I bet you'd do it jolly well.

– Well, I'll think about it, he said, secretly flattered.

During the next song, Kate put her lips to his ear and whispered: *All right if we go after this?* He nodded his assent. The bench felt uncomfortably hard, and the ponderous foreign singing was beginning to get on his nerves. He thought that on the whole he preferred Kate's way of spending an evening out. Nevertheless he defended Don's entertainment loyally when they were alone together in the lift going up to Dolores' room.

– Had a lot of atmosphere, didn't it, that beer-cellar? he ventured.

– I'll say! You could have cut it with a knife. And the smell of the river at dinner. Phew!

– I didn't notice, he lied. But did you enjoy the evening otherwise?

– Well, it was a change. Got your key? Don's a nice boy, but he's not exactly a thousand laughs, is he?

– Too serious, you mean?

– He kind of sits back and lets things happen. If nothing happens, that's fine by him. Now what I like about Vince and Greg is, they *make* things happen.

– I've had some pretty interesting talks with Don, said Timothy, as they entered his room.

– What about?

– Oh . . . the war. The concentration camps.

Kate threw up her hands.

– Wonderful! There's nothing I like more than a nice cosy chat about concentration camps.

– Vince talks about Hitler all the time, Timothy pointed out.

– Not to me, he doesn't. Listen, I think Don is a thoroughly nice guy. He's just not my type, that's all. For one thing, I can't stand a man that uses a purse.

– I think he was a bit disappointed about next weekend.

– Disappointed! I thought he was pretty fresh, myself. I don't go away for weekends with every Tom, Dick and Harry, you know.

– Well, I was supposed to go with you.

– As chaperone, huh? She put her hands on her broad hips and grinned at him. You think you could defend my virtue if it came to the pinch?

– I thought you wanted to lose it, he said cheekily. He ducked as she slapped at him, almost too hard to be playful.

– Watch it, young brother! And remember, if you ever repeat a word of what I told you last night, I'll wring your neck.

– Kate, couldn't Don come with us to Garmisch?

She looked taken aback.

– Why should he?

– Well, I think he was banking on seeing us this weekend – my last weekend. I'll ask him, if you like. I think he'd jump at it.

– I'm sure he would. But I'm not sure what Vince and Greg would think . . .

– Well, ask them.

She pondered.

– I'll see, Timothy. Now don't forget the Mercers, tomorrow.

The Mercers lived in one of the big apartment blocks the Americans had built for their personnel in South Heidelberg – America Town, as Kate's friends called it, with a slight sneer of condescension in their voices. Certainly there was nothing to remind one of Germany in the neat, rectilinear streets and the featureless, repetitive buildings. The pavements were curiously deserted, though there were plenty of cars on the broad, smooth roads – huge Fords and Pontiacs and Chryslers, that cruised past with whispering tyres. After alighting from his yellow bus, Timothy had some difficulty locating the right block, but at last he found it. Some American children lounging at the foot of the stairs fell silent and stared at him as he approached.

– Is this Lincoln Block? he asked.

– Yep, said one. Another extruded a large bubble of gum from his mouth and made it pop. As they made no move to let him pass, he stepped over them and proceeded up the stairs.

Mrs. Mercer looked blankly at him when she opened the door. She was a thin, tired-looking woman in a flowered housecoat, with her hair in plaits. A little girl about three years old, sucking her thumb and clasping a filthy ragged blanket, clung to her mother's skirts.

– Timothy who? Oh, yeah, Kate's brother, come on in, said Mrs. Mercer. Lulu, don't get in the way, now. This is Timothy, he's from England.

– Hallo, said Timothy. Lulu went on sucking.

– She's a little slow, speechwise, Mrs. Mercer explained. But the paediatrician says to talk to her all the time. No baby-talk, though.

– Well, I don't know any baby-talk.

Mrs. Mercer laughed.

– You have a wonderful accent, anyway.

– My sister doesn't think so.

– Ah, now, your sister's in a class of her own. That's what I call a beautiful English accent.

She led him into what seemed to be the living-room. He was uncertain because the furniture was strewn with large quantities of washing, some clean and some dirty. He followed her about the apartment as she searched for her sons, and every room displayed the same confusion of function. There were dirty plates in the bedrooms, toys and sports equipment in the kitchen, and a wireless playing in the empty bathroom.

– The boys must have gone out, said Mrs. Mercer. She went to the front door and shouted down the stairwell: *Larry! Con!*

In due course, the boy who had answered his enquiry at the foot of the stairs, and the one with the bubble gum, slouched into the apartment. Though they were both younger than himself, Larry was a head higher and Con almost as tall.

– Larry, Con, this is Timothy, said their mother.

– We already met, said Larry.

– I'm awful hungry, Mom, said Con. He blew another bubble.

– O.K., I'll fix you a peanut butter and jelly sandwich. Would you like a sandwich, Timothy?

He declined politely, thinking that it was too near lunchtime. After a confused exchange of remarks, he realized that the sandwich *was* lunch, and changed his mind. They ate in the kitchen, sitting on high stools before a high narrow table like the counter of a snack bar. Conversation was slow.

– Whaddya doin' in Heidelberg? Larry asked him, his mouth full of peanut butter sandwich.

– I'm on vacation, he said. The word *holiday* already sounded quaint to his ears.

– Crappy place to come for a vacation, Con remarked.

– Con! I've told you before not to use that word, said his mother.

– Don't you like it here? Timothy asked.

– Nope. Nothin' to do.

– What are you boys going to do with Timothy this afternoon? said Mrs. Mercer.

– There's a new movie downtown, said Larry.

– You went to the movies yesterday.

– Well, there's nothin' else to do.

– You could go to the pool. Have you been to the pool, Timothy?

– Yes, he said.

– He's been to the pool, said Larry, spinning round on his stool and jumping down. Can I have some money for the movie?

– I guess so, Mrs. Mercer sighed. She took some money from a purse and handed it to him.

– Aw, come on, Mom, have a heart!

– The movie is only fifty cents each.

– Yeah, but there's the popcorn, and I thought maybe he'd like a milkshake after. Larry indicated Timothy with a jerk of his head.

– Oh, all right, here you are. And put a clean shirt on, both of you, before you go out.

The two boys rooted through the laundry in the living-room till they found two clean tee-shirts. They seemed to have no personal property among the clothes, which Timothy found very strange. With the tee-shirts they wore jeans and grubby basketball boots, and before leaving the apartment they shrugged on light zipped wind-cheaters. Timothy felt rather overdressed beside them in his new jacket and trousers.

– What shire d'you come from? Larry asked him, as they jolted back to the city centre in a yellow bus.

– Shire? Timothy repeated blankly.

– Yeah, doncha call 'em shires in England, like we have states? York*shire* and Lanca*shire*.

– Oh! I come from London, that isn't in a shire, really. Where do you come from in America?

– Kentucky, most lately.

– Where they have the Kentucky Derby?

– Right! You heard of it? Larry seemed pleased, genuinely friendly for the first time.

As they approached the cinema the numbers of American children and teenagers thickened on the pavement. They sauntered along with a characteristically lazy, looselimbed gait, bright shirts hanging outside their patched jeans, never singly, always in packs, their voices twanging unselfconsciously. They seemed not to feel the compulsion Timothy always felt to camouflage himself on the streets of Heidelberg, to conceal the fact that he belonged to the enemy, the occupiers. Rather, they behaved simply as if the Germans weren't there, as if they had landed on the moon, bringing all the apparatus of their civilization with them. The first things that drew the eye in the shabby foyer of the requisitioned cinema were the shiny modern booths selling popcorn, hotdogs and soft drinks. Inside the auditorium a more mysterious modification aroused his curiosity: the arms had been removed from alternate seats in the back rows.

– Love-seats, Larry explained impassively, his hand moving rhythmically from popcorn bag to mouth and back again.

Love-seats! The idea, and its practical application all around him, distracted his attention from the cowboy film they had come to see. Love-seats: it brazenly acknowledged that people came to the cinema for that. You took your girl friend to the pictures and at the ticket booth you said, *two love-seats, please*, and nobody raised an eyebrow, apparently. Fantastic.

With half his mind he jeered at this institutionalized licence, while with the other half he coveted it. It was childish, yes, that was the word for it, for all of them, they were all childish – he felt himself to be immeasurably older than any of them, however tall they were. But it was a childhood he had never known, and he coveted it in spite of himself.

So, although he felt half bored and ill-at-ease in their company, he hung on to Larry and Con as they came out of the cinema, blinking in the sunlight (*a crime*, his mother would have called it, to waste such a glorious afternoon at the pictures) and went with them to a milk-bar nearby. It was an American establishment that he hadn't visited before, its customers mainly G.I.s and the teenagers who now crowded in noisily from the cinema. Behind the narrow, unobtrusive façade on Bergheimerstrasse a whole little America opened up, all pink neon and chromium plating. Tall, broad-shouldered soldiers sat at the counters sucking at straws, or stood leafing through the magazines and comic books displayed on a long rack by the door. A huge, monolithic jukebox, standing like an altar against the end wall, throbbed and boomed.

– They make the best ice-cream sodas in town here, Larry said. Twelve flavours.

– Howard Johnson does thirty-nine, said Con.

– I sure wish they'd open a Howard Johnson in Heidelberg, Larry sighed. Well, let's make a pool. I got one dollar fifty. He threw the scrip onto the table.

– I only have a dime, said Con. Mom always gives you all the money. How much you got? he said, turning to Timothy.

Timothy imprudently produced a five dollar bill.

– Gee! exclaimed Con, with wide eyes, we can have three each.

– Four, said Larry. Four, minimum.

Timothy felt it would be impolite to question the fairness of this arrangement. They started with a round of chocolate, and went on to pineapple and then strawberry. The ice-cream sodas were indeed superb, but Timothy found it difficult to finish his strawberry one. When, however, Larry rose unsteadily to his feet to order a fourth round, Timothy felt it would be a confession of weakness to refuse.

– What'll it be this time? Larry demanded, leaning heavily on the back of his chair.

Con leaned back at a dangerous angle to examine the printed menu posted on the wall.

– How 'bout pistachio?

Larry nodded his agreement, but appeared incapable of raising his chin from his chest.

– Pistachio it is, he said in a slurred voice, and shuffled off to the counter with his head bowed.

– What's Con short for? Timothy enquired conversationally.

Con looked abstracted, as if he hadn't heard the question, or had forgotten the answer. Then he belched and a grin of relief spread across his round, freckled face.

– Constantine, he said.

– After the Roman Emperor?

– You tryin' to be smart? After my grandpa.

Timothy changed the subject, enquiring about the purpose of the small metal boxes, fitted with buttons and knobs, that were fixed on the wall above each table.

– For the jukebox, Con explained. Remote control. Saves you walkin' over there.

Just like the love-seats. Americans!

Larry returned with the brilliantly green ice-cream sodas. Leaning forward on his elbows, sucking raptly, Larry became confiding, even maudlin, drooling on about soda-fountains at home, about hot-rod races and ball games and T.V. programmes.

– You got T.V. in England?

– Yes.

– You're lucky, there ain't nothin' here. How many channels?

– Channels?

– Yeah, like, how many different programmes can you get?

– Oh, just the one. Just the B.B.C.

– Just one? They both looked at him with pity and contempt.

– You have adverts on your television, don't you? said Timothy. We don't in England.

– Whaddya have between the programmes, then?

– Nothing. Just interludes.

– Inter*whats?*

– Well, they just show a picture of a field, or a waterfall, or something. While you wait for the next programme.

Larry looked suspicious.

– You havin' us on, or somethin'?

– I used to like the commercials, said Con. Some of them were really neat.

Timothy's attention was caught by some young girls who got up from a table on the other side of the room. They lingered, shuffling their feet to the rhythm of the jukebox, bantering with some boys who remained seated at the table. They all wore tight blue jeans, cut off and frayed at mid-calf. Larry brought his head close to Timothy's.

– See the girl in the yellow sweater? he murmured, the sickly-sweet scent of pistachio heavy on his breath.

– Yes, said Timothy, who had already picked her out.

– Her name's Gloria Rose. She shows her tits to guys for a dollar. In the garages back of Lincoln.

Con sniggered, and thrust his hands down between his thighs.

– Seems expensive, said Timothy. You can see quite a lot for nothing.

It was an instinctive reflex, the kind of cool, patronizing comment he had used so often to deflect challenges to his sexual experience and curiosity. The trouble was, it tended to put a stop to further conversation. He waited hopefully, eyeing the jutting breasts of Gloria Rose from under lowered lids. A dollar to see them, pink and bare. And how much would she show for five dollars? Everything, surely. He took a deep, distracted draught of his ice-cream soda, and felt a wave of nausea rise from his stomach.

– 'Scuse me, he said, getting up abruptly. He stumbled off

towards what he hoped was the toilet. If by any chance it wasn't the toilet, something terrible was going to happen.

It was unfortunate that the boys had invited him and Kate to dinner that evening, in their luxurious apartment on the top floor of one of the massive old houses that brooded like castles over the Neckar on the north side. The boys cooked and served the meal themselves, with considerable style. The table was beautifully laid, with gleaming cutlery and glass, stiff white linen and flowers. Clusters of red candles splayed out from special holders at each end. The food itself was obviously delicious, but, still queasy from the ice-cream sodas, Timothy had no appetite for it. He explained that he wasn't feeling well, and was allowed to leave the table before the meal was over. In the adjoining room was an amazing gramophone that changed records automatically, and the records themselves were of a long-playing type that he had never seen before. Greg had loaded the machine with a stack of records at the beginning of the evening, and Timothy was sufficiently entertained just watching the robot-like movement of the automatic changer.

Kath came in with her coffee, flushed and replete, and sank into a deep sofa.

– The boys wouldn't let me help clear up, and I didn't argue with them, she said. Listen, I had a word with them about Don, about Garmisch, and they weren't too keen.

– Oh.

– You won't mind if we don't invite him along, will you?

– No.

– As Greg said, these trips are no fun if there's one person who doesn't fit in.

– You think that's the real reason?

– What d'you mean?

– You don't think they're a bit . . . jealous?

Kate tittered.

– Well, there may be something of that too. What are you doing tomorrow?

– Going cycling with Rudolf, he said gloomily.

– Oh, yes. Well, have fun.

*

The bikes Rudolf provided were heavy, clumsy machines, with no gears, broad, feminine saddles and soft, fat tyres made of a curious whitish rubber. Not the sort of thing a subscriber to *Cycling* would normally be seen dead on, though he saw the advantage of the thick tyres as they bumped over the cobbles and tramlines of Heidelberg. Rudolf managed surprisingly well with his one arm, except for a certain awkwardness when starting off. Their route took them away from the mountains, into the flat, hazy plain that stretched towards the Rhine. Trams ran out into the country here – they looked comical running past fields full of cattle. The earth was baked and dry from the recent heatwave. Dust hung in the air, and exhaust fumes mingled with the smells of dung and hay. It was all very much more ordinary than the spectacular scenery of the Neckar valley. Just country.

Rudolf was full of enthusiasm for the English countryside, especially Cornwall, where he had been interned as a prisoner-of-war. It seemed queer to Timothy to be discussing the finer points of the English landscape in this context. He had seen German prisoners of war, once, in the railway sidings at Blyfield. They stared from the windows: sallow, ill-shaven faces under peaked caps, dressed in drab dungarees. A few British soldiers with slung rifles walked up and down beside the train. He watched the prisoners from the safe vantage point of a footbridge, with a mixture of pity and hatred. The train was kept waiting for nearly the whole day, and after it had gone there was a bad smell from the sidings. The villagers were indignant, and somebody in a shop said they should have been made to clean it up, it was all they were fit for. And now, a few years later, he cycled beside someone who had been such a prisoner, exchanging pleasant remarks about the English hedgerows. It was a queer world.

After a while, he summoned up the courage to ask Rudolf a question.

– Did you try to escape?

Rudolf laughed.

– Certainly not! Are you kidding? Escape – that is very good. You have no idea how happy we were to be prisoners.

– Happy?

– Naturally! We were safe, well-fed, medicine if we needed. It was like a vacation. Let me tell you, they billeted us in, how do you call it, a vacation camp?

– Holiday camp?

– *Ja*, holiday camp. Little huts beside the sea. Clean blankets. Even table tennis. It was the best part of the war for me.

A queer world.

They stopped for a picnic lunch at a swimming place – not a proper pool, but a stretch of river that had been cordoned off and provided with tents for changing, and picnic tables. Timothy didn't fancy the murky water and the squishy mud you would have to tread on before you got out of your depth. But he was glad of the opportunity to rest and cool off under the shade of some trees while Rudolf went for a dip.

Only Germans frequented the place. You could tell from their clothes, their picnic food, the bottles of wine. And the flies. There were never any flies in the American places in Heidelberg, not even at the riverside swimming pool. Rudolf was gone a long time, and Timothy couldn't pick him out among the splashing throng in the water. He suddenly felt very isolated. Supposing Rudolf had gone off and left him, for a joke? Supposing he had drowned . . . ? Timothy imagined himself sitting there with the two bicycles, as the shadows lengthened, tongue-tied and impotent. He would never be able to find his way back to Heidelberg alone.

Two young girls in swimsuits spread their towels on the grass not far from where he was sitting and sat down. They had broad, freckled peasant faces and long blonde hair in heavy plaits. He guessed they were about fifteen, though their breasts were well-developed, bobbing to and fro under what looked like hand-knitted woollen costumes. After a while he became uneasily aware that they were watching *him*. Every time he glanced in their direction he caught the flicker of an eye, a head belatedly turned aside, knuckles raised to stifle a giggle. They must have sensed that he was a stranger, and set themselves to make fun of him. At any moment they might say something to him, and what would he do then? He strained his eyes for a sight of Rudolf.

At last he came, carrying his wet costume and a bottle of mineral water in his one hand. Timothy wondered what his stump looked like when he was stripped for swimming, but was glad he had not had to see for himself. A damp cigarette dangled from Rudolf's lips, and waggled as he spoke.

– I am sorry to be a long time, but the swimming was so good. You must be hungry.

By arrangement, Rudolf had brought rolls and butter in his saddlebag, and Timothy some goodies from the P.X., tins of ham and frankfurters, and a little tube of mustard, like toothpaste. This last item seemed to throw the two young girls into throes of hilarity.

– You have made an impression, Rudolf observed.

– What's got into them? I've done nothing except sit here.

– You are sexy for them, said Rudolf disconcertingly. Your pale face and dark hair and eyes are unusual here.

– Good Lord, said Timothy, blushing, but not displeased.

Rudolf called something in German to the girls. They snatched up their towels and fled, giggling, their puppy-fat buttocks wagging.

– Silly geeses, said Rudolf, with a shrug. It is better without them, no?

– Yes, said Timothy, though he felt a certain regret as well as relief at their departure.

Rudolf, his meal finished, lay back on the grass. Timothy remained upright, propped on his locked arms.

– Rudolf, what was it like in the war in Germany? he said. He added: You don't have to talk about it if you don't want to.

– You must know that I was ten years only when the war started, Rudolf said. We lived in Munich, then. It was far from all the fighting. Out of range of your bombers for a long time. Naturally I was very excited by all the German victories. My father belonged to the Party, and had a safe job at home because of his medical category. At school they told us of the glorious German mission: to lead Europe, to resist the menace of Bolshevism. I joined the *Jungvolk*, naturally, swore to give up my life for Him at ten years. There was a picture of Him in every classroom.

As Rudolf went on, Timothy noticed that he never referred to Hitler by name, only as *He* or *Him*.

– Then the war began to go badly. The victories we were promised never happened. More and more young men were drafted, and everyone knew somebody who had been killed or wounded somewhere. Especially in Russia. I remember the fall of Stalingrad. Even He could not pretend that was a victory. There were four days of National Mourning. Cinemas and theatres were closed. Flags at half-mast. Solemn music on the radio. I think that was the first time I began to wonder why we had started the war. You see, we had been told that the Russian people welcomed our troops as liberators.

– Then a little while after, there was the Scholl affair – you know? No? Well, these two students at the University, Munich University, Hans and Sophie Scholl, they were brother and sister. They were organizing anti-Nazi propaganda among the students – those students who were left. I found one of their pamphlets in a trash-can, and brought it home. My father was frightened and beat me. Then someone betrayed the Scholls to the Gestapo. They were hanged, naturally.

– At fourteen years you were supposed to join the Hitler Youth. I said I didn't want to and I had a great fight with my father. I joined in the end, of course. It was dangerous not to. But there were many like me. Naturally there were some fanatics who couldn't wait to get into uniform. You had to be careful what you said. But most of us hoped that the war would be over before we were drafted. But we were not so lucky. Our last chance was when they tried to kill Him in the July Plot. You know about that?

– Yes, said Timothy, Vince – Mr. Vernon told me.

– I was called up at sixteen. Thank God they sent us west not east. We were supposed to be reserve troops, miles behind the front line. But the American break-out from Avranches took us by surprise.

– How were you captured?

– I knew nothing about it. I was unconscious from my wound. When I woke up I was afraid I was in a German hospital. Then a doctor said something in English and I was happy. I knew I would survive the war.

– It must seem strange, thinking of it now?

– Yes. What were you doing that summer, Timothy?

– I was in the country, a place called Blyfield.

– That sounds nice.

– There wasn't much to do. I used to chase butterflies.

Rudolf gave a little grunt of amusement.

– I was in the Blitz, though, said Timothy defensively. I was in a shelter and the house it belonged to was hit by a bomb. A little girl I used to play with was killed, and her mother.

It all came back to him suddenly, and it was as if a cloud had passed over the sun. Jill and Auntie Nora, killed in the garden. And Uncle Jack afterwards, shot down over Germany. He felt a sudden coldness towards Rudolf. Not that he was to blame personally: but it seemed a kind of betrayal of the dead to be, to be . . . well, too easy and friendly with a German. Surely if two countries hated each other enough to kill each other in hundreds and thousands, the hate ought to last a bit longer than six years?

As soon as he had formulated the question in his mind he saw that there could be another answer. If the hate was so short-lived, then perhaps the war itself had been pointless. But Hitler had to be stopped – even Rudolf admitted that. But then, to listen to Rudolf, you would think the Germans had hated Hitler as much as the British. But that couldn't be true, surely. It couldn't have been just one man who was responsible – there must have been plenty of others willing to do what he told them. Like the people who ran the camps. That alone must have taken quite a lot of people as wicked as Hitler.

– Did you know about the Jews? he asked recklessly.

Rudolf smiled wryly.

– Ah, that is, what do the Americans call it, the sixty-four-thousand-dollar question. Every German of a certain age lives in fear of it.

– Because they did know?

– Know what? That is the problem. Of course we knew that something nasty was happening to the Jews, believe nobody who tells you different. But most of us didn't know how nasty. And it was dangerous to ask questions.

– But if some people *had* asked . . .

Rudolf shrugged.

– I am not excusing. I am trying to explain. We lived in fear. If you cannot understand, that is lucky for you.

Something Don had said to him came into Timothy's head: *History is the verdict of the lucky on the unlucky, of those who weren't there on those who were. Historians are so goddam smug.*

Rudolf stood up and stretched.

– It is time to go. Are you rested?

– Yes, said Timothy, getting to his feet. Your parents – what happened to them?

– They survived, Rudolf said. You will meet them this afternoon.

– This afternoon? He was gripped by a sudden panic.
– Yes, they live not far from here. They will give us coffee.

Rudolf's parents lived in a small hamlet which they approached by a cart track, bumping slowly over the sunbaked ruts and potholes. The air was oppressively still and silent, disturbed only by the buzzing of flies and the scuffling of chickens in the dust of the village square – a half-cobbled, irregular open space with a pump in the middle. A small barefooted boy put his bucket down to stare at them as they dismounted. Timothy was aware of other curious glances, from behind window panes, and from shadowy doorways. He felt depressed and uneasy, and wished himself away from the place.

The silence was broken by a small mongrel bitch that came darting out of somewhere and began barking and snapping at them. An old woman scuttled out of one of the cottages and began to beat the animal savagely with the flat of her hand. It yelped and whined, dragging its belly in the dirt. Rudolf spoke to the woman in German and she straightened up with a final kick at the dog. Timothy heard the word *Englisch*, and saw the old woman shooting curious, furtive glances at him. The small boy maintained his fixed, watchful stance. Timothy had never felt so far from home.

They wheeled their bicycles down a narrow lane, smelling of honeysuckle and dung, to reach the cottage where Rudolf's parents lived. It was small and dark, overcrowded with heavy furniture, but pleasantly cool after the heat of the sun. Rudolf's mother welcomed them, kissing her son on both cheeks and shaking hands with Timothy, and led them into the parlour. She was a plump, grey-haired woman with rosy cheeks and ill-fitting false teeth. She nodded her head all the time during conversation, like a doll on the back shelf of a car.

– My father is working in the garden, said Rudolf. Shall we go out to him?

Timothy followed with a certain trepidation. From Rudolf's remarks about his childhood he had constructed a rather sinister image of the father. When they turned round behind the cottage into the garden, and saw him, dressed in singlet and trousers, squatting on the ground with his back towards them, attending to some plants, Timothy's heart missed a beat: the broad, muscle-bound shoulders, the bumpy, shaven, iron-grey skull, instantly recalled the brutal-faced man he had encountered at the drinking fountain near the castle in Heidelberg.

– *Vater!* Rudolf called.

Timothy almost flinched as he stood up and turned to face them. But it was not the face he feared. It was a rather melancholy, gentle face, an aged, sunken replica of Rudolf's own, lined and burnt by the sun. For all that, he was an ex-Nazi, the first certified specimen Timothy had met, and he experienced a slight queasiness as they shook hands, the old man wiping his own on a handkerchief first and evidently apologizing for their earthiness. He tried a few words of English on Timothy, about the heat, about Heidelberg, then led them round the garden, Rudolf commenting volubly and translating for Timothy, who made inarticulate noises of admiration and approval. They went back into the house, where Rudolf's mother had prepared coffee and cakes. The father left them for a moment and reappeared, wearing a shirt and carrying a bottle from which he poured Timothy a tiny glass of some transparent liquor. Timothy took a sip which burned his throat and made him choke. Rudolf and his father laughed, but the mother looked concerned and brought him a glass of water. He declined it politely, fearing that it had come from the village pump.

After half an hour he was impatient to be gone. He did not understand the conversation and had no real wish to. Jokes were made in German, laughed at, and handed to him in translation, like slices of cake, so that he could contribute his belated smile. Noticing, perhaps, that he was bored, Rudolf's father beckoned Timothy over to a large cabinet radio which stood in one corner of the room.

– My father asks if you would like to listen to the B.B.C., Rudolf explained. It is a very powerful set. Ten valves. My father is very proud of it.

The set began to hum as it warmed up. Then, through a crackle of static, faint, but quite audible, there came the sound of a very English voice:

. . . bowls, and Edrich pushes it away on the leg side, Stewart comes in quickly from mid-wicket, and there's no run. That's the end of Bedser's seventh over of this spell and his third maiden . . .

– Cricket! Timothy exclaimed.

Rudolf's father looked puzzled.

– Krick? he seemed to say.

Rudolf laughed.

– He thinks you mean *Krieg*: war.

– No, not war. Cricket, the game.

– I know it, I have seen them playing in Cornwall.

Rudolf explained to his father, who smiled and nodded. His mother also nodded, more vigorously than ever, as if her head was about to topple off her shoulders. He had a momentary impression of being in a room full of animated dolls, like the carved figures on German clocks, all madly nodding.

– You wish to listen? Rudolf asked him.

– Please. It's Surrey and Middlesex. I support Surrey.

So for the rest of their stay he was happily absolved from social intercourse. He sat beside the radio, in the strange German room, with the unintelligible German conversation going on around him, connected by a thin thread of sound to the place he belonged to, from which he had set out – was it only two weeks ago? He remembered going past the Oval on the bus, and seeing the overnight score. It was as if he had been cast far out into deep waters, then, to drift and swim as best he could among strange currents; and now, in the furthest, strangest place he had reached, he felt an unexpected, reassuring tug on the rope. How sane and secure and familiar it was, the commentator's voice: relaxed, good-humoured, knowledgeable, finding significance in the tiniest detail.

> *. . . and I think that Laker – yes, Laker is going round the wicket now. He's marking out his run, and Compton is taking fresh guard. And this should be very interesting. I should say that Laker's going to try and drop the ball on that spot where he got one to lift and turn quite sharply just now – and, yes, Compton is going down the wicket to have a look at it . . .*

Timothy bent his head over the set as the voice faded momentarily on the airwaves. Rudolf, listening attentively to his father, caught his eye and flashed a brief smile.

– I hope it was not too dull for you, said Rudolf, as they cycled away from the village, the small boy still staring after them.

– No, I enjoyed it. It was great, hearing the cricket.

– It is good that you see a German home, no? You must not come to Germany and meet only Americans.

– Oh yes, absolutely.

Timothy spoke sincerely. Now that the visit was behind them and they were headed back to familiar territory, he felt a glow of righteousness at having braved the German interior to mingle with the natives.

– Your parents are very nice, he said politely.

– Thank you. They are also very sad.

Rudolf proceeded to tell him something of his parents' fortunes as they cycled side by side. His father had been a local government official in Munich. At the end of the war he had lost his job and his pension because of his connections with the Party. They had moved from Munich to this village to be near Rudolf, on whom they were totally dependent. There had been two other sons, older than Rudolf: one had been drowned in a U-boat, sunk in the Atlantic; the other had been taken prisoner in Russia and never heard of since.

– It is a very poor, dull life for them here, said Rudolf. But the cottage is cheap.

From Rudolf's account of his wartime childhood earlier that day, Timothy had cast him as an enlightened rebel against a compromised and corrupt father; but Rudolf surprised him by his vehement defence of his father.

– It is not fair, you understand. The little men suffer while the big ones go free. There are many high-up Nazis in positions of power today. In government, in business, in the universities. Men with records much worse than my father. Some were sent to prison at Nuremberg, but now the Americans are releasing them in crowds, and they are better off than my father, who was no criminal.

– What did he do exactly? Timothy felt he was treading on thin ice, but an irresistible curiosity egged him on.

– He worked in the *Rathaus* of Munich, the Town Hall you would say. He worked in the taxation department. Then one day – it was in 1943 – he was transferred to the Rationing Department, and it happened that he had to stamp the ration books for the prisoners in Dachau. After the war it was told that most of the ration books belonged to dead men. I know my father never guessed that was the fact, whatever else he may have known. I remember him worrying about the black market in rations in the city. *I can't understand where the food is coming from*, he would say. He was an honest man. But after the war, no one believed him.

– Can't he appeal, or something?

– He is too proud. Sometimes I think of writing to the authorities. They are getting easier about such matters. But then he would have to answer questions and so on. It would bring back unhappy memories, and perhaps nothing would come of it in the end.

– Why don't you ask Vince, Mr. Vernon, about it?

– Miss Young's friend?

– He deals with that sort of thing in his work.

– Does he? I did not know.

– He might be able to help.

– Yes, said Rudolf thoughtfully. He seems very friendly, I must say. He always gives me a smile as he passes my office at Fichte Haus.

– 'Course, I don't know if he could do anything. It was just an idea, said Timothy, having sudden doubts. What was Rudolf's father to Vince, or to himself for that matter? What on earth was he doing, trying to help an ex-Nazi get his pension? A queer world. He pedalled on in silence for a while.

– I'm afraid I have brought you too far, said Rudolf.

– No, it's all right. I cycle a lot in England. It must be tiring for you, though, riding one-handed.

– I am used to it. But it would be fine to have a car, no? Like Mr. Vernon's Mercedes. That is quite a car.

– It's terrific. I went to Baden in it last weekend.

– Fast?

– Fantastic acceleration. But can you drive, Rudolf?

– I learned in the Army.

– I mean . . . Timothy glanced at Rudolf's damaged arm.

– Oh yes. I can hold the wheel with this (he raised his stump) and change gear with my good hand.

Timothy must have looked dubious. Rudolf laughed.

– It is quite safe, I assure you.

– Kids, said Don, I want you to meet a friend of mine from England. Timothy Young.

The class, scattered around the room in various indolent postures

– on desks, on chairs, on window ledges – regarded him with mild curiosity. A boy with thick glasses sitting at the front said, *Hi!* very loudly. Timothy smiled hesitantly from beside Don's desk. The set-up was not quite what he had expected. The class was of mixed sexes and ages, ranging from about twelve to sixteen. There was no evidence of any organized work in progress. An atmosphere of relaxed indiscipline prevailed. The pupils addressed Don by his first name. Most disconcerting of all was the presence of Gloria Rose, lolling in a seat at the back of the class, filing her nails, a book open on her desk. She said nothing all the time he was in the classroom, only making expressions of impatience at the remarks and questions volunteered by others.

– Timothy has very kindly volunteered to tell us something about his country, said Don. Timothy, it's all yours.

Don left him standing alone at the front of the class, and went to sit at one of the desks in the back row. Timothy straightened his tie (it was his school one, specially put on for the occasion) and cleared his throat.

– Well, er . . . I don't know what they want to know, he said to Don.

– What d'you want to know, kids?

After a silence, a girl with metal braces on her teeth asked:

– Does the King of England wear his crown all the time?

– No, Timothy answered confidently.

The questions began to come thick and fast then:

– Do you have Democrats and Republicans?

– Do you play baseball?

– Do British kids pet?

A titter ran round the class at that one, and Timothy looked to Don, expecting a reproof, but none was forthcoming.

– I don't know, he said. I go to a boys' school myself.

The audience laughed, as if he had made a joke.

The real difficulties started when he rashly attempted to give a geographical description of the British Isles. He drew a stylized map on the blackboard: a rough triangle for England, a bulge on one side for Wales, and another inverted triangle on top for Scotland. A parallelogram over to the left for Ireland. He marked the position of London confidently, but after that he was at something of a loss. English geography had never been his strong point. He had dropped the subject in the Fourth Form, when O-Level choices were made, and he had never been north of London in his life. He hesitated over marking in Manchester, eventually putting it in just below Scotland, in the middle. Some members of the class called out the names of various cities, Birmingham, Oxford and York, and he dotted them in vaguely around Manchester. He shaded most of the northern half of England and explained that this was the Black Country.

– It's where all the mines and factories are. There's such a lot of smoke and soot that the fields are all black. That's why it's called the Black Country.

This was what he had always assumed. The name had evoked for him a vivid mental picture of flakes of soot falling like snow and setting on the fields, black corn waving in the wind under a pall of smoke. In his mind's eye the whole of Northern England was like that. But as he uttered this description, it sounded rather improbable, and out of the corner of his eye he caught a suspicion of a grin on Don's face.

Don thanked him warmly for talking to them, first on behalf of the class, and again privately in the corridor. He said it had been very interesting, and that the kids had obviously got a kick out of it. But, going out of the school, Timothy lost his way and retraced his steps, passing Don's classroom again. He heard him saying, *Manchester, for instance, isn't quite as far north as this, and it's further west* . . . There was the scuffing of a blackboard rubber and the squeak of chalk. Timothy felt mortified but also resentful. It wasn't fair of Don to have lured him into this situation, allowing him to make a fool of himself in front of Gloria and the rest. He felt ill-rewarded for his efforts to get Don invited to join the party going to Garmisch, and rather glad, now, that he hadn't succeeded.

It served him right, of course. He had always known that it was deeply, shamefully wrong to eavesdrop on the woman next door. Time and again he had resolved, in the daylight of good intentions, to stop, to break the habit, only to find himself at the end of the day drawn irresistibly back to the cupboard and its promise of whispered, forbidden secrets. And now he was punished. God was not mocked.

He prayed to God, now, promising that if he got out of the cupboard safely, he would never open it again. And he would say the whole Rosary every night and go to Mass every morning for a month when he got home. Having hopefully offered this bargain, he tried the door again, but it didn't budge. He had never completely closed the door behind him before, always leaving it open a crack for air; but this evening he had pulled it a little too hard and the lock had clicked shut. There was no handle on the inside. How idiotic to make a cupboard like that! Anyone could easily lock themselves inside. People could suffocate. At the thought, his chest tightened and he began to gasp for air. He quelled his panic and tried to think calmly. In the darkness he explored the lock carefully with his fingers and confirmed that there was no way of dismantling it without a screwdriver.

He had two alternatives; or rather, three. He could call for help, which was out of the question – he couldn't bear to even think of the humiliation of being released by a curious crowd of women in dressing-gowns, military police, firemen . . . He could break his way out by charging the door, for it was flimsy enough, but this would alarm his nextdoor neighbour, with consequent risk of exposure. Or he could spend the night in the cupboard and break out in the morning when everybody had left the building. This was obviously the most prudent plan, but he wondered whether he had the stamina to wait out the night on the floor of the cupboard. Then there was the problem of air supply. There was the hole in the party wall, and the cracks around the door, but already the interior of the cupboard felt stuffy.

In the end he compromised. He would wait until the woman nextdoor was asleep (he could hear her radio playing) and then he would break out, hoping that, even if the noise woke her, she wouldn't know what it was or where it had come from.

Time passed very slowly. Hours seemed to pass before the radio was turned off and the light went out behind the chink in the wall. By an immense effort of will he restrained himself from moving for what he calculated was another three-quarters of an hour. At this point he was aching in every limb, soaked in perspiration and on the verge of hysteria. He couldn't wait a moment longer.

It was essential to the success of his plan that he should break out in one clean smash. One loud noise, and then silence – that was his strategy. He took a deep breath and launched himself at the door.

The door did not budge, but the cupboard boomed like a drum and about a hundred wire hangers fell to the floor. Frantically, all discretion gone, he charged the door again. And again. A panel cracked and split, but the lock, the bloody, bloody, bloody, blasted lock wouldn't give.

The light came on behind the chink in the wall, and a woman's voice said sharply:

– What's that? Who's that?

Timothy, breathing heavily and nursing his bruised shoulder, said nothing.

– Dolores? Are you back already? Is that you, Dolores? Listen, I don't know who the hell you are or what you're doing in Dolores Grey's room, but I'm going to report you right now.

– No, don't do that, Timothy said.

There was a surprised silence. Then:

– Who's that? Who are you?

– Er . . . my name's Timothy Young.

Oh God, oh God.

– Yeah? Keep talking.

– I'm locked in this cupboard.

There was a high, full-throated laugh from the next room.

– Well, I'm darned. Who locked you in there?

– I locked myself in, accidentally.

– What are you, a burglar, or something?

– No, I'm . . . I'm a friend of Dolores. She let me use her room while she was away.

– You're not American, are you?

– I'm English.

– English! How long have you been in the closet?

– About three hours, I should think.

– Jesus! You must be suffocated. I'll go get somebody to let you out.

– No, don't do that.

– Why not?

– Well, I'm not really supposed to be here. I mean, Dolores let me, but it's not official. She might get into trouble, because I'm not a woman.

– Yeah, I kind of figured that. But you can't stay in the closet till Dolores gets back from her vacation.

After a pause for thought, Timothy ventured a suggestion:

– Could *you* let me out? It just needs someone to turn the handle from outside.

– Is the door to your room locked?

– Yes, I'm afraid it is, he said miserably.

– O.K., I'll go get the master.

– Don't tell him I'm here.

She chuckled.

– How do I know you won't jump on me and rape me as soon as I open the door?

– I won't, I promise.

Again the high, full-throated laugh.

– O.K. Timothy, I'll trust you. I hope I don't live to regret it. How old are you, anyway?

– Sixteen.

– Is that all? Hold on, kid, I'll be back directly.

While she was gone he could think of nothing. His mind was as dark and vacant as the cupboard. He waited passively, like a casualty waiting for the ambulance to arrive, withdrawn into some deep centre of himself. Then he heard the sound of a key in the lock of the door to his room, and footsteps. The cupboard door opened. He blinked in the sudden light and stumbled out into the room, almost falling against the woman.

– Easy! she exclaimed, and steadied him with a firm hand. You'd better sit down for a minute.

– Thank you, he said, and sank into the armchair.

– Don't mention it. Cigarette?

She took the pack from her dressing-gown pocket.

– No thanks.

She lit a cigarette and sat down opposite him on the divan bed.

– I'm awfully sorry about this, he said. Waking you up and everything.

– Don't worry about it. I don't sleep too good, anyway. She flashed him a sudden, generously curved smile. Tell me about yourself.

He told her, briefly. She knew Kate, by sight.

– But you won't tell her about tonight, will you? he pleaded.

– I can keep a secret, she assured him. But so can you, obviously. How did you manage to live here for two weeks without anyone finding out? By the way, excuse my appearance, but I wasn't expecting company.

She gestured towards the huge plastic curlers on her head, covered by a gauze scarf. She could never, he thought, be described as pretty, even if she were looking her best. There wasn't a single feature or limb that wasn't somehow odd or out of proportion. Her face was too small, or her mouth too wide; her chest was flat and her long arms and legs jutted out at odd angles, like a grasshopper's. But there was something about her attitude, her expression, that refused to apologize for her body, and thus made it surprisingly attractive. As she crossed her legs, the skirt of her dressing-gown fell away, and she didn't pull it back into position. She didn't appear to be wearing a nightgown underneath. What he knew, or had imagined, about this woman flooded into his mind like a rush of blood. His flesh stiffened, and he folded his hands on his lap, striving to subdue and conceal it.

– You sure you feel O.K? Like some aspirin or something? I got enough pills in my room to dope an army.

– No thanks, I'll be all right now.

He stood up to indicate that she could leave.

– Let me get you some aspirin. You look kind of pale. By the way, my name's Jinx Dobell.

– Pleased to meet you, he said, feeling foolish, standing there in his pyjamas. Her green eyes were bright above a crescent smile.

– You're a big boy for your age, Timothy.

He couldn't think of anything to say to that, never having thought of himself as particularly big, especially compared with American boys of his age.

After she had gone, he discovered that the fly of his pyjama trousers was gaping open. He put on his dressing-gown and sat down in the chair again, waiting apprehensively for the woman's return. The only good thing was that she didn't seem to suspect he had been spying on her.

When she came back into the room, her face wasn't so shiny and she had taken the curlers out of her hair, so that it hung down to her shoulders. She carried a tray on which there were two glasses, a bottle of brandy and a small bottle of aspirin.

– I thought maybe you would prefer a stiff drink.

– No thank you.

– Don't smoke, don't drink . . . What's your vice? It must be girls.

– I will have a cigarette, actually, if you've got one to spare.

– Sure.

She gave him a cigarette that seemed as long as a flagpole, and he managed to puff at it without coughing. She poured herself a generous measure of brandy, and added some water from the tap. Then she perched on the bed, with her back against the wall, and her knees drawn up in front of her. She rested her sharp chin on her knees and looked at him.

– Well, she said, with a smile.

He shifted uncomfortably under her gaze.

– Pardon my asking, she said, but how d'you manage about the john?

– John who?

– I mean, the bathroom, the toilet, the . . .

– Oh, I, er, wait till no one's around.

– I can't get over it. It's like Don Juan in the harem. Ever read that poem? By Lord Byron?

– No, we haven't done Byron at school.

– You should, it's fantastic. I read it in a course I took in my Junior year, the Romantic poets.

She began telling him a story about a boy in the olden days who got into a Turkish harem, disguised as a young girl. He didn't attend very closely because he was distracted by the fact that the skirt of her dressing-gown had slipped away from her knees. Her knees were together and all he could see were two long shins and the white underpart of one thigh. But if she should open her knees . . . Even as he formed the thought, her knees parted perhaps half an inch. He felt his flesh stiffen again, and looked away hastily, at the wall, at the floor. His eyes strayed back almost at once, but all was dark shadow between the legs. Unaware of her immodest posture, she was still talking about poetry.

– I just adore the English Romantics, don't you?

– Yes, he croaked, his mouth dry.

– Who's your favourite?

– We're doing Wordsworth at school, he said. Was it his imagination, or had her knees moved another half inch further apart?

– Oh, I used to be crazy about Wordsworth!
She threw back her head and began to recite:

And I have felt
A presence that disturbs me with the joy
Of elevated thoughts; a sense sublime
Of something far more deeply interfused . . .

Her limbs loosened with every line, the white thighs parting like sticks of celery, and he realized, his heart pounding, that there was nothing accidental about it, that she was purposely letting him see.

– I can't remember how it goes on, but it's beautiful, she murmured, her eyes half-closed, legs half-open.

Fearing that this lapse of memory might break the spell, he began hoarsely to recite *The Daffodils*, which was the only Wordsworth poem he could think of:

I wandered lonely as a cloud
That floats on high o'er vales and hills . . .

– Oh yes! She picked it up:

When all at once I saw a crowd,
A host, of golden daffodils . . .

And now, in shameless abandon, her legs fell slackly apart, and he saw. But what did he see? Not the smooth, pearl-pink little dimpled cleft of his mind's eye, but hair, a beard of vivid ginger hair, dense and wiry as a fox's tail, shadowing vertical lips of loose, brownish skin. He lowered his eyes.

And then my heart with pleasure fills,
And dances with the daffodils.

She ended, and said, conversationally:
– Ever screwed a girl, Timothy?
He shook his head, not meeting her eyes.
– I figured you hadn't. Want to?

He shook his head a second time. There was a long silence. Then the bed springs creaked as she stood up.

– Well, never let it be said that I forced a virgin against his will. I enjoyed the poetry, anyway. Another time we might try Whitman. Do you know any Walt Whitman?

> *Who goes there? Hankering, gross, mystical, nude:*
> *How is it I extract strength from the beef I eat?*

– No, he whispered, shaking his head.

– No, she said, I guess you wouldn't. Goodnight, Timothy.

He sat in the chair, quite still, a long time after she had gone.

3

He woke to an unfamiliar sensation of rocking movement, and the muffled clatter and rattle of the train. In the bunk beneath him, Mel snored. Vince and Greg slept quietly in the two berths opposite, their faces eerily tinted by the blue nightlight that dimly illuminated the compartment. He turned and drew up the blind over a small window at his side. A prospect of extraordinary beauty dazzled him.

The train was winding through a fir forest overhung by huge mountains. Proper mountains – not the tree-covered humps of the Neckar valley and the Black Forest, but great soaring masses of grey rock, peaked and fissured, some still capped with snow, mountains such as he had only seen in pictures till now. The dawn cast upon their flanks a rosy reflected glow that slowly faded as he leaned on his elbow and gazed entranced. It was the fulfilment of a persistent dream of his childhood, a dream of effortless travel or exploration conducted under ideal conditions. How often, before dropping off to sleep, he had transformed his bed, in his imagination, into some fantastic and as yet uninvented vehicle – low, streamlined, caterpillar-tracked, indestructible, unstoppable, impervious to extremes of climate – and set it moving across vast deserts and icy steppes, lolling at the controls and gazing through the windscreen at the hostile but impotent landscape, devouring mile after mile, an endless journey at once heroic and luxuriously comfortable.

There was a knock on the door of the compartment, and a steward came in with steaming coffee. He switched on the light and announced:

– Garmisch-Partenkirchen thirty minutes!

The men yawned, and stretched.

– We're going through some fantastic mountains, said Timothy. You should have a look.

– The Alps, kid, said Greg.

Alps entirely surrounded the Rest Centre, a vast hotel, timbered and balconied, built on the shore of a big lake called the Eibsee, about half an hour's drive from Garmisch. Timothy had a room to himself next to Kate's, with a connecting balcony from which she pointed out to him the Zugspitz, the highest mountain in Germany. As they gazed, the calm surface of the lake was disturbed by a motor boat that came into sight, drawing behind it a man on skis.

– Is that water-skiing? he exclaimed. I've only seen it on the pictures before. Is it difficult?

– Once you get going, it's easy, or so they tell me. I've never succeeded in getting started.

– What's the water like?

– Cold, it's glacier water. But wonderfully refreshing.

He was able to verify this later. After breakfast, they all walked round the rim of the lake to a small bathing beach, with a diving raft moored a few yards out from the shore and a life-guard seated on it. Timothy and Kate were first in the water. The cold made him gasp, but afterwards, drying off in the warm sun, a delicious sense of well-being spread through his body.

– This is a fantastic place, Kate, he murmured.

At lunch Ruth suddenly said:

– Kate, isn't that your G.I. over there?

– My G.I?

– At the table by the window. The Jewish-looking guy we met at the pool that day.

– Don! Timothy exclaimed. What's he doing here?

Kate blushed and frowned.

– He's got a nerve.

– How d'you mean? Ruth asked. Did he know you were coming here?

Kate nodded.

– He was fishing for an invitation to come with us.

– How exciting! He must have it real bad.

– Don't let it worry you, Kate, said Vince. You don't have to take any notice of him.

– Well, I can't just ignore him, can I?

– I don't see why not.

Kate turned to Timothy.

– Did you know he was going to come here, Timothy?

– No, he replied, honestly. But he felt obscurely responsible for the intrusion.

– He's seen us, said Ruth, and waved.

– Ruth, for God's sake, don't, Kate scolded. But Don came boldly over to greet them.

– Well, hi, everybody! he said with a forced casualness.

– Hallo, said Kate coldly.

– Like it here, Timothy?

– It's very nice, he managed to say, smiling uncomfortably.

A chilly silence followed, which Ruth broke:

– Did you come on the overnight train, Don?

– No, I hitched a ride yesterday. Coupla guys I know were driving to Munich.

– How are you going to get back?

– Oh, I'm planning to stay on a while. I got fired from my job, you see.

– Fired? said Kate quickly. Why?

– Well, that's not what they called it, but that's what it was. Seems somebody passed the word along that I was a conscientious objector once. I guess they thought I might corrupt the kids. You can't be too careful about pinkoes these days, am I right?

He swept them with a sardonic grin and glanced at his watch.

– There's a bus trip to the Linderhof castle this afternoon – anyone going? No? Well, I'll see you around, no doubt.

When he was gone, Kate turned angrily to Vince.

– Vince, did you say anything to anyone?

– What d'you mean, honey?

– About Don. You and Greg were the only people I told.

– Not guilty, said Greg, raising his hands in a gesture of surrender.

– What's all this about? Ruth demanded.

– Ask Vince, said Kate, frowning after the departing figure of Don.

Vince explained:

– Our friend told Timothy, here, that he was a C.O. one time. Timothy told Kate and Kate told us. Now he thinks we leaked it to the Education Department. As if there were no such thing as files.

– Well, you can't blame him, can you? Kate said. She got up abruptly and followed Don into the lobby. She returned a few minutes later.

– I told him we had nothing to do with his losing his job, she announced. And I asked him to join us this evening. To show there's no ill-will.

She met Vince's eyes defiantly. He shrugged his shoulders.

– Fine, honey, if that's the way you want it.

Timothy anticipated the evening with considerable misgivings. He felt in the awkward position of a neutral country between two enemies, with reasons to be friendly to both, but driven to make a commitment one way or the other. In the event everything went much more smoothly that he had dared to hope, and it was Mel, rather than Vince, who clashed with Don. Rather to Timothy's surprise, neither Vince nor Greg tried to assert any prior claims on Kate. Kate herself, evidently anxious to atone for any offence, real or imagined, gave Don most of her attention, and danced with him a lot, while Vince devoted himself to Maria, who fairly blossomed under his charm. Greg flirted mockingly with Ruth, while Mel, who disliked dancing, got steadily drunk.

In consequence of this pairing off, Timothy found himself left alone at the table with Mel a good deal. Mel was talking obsessively about the war, which was quite interesting, except that he kept going on about the superiority of the American armies in a way that Timothy found rather annoying. He had his own convictions, imbibed somewhere in childhood, that the British were the tougher soldiers, Americans requiring a constant supply of modern comforts in the front line and frequent rest periods. The others came back from the dance floor when Mel was in full spate about the overcautiousness of Montgomery after D-Day, and Don immediately upset him by saying that of course the war was won and lost in Russia.

– Maybe that school wasn't so stupid to fire you, after all, Mel said rudely.

– Cut that out, Mel, said Ruth.

– Don's right, you know, said Vince unexpectedly. You only have to look at the casualty figures on the Eastern front. There was never a battle like Stalingrad in the West.

– I was with the Third Army – I know what I'm talking about! Mel almost shouted.

– You were Quartermaster in a catering supply depot, honey, said Ruth. You saw more cans of condensed milk than shell-cases, so stop shooting your mouth off.

Mel looked for one moment as if he was going to hit her. Kate desperately changed the subject.

– What about this Burgess and Maclean affair? Has there been any news lately?

The choice of topic was not particularly fortunate. Don perversely defended the ineptitude of British security:

– The countries with the most efficient secret services are the most repressive. Just think of Russia. America is more security-conscious than Britain, and the price we pay is McCarthy and J. Edgar Hoover.

– Joe McCarthy is a great American, Mel growled.

– McCarthy is a bum, said Vince coolly, and in due course will be shown to be one.

– Hell, whose side are you on, Vince? Mel complained.

– Yours, of course, said Vince, with his imperturbable smile. But let's face it, McCarthy is not doing America any good. All he's doing is giving liberals, like Don here, a persecution complex.

– Of course, I feel sorry for *her*, said Ruth.

– What the hell are you talking about? Mel demanded.

– Mrs. Maclean.

– We're not talking about Maclean, we're talking about McCarthy.

– You may be, but I'm not. Imagine him leaving her when she was eight months pregnant.

– I wonder if she knew, said Kate.

– Of course she knew. Think I wouldn't know if Mel were passing secrets to the Russians?

And so the conversation resumed a lighter note, more drinks were ordered, and Mel sulked in silence. Only when he was left alone with Timothy again did he unburden himself.

– It's true what that bitch of a wife of mine said, that I never saw any action personally, but I was a helluva lot closer to it than your pal Kowalski, and I was proud – I'm not ashamed to use the word – I was proud to be with the Third Army. Patton was a bastard in many ways, but he was a kind of genius, too, and he made his men do the impossible. There was never anything like it in the history of warfare, kid, the way he pushed his armour through. Those guys drove their Shermans like they were driving hot-rods down the turnpike. The Krauts were paralysed by the sheer speed of it. They still used horses and carts, you know, the Krauts, and the Russians. Our boys were the only soldiers in Europe who'd grown up with the automobile, took it for granted, and knew how to use it. And they used it with . . . well, I can't explain, but it was as if they were all in some goddam movie or something, and they were bound to win and the wounds weren't real. They were, of course.

His bloodshot rheumy eyes stared into his glass, which he rotated slowly, chinking the ice-cubes against its sides. He added:

– But it gave them a kind of courage which was very fine.

Timothy kept a respectful silence. He was strangely moved.

The next morning, after a late breakfast, everyone except Timothy went down to the shore to the water-skiing jetty. He arranged to meet them later, after attending a Mass he had seen announced for 10 o'clock in the Rest Centre. It was celebrated in the main lounge with rows of easy chairs instead of pews, in which the congregration lolled and stretched out their legs during the sermon, which the priest delivered in a casual drawl, and sprinkled liberally with jokes. It wasn't exactly religion but, like most things American, it was fun.

He was in no particular hurry to try his hand at the water skiing, though if Kate had the nerve to attempt it, he could hardly avoid doing so with honour. As it happened, he was too late. Coming out on to the terrace, blinking in the bright sunshine, he met Kate, being carried by Vince and Don. All were in wet swimming costumes. Kate tried to smile at him, but her face was white with pain. Ruth came clucking up the steps behind them, followed by Maria, and Mel.

– Just twisted my ankle a bit, Timothy, said Kate. Not to worry.

– You ought to have a doctor look at it, said Don, it's beginning to swell already.

– I'll see to it, said Ruth, as the two men carried Kate inside.

– She seemed to get her skis crossed somehow, Mel said. I've never seen it happen like that before.

– What a shame! I hope she is not broken, said Maria. I told her to give up, but she must have another try.

– We thought she was laughing because she'd taken another nose-dive starting off, said Mel. Then we realized she was in distress. Vince and Kowalski jumped in and held her up until the boat came back to pick her up. She screamed as they pulled her out of the water. Jesus! I thought she'd broken a leg for sure. But it looks like just a sprain.

The doctor confirmed this diagnosis. Kate was to rest the ankle completely. He advised her not to travel till the end of the week, at the earliest.

– Well, said Kate, grinning wanly at them as they gathered round her bed afterwards, it looks like I've got myself an extended vacation. You too, Timothy, unless you want to go back to Heidelberg with the others.

– I'd rather stay with you, he said. But what about Mum and Dad? They're expecting me back on Wednesday.

– We can wire them.

– I'd stay, if I could, honey, said Vince. But Greg and I have a meeting in Frankfurt tomorrow.

– Oh, I'll be fine, said Kate. Timothy will look after me.

– And Don's staying on – isn't that right? Ruth said.

Don, who had disappeared, now returned carrying what looked like an old-fashioned fireguard.

– I thought you might find this useful, he said to Kate.

– What in God's name is that for – to keep the flies off her face? Ruth squawked.

– No, to keep the bedclothes off her foot.

Don lifted the bedclothes at the end of the bed and inserted the fireguard, which made a hump over the injured foot.

– Well, said Ruth with a high-pitched laugh, we're leaving you in good hands, honey, that's for sure. She nudged Don as she added: I bet you're a great physiotherapist, too, huh?

Idyllic days followed. Many guests left the Rest Centre at the end of the weekend. The vast building was only half full, and the lake shore uncrowded. The weather remained fair. After a couple of days, Kate was allowed up on crutches, and the management provided a wheel-chair in which Don and Timothy could push her around for walks. In the evenings they played cards together, or listened to records in the music room, classical ones that Don chose. There was one called *Tapiola*, by Sibelius, that they liked to listen to sitting at the window as the light faded on the mountains and a mist rose from the surface of the lake.

On the Wednesday, Timothy went on the bus excursion that Don had taken earlier to Linderhof, where there was an extraordinary castle built by the mad king Ludwig of Bavaria, with a hall of mirrors and huge fountains and a grotto made out of *papier mâché*. He enjoyed the expedition so much that he went off the very next day to see another of Ludwig's castles, at Neuschwanstein. It was further away than Linderhof, and the trip would take all day. When they were about halfway to their destination, however, the bus was caught in a violent thunderstorm. The driver halted the bus on the mountain road and they cowered under a deafening bombardment of hailstones that completely obscured the valley below. In fifteen minutes the storm had passed and the sun was shining again, but a landslip further along the road blocked their progress and they had to turn back. The driver had to steer the bus in reverse for two miles, round twisting bends with a sheer drop on one side, before he reached a place where he could turn round.

Full of this adventure, Timothy hastened up to his room at the Rest Centre, dumped his belongings on his bed, and went out on to the balcony where Kate and Don often sat looking out over the lake. The balcony was empty, but Kate's french window was wide open. He walked along the balcony and looked into the room.

Kate and Don were lying on the bed. They were naked except for the bandage around Kate's ankle and the fireguard that incongruously covered it. Don had his face pillowed on one enormous milk-white breast, while his hand clasped the other, a rosy nipple peeping between his splayed fingers. Kate was lying on her back with her eyes closed, one arm thrown across Don's neck and shoulders. She was smiling in her sleep as if dreaming of something pleasant. Her belly rose and fell as she breathed. At her crotch there was a thick bush of black curly hair.

He went softly back along the balcony, through his room and down the stairs. He went out of the lobby, across the terrace, and down the road to the lake shore. All he could think of doing was to put as much space as possible between himself and Kate's room.

At the jetty where the water-skiers started from, a motor launch was filling up with passengers for a cruise on the lake. Somnambulistically, he lined up, paid his fare, and took a seat. There were not many passengers, and he wondered irritably why a plump, sandy-haired G.I. chose to sit down right beside him. The young man was festooned with leather cases of various shapes and sizes, suspended from his neck and shoulders by straps. He opened the largest of these cases and took out a film camera. As the motor launch chugged out towards the other side of the lake he began to take pictures of the receding shore.

– Great place, he remarked. Very scenic. But there's a terrible shortage of tail. You know what I mean?

Timothy thought he did, but could think of no useful comment to make.

– You found any tail since you got here?

Timothy assured him that he had not.

– Perhaps you're too young to be interested in tail?

Timothy responded with an ambiguous leer.

– I mean, what's a furlough without tail?

Timothy murmured his agreement that the question answered itself.

– The nearest I ever get to it is this goddam boat trip.

Timothy expressed puzzlement.

– You see that beach there on the other side of the lake? That's where the Krauts sunbathe in the nude. If you're in luck.

He snapped open another of his leather cases and took out a pair of binoculars, which he focused on the shore. He whistled through his teeth.

– Today we're in luck. Get a load of that.

He offered the binoculars to Timothy, who declined politely. The spectacle no longer held for him the interest it would have done once. As the boat drew nearer the shore, white figures became discernible against the dark background of trees. The G.I. fiddled with the lens of his camera, then pointed it like a gun at the shore. The apparatus whirred. The people on the beach were unquestionably nude, but unabashed by the boat's intrusion. They seemed to be mostly families with children. Some stood up and waved. Timothy waved back.

So all women had hair. Just like men, except that a woman's was more sharply defined, like a trimmed beard. It was funny, the little beard, but it was all right once you got used to the idea. He had been shocked when he saw it on the Jinx woman, but seeing it again on Kate he hadn't been shocked. It made women seem more like men. Perhaps they wouldn't find a man's thing ugly, because they weren't exactly beautiful in that part. There had been something beautiful about Kate and Don lying on the bed, but that was taking all of their bodies together. Taken all together they had looked rather beautiful, like a painting. Though all the paintings, and the photographs, he had seen of naked women had been deeply misleading.

The beach slipped away out of sight. The G.I. sighed and put away his equipment.

– Well, that's another reel for the archives, he said. Wait till the guys back home see this.

Timothy enquired about his home.

– Friend, Nebraska.

– You mean a place called Friend? Timothy stifled a giggle.

– That's right. Real friendly it is, too.

Timothy laughed outright. The G.I. didn't seem to mind. He smiled like the author of a successful joke.

Walking along the road from the lake shore towards the Rest Centre, Timothy saw Kate and Don sitting, fully dressed, on the balcony outside her room. They waved to him and he waved back. He thought of their naked entwined bodies again, and wondered whether today was the first time, or whether they had done it before. He reflected, wryly, that what his mother had suspected, what she had sent him out here to discover, he had in a sense helped to bring about. If it had not been for him, Kate would never have met Don. And what would they do now – get married? It was difficult to imagine them married, unless of course Kate was pregnant . . . He checked his wandering thoughts. They had led him sadly astray once before. What Kate did was her own business. He was not going to get involved again. Nevertheless he felt strangely pleased on Kate's behalf about what had happened, in spite of its being a sin.

As he came on to the terrace, they leaned over the balcony rail and called down to him.

– How was the castle?

– I dunno, he answered, with a shrug. We had to turn back, because of a landslide.

Kate pulled a sympathetic face.

– What a shame, she said, when he joined her on the balcony. When did you get back?

– A couple of hours ago. I took a boat trip on the lake. I thought you were probably resting.

– Yes, we were, I was. Resting.

A deep blush spread over her face and she tried in vain to meet Timothy's eye. He was amused and embarrassed, but also touched.

– Don't you think your sister's looking great? Don said.

He agreed that she was.

– The doctor says I can travel back to Heidelberg tomorrow, said Kate.

– So when shall I go back home? Timothy asked. Next Monday?

– Well, I had a letter from Vince this morning. The Heidelberg fireworks are on Saturday week, and we're all invited to a party at the boys' flat to watch. What d'you think?

– You mean, stay on another week?

– It seems a pity to miss the fireworks. It's a great display. We could send Mum and Dad another wire.

– All right, he said. Then, with a grin: They'll think I've gone mad.

– Don't you think Timothy should stay for the fireworks, Don? said Kate.

– Sure, but count me out of the party. I'll see you at dinner.

– Oh, dear, sighed Kate when he had gone. I wish Don and the boys could get on together. It's going to make things so awkward when we get back to Heidelberg.

– Well, he won't be there long, will he? Don, I mean?

– Why? Kate asked quickly.

– Well, he's been offered a place at L.S.E., hasn't he?

– Yes, but I don't know whether he's definitely accepted it . . . Decisions, decisions, she sighed. How I hate them! It's been so blissful here this past week. Nothing to worry about except my ankle.

– Perhaps you should try and twist the other one, said Timothy, and ducked as she threatened him with her crutch.

It was raining when their train drew into Heidelberg the following evening: a fine drizzle falling from low clouds that swathed the tops of the mountains. The town looked lost and blind, hemmed in by the mountains and the mist, drained of colour and shrunken into itself like a snail into its shell. But it was a measure of how long he had been away from England that coming back to Heidelberg felt almost like coming home.

The cab drew up outside Fichte Haus behind a familiar white sports car, its hood up, its paintwork beaded with moisture.

– I wonder what Vince is doing here? Kate exclaimed. Perhaps he and Greg are fixing a meal to welcome us home.

– In that case, said Don, I'll just help you in with your bags and go.

In the lobby, Rudolf sprang out of his little office to greet them, an envelope in his hand. Kate asked him if Vince was in the building.

– No, Miss Young. He and Mr. Roche have gone to Berlin for the weekend. They return tomorrow.

– But his car is outside.

– Yes, Miss Young, he has kindly borrowed it to me.

– Vince lent you his car?

Rudolf made a gesture of annoyance.

– I should say lent it, of course.

Kate did not attempt to disguise her astonishment.

– You mean he said you could drive it?

– Yes, tonight I drive to my parents. Quicker than a bicycle, no? he said, smiling at Timothy. Here is a cable for you. It came just this morning, from England.

– Mum and Dad must be in a flap, said Timothy.

– Oh Lord, perhaps they didn't get my wire, said Kate. What does it say?

He read it out to them:

– YOU PASSED GCE FIVE DISTINCTIONS THREE CREDITS STUBBINS GILLOW OFFER FIVE TEN PER WEEK EXCELLENT PROSPECTS STARTING IMMEDIATELY HEAD SAYS STAY ON CONGRATULATIONS LOVE DAD.

Kate hugged him and kissed him on both cheeks.

– Timothy! You clever boy!

Don shook his hand warmly.

– Congratulations, Timothy. All those distinctions – it sounds really impressive.

– I wish he'd told me what subjects they were, said Timothy, staring at the telegram.

– Never mind the details, Kate cried. Rudolf! Timothy's passed his examinations. Brilliantly!

– Well, I wouldn't call it brilliant, exactly, Timothy mumbled, accepting Rudolf's handshake.

– You'll go on to college now, won't you, said Don.

He looked at their faces, seeing his success reflected unselfishly there, and for the first time in his life he sensed the possibility that he might not be entirely ordinary. It was a wonderful feeling, but there was no vanity in it: he merely accepted it humbly, like a grace which had descended upon him. But the decision he had to make seemed blindingly obvious. He wanted more moments like this one.

– Yes, he said. I'll stay on at school. I'll send a telegram to Dad tonight.

– Good for you, Timothy! Don clapped him on the back.

– We can do it by phone from my room, said Kate. Come on up.

In the excitement of the news it was some time before Kate reverted to the mystery of Rudolf and Vince's car.

– I'm simply flabbergasted. I know Vince has lent it to friends occasionally, but he hardly knows Rudolf to speak to.

– Perhaps a friendship has ripened in our absence, said Don drily.

Timothy had his own theories, but did not air them. Later he went down to the lobby to get some Coke from the icebox, and found Rudolf preparing to leave. He looked smart, dressed in a new-looking zipped windcheater of a type Timothy had seen in the P.X.

– I spoke to Mr. Vernon, as you suggested, said Rudolf. He thinks he may be able to do something about my father's pension. I am most grateful for your suggestion.

Timothy followed Rudolf out into the street. He looked not at all like a porter, standing tall and proud beside the car in his smart zipped jacket.

– Beautiful, isn't it? he said, running his eyes almost lustfully over the lines of the car. Would you like a small ride? No? Then goodbye, and thank you again.

Rudolf ducked into the driver's seat. The engine started and the wipers scythed through the raindrops that had accumulated on the windscreen. The car moved slowly forward, and Timothy saw Rudolf lean forward in his seat to steady the wheel with his damaged arm as he changed gear with his good hand. Then the car roared away and disappeared round a corner.

The news of his G.C.E. succcess made Timothy suddenly anxious to get home, to reconnect himself with reality again. He had made a mistake, he felt, in agreeing to stay in Heidelberg for another week, just for the sake of seeing a fireworks display. The weekend of their return from Garmisch was dull. The rain continued. Kate was not allowed to walk any distance, and Don had no car, so they were confined to her room, passing the time by playing Canasta and Scrabble. It took him back to the ritual games of Monopoly and cribbage with Jonesy and Blinker on Saturday nights, in the years of his boyhood that now seemed so barren and empty in retrospect.

On the Monday Kate went to the Military Hospital to have her ankle examined, and Timothy took a guidebook Don had lent him and went for a walk round the town to re-examine its sights more attentively. The gardens of the castle were melancholy, rain dripping from the trees on to the gravel paths. From the eastern terrace you could see the traces of a maze laid out in the time of Elizabeth Stuart on the model of Hampton Court. According to the guidebook, *it was considered a great wonder by visiting ambassadors and in reports to their masters it became an allegory of the politics of the period*. There was a curse on the castle, apparently. A Protestant preacher had been burned alive there for heresy, and a witch had cursed the ruling prince for his cruelty and called on God to burn down the castle. The buildings were subsequently damaged by fire on several occasions, and the castle was finally destroyed by the French armies at the end of the seventeenth century. The fireworks commemorated this event.

Reading about Catholics burning Protestants always made Timothy uneasy. Mary Tudor, for instance: it was difficult to feel the same way about the Catholic martyrs under Elizabeth when you discovered that Mary had killed just as many, if not more, Protestants. It was as if you discovered that the Allies had committed atrocities in the war as well as the Nazis.

He wandered back to the town and had lunch in the snack bar where the Mercer boys had taken him. They were not there, but

Gloria was, chatting with a group of friends near the jukebox. She was wearing a white sweatshirt with the letters *U.S.* printed on the front. He thought to himself that two 50c. signs would be more appropriate, one over each breast. The coarse private joke could not suppress his awareness that he lacked the courage to speak to her. She appeared to recognize him from Don's class, for she gave him a shy but friendly smile as she left the snack bar with her friends, but he weakly failed to respond. Afterwards he tramped around the town in the rain in the unacknowledged, and unfulfilled, hope of bumping into her again.

In the evening he had dinner with Kate and Don in her room. The hospital had said that her ankle was in good shape and she could go back to work providing she kept her weight off it as much as possible.

– I told my boss, and he's going to send his driver round with an Army car to fetch me every morning – isn't that sweet of him? I was going to ask one of the boys to pick me up, but I couldn't get hold of them.

In the course of the evening Mel rang up, apparently asking about Vince and Greg. Kate put her hand over the phone and said to Timothy and Don:

– It's very mysterious, Vince and Greg were due back this morning, but nobody's seen or heard from them . . . Just a moment, Ruth is coming – she wants to speak to you, Timothy.

What Ruth had to say was that the daughter of a friend of hers was having a birthday party on the following Friday and that Timothy was invited. He declined politely but firmly.

– You should have said yes, Kate badgered him afterwards. It might have been fun.

– I wouldn't know anybody there. This girl doesn't know me from Adam. I bet Ruth bullied her into inviting me.

– Don't be silly, Timothy, you know how friendly Americans are. Anyway, she said one of this girl's friends knows you.

– Who? he demanded, anticipating, with a bitter pang of regret, what the answer would be.

– Ruth did say, but I've forgotten. Someone in your class, Don. Rose somebody.

– Maybe it was Gloria Rose. D'you remember the well-stacked brunette in the back row, Timothy?

– No, said Timothy. I don't like parties, anyway.

– Oh well, if you won't, you won't, Kate said with a shrug. But I should have thought you would be getting a bit bored, on your own in Heidelberg all day.

– I'm all right, he said doggedly.

– Hey, said Don, soothingly, I've got to go to Frankfurt on Wednesday. How would you like to come along, Timothy?

Timothy accepted, grateful for the change of subject. He went back alone to the hostel. Kate's injury made it inconvenient to practise their usual subterfuge, and in any case, now that his time in Heidelberg was drawing to a close, he had grown reckless. He walked boldly into the hostel, and, if he happened to meet anyone, looked purposefully at his watch, as if he had come to pick up a date.

He had not seen or heard anything of Jinx Dobell since he returned from Garmisch, and presumed that she had gone away for a while, perhaps on vacation. He didn't know whether to be glad or sorry if this was the case. It would be extraordinarily embarrassing to meet her again after that night, which seemed like a dream in retrospect, when she had offered to do it with him; but there were times, like tonight, when his mind played hesitantly with the idea of being given a second chance. He banged the door of Dolores' room deliberately as he went in, and moved about noisily preparing for bed. After a while he went over to the cupboard, turned the key and opened the door for the first time since he had locked himself in. There was no light or sound coming through the chink in the wall from the next room, but there was a book on the floor of the cupboard. He picked it up. It was a paperback edition of *Leaves of Grass*, by Walt Whitman. He stood perfectly motionless for some minutes, holding the book as if it were a booby trap. Then he opened it, and read an inscription on the fly-leaf: *To Don Juan, with love, J.D.* He opened the book at random, and read:

> *I mind how once we lay such a transparent morning,*
> *How you settled your head athwart my hips and gently*
> *turn'd over upon me,*
> *And parted the shirt from my bosom-bone, and plunged*
> *your tongue to my bare-stript heart*
> *And reached till you felt my beard, and reached*
> *till you held my feet.*

He locked the door of the cupboard, got into bed and began to read the poem from the beginning. But it was a very long poem and he found it difficult to follow. There didn't seem to be a story, though long poems usually had stories. His eyes felt heavy after about ten pages, and he put the book down and turned out the light. But he couldn't get to sleep. He thought of the book, ticking in the darkness of the cupboard like an unexploded bomb, for how many days? What did it mean? Why had she left it there for him? It seemed to be a kind of parting gift, which was probably just as well. He thought she was probably slightly touched.

He turned over in the bed and thought of Gloria instead. She had looked very nice in the snack bar, in her U.S. sweatshirt. As well as her breasts, she had a nice face. Smooth skin, a dark matt complexion, glossy dark brown hair parted in the middle. Gloria Rose. He turned over again.

About fifteen minutes later he sat up abruptly, switched on the bedside lamp, and picked up the telephone. He had never used it before, because it meant going through an operator. The man, however, sounded sleepy and incurious, and put him through to Fichte Haus where Rudolf connected him to Kate.

– Timothy! is anything wrong?

– No, I just wanted to tell you that I've changed my mind about that party. I'd like to go.

She laughed with relief.

– What made you change your mind?

– Oh, I don't know. I thought Ruth might be offended.

– Well, that's very thoughtful, Timothy. I'll phone her first thing tomorrow morning. It's getting kind of late now.

– You weren't asleep, were you?

– Er, no, I wasn't asleep.

She seemed to stifle a giggle, and he thought he heard Don's voice in the background.

– 'Night, then, he said.

– Goodnight, Timothy. Pleasant dreams.

The next morning he was in the P.X., buying some presents to take home, when he ran into Ruth. She was wearing knee-length shorts, a coolie hat and sandals with wooden soles. She looked more than usually excited.

– Timothy! she cried, clutching him with her long painted talons. Have you heard about Vince and Greg? I called Kate as soon as I heard the news.

– What news?

– Why, A.F.N. said this morning that two Americans were missing in Berlin. They think they must have wandered into the Soviet Zone by mistake, and been arrested, though the Ivans are claiming they don't know anything about it.

– Vince and Greg?

– Well, they didn't give any names, but it all fits. Mel and I are real worried. Imagine being locked up behind the Iron Curtain! Jesus, sometimes you never hear of people again.

– Perhaps it isn't them.

– Then where are they? She glanced at her watch. I must run.

– Did Kate say anything to you about the party? he asked anxiously.

– The fireworks party? I guess that's cancelled until further notice.

– No, I mean the birthday party. The one you phoned about last night.

– Oh yeah. Kate said you'd like to go after all, right?

– Yes please.

– Fine, I'll tell Lola Eastman, the mother of your hostess, Cherry. She's a sweet kid, you'll like her.

– Why did she invite me? I mean it's jolly decent of her, but . . .

Ruth gave a sly grin.

– Well, to tell you the truth, it was Lola who invited you. She was playing bridge with us last night and I was telling her about you. Look, I must fly.

She began to hobble towards the exit.

– But, he protested, trotting beside her, does this Cherry girl *know?*

– Don't worry about it, Timothy, there'll be about a thousand kids at this party. I just hope the goddam boat doesn't sink.

– What boat?

– Didn't I tell you that? They're hiring one of those pleasure boats on the Neckar – going for a moonlight cruise. Neckin' on the Neckar, Mel said. That's pretty smart for Mel, doncha think?

She left him with a wave and a lewd wink.

In changing his mind about the party, Timothy had prepared himself to receive some teasing and questioning from Kate and Don about his motives. When they met again, however, the only topic of conversation was the disappearance of Vince and Greg. Kate was both excited and upset. She limped up and down the apartment, smoking cigarette after cigarette, making and answering telephone calls. Don, reclining calmly on the divan, asked her if she had known they were going to Berlin.

– No, but they're always dashing off somewhere, on business or pleasure.

– Which d'you think this trip was for?

– Pleasure, I suppose, it was a weekend. But I can't see them doing anything so foolish as to wander into the Soviet Zone by mistake.

– Maybe it wasn't by mistake.

– What d'you mean?

– Maybe they went over on purpose.

– What purpose?

– I don't know, but it wouldn't surprise me a bit if those two turned out to be in the C.I.A. Maybe the Russians picked them up for spying.

– Spying! Kate repeated scornfully.

– Of course, you know them better than I do –

– I certainly do, said Kate, lighting up another cigarette. I never heard such a daft idea.

– But are you quite sure they could have no secrets from you?

– No, but you could say that about anybody. Timothy, for instance.

Don grinned at him.

– You got a secret life, Timothy?

– Not that I know of.

– What d'you think about it all? Kate asked him.

– I think they'll turn up soon, wondering what all the fuss is about. I think they've been held up somewhere, and sent a telegram which didn't arrive, or something.

Kate laughed.

– Down to earth, as usual! And I bet you're right. For all we know, they may be back already. I didn't even bother to try their number today.

She took up the telephone and put through a call to the boys' flat.

– Is that you, Vince? she said eagerly.

Timothy and Don sat up and exchanged glances. But it wasn't Vince who had answered the phone. It was a Staff Sergeant in the Military Police who was logging all incoming calls. Kate had to give him her name and identity number.

– Well, well, said Don.

– The Army must be really worried about what's happened to them, said Kate.

Timothy and Don went to Frankfurt early in the morning of the following day. Apart from glimpses of Mannheim in the dawn of his arrival, Timothy had seen no war-damaged German city. The only ruins in Heidelberg were the picturesque traces of old, historic wars, and Baden-Baden and Garmisch had lacked even those. Frankfurt was a brutal return to reality. It was like London, but London as it might have looked if England had lost the war. Street after street – simply missing. The road was there, and the pavements, and people walked on the pavements and cars passed on the roads, but on each side there was – nothing. Flat, rectangular spaces, packed mud with bricks sticking out of the soil and coarse grass sprouting unevenly. Here and there the blackened shell of a church or other public building, or the stark, raw outline of some brand-new block, marooned amid the vacant lots. Everywhere building was in progress: drills stuttered, bulldozers roared, the dust of demolished buildings hung in the air. Men, stripped to the waist and browned by the sun, worked feverishly. But the extent of the devastation seemed to mock their efforts. Timothy recalled Don's remarks, on the morning they had first met, about the Americans setting up their Headquarters in Heidelberg so that they wouldn't be reminded of what they'd done to German cities, and the idea no longer seemed so queer.

Some of the old buildings in the centre of the town had apparently survived the raids by a kind of miracle, huddled together now amid the wide open spaces. According to Don, however, they had all been destroyed in the war, and rebuilt afterwards. Timothy could hardly believe it, the restoration was so perfect, though at close quarters you could see that the paint was too bright, the stone unweathered, the angles just a little too regular. The house that had belonged to some apparently famous poet whose name sounded like Gertie was more successful. It had been largely destroyed by the bombing, but in anticipation most of the furniture had been removed to safety and, with typical German thoroughness, the exact specifications of all the rooms had been recorded so that they had been restored with complete fidelity to the originals, even down to the warped floorboards and the crooked window frames.

– The Römer – that's the old quarter – and the Goethehaus were the first buildings to be rebuilt in Frankfurt after the war, said Don, as they stood in the poet's bedroom. Isn't that fantastic? When you remember that half the population was still living in cellars and bombed-out buildings.

– It's rather impressive, in a way, said Timothy. To have that sort of feeling for history, and architecture.

– I think it goes deeper than that, said Don. Or shallower. Instead of seeing the bombing as a nemesis, or an atrocity, the Germans just tried to forget about it. Putting the bricks and mortar back just as they were, was a way of making the war, the whole Nazi thing, unhappen. Like running a movie backwards, you know?

– What d'you mean, atrocity?

– I mean the saturation bombing of civilian centres.

Timothy was about to point out that the Germans had started it with the Blitz, but he was distracted by the sound of music coming from a room beneath them. He held up his hand.

– I say! That's *God Save the King!*

– They must be playing it in your honour, said Don with a grin.

They followed the sound till they found a room on the first floor where an elderly museum official was standing before a harpsichord playing the familiar tune for an earnest group of tourists. He lowered the lid of the instrument and began speaking in German. Timothy and Don tiptoed away.

– It's an old tune that crops up in a lot of European countries, said Don. I don't think anyone knows who first composed it.

– It was queer hearing it in this place, said Timothy. I connect it with home.

Standing self-consciously in the aisle of the local cinema, turning sheepishly to face the Union Jack fluttering on the screen, furtively buttoning up your coat. Listening to the radio on Cup Final day, the strains of the military band floating across a hushed Wembley. Or sitting at the table in the dining-room on Christmas Day as the yellow December light faded outside the window, miming requests for mince-pies and a second helping of pudding, while the thin faltering voice of the King enunciated vague syllables of hope and goodwill: *at this season . . . people of every nation . . . Empire and Commonwealth . . . hope and pray . . . united effort . . . peace*. And, as the strains of the National Anthem died away, mother saying, *I thought he was better this year. Poor man, it must be a strain.*

They came out of the Goethehaus, into the roar of traffic and drills, and began to walk through the barren, vacant streets in search of a café. Timothy reverted to the subject of the bombing, which troubled him like Catholic persecution of Protestants in the Reformation. Don needed no prompting, for he had researched the subject for what he referred to as a Peace organization in America. He described the strategy of area bombing and the technique of creating firestorms in cities by dropping incendiaries on top of a carpet of high explosives. He reeled off disconcerting statistics, such as that 13,000 people were killed in the London Blitz, but 130,000 in one raid on Dresden in 1945. Or that 500,000 Germans had been killed in the raids at a cost of 160,000 Allied aircrew.

– A hundred and sixty *thousand?* Timothy repeated incredulously.

– Unbelievable, isn't it? And German civilian morale wasn't weakened by the bombing. It got stronger, if anything. Even their industrial war production went on rising right up to August 1944.

It was hard enough to face the possibility that the bombing of Germany had been excessive; that it had also been wasteful and ineffective was almost too bitter for contemplation. On the train back to Heidelberg Timothy watched his own pale reflection sharpen in the window as the German sky darkened over the German landscape, and thought of Uncle Jack and all the airmen like him who had gone to their deaths in that sky. He groped towards some imaginative reconstruction of the experience: the drop of the burning, disintegrating plane into the dark, the sickening, toppling spin of the great wings, life moving towards zero with the altimeter. But he had only the imagery of old newsreels and war films to work with, that could never express the terror and the pain of such a death. And how would it be to discover, in the total knowledge that came after death, that your terror and pain had been entirely futile? He imagined waves of reproach rolling in from the after-life and breaking upon an indifferent world. *History is the verdict of the lucky on the unlucky* . . . It was true. But what could you do about it, except go about in fear and trembling, hoping your luck would hold? *Penance*, Don said, with an ironical smile. *We can do penance, Timothy. You should know all about that.* He knew about saying three Hail Marys and an Our Father after Confession, and giving up sweets for Lent, but he didn't think that was what Don had in mind.

They had arranged to meet Kate at Fichte Haus that evening, but she was waiting for them at the station when their train drew in. She looked pale and anxious.

– The most awful thing has happened, she said. Rudolf has had a crash in Vince's car.

– I knew it, Don said grimly.

– You knew?

– I knew it was crazy letting him drive an automobile like that, with only one arm. Vernon must have been out of his mind.

– Is Rudolf all right? Timothy asked.

– He's unconscious – severe concussion. He's in the Military Hospital. Apparently he's lucky to be alive. It seems the M.P.s chased him on the autobahn, and instead of stopping when they gonged him he tried to get away. The car left the road and hit a tree. He was thrown out.

They began walking back to Fichte Haus through a thin drizzle.

– Why were they chasing him? Why didn't he stop? Timothy wondered aloud.

Kate shrugged.

– I suppose he was speeding. Or perhaps he shouldn't have been driving the car. Perhaps Vince didn't lend it to him.

– Maybe he's only allowed to drive a car with special controls, Don suggested. Or he doesn't have a licence at all.

– That sounds more like it, said Timothy. Rudolf wouldn't just . . . steal Vince's car.

– Well, I don't know what to think, said Kate. The whole thing has started some fantastic rumours, I can tell you.

– Like what? Don asked.

– Such as that Vince and Greg were spying for the Russians and that Rudolf was their contact and that's why the M.P.s were chasing him.

Don threw back his head and roared with laughter.

– It's this Burgess and Maclean business, he said. People are getting spies before the eyes.

– Well, you can talk, Don –

– I said they could be in the C.I.A., that's quite a different matter. You're not taking this rumour seriously, are you?

Kate frowned.

– I don't know what to think. It's all a mystery. I agree that it's not like Rudolf to take Vince's car without permission, but I wasn't aware they were on car-lending terms.

– Er, I think I know how Rudolf and Vince sort of got together, Timothy said hesitatingly.

– You, Timothy?

Kate came to a halt on the pavement and stared at him. When he had finished his explanation about Rudolf's father, she said, with a little nervous laugh:

– Well, you do plunge in where angels fear to tread, don't you? But it still doesn't explain why Vernon should do Rudolf another favour, by lending him his car.

– I have a theory, said Don. But I'd better keep it to myself.

Kate glanced at him, seemed about to speak, then changed her mind.

The next day, Thursday, there was hard news about the boys at last, news which made all the rumours and speculations of the previous days evaporate as quickly as the puddles in the streets of Heidelberg, as the sun shone down from a clear blue sky again. Vince and Greg were safe in West Berlin and were on their way back to Heidelberg. They had taken a walk in the woods on the outskirts of the city on the previous Sunday, strayed over the frontier into East Germany, and been arrested. They had been locked up for three days under interrogation, then, without explanation, taken back in a closed truck to the place where they had been found, and allowed to recross the frontier. Vince had rung Kate from Berlin and told her that they would be returning to Heidelberg on Saturday, and to spread the word that the fireworks party was still on.

– He seems to be taking it all very lightly, Don observed. Does he know the rumours that have been flying around?

– He said they were going to have a de-briefing in Frankfurt on their way home, and there might be an enquiry later. He treated it all as a bit of joke, but I think he was more shaken up than he was prepared to admit. Like you said, Don, the Russians suspected them of spying.

– Does Vernon know about Rudolf's crash?

– Yes, apparently he asked Rudolf to take the car in to be serviced, but Vince hadn't meant him to drive it around afterwards.

– How is Rudolf? Timothy asked.

– He's regained consciousness, which is a relief, but he's not allowed visitors yet. Another relief is to know that Vince and Greg are all right. What a tale they'll have to tell.

– Yes, said Don, dryly, I'd like to hear it.

– Well, why don't you come to their party? You're invited.

Don fingered his cleft chin, considering.

– Well, I'll see. I don't particularly want to join a demonstration of loyalty.

– What d'you mean?

– That's why they're going ahead with the party, isn't it? To show they've got nothing to hide? All their friends there to express solidarity.

– You read too much into things, Don, said Kate crossly. Of course all their friends will be there, it's a kind of welcome home party. And a farewell party for Timothy, she added, smiling at him. Two parties in two days – you're really ending your holiday with a bang!

The gaily decorated pleasure-boat, giving out strains of recorded music from its mooring just above the Old Bridge, was attracting a good deal of attention. Spectators, most of them German, hung dangerously over the parapet of the bridge and lined the road beside the river, getting in the way of the huge docile automobiles that deposited the young guests, like gift-wrapped packages, on the quay. The girls sunned themselves in the publicity, shaking out the skirts of their party frocks as they emerged from the padded depths of Buicks and Chevrolets, waving goodbye to their parents and climbing the gangplank with little screams of fear as the boat rocked slightly in the wash of passing barges. On one such barge Timothy saw a young boy, brown and barefoot, run the length of his deck to stay level with the amazing spectacle as long as possible, and then lean over the stern with mouth gaping until he was drawn out of sight into the setting sun.

Timothy arrived on foot. He was glad of the moral support of Kate and Don as he ran the gauntlet of spectators, gripping self-consciously a large box of chocolates, tied up in an enormous bow of lilac silk, which Kate had procured for him from the P.X.

– My, Timothy, you're making the social scene with a vengeance tonight, she teased him. They've even got a photographer here.

– It's unbelievable, Don murmured. Some poor slob must have spent a fortune on this circus.

– Well, he can afford it, said Kate. Cherry's father is a Major.

– I bet the boat was his wife's idea, though. Is that her in the black sequins?

– Yes, and Cherry is beside her.

– The kid looks terrified.

– She doesn't, she looks perfectly sweet.

On the deck, at the head of the gangplank, a woman with blue-tinted hair and wearing a glittering black cocktail dress stood receiving and shaking hands with the arriving guests. The brilliance of her smile was visible even from where they stood on the riverbank. Beside her a limp, mousy-haired girl in a wide-skirted white dress stood nervously fingering a small bouquet. There was a table beside them which bore a growing pile of brightly-wrapped presents. The gangplank began to fill up.

– Is the Major planning to run for President? Don enquired. It's beginning to look like a line at the White House.

– Oh stop carping, Don, you'll make Timothy wish he hadn't come, said Kate.

Timothy was already wishing exactly that. He hadn't bargained for anything so formal or so public; and whatever enticing prospects had been opened up by Mel's quip of Neckin' on the Neckar seemed firmly closed off by the emphatic presence of Mrs. Eastman, not to mention Major Eastman, who now appeared in rather dashing nautical attire – dark blue slacks, white cable-stitch sweater and peaked cap – carrying a large crate of Coca-Cola aboard, a curved yellow pipe clenched between his teeth.

– Would you like me to introduce you to the Eastmans, Timothy? Kate asked.

– Yes, please.

He followed her up the gangplank, shook hands with his hostesses and handed over his bulky package with relief.

– My, what a darling ribbon! Mrs. Eastman enthused. It matches your sash, honey, see?

– Thank you very much, Cherry murmured listlessly. Her hand was limp and moist.

– It's so kind of you to invite Timothy, I'm sure he'll have a great time, said Kate.

– It's a real pleasure, Mrs. Eastman beamed. We've been hearing so much about you, Timothy.

He grinned feebly.

– We should be back by ten-thirty, Mrs. Eastman said to Kate. I think that will be long enough for me, if not for the kids. She laughed, showing her white teeth.

– You needn't bother to meet me, Kate, he said.

– O.K. my pet. Enjoy yourself.

To his embarrassment, she pecked him on the cheek before teetering down the gangplank to the riverside pavement. He saw her link arms with Don and they disappeared into the crowd.

– Now, said Mrs. Eastman, I guess you don't know anyone here, do you, Timothy? She examined him with a frown, as if he was a puzzle on whose solution her self-esteem depended.

– No, I don't think so, he said, looking round. He saw Gloria leaning on the stern rail, but did not feel equal to claiming her acquaintance this early in the proceedings.

– Baby! Mrs. Eastman grabbed the arm of a smaller edition of Cherry who was twirling round on the deck to admire her skirt. Timothy – this is Cherry's sister, we call her Baby because she's our youngest. Baby, this is Timothy, he's from England. Get him a Coke or something, will you honey, and introduce him to some nice kids?

Baby pulled a face.

– Aw, Mom . . .

– *Baby!* said Mrs. Eastman threateningly.

– Oh, all *right*. C'mon.

She jerked her head as a signal that Timothy should follow her, and led him to a pile of crates containing soft drinks.

– Coke or Pepsi?
– Coke, please.
– Help yourself.

While he was fiddling with the bottle-opener, she disappeared. He was not sorry. He took his Coke round to the other side of the boat, out of Mrs. Eastman's sight, and leaned on the rail, feigning absorption in the view of the river and the far bank. The ship's whistle emitted a shrill, comical shriek, and there was an answering yell of excitement from the passengers. The engine throbbed, and the boat began to move slowly away from the smiling, waving spectators on the bank. The loudspeaker crackled:

– Hallo everybody, this is Harold Eastman speaking, that's Cherry's old man in case any of you don't know. (There were cheers and a few jeers.) I'd like to welcome you all aboard this birthday party . . . (He paused to receive some polite laughter) . . . and to say how pleased we are, Cherry's Mom and myself, to have you all here to celebrate this very special day in her life. Now we want you to have a lot of fun. There's enough Coke and Pepsi on board to turn the Neckar pink. There's all kinds of food in the saloon under the bridge. Just help yourselves. The top deck has been cleared for dancing. Just one serious word: we don't want to spoil the party with an accident, so please don't sit on the rails or lean over the side of the ship. That's all. Enjoy yourselves!

There was a cheer from the guests, and the music resumed over the loudspeakers. The boat paused to negotiate the lock above the Old Bridge and then headed upstream into the Neckar valley. At first the mountains sloped gently away from the river, but as it twisted its way further eastwards they heaved up more steeply. Some of the mountains were capped by tiny medieval-looking villages with fortified walls. Through this vast spectacular scenery the little craft made its way, spilling its music and chatter and laughter into the brooding silence of forest and mountain.

Some of the older and more sophisticated guests began to dance under the awning on the top deck, but for the most part they gathered in groups, talking and laughing, the girls sitting shoulder to shoulder while the boys stood round them, lightly butting and punching each other, displaying themselves, prancing up to the tight knot of girls and then backing off again, tossing back bottles of Coke with a manly swagger. He saw Gloria Rose, looking very vivid and ripe in a wide red skirt and white peasant-style blouse threaded at the neckline with red ribbon, her long dark freshly-washed hair fanning out over her shoulders. She was engaged in animated conversation with two plainer girls seated on each side of her, and affected to ignore the attempts of one of the boys in her circle to untie the ribbon in her blouse, flicking her shoulder out of the way with a scornful shrug. He only needed to walk up to her and smile and say, *Didn't I see you the other day in Mr. Kowalski's class?* But what then? Supposing she said no? Even if she said yes, he couldn't imagine himself joining the puppyish circle of boys romping at her feet. He felt, as he had felt with the Mercer boys, rich in experience that was of no use to him, that simply didn't apply.

As if to enforce the point, Larry himself appeared from the stairway leading to the saloon, a hot dog clenched between his teeth like a huge cigar, another in his right hand and a Coke in his left. Like most of the boys on the boat, he was wearing a rather gaudy jacket of lightweight checked material, a white shirt and a clip-on bow tie. His closely cropped hair had a downy sheen. Glad to end his conspicuous isolation, Timothy greeted him warmly.

– I didn't know you knew Cherry Eastman, Larry mumbled through his hot dog.

– I don't.

– Whaddya doin' here, then?

Timothy explained.

– I didn't want to come myself, to tell you the truth, said Larry. I hate gettin' all dolled up. I only came to make Con mad, because he wasn't invited. He *was* mad, too.

– Perhaps he thought there would be ice-cream sodas, said Timothy.

Larry slapped his thigh and guffawed.

– Holy mackerel! I'll never forget that! How many did we have? Was it five?

– Four.

– I thought it was five. Lemme see, we had chocolate first, and the strawberry . . .

– No, pineapple.

– Right: pineapple, and *then* strawberry, and then . . .

– Pistachio.
– Didn't we have another one after the pistachio?
– You may've, but I didn't.
Larry nudged him in the ribs.
– I remember, you had to go to the john. Con threw up on the bus goin' home. Boy, was the driver mad! I threw up at home, in the livin' room. Just couldn't make it to the bathroom.

Larry shook his head wistfully. A numb despair settled on Timothy's spirits as their conversation dribbled on. It was as if Larry and himself were juvenile parodies of two old men at a ball or a wedding, two old, neglected boozers reminiscing about past excesses while the young people danced and flirted obliviously under their noses. He broke away abruptly on the pretext of getting something to eat.

– Be seein' ya, said Larry.

The saloon was crowded with young guests pillaging the tables spread with sandwiches, pickles, pies and potato crisps. At the end of the room Major Eastman, in striped apron and chef's hat, was slicing rolls and filling them with bright red sausages which he lifted from a large saucepan with a pair of tongs. *Hot dawgs! Hot dawgs!* he chanted, *Mustard one cent extra!*

– Thank you very much, Timothy said as he was served.

– Do I detect a British accent? Major Eastman enquired with a twinkle. You must be the young man Ruth Fallert has been telling us so much about.

– I'm Timothy Young.

Major Eastman wiped his hand on his apron and held it out.

– Glad to meet you, Timothy. I was stationed in England in the war. Place called Scarborough – know it?

– No, I'm afraid I don't.

– In Yorkshire, where the pudding comes from, isn't that right, Gloria?

The question was addressed over Timothy's shoulder. He turned to find himself in sudden proximity to Gloria, all warm, breathing flesh.

– I beg your pardon, Major Eastman? she said.

– Never heard of Yorkshire pudding?

– Gloria hasn't even heard of Yorkshire, sir, one of the boys behind her quipped.

– I have, too, she pouted. She indicated Timothy. He told us, in Mr. Kowalski's class. It's near Scotland, isn't it?

Timothy nodded, tongue-tied.

– Oh, so you've met Timothy already? said Major Eastman, handing Gloria a hot dog wrapped in a paper serviette.

– Yes, he drew us a map of the British Isles. I copied it.

She smiled at him, and he managed to say:

– I hope you never have to use it. You're bound to get lost.

It was apparently as easy as that. He was somehow magically, effortlessly assimilated into Gloria's group. When they had finished eating he followed them upstairs on to the deck again, where they arranged themselves around the stern rails in a new, significant pattern: boy-girl-boy-girl. The fading light allowed this adjustment to be made inconspicuously. Behind them a ruddy sunset still stained the sky, but the boat's bows were headed into a tunnel of darkness. Timothy, with a cool stealth that surprised himself, took up a position on one side of Gloria. She shivered slightly in a puff of wind that blew off the river.

– Gee, I should have brought a wrap.

The boy on the other side of her sniggered.

– I got something to warm you up.

He produced a flat bottle from his inside pocket. The others crowded round him whispering and giggling.

– What you got there, Ray?

– Is that rum?

– Hey, Ray has some rum!

– Hot dog!

– Ssh!

– Anyone got a bottle of Coke?

– Rum'n Coke, *dee-lishus!*

– Don't tell the whole boat, for Chrissake!

They emptied half the contents of a bottle of Coke over the side, and topped it up with rum. Then it was solemnly circulated among the boys, the girls declining to drink. The boys smacked their lips, wiped their mouths with the backs of their hands and murmured, *Boy, that hit the spot!* Timothy gulped down a mouthful of the sweet, aromatic concoction and passed the bottle on.

– Do you really like it? Gloria asked him.

– It's not bad. I prefer rum omelettes.

– Rum omelettes? I never heard of a rum omelette before.

– It's nicer than Yorkshire pudding, any day, he said, and was rewarded by her answering smile.

– Go on, try it, Gloria, Ray urged her.

– I know what you're trying to do, Ray Dillon, she said archly.

– Aw, this won't make you drunk. He took another swig and wiped the neck of the bottle chivalrously with his tie.

– Well, just a little sip.

As she lifted the bottle cautiously to her lips, Ray tilted it. She swallowed and spluttered.

– Ugh! You sneaky –

– Ssh! We don't want Ma Eastman up here.

– It tastes horrible, anyway.

– Just wait a minute and you'll feel all warm inside. Pass the bottle.

She passed it to Timothy.

– I'm sorry, she said, I don't have a handkerchief.

– It doesn't matter, he said, raising the bottle, moist with her spittle and warm from her lips, to his mouth. One of the boys coughed loudly and somebody kicked him sharply in the shin. Mrs. Eastman had appeared out of the shadows. He was holding the bottle.

– Hallo! she greeted them gaily. What are you kids hiding away up here for?

– Oh, just enjoying the view, Mrs. Eastman.

– It's such a lovely evening, Mrs. Eastman.

– Swell party, Mrs. Eastman.

– Well, as long as you're enjoying yourselves . . . but I'd like to see more of you young folk dancing. There seems to be a funny odour around here, she said, sniffing.

They all began to sniff extravagantly, with deep inhalings and exhalings.

– I don't smell anything, Mrs. Eastman.

– You do get funny odours on the river sometimes, Mrs. Eastman.

– It's not that kind of odour at all, she said, drawing closer to Timothy.

– Perhaps it's my hair oil, he said. It has bay rum in it.

– So that's what it is, she laughed. I didn't know British boys were such dandies, Timothy.

They all burst into uproarious laughter, strident with released tension. Mrs. Eastman went away with the pleased air of a successful humorist. When she was out of earshot they burst into further hilarity, the girls convulsed with giggles, the boys doubled up, shaking their heads, punching each other, eyes watering, gasping and wheezing. Only Timothy kept his poise, smiling, accepting their tributes.

– Say, that was pretty cool, one of the boys said, when relative calm had returned. Howja think of it, just like that? The hair-oil bit?

– I dunno, it just came into my head, he said. The barber I go to in London, he has a bottle of Bay Rum hair oil on the counter. I always thought it was a funny thing to put on your hair. It sort of stuck in my mind.

– You don't really use it, then? Gloria asked him.

– Good Lord, no.

– That was real neat, though, to think of saying it.

While he was savouring this delicious compliment, more lights on the deck suddenly came on, casting golden reflections on the water. *Oohs* and *Aahs* of admiration were heard, but from the little group at the stern only suppressed groans.

– That's Ma Eastman trying to flush us out.

– *Come on, boys and girls, I want to see everyone dancing!* they heard her cry from the distance.

– Huh! Who wants to dance with her staring at you all the time?

– And the records are such crap.

– I reckon she bought them for her own sixteenth birthday.

– We can fix the lights, anyway, Ray said.

– Whaddya gonna do, Ray?

– Wait and see. He winked and moved off.

– What did he say? a girl asked.

– He's gonna fix the lights.

– He's crazy. Ray's crazy.

– He's had too much rum.

– Too much hair oil.

They sniggered and nudged each other, elated and expectant. Whatever Ray was going to do, Timothy hoped it would occupy him for some time. His departure had evened up the numbers and left Timothy in conversational possession of Gloria. But this advantage was short-lived.

– *I want everybody on the floor for a mixer! Come on, boys and girls.*

– Oh, no! Gloria groaned.

– What's a mixer?

– Oh, its a corny kind of dance where you all walk around in two circles until the music stops and then you dance with the person who's opposite.

– I can't dance, said Timothy, seeing a desperate choice looming up, between making a fool of himself on the dance floor and losing Gloria for ever.

– Don't let it worry you – neither can half the kids here.

Major Eastman appeared, grinning jovially.

– Come on, now, everybody! On the dance deck – Captain's orders.

– I can't dance, said Timothy.

– Well, now's the time to learn, young man, said the Major, herding them towards the centre of the boat.

They were halfway up the stairs that led to the dancing deck when the lights went out and the music from the loudspeakers died with a groan. There were several screams, whoops, whistles, and some laughter; then a buzz of voices, above which Major Eastman's was raised in tones of military authority.

– O.K., hold it, everybody. Don't panic! Don't move. Stay right where you are. We'll have this sorted out in just a moment.

A few matches and cigarette lighters flickered briefly in the darkness. A girl's voice said sharply, *Cut that out!* and a titter ran through the close-packed crowd. Timothy, standing on the stairs below Gloria, was aware of her skirt brushing his face.

– I'm losing my balance, she said, swaying back.

– Hold on to me, he said.

– Thanks.

He would happily have stayed there for the remainder of the voyage, with Gloria's faintly perfumed, rustling silks enveloping him, her hand resting lightly on his shoulder; but almost immediately the lights went on again, the record groaned into life and speeded up. A few couples were discovered clasped together, and there were whistles and catcalls as they hastily separated. Timothy wondered whether Gloria would have been willing to take the same advantage of the darkness. He rather thought she would have been.

Major Eastman bustled up behind them.

– Right, he said, panting a little, it seems that some joker threw the main lighting switch. If I catch him, he'll be court-martialled. There was a perceptible edge of anger to his joviality.

– Who says it was a he? someone murmured, and those who heard giggled. Timothy sensed mutiny in the air. The extinguishing of the lights had touched some nerve of rebellion in the young guests. They were flushed and excited, grimacing at each other, unco-operative as Major and Mrs. Eastman organized them into two large circles on the dancing deck, the girls inside and the boys outside. Gloria, facing Timothy, smiled.

– Relax, it won't hurt.

– I don't know what to do, he said, I haven't the faintest idea.

– Oh, just kind of move around to the rhythm. She shuffled her feet and swayed her hips under the red skirt.

Major Eastman stepped into the centre of the inner ring.

– Everybody ready? You all know the drill. Boys walk clockwise, girls anticlockwise. When the music stops the person opposite you is your partner for the next dance. O.K?

– I hope you're opposite me, he said.

– I guess the odds are against it, she said, with a smile.

– It's like roulette, he said miserably.

Major Eastman began a countdown:

– Five, four, three, two, one, *ZERO!*

There was a popping explosion and the lights went out again. Cheers and groans rent the sky. Timothy felt bodies colliding against him as Major Eastman pushed his way roughly to the stairhead, swearing under his breath. Timothy groped forward and touched a soft, smooth arm.

– Is that you, Gloria?

– Timothy?

She suddenly staggered against him.

– Hey, quit pushing! she cried to some invisible person. Sorry, she said to Timothy.

– It's all right.

– It's kind of scary, all these people in the dark.

A sudden movement in the crowd sent them staggering again, but he held on to her arm. Somewhere Mrs. Eastman could be heard begging people to stay where they were, the lights would be fixed any moment. There was hysteria in her voice. From the bridge came guttural shouts in German.

– Shall we get off this deck? Timothy suggested.

– How can we find our way? I can't see a thing.

– Just hold on to me.

With his free hand he groped for the rail, then followed it round till he came to the stairhead.

– Here's the staircase. Hold on to the rail, here.

– Whew! she said as they reached the bottom of the stairs. I don't know how you do it.

– I suppose I learned to find my way about in the dark in the blackout.

– What blackout?

He explained.

– Gee, that must have been scary.

– Oh, you got used to it.

– I guess I'm beginning to get used to it now. I can see you, more or less.

– I can see you, too.

They fell silent. He was still holding her hand.

– It's taking them a long time to mend the lights, she said eventually.

– He must have fused them, the second time.

– Ray? D'you really think so? He's crazy.

– Well, he saved me from having to dance, anyway.

– Have you really never danced before in your whole life?

– Never. He cleared his throat and added: I've never kissed a girl, either.

There was a silence. Then she murmured:

– Why did you tell me that, Timothy?

He laughed nervously.

– Well, I'd like to kiss you, but I'm afraid I'll make a mess of it.

– You're a funny boy, she said, not unkindly. Are all British boys like you?

He thought for a moment.

– Quite a lot are, I think.

Another silence. Her face, pale and dim, was lifted to his. He bent towards her and closed his eyes. The kiss landed high up on her cheekbone and his glasses, striking her forehead, slipped sideways on his nose.

– See? he said.

By way of reply, she removed his glasses and kissed him gently on the lips. He clasped her clumsily round the waist. She nestled against him and he felt her breasts yielding against his chest, and her cool fingers on the base of his neck. He kissed her again. And again. And again.

The sixth time, she forced his lips apart and pushed her tongue between his teeth. It came into his mouth like a live thing, long warm wet supple strong.

– What did you do that for? he said distractedly.

– Don't you like it?

– Oh yes!

– It's called French kissing, she whispered. Some kids call it soul-kissing.

Because you lose your immortal soul? he wondered; and did it back to her, at greater length.

– Hey! she panted, surfacing.

– *Baby! Is that you, Baby?*

Mrs. Eastman was approaching. Timothy pulled Gloria into the deeper darkness of an alcove beneath the staircase, and they heard her pass, bumping against deckchairs, followed by her husband muttering murderous threats under his breath.

– Have you got the lifebelt, Harold? Mrs. Eastman wailed.

– She hasn't fallen overboard, for Chrissake, Lola!

– Then where is she? *Baby!* Why don't you *do* something?

– The crew are working on the fuse. There's nothing I can do.

Mrs. Eastman sobbed.

– Poor Cherry! Her party's ruined. Who could have done it?

– If I find him, said Major Eastman grimly, I will personally tie a knot in his balls. A reef knot.

Gloria buried her face in Timothy's shoulder, heaving with suppressed giggles.

– Did you hear him cuss? she whispered breathlessly, as the Eastmans stumbled out of earshot. That she had heard the crude words excited him, and he kissed her again, passionately straining her body against his.

– Oh Timothy, she whimpered.

– Oh Gloria!

Eventually the lights came on again, but the party had fragmented beyond repair. Couples danced where they stood, in the shadows of the lower decks, draped over each other's shoulders, and swaying only just perceptibly to the music. In other shadows other couples necked without the pretence of dancing. The Eastmans had retired, evidently defeated, having found Baby asleep in the saloon. Timothy and Gloria stayed huddled in their alcove. He didn't suggest that they should sit down, because he wasn't sure he could comfortably do so.

– Those must be the lights of Heidelberg, he said.

– Really? I didn't even know we'd turned back. Is it late?

He squinted at the luminous dial of his watch.

– About half-past ten, I make it.

– Harf-parst ten, she mimicked him. You mean ten thirty.

He wondered whether he dared to touch her breast. He touched it, lightly, holding his breath.

– I don't want this boat ever to stop, she said.

– Neither do I, he said, stroking her breast more firmly. It felt lovely. Gloria, where are you going when we get back?

– Home, I guess.

– Couldn't we go somewhere, first?

– I can't, I have to go home. Where to, anyway?

– We could go to my room. I have my own room.

He had a very clear picture in his mind, so clear he could have drawn it: their two naked bodies on the bed in Dolores' room, his head pillowed on one breast, his hand clasping the other, a rosy nipple peeping between his splayed fingers.

– Are you staying at a hotel?

– No, a kind of hostel.

– They let you bring girls in? What are you laughing at?

– It's a girls' hostel, he said.

It seemed a good joke, and they giggled over it for a little while.

– Don't you feel funny, living in a girls' hostel?

– You get used to it.

– Like the blackout?

– Like the blackout.

– You know something, Timothy? You're real cool.

– Am I? I don't feel it.

– Well, you are, I'm telling you.

– Will you come then? Back to my room?

– I have to go home, really I do. My girl friend Edith, her father's driving me home. My folks will raise all hell if I don't go back with her.

– What about tomorrow then? Can I see you tomorrow?

– Tomorrow's Saturday. I'm supposed to be watching the fireworks with my folks.

– So am I. What about the daytime? Tomorrow afternoon?

– I said I'd go to the pool with Edith. You could meet us at the pool.

– Not with Edith. Let's meet on our own.

– Well, maybe.

– Please, he said urgently.

Eventually they made a date for half-past one on the following afternoon, outside the Stadtgarten. As the boat was tying up, Timothy took Gloria round to the other side of the deck for a last long kiss, with bruised, aching lips.

– See you tomorrow, then, he said.

She nodded, smiled, and left him. He went into the lavatory. His face in the mirror over the washbasin surprised him, ruddy and smeared with lipstick as if by the blood of combat. He washed it off. Coming out of the lavatory he met Larry, tilting a bottle of Coke to his lips.

– Last one! He brandished the bottle proudly, and belched. Say, what happened to you all evening?

– Oh, everything! he said gaily, and slapped the astonished Larry on the back. Goodnight!

Well, nearly everything, he corrected himself. Everything was for the following afternoon.

By the end of the following afternoon, Timothy was in a state approaching delirium, and far beyond anything he recognized as pleasure. He had got so far towards the consummation of his desire that he was stretched out on the bed with Gloria, and they were both partially unclothed; but it had been a long, exhausting process, and now, at what he thought must be near the climax, he wondered whether he was capable of commanding his perspiring, aching flesh any further.

The fault was entirely his. It had taken him a long, long time to realize that Gloria was of the same mind as himself, and would not resist any of his advances. When, no doubt impatient with his ineffective plucking at the straps of her brassiere, she suddenly sat up, put her hands behind her back and deftly unfastened the catch, and her breasts tumbled into his hands, he felt as if he had reached an ultimate plateau of delight on which he would be content to rest for ever, enraptured by their pliant weight, fascinated by the different shape they had when freed from the sharp, conical cups of the brassiere, flatter and rounder and wider apart, falling to each side like arms opening in a gesture of submission, tipped with blunt nipples that hardened mysteriously under his touch.

Then he had made an almost fatal error, recalling facetiously the way in which Larry had first called his attention to her. She had responded with indignation, and a determined doing up of hooks and buttons. She denied the story and reproached him for believing it. Later, much later, when he had coaxed her back into a loving disposition, she admitted that she had shown her breasts once, for a dare, a long time ago, but that she hadn't taken any money from the boy, only from the girl who had bet her a dollar she wouldn't do it. Then slowly, hesitantly, he had made up his lost ground.

All that was a long time ago, or so it seemed to him. Her brassiere was on the floor beside the bed now, a strange, forlorn-looking object, like a pair of empty conch-shells stranded on the beach, along with her blouse and his shirt. His cheek was pressed against her left breast, but its nakedness, though agreeable, no longer seemed so extraordinary. His thoughts and his nerves were active down below, with his fingers, and her fingers. His fingers had crept underneath the loosened waistband of her jeans, underneath the elastic of her knickers, over the warm swell of her belly, to be halted by the expected but still electrifying brush of her hair. And her fingers had plucked his vest from its moorings, scampered over his torso, unbuckled his belt, unzipped his fly, and were now, holy God, stroking through his underpants the hard, rocklike pillar of his straining flesh.

They had not spoken for perhaps twenty minutes, just lying there almost immobile, exploring each other with their fingers, their eyes closed. At least, his eyes were closed; he didn't know about hers. He had always thought he would want to look, but now he would have been grateful for darkness, pitch darkness. The green curtains were drawn, but the room still seemed uncomfortably bright, the furniture and fittings too sharply defined, crowding round the bed like inquisitive and disapproving presences.

A squadron of jets suddenly screamed overhead, making the windows rattle. Feeling a commotion beside him, he opened his eyes and saw Gloria arch her back, kick, and the blue jeans flew off her brown legs. He shut his eyes again. His hand now moved freely under the light tension of her flimsy briefs. He ran his hand over the fine, springy nest of hair, and reached a moist crevice. There was a distant rumble, as of bombs or guns. The sound barrier. He heard her breathing quickly beside him. He scarcely dared to breathe himself. She spread her legs and his index finger slipped in like a seal into a rock pool, slithering against the slippery walls, and touching something that quivered and contracted, fluttering like a shrimp under bare toes at low tide, and he thought he must be losing his senses, for there was a strange smell of shrimps in the room. She moaned and began to rub herself against his finger. His heart pounded, and there was almost terror in the pounding, for he was afraid of the strange powerful rhythms he had started in her, as though he had her whole body balanced effortlessly on his finger tip, and could make her do anything, split open like a pea-pod, turn herself inside out, at the slightest extra pressure; and afraid for himself, afraid to move, though this was obviously the moment to do it, because if he moved, if his tensed, straining body were disturbed in its balance by even a millimetre, he knew he would spill, he would burst, he would fountain.

Then she slipped her hand under the elastic waistband of his underpants, and at the first touch of her fingers he gave a despairing cry and he spilled, he burst, he fountained. He tried to stop himself, he bit his lip, he clenched his fists, and twisted aside; but he could not stop, he did not want to stop, he only wanted to reach oblivion, to die, like a wasp dying in jam, clogged and sticky and exhausted.

When the last spasm had spent itself, he rolled over on to his stomach and buried his face in the pillow. He was ashamed to look at her. He hoped she would dress quickly and go away. But she made no move. After a few minutes he felt her hand creep under his vest and draw a line down his backbone.

– Hey, she said softly.

– I'm sorry, he said hoarsely, keeping his head turned away from her.

– What for?

– I'm sorry I . . . you know.

– You wanted to, didn't you?

– No. Well, not like that.

– Like what then?

– Well, you know . . . inside you.

– You're crazy, she snorted, but she didn't sound angry or disgusted.

He stared out over the edge of the bed at the room, at the washbasin and the cupboard and the armchair, Dolores' books and the green curtains drawn against the sun, and a pair of socks hanging over the radiator to dry. They were all charged with an an insistent reality, like objects in a still-life, and he felt as if it had been drawn out of himself. He felt hollow, as if the marrow had been sucked out of his bones.

– Why am I crazy? he said.

She sighed, and nuzzled his neck.

– Don't you know anything? That's how girls get pregnant.

– I know, he said, but not every time, do they?

– Nope. But who would take the risk? Anyway, I don't think it's right.

He was somewhat staggered by that.

– You don't think what's right?

– Going all the way with a guy, unless you're going to marry him. And even then . . .

– Even then, what?

– Even then I think you should save it up, so there's something special about getting married, don't you?

He turned to face her, propping himself up on his elbow. She looked very vulnerable and waif-like, with her white, tender breasts and her long bare brown legs and the brief blue pants.

– Gloria . . .

– Yes?

– D'you think this is right then? What we just did?

– Don't you?

– It's a sin, he said.

He thought to himself: I must go to Confession tomorrow before I leave for home. Trains could crash, ships could sink. Gloria looked uncomfortable, and crossed her arms over her breasts.

– Are you a Christian? she asked.

– I'm a Catholic.

– That's a Christian, isn't it?

– Yes. What are you?

– I'm not anything, much. We're sort of Jewish, but we don't go to Temple or anything.

He lay back on the bed, his hands behind his head.

– I never met any Jews until I came out here, he mused.

– Aren't there any Jews in England?

– Oh yes, lots. Petticoat Lane, for instance. But I mean to talk to.

– Petticoat Lane, that sounds kind of cute.

– It's a Jewish market in London – they're allowed to open on Sundays.

– Do they sell only petticoats?

– Oh no, anything. Mostly second-hand stuff. My father took me there to buy my first bike.

Her face softened.

– Your folks were pretty poor, huh?

– Well, they're not exactly well-off, but . . .

– You said you had a second-hand bike.

– Oh, you couldn't get new bikes then, he laughed. It was just after the war.

– I guess we didn't know much about the war in the States, when I was a kid.

– How d'you feel about living in Germany now?

– How d'you mean?

– Well, after what happened to the Jews.

– I don't think about it much. I don't like to.

– Oh, but you should, he said.

– It doesn't seem real. I can't believe it happened.

– That's why people should think about it, he said. That's why it happened in the first place, because people couldn't believe it was happening. The Jews didn't think it was real. They queued up for the gas chambers.

– Don't, she winced.

– You see, I have a sort of theory that the worst things that happen are the things you never think will happen.

– Oh no! The nicest things are always unexpected. Like us meeting on the boat. I didn't expect that.

– I did – I told you. That's why I went to the party.

– Tell me again, she said, wriggling comfortably against him.

– Just a minute.

He had a thread of thought between his fingers and he didn't want to lose it. It was something he had never put into words before.

– Don't you think that when something really rotten happens, it's much worse if you don't expect it – if it's a nasty surprise?

– Mmm . . . I guess so, she conceded.

– And don't you try and stop rotten things happening by thinking that they *might* happen, in advance?

– How would that stop them? If something's gonna happen, it's gonna happen.

– I don't know, but it always seems to me that you can. For instance, examinations. I always tell myself I've done badly, and then I usually do quite well.

She laughed.

– I always reckon I've done O.K. and I usually flunk.

– Try my system next time, he advised her earnestly.

– It's no use if you haven't got the brains! She laughed again. I think your system's crazy.

– It isn't crazy.

– It is, too. Are you trying to tell me that if you could think of all the lousy breaks in the world, none of them would ever happen?

– If you knew enough to think of them all . . . Well, I'm not saying that none of them would ever happen, but I still think you could stop quite a few.

She chuckled.

– For instance, this morning, he went on. I kept telling myself that you wouldn't come. And then you came.

– I wanted to come.

– But you mightn't have.

– That wouldn't have had anything to do with what you were thinking.

– How could you prove it?

She held her breath for a moment as she groped for an an answer, then exhaled in a spluttering laugh:

– It's obvious. *Che sarà, sarà.*

– What's that?

– Italian. What will be, will be.

– You're a fatalist.

– You're superstitious.

– I'm not. I don't believe in lucky numbers. I always walk under ladders on purpose.

– Your system's superstitious.

– It's not, it's based on reason. You have to be able to think of things.

– Do you think all the time?

– Of course, you can't stop thinking. *Cogito, ergo sum.*

– What's that?

– Latin. I think therefore I am. He grinned, adding: That makes us one all.

– Timothy . . .

– Yes?

– Were you thinking when we were petting just now?

– Not at the end.

– Only at the end? I reckon that's why you felt bad afterwards. You're afraid of not thinking.

– I am afraid, in a way, he admitted.

She gazed earnestly into his eyes.

– But that's what it's all about, between guys and girls. To feel and not think. That's good sometimes.

– Yes, he said, wavering. I can see that. If you're grown up. Married.

– Oh, married! Who can wait that long? You might be dead before. We might all be dead, from the atom bomb.

– Do you really think that?

– Sometimes. Don't you?

– No, not really, he said, and grinned. That's something we've thought about. We've got it covered.

She punched him lightly in the ribs.

– You're crazy. She took his hand and turned his wrist to read his watch. Jeepers! I must go.

– Don't go.

– I have to. Can I wash up here? Don't look, promise?

– I promise.

He turned to face the wall, and heard taps running. If he wasn't to look she must be washing herself all over. He pictured her standing naked at the sink and his inordinate flesh began to stiffen again.

– O.K., said Gloria.

He turned to find her all clean and shining, clothes neatly tucked, buttoned and fastened, combing her hair in a mirror on the wall. He felt soiled and ill-smelling and sweaty as he stood up and adjusted his own dress. He went over to the washbasin.

– I'm afraid the carpet's kind of wet. And I used your towel.

– That's all right.

He rinsed his face and hands, and dried them on the damp towel, that smelled of her body and his.

– Well, she said, giving a final pat to her hair, and sheathing the comb in the back pocket of her jeans.

– I'll see you to the bus, he said, putting on his shoes.

– No, skip it.

– I'd like to.

– No, there'll be lots of kids around. I'd rather leave you here.

She turned back to the mirror and fiddled with her hair again. He went over and put his arm clumsily round her waist, looking at her reflection in the mirror and his own, two strange people.

– Can I see you tomorrow? he said.

– I guess not. We're having a picnic in the Black Forest. Unless you'd like to come?

– I'd like to, he said, but I have to catch my train in the evening.

She nodded, without speaking.

– Won't I see you again, then? he said.

– Doesn't look like it, does it?

– I hadn't thought of that, he said glumly.

– There you go again, she said, with a choked laugh.

– I don't know what to say, Gloria, he mumbled, dropping his eyes from the mirror reflections, buffeted by emotions he could not put a name to.

– Don't say anything, or I'll bawl, she said, moving towards the door.

– Wait! Give me your address. I'll write.

Exchanging addresses calmed them a little.

– I'll write as soon as I get home, he promised.

– I'll look forward to that.

– And you'll write too?

– I'll try. I'm not much of a letter-writer, to tell you the truth.
– Perhaps you'll come to England on holiday one of these days.
– Maybe. Will you be coming back to Heidelberg?
– Yes, if my sister's still here.

They stood in silence for a while, holding hands, not really believing in these remote possibilities.

– I suppose you'd better go, then, he said.
– Yes.
– I don't want you to –

She kissed him once on the lips and slipped out of the room, pulling the door shut behind her. The room seemed dead, empty. He went over to the bed and threw himself down on it.

He woke suddenly, with no memory of having fallen asleep. The room was dark, and he thought at first that he had slept through the fireworks and the party. But when he drew the curtains he saw that it was still early in the evening. He was in no hurry to get to the party, except that he felt ravenously hungry. He washed himself thoroughly at the sink, dried off briskly and brushed his teeth. He put on fresh underwear and a clean shirt. The clothes were cool to his skin. Physically he had a great sense of wellbeing. In himself he felt – not sad exactly, and not happy either, but . . . solemn. And old. Old and wise and experienced. He examined himself gravely in the mirror, and wondered whether he looked different.

He checked his watch. It was time to leave, but he was reluctant to break the silence and solitude of his own mind, which calmed him now, like an empty church. He looked round the room and it suddenly struck him as squalid and untidy. With a burst of energy and efficiency, he began to tidy up, making the rumpled bed, collecting his dirty laundry together, throwing waste paper into the bin, opening the windows wide to air the room.

A key turned in the lock, and he swung round, expecting to see Jinx Dobell. But it was Dolores who nudged her way into the room, a suitcase in each hand. Her jaw dropped as she saw him.

– Oh! she gasped, dropping the suitcases.
– You've come back? he said.
– You're Kate Young's brother, aren't you? Timothy? I'd forgotten all about you.

She looked tired and drawn beneath her tanned skin. Leaving her cases where they had fallen, she sank into an armchair and closed her eyes.

– Yes. I decided to take your offer, in the end.

– So I see. I didn't know you were staying this long.

– I didn't intend to. I'm going home tomorrow.

– Tomorrow.

– I – we – thought you were coming back next week.

– I was. I'm a refugee from dysentery, or some goddam thing.

– You mean you're ill?

She nodded, without opening her eyes.

– Well, he said, I expect I can find somewhere else to sleep tonight.

She nodded again.

– You do that, Timothy.

– I'll just pack my bag, then I could call and collect it tomorrow.

He moved swiftly around the room, emptying drawers and cupboards. Dolores sat immobile in the armchair. She spoke once.

– How did you make out here?

– Oh, fine. I'm jolly grateful . . .

He put a toothbrush and a pair of pyjamas in a paper bag to take with him.

– Well, I'm ready now. Will you be all right?

– You might just knock on the door of my next-door neighbour. Her name's Jinx, Jinx Dobell. Ask her if she could drop by.

– I don't think she's there.

Dolores opened her eyes, with a flicker of curiosity.

– It's been very quiet next door, he said, for the past week.

– Oh yeah, I remember, she was taking a vacation about now. Well, I'll call someone else, don't worry.

He left her sitting in her chair, with her eyes still closed.

The streets seemed strangely hushed and deserted for the hour, but, preoccupied with his own thoughts, Timothy did no more than vaguely register the fact. Though he was now late for the party, he did not hurry. He considered with awe his narrow escape. If Dolores had come back an hour earlier, if the door had swung open while he and Gloria . . . He couldn't bear even to imagine it. And if she had come back earlier still, he would never have been alone with Gloria at all, he would have had no room of his own to take her to, he would be walking through the streets of Heidelberg now as ignorant, as innocent, as he had been yesterday. It was extraordinarily lucky. But luck seemed too trivial a word for the occasion. He felt it rather as a kind of dark grace that was granted to those who took the plunge into experience.

He tried to decide how he really felt about what had happened. He felt a certain guilt, but not in the ashamed, despairing way he had felt immediately after he had spilled. The talk they had shared had changed that. A wave of tenderness surged through him, so strong that it almost brought him to a halt on the pavement, as he remembered her lying beside him in her blue briefs, with her arms crossed over her breasts. I shall not go to Confession tomorrow, he decided suddenly, I shall wait until I get back to England. And though it made no kind of sense, he laid the risk to his unshriven soul as a gift at Gloria's feet.

He suddenly realized that the humming murmur he had been vaguely aware of as he paced the empty streets was the noise of a vast, excited crowd, and as he approached the New Bridge he found himself on the edge of it. The pavement on one side of the bridge was lined with people standing or sitting five or six deep, as were both banks of the river stretching down towards the Old Bridge. The river itself was crowded with craft of every description – pleasure boats, barges, tugs and rowing boats, many of the latter with Chinese lanterns hanging over their sterns in clusters, suspended from slender wands, casting pretty reflections on the water. The windows of every house that faced the river were open and dark with heads. People stood on benches, on ledges, on the plinths of statues, or perched on the roofs of parked cars. And every face was turned towards the east, where the darkness of the mountains was already merging into the darkness of the sky. As the light faded, the buzz of expectation, the laughter and the chatter, subtly intensified.

He made his way slowly along the edge of the crowd, across the bridge, and along the northern bank towards Vince and Greg's flat. As he climbed through the dank garden, he could hear strains of jazz and saw lights shining from the uncurtained windows of the top floor. The front door of the building was open and bore the handwritten direction, *Come On Up*. He climbed the polished wooden stairs. The door of the flat was ajar, and he went in.

He put down his paper bag in the hall, and paused on the threshold of the main room. The guests were standing in small groups, talking and gesticulating, blowing cigarette smoke into the air and swirling the ice in their drinks. Kate, fidgeting with the neckline of her dress, was talking to Maria in one corner. Mel and Ruth were there, and Dot, and most of the other faces were vaguely familiar. He couldn't see Don. Vince, with a cocktail shaker, and Greg, with a platter of food, moved among the guests. It was some time before anyone noticed him, and he felt queerly detached from the party, as if he were invisible, observing without being observed, and somehow getting a sharper, less dazzled view of the people than he had ever had before. They looked so middle-aged, if not positively old. He was aware of thinning hair, ugly rolls of surplus flesh, lines and wrinkles caked with make-up. Smiles seemed strained, eyes empty and desperate, grimaces and gestures like nervous tics. What was he doing here? He wished he could be standing down in the crowds below, holding Gloria's hand in the twilight, waiting for the fireworks to begin. Then Kate saw him, and came eagerly across the room.

– Timothy! Where have you been? I was getting worried . . .

She kissed him: a sisterly, aunt-like kiss, smelling of face-powder and perfume.

– Bit of a hitch, he said.

He told her about Dolores' illness and premature return.

– What a nuisance, she said.

– It could have been worse.

– You seem to be taking it in your stride, anyway, she said, brushing back his forelock, with a smile. How was the party last night?

– It was O.K.

He scanned the room, looking for distraction from this topic. Ruth saw him and blew a kiss. He waved back. Vince came up.

– Hi, Timothy, how are things?

– Fine, thanks. What about you? Were you scared the Russians wouldn't let you go?

– Not really. Have a Manhattan.

– Have you got a Coke?

– There may be some in the kitchen, but why not live a little? This is your last night, isn't it?

– Yes, and just as well, because Dolores has come back from her holiday.

– Dolores? Oh, *Dolores!* Hell, where will you sleep tonight, then?

– I'll get him a room somewhere, said Kate. It's only for one night.

– A room? You mean in a hotel? On fireworks night?

Kate bit her lip.

– I suppose they'll all be full.

– You bet. But Timothy can stay here – no problem.

– That's jolly nice of you, said Timothy, relieved.

Kate looked doubtful.

– Well, I don't know. Your couch is in here, and who knows when this party is going to end?

– Don't worry, honey, I'll see he gets his beauty sleep. Tell you what, he can have my bed and I'll sleep on the couch. I don't plan to go to bed tonight, anyway. Let's have no more discussion. Let's have another drink.

– No thanks, Vince, I'm fine. Kate covered her glass with her hand.

– Oh come on, honey, pull your weight, we're all going to get high tonight. It's a hail and farewell party: hail us and farewell Timothy.

Vince tried to pour into her glass and splashed the liquor over her hand and on to the carpet.

– There! she said, upset.

– Don't worry, it's a good mothkiller, said Greg, coming up to dab the carpet with a cloth. First the moths get drunk, then they go out and get knocked down by automobiles. Hi, Timothy! Are you glad to be going back to Blighty?

– Yes and no.

– That's a good answer, I must remember it when I get married. He stood upright, shoulder to shoulder with Kate. *Do you take this woman to be your lawful wedded wife? Well, yes and no.*

Timothy laughed. Encouraged, Greg put his face close to Kate's and ran a finger lightly over her bosom. He murmured:

– Honey, are we going to elope tonight or do you want to die without knowing?

This did not go down well with Kate. She flinched and pulled away.

– Come on, Timothy, she said. I'll get you that Coke.

Kate pushed the kitchen door shut behind them before she opened the huge refrigerator.

– I don't like the way the boys are acting tonight. I've seen them before in this mood. They don't get drunk very often, but when they do . . . I'd rather you weren't staying here, really.

– I'll be all right.

– I suppose it's natural they should want to let off steam a bit after Berlin. Greg said there were fleas in their cell and the food was uneatable.

– Is Don coming tonight?

– I think not. He said he would drop by the hospital to see how Rudolf was. He's off the danger-list, anyway, which is a relief.

– Good. Er, I'm terrifically hungry, Kate . . .

– Come back into the dining-room – Greg's made a marvellous terrine.

She led him to a table spread with a cold buffet. Ruth was there, pecking greedily at the delicacies.

– Hi, Timothy. Like some chocolate ants?

He stared incredulously, then blenched.

– No thanks.

– Mmm, they're delicious.

She scooped the chocolate-coated insects into her mouth with her long talons. A faint crunching sound came from her moving jaws. Timothy felt slightly nauseous, but, biting into an open sandwich of cream cheese and chopped ham, immediately felt his appetite return.

– Hey! Ruth said, a gleam in her dark eyes. Was it you who turned out the lights on the boat last night?

– What's this? Kate pricked her ears.

– Didncha hear about the birthday party, Kate? Some kid fused the lights and it turned into some kinda teenage orgy.

– Really?

– No, not really, said Timothy, busying himself with the pâté.

– Well, Lola Eastman had hysterics after they got back. What with trying to keep the kids out of each other's pants and stopping them from falling into the river . . . Never again, she says.

– Well! Kate exclaimed, her eyebrows arching. I want to hear all about this, Timothy.

He was rescued by a sudden huge murmur from outside, and a cheer that rolled down the valley. They crowded to the windows, to see that the streetlights had been extinguished all along the river-banks. Vince clapped his hands

– Fill up your glasses, folks! The lights are going out all over Heidelberg. Everyone out on the balcony.

He went round the room, turning off every light except one low table lamp with an almost opaque red shade. They squeezed out on to the balcony, but it was not big enough to take them all, and some of the guests stood on chairs just inside the room. Timothy, however, had a place at the balustrade. It was quite dark, except for the headlights of cars crossing the New Bridge and a few lights on the river craft. The shapes of the town and the mountains were lost in the blackness, and the floodlights had gone from the castle. An expectant hush had settled over the crowd below and communicated itself to their own tight-packed group. A plane droned somewhere overhead.

– Well, what are we waiting for? Mel grumbled in the darkness.

– Someone forgot to bring the matches, Greg quipped, and they all laughed wildly.

– It's like waiting for an artillery barrage to begin, Mel complained.

Three rockets soared into the velvet black sky and burst with loud explosions into stars, red, green, blue. A long *Ooh!* was exhaled from the crowd below.

– That's the signal to begin, said Kate.

The embers of the rockets faded as they fell, and darkness returned again. Then, magically, the castle materialized, as if floating in the night sky opposite them, burning like an airship on fire. It seemed enveloped in red flames, licking round the walls and battlements, and there was a glow from inside the buildings, throwing the ruined façades into silhouette against the brightly lit windows, where one could easily imagine figures fighting desperately to escape.

– Boy! Vince murmured from somewhere at the back, I never get tired of that. Timothy remembered him quoting in the Mercedes on the way to Baden, *We shall drag a world with us, a world in flames.*

The spectacle lasted for about ten minutes before the red glow began to fade, and the castle slowly melted back into the blackness of the night. Then, to a great gasp from the crowd, the Old Bridge burst into view, its twin towers, arches and parapet outlined in molten gold and silver that cascaded into the dark river and sent reflections bouncing and spinning like new coin across the surface of the water. And as that display spent itself, a tremendous rocket barrage began in the valley beyond the bridge. The rockets illuminated the whole town as they burst, scattering their seeds of fire, jewel-coloured stars that exploded again and again, throwing out new galaxies of colour as their predecessors faded. Each cluster of rockets seemed to outdo the previous one in splendour. The valley boomed and echoed with thunderous explosions. You felt it could not go on, and yet you willed it to go on, to go on surpassing itself. And when the obvious climax came, when a great necklace of diamonds, rubies and sapphires was thrown across the throat of the valley, and hung there in exquisite symmetry for a few fragile seconds, and then slowly, poignantly, began to waver, to melt, to disintegrate, to fall, and fell, and went out, star by star, leaving the dark backcloth still and vacant, the spectators could not resign themselves to its being the end, but waited in suspense until the streetlights came on again. Then there was a great collective sigh of mingled satisfaction and regret, and bursts of clapping and cheers, and the crowds began to break up and disperse, cars started their engines, and the boats on the river began to churn the water. On the balcony they stirred, and shuffled round to go back into the room.

– Well, said Kate to Timothy, what did you –

Her question was cut short by a woman's piercing scream from in front of them. The people in between swayed back, forcing himself and Kate dangerously against the balustrade, then lurched forward again, and they all tumbled into the room. It was obvious what had provoked the scream, and Timothy himself experienced a momentary shock of fear when he saw, standing quite still, in the far corner of the room, with his back towards them, hands clasped behind his back, his sinister shadow thrown on the wall by the dim red lamp, a German Army officer in the unmistakable uniform of the Second World War – the long, full-skirted topcoat, the high-crowned peaked cap, the black, shiny jackboots.

– What the hell? Mel blurted out.

Vince wheeled on them, clicked his heels and shot out his arm.

– *Heil Hitler!*

Then he lowered his arm until it was merely pointing a derisive finger at them, and sweeping it round in an arc, he threw back his head and roared with laughter.

The guests responded variously. Some were amused, some pretended amusement, and a few were openly disapproving. Kate was among the latter.

– I don't think that was very funny, Vince, she said. You've upset Maria.

Maria was crouched in an armchair, with her head in her hands, trembling.

– Oh Maria, you're not really upset? Vince cajoled. It was just a joke.

Maria looked up and smiled weakly, shaking her head.

– It may be a joke to you, said Kate, but Maria has reason to be afraid of that uniform.

Timothy remembered her telling him that Maria had been in Holland under the Nazi occupation. Kate looked at her for support, but Maria was, as usual, too humble to say anything.

– I'm sorry, Maria, said Vince. I apologize. Is that all right? Am I forgiven?

Maria nodded.

– What you need is a drink.

– She's not the only one, said Dot, feelingly.

There was a general rush to the bar. Greg slipped a record onto the turntable and began to roll up the carpet.

– First dance, Kate? he called.

She shook her head.

– No, Greg, not just now.

– Here, said Vince, coming up with a drink for Maria, and another which he pressed on the reluctant Kate.

– Say, Vince, that was a helluva trick you played on us, Mel said. You must have cut off while we were watching the rockets.

– That's right. Vince winked at Timothy. Did I scare you, kid?

– Just a bit.

Dot joined them.

– Where'd you get the togs, Vince?

– Oh, here and there.

– I hope you've had 'em cleaned. You don't know where they've been, as they say. She giggled.

– Sure, but they couldn't get rid of the bloodstains, see? This was where the guy got hit.

They crowded round to see the bullet hole in the chest, slightly frayed around the edge, and the brownish stains of old blood. Encouraged by their interest, Vince opened up his entire collection of Nazi souvenirs, which proved astonishingly extensive – uniforms, hats, helmets, belts, boots, weapons and badges and medals, dragging them out of drawers and cupboards, and spreading them over the floor of the main room. The guests handled them with a mixture of repulsion and fascination; and then, on a sudden whim, a few began trying on the clothing themselves. In the tipsy, excited mood of the party, nerves still tingling from the power of the fireworks and the shock of Vince's tableau, the idea of dressing up caught on rapidly, and soon they were all scrambling hilariously among the clothes and objects, struggling into various items of uniform and equipment, posing before mirrors, strutting about and clicking their heels and giving each other the Nazi salute. Greg was urging them on with spluttering announcements delivered through an old tin megaphone: *Achtung! Achtung! Until further notice the National Socialist Party will be known as the National Socialist Cocktail Party!* One of the girls was wrapped in a swastika flag and acclaimed Miss Gestapo. Dot was going around holding out an Iron Cross.

– Decorate me, she invited Timothy.

Sheepishly, he obeyed. Kate had pointedly turned her back on the charade, and was talking to Maria. He heard her asking the Dutch girl if she would like to leave, and hoped that this wouldn't mean he would be packed off to bed. Though he had no wish to take part in the masquerade, which struck him as being, in a queer way, almost blasphemous, it held him with a morbid fascination. In the dim red light of the lamp, which might have been the reflected glow of the castle burning on the other side of the valley, the spectacle had an eerie and almost frightening reality. Although the faces beneath the death's head cap-badges were foolishly grinning, and the swastika armbands were tied on the sleeves of cocktail dresses, and the creased tunics were buttoned over jazzy silk ties, the incongruity did not make these grim relics entirely absurd. Like children meddling naughtily with old spells, the guests had conjured an element of genuine evil in the room.

Mel came over to Timothy, fondling an automatic pistol.

– Take a look at this, kid.

It was so unexpectedly heavy that he nearly dropped it. Kate snatched it from his hand.

– Give that to me! You're a fool, Mel, how d'you know it's not loaded?

– It's not loaded, relax. None of the weapons is loaded, Vince said, as he came up to them. He took the pistol from Kate. He was still wearing his long overcoat, though his forehead was beaded with perspiration.

– Vince, can I take Timothy to your bedroom, please?

– You're not sending the kid to bed already?

– I'm taking Maria home, and I want to see that he's in bed before I leave.

– I don't have to go straightaway, said Maria anxiously.

Kate looked vexed.

– Timothy ought to go to bed anyway, he has a long journey ahead of him tomorrow. And I want to leave myself.

– Oh, come on, Kate! You can't go just when the party's beginning to swing. Get with it, baby! Have another drink. You've gone all serious on us. You've been seeing too much of that Commie schoolteacher.

Kate's face was red, angry.

– Vince, I believe you did report him after all.

– What are you talking about? Do you know what she's talking about, Greg?

– Nope, but she looks adorable when she's mad, doesn't she? Come on, honey, let's tango.

Greg put his arm round her waist, but she pushed him away, almost violently.

– I wouldn't dance with that . . . rabble. It's disgusting. She turned to Mel. I'm surprised at you, Mel, why don't you make them stop it?

She looked upset, almost hysterical. Mel looked merely embarrassed.

– Aw, come on, Kate, you know it's just for laughs. We have to be so goddam tactful with the Krauts these days, it's a relief to let go once in a while.

– It does look pretty wild, doesn't it? Vince murmured, surveying the dance floor with a certain awe. Packed close together in the dim red light, sweating in their hats and helmets and uniforms, the dancers heaved and jostled, swaying to the music, some laughing and chattering, others almost asleep, propping each other up.

– I'm going to have one more cigarette, Kate declared, then Timothy's going to bed and I'm going home.

Her fingers trembled slightly as she extracted the cigarette from her case. Vince supplied her with a light from his Ronson, without appearing to take his eyes from the dancers.

– You know what, he mused, it must have been like this the night Adolf shot himself in the Berlin bunker.

– Not as merry as this, surely? said Mel.

– That's what you might think, but there's a strange story about that night, perhaps the strangest Hitler story of all. (He paused to take a swig from his glass.) Of course, they were all out of their minds by then. Most of them had been living underground for days. The Russians were closing in, shells were falling in the Chancellery garden, the whole of Berlin was in flames, Adolf was throwing fits every hour, on the hour. Then there was the wedding with Eva.

Kate stubbed out her cigarette, only half-smoked.

– Come on, Timothy.

– Wait a minute, Kate. I'm telling the kid a story here. It's a history lesson.

– Yeah, hold it, Kate, said Mel. This is interesting. So he married Eva Braun, yeah?

– So he married Eva Braun and . . . d'you know the name of the guy who married them?

– Wagner, said Timothy.

– Right! You remembered. Vince grinned at him. You're a smart kid, Timothy. You don't forget things. You won't forget tonight in a hurry, huh?

– Vince, said Kate impatiently.

– O.K., O.K. So Adolf and Eva got hooked, and they had a wedding breakfast, with champagne and all, but that was something of a flop, not surprisingly, since the happy couple had declared their intention of shooting themselves within the next twenty-four hours. That kind of puts a damper on a wedding. Adolf didn't even go to bed with his bride. He spent the night composing his last will and testament. Next day the news arrives that Mussolini and his mistress have been shot by partisans and strung up by their heels.

That must have made up Adolf's mind, if he was still hesitating. He had his dog, Blondi, poisoned. He handed poison capsules to his two secretaries, to save themselves from the Russians. Then he sent word that nobody was to go to bed until further orders. Some time after midnight, they were all summoned to the dining-room, and he walked down the line, shaking hands with the women, and mumbling something that nobody could hear, not looking at them, looking far away . . .

Vince's own eyes seemed to be looking far way. His listeners, even Kate, were quiet, attentive, still, anxious not to miss his words against the noise of the dancing.

– Then a strange thing happened. They all knew that this was Hitler's farewell, that he was going to kill himself, and remember that most of these people were devoted to him. Most of them had volunteered to stay with him in the Bunker until the end. But d'you know what they did? Afterwards, after he'd gone back into his room? They went to the canteen and they had a party. A party! They danced. *Danced!* They made so much noise that Hitler sent a message asking them to be quiet. But they went on dancing. Can you imagine? With the Russians half a mile away, Berlin about to fall, what was left of it, and knowing that they'd be dead themselves soon if they didn't get the hell out . . . they danced.

He stopped, and took another sip of his drink.

– And what was Hitler doing? Timothy asked

– Who knows? said Vince, abstractedly. Perhaps he was waiting, with his finger on the trigger . . . Vince raised the automatic and looked into the barrel. Perhaps he was hoping for a miracle, a miracle that didn't come. So . . .

Vince put the barrel to his head and squeezed the trigger.

– *Bang!* said someone from behind, and they all jumped.

– Jesus Christ! said Mel.

– Don! Kate exclaimed.

– Well, well, said Vince, the Russians have arrived.

– The door was open, so I came in, said Don. He looked around the room. Fun and games.

– You missed the fireworks, Vince said.

– Yeah, I was at the hospital, visiting a friend of yours.

– Rudolf? How is the guy?

– Much better.

Vince nodded.

– Good, I feel kind of responsible. I'll have to go round there tomorrow. I didn't know he was allowed visitors.

– Tonight was the first time. Apart from the military. I gather he's been seeing a lot of the military. He looked challengingly at Vince, who did not reply, but lit a cigarette. It's my guess that you're in deep trouble, Vernon.

Vince gave an odd, derisive snort.

– What would you know about the trouble I'm in?

Don looked at Kate.

– Are you and Timothy ready to leave?

– Yes, I'll come, but Timothy's staying here for the night.

Don stared.

– Staying here?

– Yes, Dolores turned up unexpectedly and –

– You must be out of your mind. Come on, let's go. Don took Timothy's arm.

– Now just a minute! Vince grabbed Timothy's other arm. Who the hell do you think you are?

– Leave him alone, both of you!

Kate clutched at Timothy protectively, and for a moment he had the bewildered sense of being tugged and pulled between the three of them. He made no resistance, for he had no idea of what was going on, and nobody seemed to be taking any notice. Mel had shuffled off after Don's arrival and the dancing was still continuing.

– I think I know what *you* are, Vernon, said Don. You get off on one-armed guys, do you?

Timothy felt Vince's grip loosen on his sleeve and fall away.

– That Kraut . . . he said thickly.

– He didn't say much, but I can read between the lines, said Don. Come on Kate, let's get out of here. He bore them away.

– Kate! Vince called after them, low but urgently. She turned a white, frightened face towards him, but did not stop. Don, however, paused by the door. He stooped, and with a quick, violent movement, pulled an electric plug from its socket. The music died with a groan. He straightened up, and switched on the ceiling lights. The dancers staggered to a halt, and looked round bemusedly, blinking in the glare. The uniforms and equipment with which they were decked looked suddenly tawdry and unfrightening.

Epilogue

The motel was one of the pleasantest they had stayed at, built in a vaguely Spanish style on three sides of a courtyard, with a swimming pool on the fourth side. Their main room (it was a residential motel, designed for vacationers, and each unit comprised two rooms, shower and kitchenette) opened out on to a small terrace overhung with some kind of flowering vine. He sniffed its perfume appreciatively as he came out, a well-iced gin and tonic clinking in each hand, and lifted his face to the starlit sky and the black silhouettes of the palm trees. Shouts and splashes carried across the courtyard from a party of late bathers.

– Nice idea, he said, swimming in the dark. We must try it. It's almost too hot in the day-time, even for swimming.

– You'll have to watch the children's feet on the concrete.

– Yes, they've got those rubber sandal things, but Michael won't keep them on.

He put her drink down on a low table and sat down beside her. She was lying on a wicker chaise longue, her face in shadow.

– They're gorgeous, the children.

– They're not bad kids, really. They get a bit fractious in the car, but that's not surprising.

– It certainly isn't, considering the distance you've covered. I think they're marvellous.

– We took it easy, mind you. About two hundred miles a day, maybe two-fifty.

– You've seen more of the States than I have in – what is it – fourteen years?

– I expect we've seen more than most native Americans, come to that. Thanks to the Fellowship.

– What a marvellous thing to have! And they gave you the car too? I suppose you have to be terribly brilliant to get it.

– And terribly lucky. They don't have many applicants in my field, I think that was in my favour.

– I know you've explained to me what it is, in your letters, Timothy, but I can never quite . . .

– Environmental Studies. It's a pretty new academic subject, actually. My own special line is urban renewal. I did my Ph.D. on planning blight.

He talked for a while about his research until her silence indicated to him that he had more than satisfied her curiosity. The problems of urban renewal were not, he reflected, likely to be of keen interest to someone living in a Californian desert resort, where nothing looked more than twenty years old except the residents.

– Isn't Sheila coming outside? Kate asked.

– In a minute. She's writing a letter to her mother.

– She's a lovely girl, Timothy. You're very lucky.

– Yes, I am.

– Of course, she is too. What are you grinning at?

– You sound just like Mum. When we told her we were getting engaged, she kept looking at Sheila as if she'd just won first prize in a raffle.

Kate chuckled in the shadows.

– You don't know how good it is to see you, Timothy, you and your little family. I can't believe you're really here.

– Oh, we're here all right. And jolly nice it is too. He leaned back in his chair and sipped the cold, clean drink. I love sitting outdoors at night, it's never warm enough in England. I remember that was one of the things I enjoyed about Germany – d'you remember my first evening in Heidelberg? Dining outside that restaurant halfway up the mountain?

– The Molkenkur. You had Chicken-in-the-Rough, remember?

– Could I ever forget!

– How you ate!

They laughed together at the memory.

– I ordered Chicken-in-the-Rough in Denver a couple of weeks ago, he said. But it wasn't the same.

– I suppose you can get as much chicken as you like, now, in England. It must be difficult to remember what rationing was like.

– Mm. Though I don't think you ever forget it really. There's a gap opening up, getting wider all the time, between those who remember the war, rationing, austerity and so on, and those who were too young to remember, or born afterwards.

– You talk like an old man, she teased him.

– Well, thirty *is* old nowadays. You know what the students say: never trust anyone over thirty. If you work it out, thirty is just about the dividing line between those who can remember the war and those who can't.

– They seem to cause so much trouble, these days, students.

– They take more for granted, so their dreams are more ambitious. Growing up in the war and just after, one didn't really expect much. Any improvement was something to be grateful for.

– Yes, she sighed, the younger generation don't know how well off they are.

– Well, you can be so grateful for being where you are that you don't want to move on, in case things get worse. I recognize that tendency in myself.

– You, Timothy? But you've done so much.

– Not all that much. And I have to push myself all the time. Like that trip to Heidelberg. I didn't really want to go, but I made the effort – and was I glad! I doubt whether I'd be here now, otherwise.

– Really?

– Really. It was a turning-point for me. It brought me out of my shell, enlarged my horizons. I learned an awful lot in those few weeks.

They fell silent, thinking back. The bathers had departed from the pool, and the only sound was the rhythmical hiss of the water sprinklers, rotating in the shrubbery beneath the palm trees.

– Do you ever hear from Vince and Greg? he asked at length.

– Never. A girl friend of mine said they went to South America, but I don't know.

– Did anyone ever discover the truth of that Berlin business?

– I don't think so, no. It was hushed up. There was an inquiry, of course. The story going round was that they tried to make contact with the East Germans to sell them a list of ex-Nazis in high places in the Federal Government, but the East Germans wouldn't do a deal.

– But it was never proved?

– No, it was never proved. It just smelled badly enough for them to have to resign. Then there was the Rudolf affair – that alone would have made them security risks. You know what that was all about, I suppose?

– Some kind of homosexual thing, I suppose?

– They never, er, tried any funny business with you, did they?

– No, never.

– Thank goodness, she sighed. It often worried me, but I could never bring myself to put it in a letter.

– Did you know they were gay?

– It never entered my head. Shows how innocent I was.

– They were pretty discreet, I suppose.

– Some people must have had their suspicions. Don certainly did. But as they were always going round with me . . . I was a kind of alibi. She gave a short, dry laugh.

– Why did they try to do a deal with the East Germans? They weren't fellow-travellers, surely?

– No, I think they just needed the money. Vince had been losing a lot at gambling. I used to think they had unlimited funds, but I guess they were living above their incomes all the time.

– It makes me feel badly, in a way, he said. All the time I was sponging off them, letting them pay for me everywhere, they must have been desperate for money.

– I shouldn't let it worry you. They were like that. They took a pride in being extravagant. Childish, really.

– All the same . . .

– I can't work up much sympathy for them, I'm afraid. I feel they made a fool of me.

– It doesn't mean that they didn't like you, Kate, he said gently. It's society that makes them deceitful.

In the silence that followed, this last remark sounded more and more pompous and affected. He broke it desperately.

– What about Don? You know that he's full professor at Ann Arbor, now?

– Yes, we still exchange Christmas cards, but that's about all.

– You know, Kate, I thought perhaps the two of you . . .

– What?

– Well, I was only a kid, of course, but it seemed to me that you were quite keen on each other.

– We had a brief affair, actually.

– An affair? He hoped he sounded surprised.

– It started that week in Garmisch. You remember? When I twisted my ankle.

– Oh yes, I remember.

She laughed a little selfconsciously.

– I don't know why I'm telling you this after all these years. I've never told a single soul before. But I'd just like one person in the world to know. Does that seem silly?

– No, of course not.

– Don asked me to marry him, actually.

– Did he? This time his surprise was genuine.

– Yes, the week after you went home.

– And you said no?

– I said no.

– You didn't think it would work?

– I didn't see how it could. He was determined to go to college in London . . . I just couldn't see myself as a student's wife, living in a bedsitter, working in some crummy office to make ends meet. And then I'm not the intellectual type, never was. There were times when I'd say something about the news, or a book, or a movie, and he'd sort of look at me, as if he was wondering whether to set me straight or let it pass. I could imagine him looking at me like that for the rest of our lives.

– I know what you mean, he said. Don was an intelligent man, a sincere man. He taught me a lot. But he was a bit of a moral bully at heart.

– He's been married and divorced since.

– Has he?

– Who are you talking about? said Sheila, as she came out on to the terrace.

– Oh, no one you know, darling, he said. Like a drink?

– No thanks, not just now.

She sat down on his knees.

– Children all right? said Kate.

– Sound asleep, both of them. This is a super place, Kate. We're ever so grateful to you for finding it.

– I thought it was the best kind of place for you, with the children. And as the season is just over, it's quite cheap really.

– I was amazed, said Timothy, fondling Sheila's waist. He thought to himself: two rooms – tonight we can make love.

– Gosh, it's so warm still, Sheila said.

– Some people were swimming just now.

– That sounds fun. What about it, Tim?

– I'm too comfortable here.

– I'll just have a quick dip.

– She's got such energy, said Kate, as Sheila went indoors to change.

– Wears me out, sometimes, he said. Would you like another drink?

– No thanks. How do you manage about religion, if I'm not being nosy?

– Oh, no problems. Sheila doesn't mind the kids being brought up as Catholics. I don't mind her planning when to have them.

– I've gone back to the Church, you know.

– Have you?

– As you get older, you feel the need of something, especially living on your own. Mind you, it's all changed, it seems to me.

– Not before time.

– More like the Protestants, now, wouldn't you say? It's funny, I miss the Latin mass, though I used to find it boring.

– Mum and Dad will be glad you're still practising.

– Did they ever know I'd stopped?

– I think they guessed. D'you ever think of coming home, Kate? I don't mean for good, but for a visit.

– It's the old story, I keep putting it off. I don't fancy the journey either. I was in a plane that nearly crashed, and it's put me off flying. But since you arrived I've been thinking that perhaps I really should make the effort. I'd like to see you and Sheila and the children again. I think it was the idea of going back and finding everybody older, the same but older, that depressed me.

– You can stay with us as long as you like, he said. We're going to get a bigger house when we go back.

Sheila came out through the french windows, a towelling robe over her two-piece swimming costume, and passed them with a wave of her hand.

– Have a nice swim, Kate said.

They watched the white robe move like a ghost through the shrubbery.

– Talking of Heidelberg, Timothy said, I suppose you never heard anything about a girl called Gloria Rose, did you?

– It doesn't ring a bell. Who was she?

– Oh, just a girl I met at that party on the river-boat. Don taught her.

– Party on a river-boat? Oh, yes, I remember. Something happened, didn't it? Someone fell overboard or –

– Someone fused the lights.

– That's it, it comes back to me now. What about this Gloria, then? Kate was full of womanish curiosity.

– Oh, she was just a girl I got friendly with. We wrote to each other a few times after I went home, then we lost touch. It was just a long shot, asking you.

They heard a splash from the pool, as Sheila dived in. He looked towards the sound, rather yearningly it must have seemed, for Kate said:

– Why don't you join her?

– I wouldn't mind a dip, actually. Won't you come too?

– No thanks, I'm getting too old for midnight swims. I'll stay here, in case the children wake.

– Well, perhaps I will.

He went indoors, and changed into his swimming trunks. Coming out, with just a towel over his shoulders, he said humorously:

– Hmm, it doesn't seem quite so warm now.

– What?

There was a catch in her voice, and he realized she was crying quietly.

– Kate, what's up?

– Nothing . . . take no notice.

– You're upset.

– No, it's just . . . I haven't talked to anyone about those days for so long.

– I understand.

He stood, hesitating.

– Go on, have your swim.

Arc lights fixed in the palm trees illuminated the pool, but did not penetrate its depths. Sheila disturbed the reflections as she swam up and down in a tidy, deliberate crawl. She was a much better swimmer than he was. Seeing him, she stopped and trod water in the middle of the pool.

– Coming in after all? she called. It's gorgeous. Warm as anything.

– They heat the water, he said.

– I know. Doesn't it seem extravagant, in this climate? Delicious, though.

He dropped his towel, kicked off his sandals, and dived into the black, lukewarm water. He surfaced and swam over to Sheila. He put his arms round her waist and kissed her wet lips. They sank slowly together, separated, and bobbed up again into the air.

– Idiot! Sheila spluttered.

He came close again, stroking her body under the water.

– Make love tonight? he said.

– Mmm.

He tried to put his hand inside her bikini briefs, but she wriggled away and swam off, too fast for him to pursue. She dragged herself out of the pool, and paddled along the side to the diving boards. He floated on his back and admired the sleek, supple movements of her limbs as she climbed the ladder. She stood on the top platform and pushed back wet tendrils of hair from her face, panting from the climb. Rocked in the warm water, under the huge serene sky, he felt an excess of happiness well up inside him. It seemed to be a moment of perfect content. He could not think of a single, even trivial care or dissatisfaction troubling him, and in the big things of life he had always been lucky. He was so lucky it was almost a scandal, he thought to himself, mindful of Kate weeping in the shadows on the other side of the courtyard. And Don, divorced, Vince and Greg driven out into the wilderness, his parents growing dully old, shedding one human interest after another, like leaves falling singly from a tree on a windless day. When one thought of all the thwarted, broken, cramped lives . . . and the deaths. The unnumbered dead of the war, of his war and all the wars, lives cut off unseasonably, at random, with no reason. For he could think of no particular reason why it should be Sheila who stood on the diving platform now, her breasts rising and falling as she drew the air into her lungs, and not Jill, who had been born in the same year, whose breasts were ghosts – not even ghosts, never grown.

Then it came on him again – the familiar fear that he could never entirely eradicate – that his happiness was only a ripening target for fate; that somewhere, around the corner, some disaster awaited him, as he blithely approached. A car smash. A mortal disease. A madman scattering bullets. He fought it down, as he had fought it many times before, treading water in the middle of the pool. But he called out:

– Better not, Sheila! It's too dark for high diving.

She pulled a face, rose on her toes, and dived. Her body flashed through the air and cleaved the dark water. The shattered reflections of the lamps rocked and danced crazily across the surface, and then began to re-form. A craven prayer forced itself to his lips, and he bit it back. He began to count, instead, silently.

When he reached nine, she surfaced several yards behind him, gasping for breath.

– Sheila! he cried, and struck out towards her.